VISITORS

VISITORS

Bob Chapman

ATHENA PRESS
LONDON

VISITORS
Copyright © Bob Chapman 2006

ISBN 1 84401 693 5

First Published 2006 by
ATHENA PRESS
Queen's House, 2 Holly Road
Twickenham TW1 4EG
United Kingdom

Printed for Athena Press

This book is for my grandson. I penned it when he was just two years old.

Curiously, before he started school when he was four he could already read quite competently. Strangely though, he just can't seem to manage to open the door of the garden shed…

Chapter One

Teetering precariously on the edge of the bathroom stool, Travis pulled himself up by grabbing the edge of the washbasin. He peered into the mirror. Not quite tall enough, he thought. He could see his slate-grey eyes but not down past his nose. Still grasping and wiggling the offending tooth, he climbed down, ran into his mum's bedroom and stared into the dressing table mirror. Another wiggle... *ouch*! No tooth fairy for me tonight – still too tight! he thought. When you're only seven, the arrival of the tooth fairy is a very important event – providing she doesn't forget to bring the fifty pence piece with her. As he turned to leave, he knew he was being watched, but he didn't even turn to see if there was anybody there. Instead he ran down the stairs (he ran everywhere), and into the kitchen.

'I've just had a visitor, Mum,' he announced.

'Have you, dear?' his mother said without looking up. 'That's nice!' And she continued to chop away at the garlic that she was preparing.

Travis ran out into the garden, which was his mother's pride and joy; it was quite large, with all sorts of interesting nooks and crannies, great for children playing hide-and-seek. It was filled with all sorts of plants, shrubs and trees that Travis could never remember the names of, although his mum had patiently told him time and time again.

At the top of the garden, in the left-hand corner, was an eight by six wooden shed. What a contrast to the rest of the garden! It had never been painted, had some timbers rotting away, and was partly hidden from the house by an oversized pampas grass. The shed was rickety, to say the least. The felt was ripped and hanging from its roof and there were great gaps in its sides, and even if you peered through them you could never see inside. The door had no lock or bolt, but it just would not open, no matter what you did; and Travis had given up trying a long, long time ago.

The shed didn't have any windows, which Travis found to be odd, since all sheds need windows. His dad told him that in their shed they weren't necessary. Above the door, somewhat faded but still legible, it said, in rather ornate gold copperplate writing: PLATFORM 731.

His dad used to disappear into the shed for hours and hours on end. He said it was to do his work, but what sort of work you could do in there Travis couldn't see. Strangely, if he knew his dad was in the shed when it was dark, no light ever shone through all those cracks – no light at all – and Travis knew that couldn't be right. Whenever it rained the shed would appear to be quite dry. It was as if the rain never landed on it, and Travis knew that couldn't be right either. One day he could remember it snowed, but when he looked out of the window, although the garden was coated in white the shed was untouched. He asked his mum about it but all she would say was his dad had that probably already cleared it off, as the shed was so rickety.

Travis's mum was a round little woman, always well presented ('immaculate and fragrant', his dad always described her), who never seemed to get flustered about anything at all. She always seemed totally unflappable. The world seemed to sail past her while she was totally wrapped up in hers, and Travis knew that he had the best mum in the whole wide world.

Travis's mother seemed to spend her time either in the kitchen, creating delicious smells, or making the garden look beautiful. When she wasn't hanging out the washing she was ironing or cleaning; she never seemed to stop. Travis once told her with all that energy she should run the London Marathon. His mother only laughed and said, 'What's that – in the roly-poly class then, Travis?'

Travis came back in the kitchen and said, 'Mum, can I go round and see Alex, please? I'm bored.'

'Yes, all right, but don't be too long. I've got your favourite for lunch.'

Travis's mum didn't really like Travis hanging around with Alex as Alex asked too many awkward questions, which Travis then asked in turn, and he always seemed to be getting Travis in trouble at school.

His latest query was about what Travis's dad did for a job, and why Travis was called Travis Travis.

Alex Macintosh was three months older than Travis and a good three inches taller.

But then all Travis's friends were taller than him. Alex was as thin as Travis was chunky. He also had a shock of bright red hair, which seemed to have a mind of its own, and freckles, whereas Travis had fair wavy hair that his mum said she'd die for. But why anyone would want to die for a head of hair Travis couldn't imagine.

Alex was called 'Raincoat' by all his friends, but never when Alex's Glaswegian mother was around. Travis didn't know why, until one day he called him Raincoat in front of her.

'His name is Alexander – that's A-L-E-X-A-N-D-E-R!' she bellowed at him. Travis didn't really understand a word she said after that, but as he ran away he knew he was in big trouble. He always remembered afterwards.

Alex had a younger sister called Kirsty who spent all her time trying to follow Travis around; she thought he was lovely. She would just stand and stare up at Travis's face, which Travis found most disconcerting. Travis, for his part, spent all his time avoiding her like the plague. The only thing they had in common, he told Alex once, was that they both hated spiders. She was a typical girl and Travis couldn't work out why they were even put on the planet.

Alex was always in trouble at school and had a tendency to drag Travis down with him. The teachers had unsuccessfully tried to keep them apart, but Alex and Travis were great chums and aimed to stay that way.

Alex lived next door but one to Travis, and Travis always cut through Mr Pomphrey's garden to get there. Mr Pomphrey didn't mind in the least; he thought it was the safest option.

Mr Pomphrey was a jolly old man who lived all alone. He had an enormous stomach and Travis thought that if it rained he could stay quite dry if he stood underneath it. He also had a huge white moustache and a bald head. His eyebrows were wild and he had the odd long hair sprouting from each of them. Travis thought he looked like a kind walrus with a bright red face.

Summer and winter, indoors or out, he wore a suit – complete with a waistcoat which sported a gold albert chain and watch – and he always wore a collar and tie. On every Remembrance Day he would wear his ribbons and medals from the Second World War, of which he was very proud, and he was always regaling Travis with 'tin hat stories', as he called them, from the war.

He was always giving Travis sweets, much to the annoyance of Travis's mum. 'Bad for his teeth,' she'd say. Travis thought there might be something in that, because all of his teeth were falling out. Teeth or no teeth, Travis liked Mr Pomphrey.

Every day, just a little after four, when he had woken up following his afternoon snooze, Mr Pomphrey would put the kettle on, get two pens and two pieces of paper and await the arrival of Travis. Travis always tried to go to Mr Pomphrey's in the afternoons, even if he was at school. He'd rush home in order to sit in front of Mr Pomphrey's television by four fifteen.

Ever since Travis had been a baby, *Countdown* had fascinated him; he'd gurgle and laugh at the screen, and if his mother turned to another channel he'd start to cry. By the time he was three he could already make up four- and five-letter words, and by the time he was six, he would regularly do the nine-letter conundrum.

Although Travis was not yet eight years old, the teachers at school told Mrs Travis his reading age was that of an adult. In fact he could read better than many of them, and by the time he had just turned seven, Travis had already read most of Arthur Ransome's children's books, and regularly read the Sunday supplements as well. Travis's dad made the observation that Travis ate books, he didn't read them.

Mr Pomphrey loved the arrival of Travis, as he only ever saw the meals on wheels lady, or had an occasional visit from Mrs Travis, who was usually there to complain about the sweets he gave her son, or to give him some of her home-made fare.

Mr Pomphrey always got the numbers game right. He explained to Travis that if you let them the numbers would jump right off the page and talk to you. Travis knew exactly what Mr Pomphrey meant; he felt the same about letters and words. Mr Pomphrey always beat Travis at the numbers game and Travis always beat him at the conundrum, except on one occasion when Mr Pomphrey couldn't believe his luck, and shouted out after just two seconds, '*Marmalade*! I just saw it, I just saw it, just like that!'

'But Mr Pomphrey,' Travis said, 'that's how it works.'

Alex had gone round to Mr Pomphrey's with Travis, but only the once. He thought it was a stupid game, and why anyone would want to sit in a chair and do that, he couldn't understand, especially as there were no prizes. And why were they always going on about Richard thingy's wig, he didn't know. Nobody with any brains would spend good money on a wig that looked like that; and as for the woman who was good at sums, well she was just making it bad for everybody else. After *Countdown*, Travis would thank Mr Pomphrey very much, and, with his pockets laden with sweets, go home for tea.

'I can't stop long, Raincoat,' Travis said. 'Mum's creating a culinary miracle for lunch.'

Alex looked at him blankly.

Travis hopped upon Alex's bed and sat cross-legged; he offered Alex a sweet and waited for the inevitable questions.

'Come on then, Travis! Spill the beans,' Alex said.

'What?' Travis asked.

'You know what! Why are you called "Travis Travis", and what does your dad do with himself?'

'Questions, questions – you're always the same, Raincoat! Sometimes I think you invented the question mark. I'm called Travis Travis because Dad said Travis goes with Travis better than anything else, and Dad said to tell you he is a genealogist, whatever that means.'

'Never heard of it… sounds like someone who studies genies,' Alex said. 'Let's play hide-and-seek.'

Mrs Travis was just dishing up lunch when Travis came in. 'Wash your hands then, Travis,' she said.

'How do you know I haven't, Mum?'

'Because I know you too well, Travis Travis,' she replied.

Travis could never understand why you needed clean hands if you were going to use a knife and fork. He whipped upstairs, showed his hands to the washbasin taps and ran quickly back down.

'When's Dad coming home, Mum? I don't half miss him.'

Mrs Travis put Travis's lunch in front of him. 'When his work's done,' she answered.

Travis looked at his plate. It was his favourite: tinned corn beef sliced, jacket potato and baked beans, to which Mrs Travis had added Madras curry paste, some raisins and chopped garlic. Travis opened the brown sauce bottle and, very carefully for a seven-year-old, let it drizzle onto the corned beef. He once told Alex, 'You can overdo the brown sauce, you know.'

Travis's mum sat opposite him at the dining table. 'What have you been up to at Alex's, then, Travis?'

'Nothing much, Mum,' Travis answered, 'but he was asking about our garden shed.'

Mrs Travis realised she shouldn't have asked that question, and quickly changed the subject. 'Looking forward to going back to school next week, are you?'

'Not half, Mum! I want to see my school friends. I'm starting to get bored and I'm running out of things to do.'

Travis carried on eating in silence. Then he suddenly looked up and said to his mother, 'I had a funny dream last night, Mum. I was in a bright room and a man called Mentor was talking to me. I couldn't actually see him, but I know he was there, and I can't remember all he said… but Mum, what is a scarper button?'

His mother's mouth fell open and she dropped her knife and fork on her plate with a clatter.

'What's the matter, Mum, are you all right?' Travis looked at his mum and felt quite concerned. Her colour had drained away and she looked startled.

Mrs Travis quickly regained her composure, however. She replied, 'It's all right, dear. Something went down the wrong way, that's all. I'll be all right in a minute.'

Chapter Two

Travis's dad hadn't come home by the time he went to bed that night and Travis felt very disappointed. He didn't ever seem to see much of his dad. They work very long hours, these genealogists, he thought.

Mr Travis eventually came in at nearly ten o'clock. He was the same build as Travis and not very tall. The usual twinkle in his eye had deserted him for once, and his broad shoulders sagged as he flopped into the nearest chair. Mrs Travis knew her husband well enough to let him unwind before she mentioned what was uppermost in her mind.

Without speaking, she went into the kitchen and brought back two large brandies and lemonade. She passed one to her husband and sat opposite him, nursing her drink on her lap.

Mr Travis sipped his drink, looked at her and said, 'What's the problem then, Mother?' Tom Travis also knew his wife well enough to know she rarely drank in the evening, and especially at that time of night.

Mrs Travis took a gulp of her drink. 'It's Travis, Tom. He's been dreaming. He wanted to know about the scarper button.'

Tom downed his drink in one go. 'It's started, then, Mother… but Travis is only seven, and that's very young.'

'Seven and three quarters,' replied Mrs Travis. She had a worried look on her face. 'Tom, what are we going to do?'

Tom stared at his empty glass, paused and said, 'We'll go and see Auntie Jennison, that's what we'll do, Mother.'

By the time Travis got up the next morning, his dad was long gone, but had left him a note to say how much he loved him and would see him at the weekend. Travis read the note, but as today was only Tuesday the weekend was simply years and years away.

Travis sat down to breakfast to find his mother scribbling away at a letter.

'Who are you writing to, Mum?'

'It's *to whom are you writing*, Travis, and the answer is your Auntie Jennison. Your dad and I thought it would be a nice idea to pay her a visit. After all, you'll be back at school next week, and then you won't see her until Christmas.'

Auntie Jennison didn't believe in telephones, so it was write or nothing.

Oh no! Travis thought. Not Auntie Jennison – anything but Auntie Jennison! If I never see her again, it will be a hundred years too soon. The very thought of the car journey alone was bad enough. It took for ever to get there, and although Dad said it was only an hour and forty minutes Travis was sure it was at least five hours.

Travis cast his mind back to the last visit. The way she grabbed you, smothered you in slobbery kisses and cackled right in your ear... her fearsome grip... *ugh*! He thought it was like kissing a slimy wet old ashtray.

'I don't want to go, Mum,' Travis said. 'Can't I go to my sister's instead, and you and Dad go on your own?'

Travis's sister lived in the opposite direction and she was some thirteen years older than Travis.

Becky Travis – or Becky Collier, now that she was married – had been swept off her feet by a 25-year-old plumber called Mark, who had come to do some repairs. Unfortunately, they had had to move away some sixty miles because the newly-weds just couldn't afford to buy a house near either of their parents.

'No dear, you know that Becky's away for the weekend, and anyway it was you who said that you didn't see enough of your dad, so now's your chance. Listen, Travis, I know we've had this conversation before, but remember both your real grans are dead, so please try to think of Auntie Jennison as one of them.'

'No way, José!' Travis muttered under his breath. 'Never in ten thousand million trillion years.'

Travis's mother spent nearly all day Saturday preparing for the visit to Auntie Jennison. First she cooked garibaldi biscuits, went out and bought four hundred Rothman cigarettes and some Earl Grey tea. 'They're your auntie's favourites,' she explained.

Travis could never understand why she was called 'Auntie

Jennison'. She certainly wasn't his auntie; in fact, he wondered if she was anybody's auntie. Who'd want an auntie like Auntie Jennison anyway?

Travis knew it would do no good to argue. But the thought of Auntie Jennison... *ugh*! Double *ugh*!

Then of course there was also the dog from hell. Auntie Jennison owned a King Charles spaniel called 'Scampi'. The last thing a King Charles needs is a pair of oversized ears; unfortunately the poor thing had ears which dragged on the ground, owing to some glitch in his pedigree. Auntie Jennison liberally coated them with Sudocrem every day, so they were always covered in a bright white cream, and all sorts of bits and pieces of rubbish that the dog had managed to drag up from the ground. Despite the cream and the ears, the dog seemed perfectly happy, especially when he was chasing Travis. The dog hated Travis with a vengeance, and Travis hated the dog. But the dog was crafty; as soon as the Travis family turned up, he would run round and round, excitedly jump up on Travis, licking him and whining, and wait to be smoothed.

'Oh, look at him!' Auntie Jennison would exclaim. 'What a sweetie! He loves you, Travis – here, give him a biscuit.'

Scampi would sit in front of Travis, wag his tail, pant and wait obediently for the biscuit, which he would take ever so gently.

It was a very different matter as soon as Travis and the dog were alone. Scampi's upper lip would curl and a growl would emerge which seemed to come right from the dog's boots, if he had had any. Then the chase would begin. Travis had never been actually bitten by the dog but he had had some pretty close calls. It usually ended in Travis sitting on something high up with his feet dangling just out of harm's way.

Travis, for his part, was never cruel to the dog and just tried to avoid him. He suspected the dog was jealous of him because Auntie Jennison doted on him. Scampi could have Auntie Jennison all to himself as far as he was concerned.

Auntie Jennison stood well over six feet tall. Travis thought she looked like a very skinny John Cleese without the moustache, although she was doing her best to grow one. She wore a white wig which had a browny-yellow streak up the front caused by cigarette smoke. Her teeth were the same colour (what few teeth she had) as the cigars she would occasionally smoke. She had a large wart on the side of her chin which sprouted three or four long black hairs, and another one on the other side of her upper lip to even things up a bit. Her oversized feet were clad in an ancient pair of plimsolls which had started off in life white but were now a uniform grey. She wore ankle-length grey socks which matched the plimsolls and her paisley-patterned dress finished a couple of inches above them. She wore a wrap-around pinafore like the ones they wore in the middle of the last century, and at the front there was a huge pocket like the ones painters and decorators have. Over her wig she wore a red and white che- quered headscarf, the ends tied tightly under her chin. A large knitted navy blue woollen cardigan completed the ensemble, and she persistently complained about the cold.

She sucked sticky peppermints, which she kept loose in her pinny pocket, between puffs on her cigarette. They were always covered in fluff, dirt and stuff, and of course Auntie Jennison insisted that Travis joined her – fluff, dirt, stuff and all.

Of course the peppermints caused havoc with Auntie Jennison's digestive system, and she seemed to break wind continually; however, strangely and thankfully these events were always odour-free. Almost every time she blew off she would immediately draw attention to the fact, even if it was inaudible, by lifting her head to the heavens and declaring, 'There goes another one!' And sometimes she'd add, 'Shows I've got a healthy gullet.'

Now, Travis knew enough about good manners to know that blowing off in company wasn't acceptable, and you had to hold it in.

Among family and friends it was different. In fact Alex and Travis would sometimes fall about laughing if one of them farted. Sometimes they would even compete with each other to see who could produce the best one. Unfortunately it all ended in tears one day, when Alex had to run home after getting too carried away…

Travis thought Auntie Jennison was quite mad. As mad as a hatter, even. 'She's just a little eccentric, dear,' his mother informed him.

Travis knew all about being as mad as a hatter. His dad had explained the term to him, and once Travis had used it in a story he wrote at school.

The teacher had asked Travis if he knew where the expression came from.

'Yes, miss,' Travis had answered, 'it comes from the olden days when people who made felt hats used mercury, and it poisoned them, miss, and sent them mad.'

'That's very good, Travis,' the teacher had said. 'How did you know that?'

'Because, miss, my dad told me and he knows everything you need to know about history.'

'Mmm,' said the teacher.

Auntie Jennison's whole house was a shrine to the tobacco industry; wherever you looked there were discarded cigarette packets, matches, lighters, snuffboxes, ashtrays and half-smoked cigars. The huge pocket in the front of her pinny contained just about everything the smoker needed. Auntie Jennison seemed to acquire cigarette brands that Travis had never heard of. Amongst the old packets scattered around there were Strand, Passing Clouds, Kensitas, Guards and Bristols. Travis wondered where they had all come from.

Auntie Jennison had the knack of holding a conversation with a cigarette – or 'fag', as she called it – dangling from her mouth, while sucking a peppermint; and no matter what, just as you thought she'd lose the ash when it was about an inch or so long, she'd whip the fag out of her mouth and deftly flick the ash into an ashtray.

Travis had once counted most of Auntie Jennison's ashtrays, which were all full to overflowing; there were twenty-seven in the living room alone, and a further sixteen in the dining room, not to mention the others which seemed to litter the house. He often wondered why she needed so many.

Auntie Jennison's dining room had a large oblong table in the middle, covered with a bottle green, fringed chenille tablecloth. The tablecloth was coated with the occasional bit of cigarette ash, bird droppings, feathers, and spent seed from the bright yellow canary that lived in the cage above hanging from the ceiling. About a foot away from the canary's cage, attached to the ceiling with a drawing pin, was a long, sticky yellow flypaper, absolutely black and full with the corpses of flies but with more live ones trying their best to get on. The canary would now and again make a desperate if unsuccessful effort to catch one, and would send showers of seed husks, droppings and feathers floating down.

'Not very hygienic,' Mrs Travis once observed.

Auntie Jennison had a succession of canaries, and irrespective of their sex they were all called Charlie and always bright yellow in colour.

'Of course,' she'd say, 'canaries don't live for ever.'

Travis suspected cigarettes had something to do with it.

Then of course there were the inevitable ashtrays all over the table – eleven of them, all full right up, as he remembered.

Travis's dad said that the late Andy Warhol should have taken photos of them, whoever he was. Travis told Alex what his dad had said, and Alex said that he thought that if this Andy bloke was going to be late they ought to get somebody else.

Along the back wall of the dining room was a tall Welsh dresser, full of willow pattern china. This had started up in life blue and white but now, like the walls and ceiling, was a uniform muddy brown. On top of the dresser was a large marble shelf clock which almost touched the dark brown nicotine-stained ceiling. Every quarter of an hour, the clock came to life. It let out thunderous chimes and on the hour made noises Big Ben would have been proud of. No one could hear themselves speak at these times, but Auntie Jennison never seemed to notice. She would just raise her voice and take on the clock in direct competition. Auntie Jennison always won.

The journey to Auntie Jennison's on Sunday took longer than expected – at least two hours longer, according to Travis; in the event it was only seventeen minutes. To while away the time, they all played a game while they travelled up the motorway. It was called 'Spot the Eddie'. Whoever spotted an Eddie Stobart lorry got three points, but they had to shout 'Eddie!' before anyone else to get the points. Travis thought his parents were a little slow, as he always won.

Chapter Three

'*Come in, come in*!' shrieked Auntie Jennison. 'Shut the door, Travis, there's a love! Do you want your old Auntie to catch her death?'

Travis sometimes wondered if she was already dead. He noticed that despite her incessant smoking she never coughed. He had asked his mum once how old Auntie Jennison was, but she was very vague about it and could only say, 'Very, very old.'

The fact that outside the temperature was in the mid-seventies made no difference to Auntie Jennison; she wrapped her cardigan around herself, hurried off to the old-fashioned log fire and gave it a good poke. The flames shot up the chimney and red-hot sparks went everywhere; the heat was unbearable.

'That's more like it!' Auntie Jennison declared, smacking her lips. 'Come over here, young Travis, my heart's desire, and give me a kiss.'

The ordeal had begun; she grasped Travis with her long, mitten-encased, talon-like hands, lifted him effortlessly off the floor, and, as far as Travis was concerned, began to devour him. The stench of tobacco and peppermint was overpowering, and the look on his face gave it all away. He well knew by now any form of resistance was useless and resigned himself to his fate.

'Yes, young Travis!' Her voice started to rise. '*Never, never, smoke, you hear*? *Never, ever*! Cigarettes will make your breath smell, they will make you smell, make you short of breath and short of money. They will kill you.' She raised her voice again. '*Kill you, kill you, do you hear*?' Then she added softly, 'But they can't kill me…'

She deposited him back on the floor. 'Here you are, young Travis; your old Auntie's got a present for you.'

Travis took the package and, trying to show some enthusiasm, started to open it. He already knew exactly what would be inside. There would be knitted gloves, always navy blue in colour; and if he was very very lucky there would be five fingers on each hand. But no matter what, the fingers would be too short for his fingers and would be in the wrong place. Auntie Jennison gave Travis gloves at least twice a year, on his birthday and at Christmas, and sometimes in between as well. Travis thought with all the knitting practice she got she just had to improve, but upon looking at his latest acquisition he knew she had a long way to go.

Travis's mum had long given up on trying to unpick and redo the knitting.

'Thank you very much, Auntie Jennison,' Travis said sweetly.

'I bet that was a nice surprise for you, Travis?' Auntie Jennison said.

Yes, Travis thought, she's as mad as a hatter.

Auntie Jennison picked Travis up, cuddled him and squeezed him and then carried him to the dining room. Then, just as he thought he was about to be smothered, she deposited him on the battered, old leather chaise longue which ran down the length of one side of the dining room table; the second part of the ordeal had begun.

They all settled around the table. The canary, on seeing Auntie Jennison, grew more and more excited. Showers of feathers, more droppings and seed husks rained down. He began twittering and singing at the top of his little voice.

'Oh, love him!' Auntie Jennison said. 'He's gasping for a fag.'

Tizer, limeade and orangeade appeared. Travis was asked to select one. On the basis that it seemed it was the very same three bottles that were there on the occasion of their last visit some four months ago, he chose the limeade; somehow it looked like it had more fizz than the rest, but he was wrong. The garibaldi biscuits were produced and Auntie Jennison poured the tea.

With a garibaldi in one hand, Auntie Jennison deftly lit a cigarette with the other. Travis noticed she was still sucking a peppermint. Immediately the canary started round and round his cage like a whirling dervish, flapping his wings and bounding from one perch to another.

The adults quickly covered the top of their cups with one hand and shielded their garibaldis with the other; they'd seen it all before. Auntie Jennison appeared quite oblivious to all this and carried on sucking away at her cigarette while still chewing away at the peppermint.

Now, Auntie Jennison was of the old school, who believed children should be seen and not heard. Travis knew enough to sit in silence while the adults made small talk, as one glance from Auntie Jennison would strike fear into the heart of an all-in wrestler.

After what seemed like an age, limeade and garibaldi finished, Travis asked if he could leave the table.

'Off you go and play in the garden,' Auntie Jennison commanded.

Travis ran out, heaving sighs of relief and muttering under his breath, 'I'm free, I'm free.' The garden, by his mother's standards, was no garden at all; there was a small flagstone-covered yard, three steps up to a small area of closely cut lawn, some chicken wire and then a wilderness.

Just opposite the back door was what passed for Auntie Jennison's toilet. It was a small, stone-built building with a door painted bright green, which no matter what you did wouldn't close properly. Inside, far too high up, was a built-in seat, completely round. Travis was always scared that he might fall right in. He could remember dropping a small stone down there once and he counted three and a bit before he heard a distant splash. The seat itself was timber scrubbed so white it glowed in the gloom of the otherwise dark toilet.

Hanging up on a loop of string by the side were carefully cut squares of the *Daily Mirror* newspaper which served as toilet paper.

'I used to use the *Radio Times*, but it's no good now, it's too glossy,' Auntie Jennison once remarked.

Travis's mum had once presented Auntie Jennison with some soft toilet tissue but it immediately disappeared and was never to be seen again.

Travis ran up the three steps to the lawned area on the left-hand side. There was another stone-built building which was referred to as the 'workshop', but for the life of him Travis couldn't see how any work could be done in there. Looking through the smeary window he could see that there was a long wooden bench inside. It was covered with all sorts of tools and a thick layer of dust. Travis somehow knew that lurking in amongst them there were sure to be the biggest spiders in the whole world.

He decided to go up towards the wilderness instead of investigating the workshop. Chicken wire ran across the width of the garden and the wilderness lay beyond. On the right-hand side of the chicken wire there was a small rickety gate which fortunately opened towards the house. Travis tentatively pushed his way into the wilderness. He wasn't scared; of course I'm not scared, he told himself.

Suddenly he had a brainwave.

In the workshop, on the bench, he had spotted a large ball of twine.

I could tie that to the gate, he thought, and pay it out; then I won't get lost in the wilderness. Of course there was the question of the massive spiders, which grew bigger the more that Travis thought about them.

He decided to just rush into the workshop, grab the twine and run. In the event it all worked a treat; he grabbed his prize and made a headlong dash for the door.

It was only when he was tying the twine on the gate that the spider living in the ball of twine put in an appearance. It was enormous, black and hairy, and Travis thought it had a least ten legs. He screamed loudly, dropped the ball of twine and made a dash for the safety of the house.

As he ran into the passageway leading to the dining room he could hear the adults talking. Deciding that facing the spider might be a better bet than incurring Auntie Jennison's wrath, he ran back out in the garden.

Auntie Jennison peered at Tom across the table. 'Come on, Tom, what's the problem?' she enquired. 'I've only got to look at you to see something's wrong.'

'I think,' he faltered, 'I think, Auntie Jennison, that Travis is being called…'

Without a word, Auntie Jennison rose from her seat and pushed her way through the pall of cigarette smoke. Beckoning for them to follow, she left the room. They followed her along the corridor back towards her living room. Abruptly she stopped in front of a door which Tom and his wife had always believed to be a cupboard. Then, producing a large brass key from her pinny pocket, she opened the door. It wasn't a cupboard. It was another room.

What a contrast from the rest of the house! It was scrupulously clean, and the whole room seemed to glow a bluey-white. Shelves covered three of the walls, and scattered over them were books, some the size of small suitcases, some very small – the size of matchboxes, even. In the middle there was a splendid desk of mahogany with a rosewood and leather top. A large, comfortable-looking black leather chair stood invitingly behind the desk.

Auntie Jennison discarded her cigarette by the doorway. 'I never smoke in the records room,' she explained. 'Come in, come in, but, Tom, please keep the door ajar in case young Travis comes back in.'

Travis, however, had other things on his mind. Bravely, he had retrieved the ball of twine, after prodding it several times with the longest piece of stick he could find; and, once convinced the spider had gone, he tied the end to the gate. Fortunately for Travis, he didn't see the spider crawl silently away into the grass.

He now set out into the wilderness, paying out the twine as he went. 'I wonder if I'll see any giraffes or monkeys or things,' he said to himself. 'I hope there aren't any lions or tigers.' Travis knew that lions and tigers didn't live in England, but now and again he liked to scare himself a bit.

Back indoors, Auntie Jennison went over to one of the shelves, selected a red, leather-bound book the size of an old family Bible and placed it carefully on the desk.

Although upside down to him, Tom could see the one word 'Travis', printed in gold leaf on the front cover.

Auntie Jennison stroked the book almost lovingly and said, 'This is the book of the Family Travis; the records show all who've been called, and all those who haven't.'

She carefully opened the book and stared at the entries. Then she looked back up and said, 'It's here: Travis Travis, first calling, twenty-third of August 2001.'

Tom interrupted. 'But Auntie Jennison, the boy's only seven years old.'

'Can't you remember when you were called, Tom? After all,

you were only thirteen yourself, and as I remember it your father decided you were too young.'

'Yes, but Auntie Jennison…'

'There can be no buts, it's already been decided, and you know that. Look on the bright side; once Travis is ready you'll be heading for a well-deserved retirement.'

'Auntie, I'm only thirty-nine years old now, and there's so much left to do! Even if Travis takes three years before he's ready, I'll be only forty-two.'

Auntie Jennison looked straight at Tom, stroked his arm and said rather sympathetically, 'Tom, you know that once he's ready the door just won't open for you again, don't you?'

'Yes, I know you're right,' Tom replied rather despondently.

Auntie Jennison gazed into space for a second and then turned back to the book; she carefully flicked through the pages and then stopped, read an entry and looked back up.

'There's an entry here for 1692, when a boy called Tremain Travis was called, and he was only eight. But in any case, Tom, you knew it was probably going to happen some time, especially after Becky was passed by – so I can't understand why you're taking it so badly. Do you know the name of his guide yet?' she asked.

'Well, he mentioned a name… I think it was Mentor.'

'Well, that's a relief,' Auntie Jennison said. 'Actually Tom, his full name is Mentor Ath-a-*nay*-shus – well, that's the way it's pronounced. *Athanasius* is old Greek for "immortal"; no need to worry – he's in safe hands there. He was my guide, you know.'

Meanwhile, Travis was almost at the end of the twine. He hadn't seen any giraffes, monkeys, lions or anything really; only rough grass taller than he was.

Just as the twine was about to run out, the wilderness came to an abrupt end. Instead there was a row of paving slabs and immediately in front of him was a garden shed. It wasn't any old shed, but it was identical to the shed in Travis's own garden. Travis stared in amazement. No windows, great gaps in the ancient timbers, the felt hanging off the roof. But it's our shed, he thought. What's it doing here? Travis ran up to the door. No catch, bolt or lock. He tugged and heaved on the door, to no avail;

it wouldn't open. Just like ours, he thought. He couldn't believe it.

But it *is* our shed. Travis was convinced. He stood back and stared, then he noticed above the door, faded but still readable: PLATFORM 766. Ours is 731, he remembered. Tentatively, he approached the shed door again, stretched out his hand and pulled. No good, he thought, and made his way back along the ball of twine, winding it up as he went. Auntie Jennison was just relocking the records room door when Travis came rushing in.

'Auntie Jennison, Auntie Jennison!' he said excitedly. 'Our shed's in your garden!'

'Is it, dear? I wonder what it's doing there,' Auntie Jennison replied.

'Well it's not really our shed, but it is the same except for the number. It says "Platform 766".'

'Well you see, Travis, "Platform" is the name of a company that make sheds, and the number is the model number,' Auntie Jennison said. That seemed to satisfy Travis, and he went skipping off.

Tom tossed Auntie Jennison a glance; he didn't believe in lying to children.

Auntie Jennison knew exactly what the glance meant. She said, 'Tom, it would be really too much for him to take in at this moment. Leave it to his guide to choose the time.'

The journey back home was uneventful. In fact, Travis slept most of the way. But dream...? Didn't he just dream! And that's the way it was for the next two years.

Chapter Four

Alex wasn't sure if he and Travis could remain friends for much longer. Travis, although three months younger, seemed ten years older. It wasn't that Travis was nasty; in fact, if anything, he seemed gentler and kinder than he could remember.

But Travis had secrets which he said he couldn't share with anyone, and Alex didn't like that. After all, they were supposed to be friends.

And Alex, who had questions about everything, found that Travis had most of the answers, and he didn't like that either. It made him feel inferior. Only that morning, Alex had said to Travis, 'Do you believe in ghosts?'

Travis said, 'I'll explain it to you if you want, Raincoat.'

Alex wished he hadn't asked, as Travis's explanations seemed to go on all day.

'Right then, Raincoat, the first thing is, there are no such things as ghosts. People who think they hear or see ghosts are seeing visitors. Visitors are people just like you and me, who are alive, not dead, and there is no need to be frightened of them. You see, they're only observers and they can't hurt you.'

At this point Travis stopped. Alex couldn't believe his luck, but before he had time to think he heard himself saying, 'OK, Travis, but where do they come from then, these visitors?'

'Can't tell you that – it's a secret.' Travis's answer was even shorter and not one Alex wanted to hear. The thing was, though, Travis didn't really know the answer himself.

'Secrets, secrets, secrets! That's all I ever get from you these days,' said Alex, and immediately went into a sulk.

Later the same day, Travis heard Mentor's voice inside his head; this came as a bit of a shock, as he had heard him plenty of times in his dreams, but this was the first time when awake.

'Now don't be frightened, Travis. You need to talk to your dad. Tell him that Mentor says you're ready now.'

Feeling rather foolish, Travis said aloud, 'Is that really you, Mentor?'

The reply came back instantly. 'Yes... you must talk to Mr Travis.'

Travis went running off to find his mum, who for once was sitting doing absolutely nothing.

'What time is Dad home, Mum? Only, I'm ready now.'

'Ready for what, Travis?'

'I don't know, but Mentor said I've got to talk to Dad.'

All on purpose, Travis's dad was even later than ever, and it was Travis's bedtime.

'Come on, Travis, bed,' his mum said. 'I'll send your dad in to see you as soon as he gets back.'

'Oh, *Mum*!'

'No "oh, Mums" – bed right now!'

Travis fought to stay awake, but gradually sleep took over, and for the first time in over two years he slept a dreamless sleep.

Mr Travis didn't get home until gone eleven. He dutifully looked in on Travis but the boy didn't stir. It would all have to wait until tomorrow.

The next morning Travis woke to the sun shining through the bedroom window and the birds singing and twittering in the garden. His first thoughts were of his dad. He ran into his parents' bedroom, but there was no one there and the bed was already made. He glanced at the bedside alarm clock. Ten to eleven! He couldn't believe the time as he never usually slept for that long. When he eventually got downstairs, his mother was, as usual, busying herself in the kitchen.

'Good morning, dear! You've certainly had a good sleep,' she said.

'Where's Dad? Mum, I must talk to him – it's very, very, very important.'

'Your dad promised he would be back by seven tonight and he said you could have him all to yourself then.'

Travis prepared himself to spend the longest eight hours of his life. Alex was out with his parents for the day and even Mr Pomphrey had taken an unexpected trip to the Day Centre. Seven o'clock will never come, thought Travis.

But it did, and true to his word Tom was home a little before seven.

'Dad, Dad! Mentor told me to tell you I'm ready.'

'OK, son; we'll go and sit in the garden.'

Tom and Travis went through the living room, where Mrs Travis was just settling down to watch *Emmerdale*. Mrs Travis liked *Emmerdale*, *EastEnders*, *Coronation Street* and *Brookside* and had to juggle her life and the two video recorders they had to fit them all in. Mr Travis couldn't stand any of it and referred to it all as 'poo TV'.

'I'm going into the garden with Travis, Mother,' he said as they passed through the living room.

'That's all right dear, I've got plenty of my poo to watch to-night,' replied Mrs Travis, chuckling.

This was just as well, for Travis and his dad were going to be outside for rather a long time.

About a third of the way up the garden was a two-seater rustic bench. It faced the old shed, which was just in sight. Tom beckoned for Travis to sit down. Then he put his arm around his son, and when they were both comfortable, he began.

'Twenty-five years ago, your grandfather sat on this very seat and explained things to me. I'm going to try to do it the same way as your grandfather told me all those years ago, which was the way his father explained it to him, and his father before him…'

'What happened to Granddad, Dad?' Travis asked.

'Please don't interrupt, Travis. I hope you'll understand by the time I've finished.'

Travis settled back to listen.

'There are some things I'm going to tell you that you'll realise you already know. That is because if Mentor has done his job properly, and I'm sure he has, that knowledge is already inside your head.'

'What – like the scarper button, Dad?' Travis asked.

'Yes, just like the scarper button.'

'But why don't I know what it is or what it's for?'

'Well, you see, your brain is like a big sponge, and for the last couple of years Mentor has been putting more and more information into it. Now sometimes, just like a sponge when water leaks out, some of the information leaks out as well. That's why you can only remember bits and pieces. But don't worry, it's all going to come clear tonight and in the future.

'Now listen, when the world was created it was done so that everything balanced and had an opposite. For example, there's day and there's night, there's up and there's down, there's male and there's female. Get the idea?'

'Yes, Dad,' Travis replied, 'like summer and winter.'

'Exactly; and then there's good and evil. That's where we come in, and I'm glad to say, we're the good guys. But you already know that, don't you, Travis?'

Travis looked at his dad and said, 'Yes, I do. Did Mentor tell me?'

'Yes, Travis, and as I go on you'll realise he's told you a lot more besides. Right, good and evil. When the universe was created, as I've said, everything had an opposite and the opposites matched. You had just as much good as you had evil; there was a balance. But as time went on and man progressed and evolved, the evil grew while the good diminished. That's where the good guys come in… but more of that later.

'Now, Travis, I want to tell you about the past. About yesterday, the day before yesterday, the day before that and so on. The past is the past, it's done and dusted; it's finished; it can't be added to, altered in any way or moved. It's set in stone. We are all on a journey through time; an hour ago, a minute ago, even a second ago recedes farther and farther away as I speak, and it's finished with. But you already knew that as well, didn't you?'

'Dad…'

'Please don't interrupt, Travis,' Tom said.

'But it's ever so important, Dad.'

'OK, son, what is it?'

'I need a pee, Dad.'

Tom Travis suddenly realised that although Travis was very grown-up in a lot of ways, he was still only a child.

While Travis was in the house, Tom stared up towards the shed and remembered that fateful night twenty-five years ago. He could remember his father turning, smiling and waving as he went into the shed. It was the last time he ever saw him alive. His thoughts then turned to his mother; after Thomas Travis had disappeared, she withdrew into a world of her own. True, she still looked after Tom, who was only sixteen after all, but as he grew into a man she became more and more withdrawn. Finally, on his twenty-first birthday, she said to him, 'I can do no more for you now, Tom Travis.'

Within three weeks she'd died of a broken heart. Tom felt the tears well up in his eyes at the memory, just as Travis reappeared.

'What's up, Dad?' Travis asked.

Tom composed himself. 'I'm all right,' he said. 'Come on, sit back down, we have a lot to get through. Is your mum all right?'

'Yes, she's fine; she says she's got plenty of her poo to watch.'

Tom grinned. 'Right, now, where were we?'

'The past, Dad, you were telling me about the past.'

'Yes, as I was saying, you can't interfere with the past. But now, the future – that's something different altogether.'

Travis listened intently to his father, but just as he'd told him, nothing he had said was surprising him, and he felt quite comfortable with all of it.

Tom continued. 'Back in the past, many, many years ago, evil took over from good and the natural balance was upset. It was then that the visitors came about. Visitors are selected from families and are usually handed down, father to son or daughter and so on. No one visitor can right every wrong, although they would like to be able to, but most of them all do their bit. Then their children do theirs and so on, and all the time they are trying to restore the balance.'

'Who invented the visitors, Dad? Are we aliens?'

Tom laughed. 'No, we're not aliens, son! We're just ordinary people put here to do a job.'

'But who put us here?'

In answer Tom cast his eyes skywards. 'Now let me tell you about your grandfather. Your grandfather was a visitor, and when I was ready I was to take on his job. Just like you, my guide—'

Travis interrupted. 'What was his name, your guide?'

'My guide was a she,' Tom said. 'Her name was Ennia.'

'Is she still with you, Dad?' Travis asked.

'No, Travis, she's long gone. Your guide only stays with you until you're ready to go it alone.'

'Dad, what is a scarper button? Have you got one?'

'Yes, Travis, I've got one.'

'Can I see it then, please?' Travis asked.

Tom laughed. 'Travis, you've seen it hundreds of times!'

Tom undid the top two buttons of his shirt and pulled out a chunky, gold-looking cross on a thick chain. In the middle of the cross was a large stone. It didn't appear to be a diamond, but it was something similar, and in different lights it took on different colours.

'That's a scarper button!'

Travis didn't know what to expect, but he wasn't expecting a cross. 'Will I be getting one?' Travis asked, but he realised he already knew the answer. 'I'll be getting yours, Dad, won't I?'

'Yes, Travis,' with that his father reached each side of his neck, lifted the cross and chain over his head and slipped it over Travis's.

'Now, you understand that once it's on, you can't get it off, don't you?'

'Yes, Dad, I understand,' said Travis, and just to show his father he lifted it up, but it wouldn't go beyond his ears, although it had slipped over Tom's head so easily.

'That's it then, Travis. I'm finished now. I'm here to stay, but at least your mum will be pleased. And there was so much left to do.'

'Dad, was this Granddad's scarper button before you had it?'

'No, son, Granddad's disappeared with him. Now, Travis, let me tell you some more about your grandfather. Your grandfather was sitting by the side of me much as we are all those years ago and when we came to the scarper button, he said, "Tom, I don't want you to have it tonight as I've some unfinished business with Ivan Roberts. You shall have it when I get back. It's very important that I take one last journey." He disappeared into the shed, and that was it – he never returned. I never saw him alive again, but whenever I've had the chance over the last twenty-five years I've searched for him. I've searched time and time again, but it's all been a waste of time...' His voice trailed away.

'So who exactly is Ivan Roberts, Dad?'

'That's just it, son, he doesn't or didn't seem to exist. I've spent twenty-five years, every spare moment, looking for your grandfather and trying to track down the elusive Mr Roberts, or "Ivan the Terrible", as your granddad used to call him, because I'm sure he's the key to your grandfather's disappearance. I'm absolutely convinced of it. You see, Travis, I think that perhaps Ivan Roberts was a good guy gone bad. Sometimes, with the powers we're blessed with, some of us get tempted and take the wrong road. I used to think that Ivan Roberts was one of those people, but there is no record of any such person.'

'So where have you looked then, Dad? The library?'

Tom chuckled. 'You don't get a list like that in the library. No, I asked Auntie Jennison, because if anyone would know she would. But she couldn't help.'

Tom's shoulders started to shake and he sobbed at the thought of his father. Travis tried to get his arm round his dad but it only went halfway and he began to cry as well.

'Come on, you two!' It was Travis's mum. 'Whatever's going on out here?'

'Dad's a bit upset because of Granddad,' Travis replied.

'He's not the only one, looking at you,' his mum said. 'Do either of you want anything?'

'No, thank you,' they chorused, and both dabbed at their eyes and blew their noses.

The smell of the jasmine and the honeysuckle in the garden was a delight as the day turned to twilight, but neither Travis nor Tom even noticed. When Travis's mum went back into the house they returned to their conversation.

'Dad, do you know why I've been called?'

'I don't know, son, I just don't know,' Tom said. He reached into his trouser pocket and fished out a small silver box. 'This is for you, Travis; it's very important that tomorrow you wear it.'

He opened the box. Inside was a Casio digital wristwatch, with an alarm. 'The first time you go you will find it very tiring,' Tom went on. 'You must promise me that after ten minutes you will come back; that's what the alarm is for. It's all a new experience, and you'll find that your strength will go very quickly. You will gradually get used to it, but it will never come easy, and you will only ever manage a couple of hours at a time.'

Travis realised why for all these years his dad came home from work looking drained.

'OK, Dad, I promise – ten minutes. But Dad, where am I going?'

'That's entirely up to you, but I don't expect it will be too far away.'

The last rays of daylight were fast fading. The garden lights automatically came on and the garden took on a whole new look.

Travis snuggled down against his dad's chest.

'I've found things a bit difficult to explain tonight, Travis,' Tom said. 'I might have got things in the wrong order and I might not have made everything very clear, but over the days, weeks and months you will gradually understand. If there's anything you need to know, ask now and I'll try to explain.'

Tom Travis looked down at his boy; it had all been too much. Travis was sleeping like a baby. Tom swept him up with his big powerful arms and carried the sleeping boy in past his mother and up to Travis's room. Mrs Travis followed on behind.

Between them they gently undressed him and slid him into his bed. Travis didn't stir; Mentor was already talking to him.

Chapter Five

On coming down to breakfast, Travis couldn't believe his eyes. His dad was sitting directly opposite his mother, and he couldn't remember his mother looking so radiant and contented.

'Look who's joined us for breakfast, Travis!' she said.

Travis ran to his dad, who ruffled his son's hair. 'Here's my special boy, then,' he said.

'Dad, Dad, when can I get started?' Travis asked.

'After we've discussed the rules,' replied Tom.

'Rules?' Travis was confused. 'But hasn't Mentor told me them?'

'Not Mentor's rules – my rules. I'm going to tell you again what it was I said to you last night: only ten minutes to start with, as it's very tiring. You mustn't neglect your school work, although it will be very tempting. You'll find you should be top of the class in history and other things as well, because you'll have an advantage. You must never confide your gift in anyone – anyone at all. At best you will be branded as a liar and at worst a madman. You must not allow your advantages to make you big-headed and arrogant, and I want you to remember that absolutely nothing can happen to you as long as you stick with the past. It's the present that's the danger, as is the future. Finally, never ever forget why you have been given the gift. Do you understand?'

'Yes, Dad… when can I start?'

'Not until you've had something to eat,' interjected his mother.

But Travis was too excited. Try as he may, the toast just went round and round in his mouth.

'OK then, son, off you go – and remember, only ten minutes.'

Travis kissed his mum, hugged his dad and ran out into the garden towards the garden shed.

Travis's mum stood at the window watching as her son made his way towards the shed. Travis's dad turned away and instead stared intently at the clock.

'Morning, Travis.'

'Morning, Mentor.'

'Well, Travis, today's the day; you know what to do, don't you?'

'Yes, Mentor,' Travis replied under his breath.

Travis came to the shed door. He paused, looked at it and uncertainly stretched out his hand. His fingers gently wrapped themselves around the timbers and he pulled. The door swung open, noiselessly and without any effort.

He stared inside. Totally black. Quickly, he stepped inside as he knew he had to; the door swung shut behind him. Instantly the gloom was transformed into a soft yellow moon-like light.

'So far so good then, young Travis,' said Mentor.

Travis didn't answer; he was too busy trying to take it all in.

A corridor stretched away before him. He started to walk down it, and for the first time in his life he was in no hurry and strolled rather than ran. As he got farther along the passageway the light gradually got brighter and brighter until it seemed like daylight. Then in front of him were steps, thirteen in all. He made his way gingerly to the bottom of them. Immediately in front of him the corridor split in two. Travis instinctively knew he was to take the corridor to the left. Within a few short paces the corridor ended abruptly and he couldn't believe what he saw next: he had emerged onto a railway platform! There, hanging down on large chains to his right, was an enormous clock, in dark, almost black, wood, bearing an inscription at the top – 'NLRY' – and lower down 'Thwaites and Reed. Clerkenwell'. The face was in black roman numerals on a white background, and the two large hands left one in no doubt as to what time it was. Immediately in front of him, standing waiting was a solitary Pullman railway carriage.

'Wow, it's a train!' exclaimed Travis, stating the obvious.

'What did you expect – a DeLoreon?' Mentor replied, chuckling.

'But there's no engine,' observed Travis.

Mentor was still laughing. 'This isn't *Back to the Future*, you know. Why do you think you need an engine?'

'Well, to pull the carriage, of course.'

Mentor roared.

The Pullman carriage was turned out in an immaculate umber and cream livery and looked spotless.

'It was built in 1927,' said Mentor. 'It was your great-grandfather's idea; you can change it if you want.'

'No, thank you, Mentor; I think I rather like it.'

Along the side at almost roof level was the inscription 'Pullman' and below the row of windows in copperplate script was emblazoned the name 'Travis'. More discreetly, near the bottom of the bodywork, Travis could make out 'Pullman 4129'.

Travis hurried to the open door.

'This is where I leave you, then, Travis,' said Mentor, 'but I'll be waiting right here when you get back.'

'Oh yes,' said Travis, 'I forgot – you won't be coming with me, will you?'

'Not for a long time yet, Travis.'

Travis climbed up the step and went inside the Pullman; the walls were panelled in a variety of timbers with ornate marquetry panels inset. The arched roof was cream with old-fashioned looking lamps suspended from it. The curtains were of a rich yellow material and there was an old, comfortable-looking, dark green leather armchair. Just like a living room, thought Travis. Several feet behind the armchair stood a table and four chairs. A cream tablecloth had been perfectly placed over the table, which was set for dinner. Beautiful gleaming silverware reflected the light, and there was a solitary rose in a crystal stem vase sitting almost precisely in the middle of the table.

Travis settled into the armchair, as he knew he had to, and looked straight at the panel in front of him. It was just as he had seen it in his dreams.

At the top of the panel, at Travis's eye level, were rows of numbers, and below them a row of brass dials. Below them were more of the same. To the untrained eye it was a hotchpotch of numbers, dials and letters, but Travis knew exactly what they meant and what he had to do. At the side of the armchair, just within reach, were two very large books, bound in the same colour leather as the armchair. Travis knew he wouldn't need either of them this time.

Right, where shall I go? he thought. Not too far for the first time… He turned the necessary dials until they read '22nd August 2001, 11.30 a.m.'. Below the dials was a round, raised, red dome-like button. Travis set a ten-minute alarm on his watch, hesitated slightly, and then with both hands firmly pushed the button.

Nothing's happened, he thought. Everything was exactly the same; he hadn't moved. 'What a swizz!' he said aloud.

Travis climbed out of the Pullman and made his way back up the thirteen stairs. It was only when he tried to push the shed door open and his arm passed right through that he knew it had worked.

'Wow!' he exclaimed.

He stepped through the shed door and out into the bright sunlight. He took a good long look around himself. There, over in the corner, was the silver birch tree looking considerably smaller than it had been that morning, and the shrubs seemed to have shrunk as well. Travis made his way towards the house. It was a weird feeling; he wasn't actually walking, he wasn't exactly flying either – it was more of a floating sensation, and yet now and again his feet would touch the ground. He drifted into the kitchen. His mother was facing him but looking down at the table in front of her.

'Mum,' he said, rather tentatively.

Mrs Travis didn't look up. He walked over to his mother and waved the flat of his hand just inches from her face. Wow, double wow, I'm invisible, he thought. Travis continued through the house and up the stairs to his bedroom. Toys he had long forgotten littered the floor and his TV was playing quietly to itself. You'll be in trouble for leaving that on, Travis, he thought to himself. I wonder if I can see myself in a mirror, he thought, and went into the bathroom. Standing on tiptoes, he stared into the mirror but all he could see was the tiled wall behind him. *Wicked!*

Hearing footsteps running up the stairs, he perched himself on the edge of the bath. Into the bathroom bounded Travis. Teetering precariously on the edge of the bathroom stool, he grabbed the washbasin, pulled himself up and peered into the mirror. He wiggled his tooth and then, as quickly as he had arrived, he was gone.

It was all too much for Travis. He remained motionless. That was me, he thought. I haven't grown all that much, though, have I? he asked himself. He didn't know how long he sat there trying to come to terms with things, but suddenly the infuriating buzzing of his watch told him time was up.

Travis raced down the stairs, out through the kitchen and up the garden. Forgetting himself, he made a grab for the shed door. He passed straight through, along the corridor, down the steps and into the carriage. It was only as he settled into the armchair that he remembered what Mentor had told him.

'All you need to do to come back, Travis, is push the scarper button at any time in any place.'

What a dummy! he thought. He reached inside his shirt and pushed. Again, nothing seemed to happen, but Travis had more confidence this time, and when he made his way back out of the shed, he had to physically open the shed door and he could see that the silver birch had regrown and everything else was back to normal.

Waves of tiredness swept over him, and by the time he got to the house, he was yawning and almost asleep. Excitement woke him up, however, for as soon as he saw his mum and dad, he shouted, 'Mum, Dad! I saw you, Mum, and I saw me!'

'All right, Travis, calm down,' said Mr Travis. 'You go and have a nap, and then you can tell us all about it later.'

'Yes, Dad,' replied Travis, yawning. 'I've had it.'

'You must be tired, young man,' said his mother. 'I've never known you in a hurry to go to bed.'

Travis went up to his bedroom and collapsed on the bed. Pretty tiring, this time travelling, he thought, and almost instantly was sound asleep.

Just after one o'clock that afternoon, Travis stirred. Lying there on his back, he pieced things together and began to wonder if it had been all a dream.

Travis joined his parents just as his mother was dishing up lunch.

'I was just about to call you, dear,' said Mrs Travis. 'Have you washed your hands?'

Settling at the table, this time with clean hands, Travis glanced at his mum and dad. They both sat there looking at him expectantly.

'Well?' his dad asked.

Travis related to them almost exactly what had happened to him that morning and then said, 'There are a couple of things I don't really understand...'

His dad interrupted. 'Probably more than a couple, Travis, but as you use your gift more and more things will become clear to you.'

'But I don't know what I'm supposed to do.'

'I'm afraid I don't know why you've been called so early, Travis, but believe me there will be a good reason. Now I want you to promise me that you'll only visit once a day, until you get used to it. Do you understand?'

'OK, Dad, I understand,' said Travis.

Later that afternoon he went round to visit Mr Pomphrey. He had a job concentrating on *Countdown* as he had so much going on inside his head.

'Not your usual self today, Travis, are you?' Mr Pomphrey remarked. 'I'm already ten points up on you and it's only just started.'

'I've had a very traumatic experience this morning,' said Travis in a very grown-up fashion.

'Really? Traumatic, eh? I'm surprised you even understand the word,' Mr Pomphrey laughed.

'It's nothing to laugh about, Mr Pomphrey,' said Travis seriously.

He was itching to tell Mr Pomphrey all about his adventure, but he knew he just couldn't.

The adverts came on and Mr Pomphrey went out into the kitchen and got himself another cup of tea and a cold Coke for Travis.

When he came back he settled himself into his chair, turned to Travis and was about to speak when Travis noticed his eyes. They were looking first at Travis, then very quickly turning and looking to the right of the television, and back again and so forth.

'What's the matter, Mr Pomphrey?' Travis said. 'Are you all right?'

'Be a love, Travis, pass me the brandy bottle and a glass from the cupboard there.' He gestured towards the cupboard.

Travis hastily fetched the brandy. Mr Pomphrey poured himself a generous measure and gulped it down all in one go.

'Are you sure you're all right, Mr Pomphrey?' Travis was growing concerned.

Mr Pomphrey didn't answer for a few seconds. Then he said, 'It must have been a trick of the light. For a minute there I thought I saw...' His voice faltered. 'I thought I saw... Oh, never mind. Come on, we're missing *Countdown*.'

The next day, although excited at the prospect of another trip, Travis decided that as it was so tiring he would leave it until the evening; then he could go straight to bed afterwards.

Travis's parents confided in each other that they were surprised and pleased that Travis was already adopting a sensible attitude to his new gift.

Travis spent some of the day sorting out his school books and doing some work set by his teacher. With everything else going on he had totally forgotten that the work had to be handed in on the first day of the autumn term. He paid a fleeting visit to Alex, but somehow Alex's interests weren't Travis's any more.

That evening he said goodbye to his mum and dad and walked towards the shed.

'Good evening, Travis.' It was Mentor.

'Hello, Mentor, how are you?' Travis asked.

'I don't know how it is to be anything other than well, thank you, Travis. It's not a concept I am really familiar with, but thank you for asking. Where do you intend to go today?'

'Well, I've been set some history homework by Mr Dalziel,' replied Travis, 'so I'm going to visit Dunkirk.'

'Try to remember the scarper button today, Travis.'

Travis opened the shed door and went straight in. This time he couldn't get down the thirteen steps fast enough. Arriving inside the Pullman, he settled into the armchair. Now, he thought, I'll need one of the books; he reached over. On the leather-bound cover of the top book it displayed the word 'Places'. That's the one, he thought. It was large and bulky and Travis needed both hands to pick it up. He thumbed through the well-worn pages. 'Ah, here we are… Dunkirk. Oh, there are three with platforms,' he said aloud. 'Right, Dunkirk, France, Platform 1069.'

He punched the coordinates into the panel. 'Now the date,' he said. He took a piece of paper from his pocket and read '2nd June 1940'. 'Right – now, the time. Shall we say 4 p.m.?' he asked himself. 'Why not?'

He set the time, then his alarm wristwatch, and, with more confidence this time, pushed the button. Just as before, nothing seemed to have happened, but this time Travis knew instinctively that it had. He rose quickly from his chair, as he knew he had barely ten minutes, and hurried to the shed door. He ran out into a patch of rough ground; a road almost destroyed by bombs and mortar fire lay beyond. A broken sign with an arrow pointed to his right; it displayed the words: *'Dunkerque – la plage'*. In the distance he could hear the chatter of machine-gun fire, the occasional deep booming of larger artillery and the scream of fighter planes swooping overhead. He hurried through a group of German soldiers who were standing around chatting and smoking; more Germans were at the edge of the beach, all firing their rifles towards the sea.

As he approached the beach, he could see that the sky was black with smoke from burning fuel, boats and tanks, and the stench of burning flesh was indescribable. The staccato sound of gunfire filled the air and a deeper *boom, boom, boom* came from far away. The sand stretched away from him to a flat, distant black sea. Cowering in small groups all over the beach were soldiers, some praying, some crying softly, mostly silent. He could hear the wounded calling for help as he started to pick his way across the beach through the groups of men, some bleeding, some dying. There, sitting facing him, was a fresh-faced young soldier with just the hint of a wispy moustache, his tunic ripped and dirty and his trousers torn. His helmet was long gone but he still clung to his trusty rifle. Travis didn't have to look twice; he knew immediately. My God, he thought, it's Mr Pomphrey.

Without thinking, Travis said aloud, 'You're going to be all right, Mr Pomphrey.'

Travis turned and saw long snakes of men in single file wading out to the waiting boats, some with their rifles held with both hands above their heads. Suddenly there was a loud explosion and a plume of water raced upwards towards the sky. Some of the men in one of the columns had gone, some were floating face down in the water. He could hear people screaming. It was all too much for Travis, and he pushed the scarper button.

The holidays over, Travis went back to school on the following Tuesday. He hadn't ventured into the shed since his trip to Dunkirk. Travis handed his homework in to Mr Dalziel with a flourish. He was rather proud of the research he'd done about Dunkirk; of course, he couldn't mention his trip.

'Well, Travis,' said Mr Dalziel, 'you look so pleased with yourself, I think you can read your homework out to the whole class.'

'My pleasure, sir,' said Travis just a little too cockily, and stood up.

'General John Gort, who had won a VC in the First World War, commanded the British Expeditionary Force in France, and by May 1940, there were 394,165 men there under his control. However, the opposing German army proved too powerful and they were forced to retreat to Dunkirk. Winston Churchill, the prime minister at the time, decided to try to rescue the troops that were stranded there and set up Operation Dynamo. They mobilised every craft that could get across the Channel and started the rescue operation. It lasted from 27th May 1940 to 4th June. On 2nd June alone, 6,695 souls were rescued from the beach. All that needless waste of life and suffering shows the futility of war,' Travis concluded, and sat down.

'Travis,' Mr Dalziel said, 'it's too short, and it might be historically correct, but I doubt very much that you're in any position to comment on war unless you've experienced it personally. Six out of ten.'

Travis bit his tongue.

Immediately after the history lesson came the games lesson. Alex and Travis were changing into their shorts and singlets when Butch Jenkins came wandering over.

Butch – or Paul, as was his proper name – was the school bully; he stood a good six inches taller than Travis and was bigger about. But in his case it was all flab and no muscle. He had piggy little eyes set too close together, and once Alex had observed that even his eyelids were overweight. His favourite was to pick bogies out of his nose and make the first year children lick his fingers, while chanting,

'Hot snot, bogie pie
Eyeballs dipped in phlegm
A cup of cold sick to wash it down
And bring it up again.'

'What's that round your neck then, Travis?' Butch asked. 'You look like a little girl. *Girlie, girlie, girlie!*'

Travis started to bristle but said nothing.

'You know the school rules about jewellery! Give it here – I'm going to take it to Teacher.'

He made a grab at Travis's scarper button. Travis ducked, and as he straightened up, he caught Butch under the chin with the top of his head. In pain, Butch lurched forward clumsily, but Travis's dad had taught him the rudiments of boxing and Travis ducked again, stepped to one side and hit Butch right in the left eye.

Mr Dalziel, who came in at that point, told the other teachers secretly later on that it was one of the best right-handers he'd ever seen.

'Travis, Jenkins, go to the headmaster's study right *now!*'

Travis, Jenkins and Mr Dalziel faced Mr Fear, the headmaster, across his desk.

'Well, Headmaster,' said Mr Dalziel, 'this young man standing in front of you was telling me not ten minutes ago about the futility of war... now look at his companion!'

Butch already had a bruise darkening on his chin and his left eye was swelling, closing and changing colour all at the same time. He had the slumped shoulders of a beaten man.

'Right! What have you got to say for yourself then, Travis?' the headmaster asked.

'Nothing, sir.'

'*Nothing, sir,*' the headmaster mimicked.

'And how about you, Jenkins?'

'Travis is wearing jewellery, sir, and he hit me for no reason, sir.'

'Is that true, Travis?'

'Yes and no, sir,' Travis said.

'What d'you mean, boy?' The headmaster was losing his temper.

'I mean, yes, I'm wearing something, and no, I didn't hit him for no reason.'

'Let me see what you've got on,' the headmaster said.

Travis showed him the scarper button.

'Take it off, boy, I'm confiscating it! Take it off, do you hear?'

'It won't come off and you can't make me,' Travis protested, and started to cry.

There was a tap on the headmaster's study door and as it opened, Travis seized his chance. He ducked under Mr Dalziel's outstretched arm and legged it for home.

When he got home, breathless and frightened all at the same time, his mum and dad were just getting into the car to go shopping. On seeing Travis, Mr Travis turned the engine off and climbed out of the car. His son was in floods of tears.

'He... he...' Travis couldn't speak. Ten minutes and several tissues later, Mr and Mrs Travis had the whole story. Mr Travis bundled Travis into the car and drove him back to school. 'Stay here, Travis,' he said. He jumped out of the car and strode towards the school. Travis had never seen him looking so angry.

'What's Dad going to do, Mum?' he asked.

'Don't worry, dear, trust your dad.'

They sat there in silence. A good few minutes went by and then Mr Travis, accompanied by the headmaster, approached the car.

His father was all smiles. Travis's dad opened the back door and said, 'Hop out, Travis. The headmaster has got something he wants to say to you.'

'Yes, you can wear your jewellery, and I'd like you to come back to school,' said the head.

'*Please*!' Mr Travis raised his voice.

'Please,' repeated the headmaster sheepishly.

By play time Travis was the class hero, by lunch time the school's.

'So what was it your dad said to Mr Fear, then?' Alex asked.

'I don't know, but whatever it was, it did the trick,' Travis replied.

Butch had been sent home nursing his eye and his bruised pride; things would never be the same for him again.

It was another three weeks before Travis felt confident enough to venture back to the shed. Mentor greeted him on the way in as usual and Travis, almost as nervous as the first time, chose to go just a few weeks into the past – just to get used to it again, as he told his dad.

'Where are you off today then, Travis?' Mentor asked.

'I'm going back to school.' Travis started laughing.

Travis was already in the headmaster's study by the time Mr Travis knocked on the door.

'Come in,' said Mr Fear. 'Ah, Mr Travis, I'm glad you've come to see me. Your boy's in very serious trouble and I'm considering suspending him.'

Mr Travis faced the headmaster and said in a quiet, even voice, 'I haven't got time to stand here and discuss the rights and wrongs of your school rules, or what happened today. My boy has given me an account of them and he doesn't tell lies. So I'll tell you the way that things are. Travis *will* wear his jewellery, and nothing more will be said about him putting the school bully in his place – something you should have done a long time ago. Otherwise the education authorities will learn what it is you do every lunch time, and with whom…'

The headmaster blanched. 'But tha-that's, that's *blackmail*,' he stuttered.

'That's very perceptive of you,' replied Travis's dad. 'Now come out to the car and fetch Travis.'

Travis was listening intently. He hadn't really understood what it all meant, but whatever it was, it had worked. He watched as his dad strode out of the room, with a very sheepish-looking headmaster obediently scuttling behind him.

Chapter Six

Two weeks before half term, Travis finished school, hurried home, dropped off his school bag and slipped through the fence to Mr Pomphrey's. As usual, he let himself in through the back door, calling for Mr Pomphrey as he went. No answer. That's funny, thought Travis, and he called out again. He walked into the living room. No sign of anyone. He called out again. Silence. He pushed open the passage door and could see a foot poking round the bottom of the stairs. '*Oh no!*' Travis exclaimed.

As he ran forward, Mr Pomphrey came into view; he was crumpled up at the foot of the stairs, and Travis could see that there was a slight trickle of blood coming from the side of his head.

Travis didn't panic; instead he walked quickly to the telephone, dialled 999 and called for an ambulance.

He went into the kitchen, found a cloth, ran it under the tap, wrung it out and made his way back to Mr Pomphrey. Very gingerly, Travis dabbed the wound on the side of Mr Pomphrey's head.

Mr Pomphrey started to stir. 'What happened?' he asked.

'I think you must have fallen down the stairs, but you're going to be all right, Mr Pomphrey.'

Mr Pomphrey reached up and gripped Travis's arm tightly. 'What did you say then, Travis?' he asked.

'I said I think you fell down the stairs, Mr Pomphrey.'

'No,' said Mr Pomphrey, 'after that…'

'I said, "You're going to be all right, Mr Pomphrey".'

Mr Pomphrey pulled himself up on one arm and was about to say something, but he stopped and just stared at Travis.

'Lie still, Mr Pomphrey. There's an ambulance on the way.'

'Honestly, Travis, I'll be all right.'

Travis heard the wailing of the sirens in the distance. 'They're here now, Mr Pomphrey, just lie still, please.'

Mr Pomphrey did as he was told.

As soon as the ambulance men arrived, Travis ran home to tell his mum and dad, and they immediately hurried round to Mr Pomphrey's house.

'It's all right, Travis, I'll go with Mr Pomphrey. You stay here and look after your mum,' said Tom.

As the ambulance men carried Mr Pomphrey out through the front door, Mr Pomphrey took Travis's arm and said, 'You're a good boy, Travis, thank you.' Travis felt ten feet tall.

Tom came home from the hospital just after nine. Both Travis and his mum were listening for the car to pull up.

'Good news,' said Tom, 'he's going to be all right. He has a slight concussion, some bruising, and he's had a couple of stitches in the side of his head. They're keeping him in overnight for observation, and he will be home tomorrow if everything is OK.'

'Can I come with you to pick him up, please, Dad? After all, there's no school tomorrow.'

'Of course you can, Travis. I'm very pleased with you and what you did today, you've made me very proud.'

Travis felt twenty feet tall now.

On Saturday morning, Travis and Tom fetched Mr Pomphrey from hospital, but it wasn't until teatime on Monday that he and Travis were on their own together. They watched *Countdown* as usual, and as Travis was about to say his goodbyes, Mr Pomphrey said to him, 'Are you in any hurry, Travis? Only I'd like to tell you a story.'

'Sure thing, Mr Pomphrey, I like stories,' said Travis, settling himself back in the chair.

'Back in 1939,' Mr Pomphrey started, 'I volunteered to join the army. I was not quite seventeen but I lied about my age in order to join up. I joined the Tigers – that's the Second Battalion, Hampshire Regiment to you, or "the Incomparables", as we were known. Almost immediately after training we were sent with the British Expeditionary Force to fight in France. We were the first to disembark in France, you know, and we were the last to leave, and we still had all our equipment intact.'

Travis could tell Mr Pomphrey was very proud of all this.

Mr Pomphrey continued. 'On the boat going over I got chatting with another youngster. He was older than me – almost twenty. We hit it off from the first. His name was Richard Webber, and he came from up north somewhere. His parents had been killed in a motorbike accident some months before and he decided to join the army. He said he wanted to kill a few Germans before it was too late; I didn't understand what he meant at the time. Anyway, things got quite tough in France, but we always looked out for each other.

'One night, it was very late and we were in a ditch listening to the mortars whistling overhead. "Bill," he said to me (Travis had never realised that Mr Pomphrey was called Bill), "I've a secret that I need to share. You see, I won't be around much longer, and you're the only person I know who won't ridicule me when I tell you what I need to say." I didn't interrupt him, Travis; I could see he was deadly serious. He looked straight at me, and although it was nearly dark I could see the truth in his eyes.'

'What happened next, Mr Pomphrey?'

'He told me he was a "visitor" and all that that meant. I believed every word he said, and I told him so. After that, he thanked me and shook my hand. The next day he got killed; he already knew it was going to happen.'

Travis thought he'd better keep quiet.

'So all this brings me round to you, young Travis. When I was on the beach at Dunkirk waiting for my turn in the boat, above all that noise and confusion I heard a voice, plain as you like, and the voice said, "You'll be all right, Mr Pomphrey." No one ever called me Mr Pomphrey in those days, and it's funny, but I've heard that same voice again recently…'

Travis didn't answer.

'Then there was the time we were watching *Countdown*, you were sitting beside me, and then for an instant you were standing there as well, right beside yourself – there were two of you! From my bedroom window I've watched your dad go into the shed, and now you. You're the same as Richard Webber… you're a visitor, aren't you, Travis?'

Travis hesitated. 'I'm not allowed to say, Mr Pomphrey.'

At this, Mr Pomphrey grew quite excited. He bounced up and down in his chair. 'I'm right, I knew I was right! Travis, that's wonderful – come and give us a hug!'

'I'll be in all sorts of trouble if Dad finds out I've told you,' Travis said.

'But you've told me nothing, Travis, nothing at all. But if you're worried, I won't say anything. So instead of my tin hat stories, think of the stories you'll be able to tell me.'

Travis slept well that night; he was glad Mr Pomphrey knew.

Half term arrived, and, with it, Travis's sister, Becky. Travis was over the moon, especially as she was all on her own. It wasn't as if he disliked her husband, Mark; in fact, he was very nice, but he didn't give him sweets like Mr Pomphrey did.

Becky took Travis to the zoo on the Monday; Travis had mixed feelings about animals being kept in cages, but for once, as he was so pleased to see his sister, he decided to just enjoy himself.

Becky knew nothing of 'visiting'. Tom thought it would be best if Becky was told all about it, but Mrs Travis would have none of it, so Becky had always been kept in the dark. This meant their dad had to pretend to go to work, and of course Travis had to stay at home, so there was to be no visiting for him. The week quickly passed and by the following Monday Becky was just a memory again.

'Dad?' It was Travis.

'Yes, son?' said Tom.

'All this visiting is all right but I don't seem to be doing any good. I know I've learnt a lot about history and stuff, but—'

Tom interrupted. 'What you're trying to say, Travis, is that you don't seem to have any direction or purpose – is that it?'

'Yes that's exactly it, Dad.'

'You see, Travis, I know you think that your dad can walk on water, but I've puzzled and puzzled trying to understand why you've been called so early, and why, and I just don't know. You see, one day you'll be called on to do your bit; it might be as a detective, historian – maybe something else, I really don't know. But one thing I *do* know is that there will be a good reason.'

It was mid-November when Travis's mum dropped the bombshell. They were all sitting down to breakfast, and Mrs Travis was reading some post. 'Oh, that's good,' she said, almost to herself, 'I've got some news, Tom, Travis. Becky is going to stay with her in-laws for Christmas, but she will be round on Christmas morning and Boxing Day. That means of course that her bedroom will be free, so I've invited Auntie Jennison for the holiday, and she's just written to say she'll come.'

A stunned silence from Travis. A more enthusiastic, 'Oh, lovely, that's nice; she won't be on her own this year,' from Tom.

Travis quickly regained his composure. 'But what about all that horrible cigarette smoke?' he asked.

'Auntie Jennison said she'd only smoke in the garden or in Becky's old room,' replied his mother.

'Well, then there's Scampi,' said Travis. 'She can't possibly leave him; he's got to be fed.'

'It's all right, Travis. Auntie Jennison's bringing him along,' Mrs Travis said.

'But what about those huge holes in the fence? He'll get out.'

'Your dad's got plenty of time on his hands now, and it's about time they were mended anyway.'

'But I won't be able to cut through Mr Pomphrey's garden!' Travis was putting up every objection possible.

'Well, it's about time you walked around, anyway,' said Tom. 'You're old enough now.'

'Well, it's not fair for her to leave the canary.' Travis thought he'd try one last ploy.

'The canary's coming with her,' said Mrs Travis.

Travis finished his breakfast in stony silence.

The day before Travis's tenth birthday, he was reminded of Auntie Jennison's impending visit.

'Postman's been, Travis,' said his mother. 'There's a parcel for you.'

Travis immediately recognised the shaky, spidery handwriting.

'It's from Auntie Jennison,' he said, in rather a flat tone. 'Bet it's another pair of gloves.'

Travis's dad looked up from his breakfast.

'Don't be so ungrateful, Travis; you know your Auntie Jennison means well.'

Inside the parcel was a birthday card. Covered in flowers, it was obviously meant for a girl. 'Oh, lovely, blooming lovely,' said Travis, and threw the card down on the table.

Travis's father looked across the table sternly at his son. 'You're not too old to get a smack, Travis! Auntie Jennison thinks the world of you, so just be grateful and accept her gifts with good grace.'

Travis opened the package inside the parcel. He spotted the navy blue colour first. Gloves, he thought. He tried his best to look pleased, as he knew his dad was watching him. Travis tugged at the contents.

'Wow, look at this!' said Travis. 'It's a scarf!' He wrapped it around his neck. It was warm and cosy. 'Wow,' he said again, 'it's OK, it really is.'

Inside the wrapping paper was a note, which Travis read aloud.

'Dear Travis, A little something to keep you warm through the winter. Your poor old Auntie just can't concentrate enough to knit gloves any more and if I can't knit them perfectly like I used to, I'm not going to knit them at all. Love, Auntie J.'

After the laughter had subsided, Travis looked at his parents, and with a mischievous grin said, 'Oh, no! How am I going to manage for gloves now?'

Later that day Travis told Mr Pomphrey all about Auntie Jennison sending him a scarf for his birthday.

'It's all right, Travis, I've remembered it's your birthday tomorrow, never fear.'

'Oh, Mr Pomphrey, I never told you about Auntie Jennison for that.' Travis felt quite embarrassed.

Travis had never said too much about Auntie Jennison to Mr Pomphrey before, but he felt now was a good time to tell him about all her quirks and foibles. He was very careful to leave out the blowing off bit, however.

'She's quite a character, by the sound of it,' said Mr Pomphrey, 'I think I'd rather like to meet her. You know, all these years that I've lived here and I've never had the chance to meet her.'

'Believe me, Mr Pomphrey, you don't want to,' Travis replied.

9th December dawned grey, dank and miserable – quite the

opposite to Travis's mood. I'm ten, I'm ten, he thought. Happy birthday to me, happy birthday to me!

Travis rushed downstairs and found the postman had already been. Quite a pile of envelopes was on the floor behind the front door, and Travis quickly went through them. Nine for me, he thought. Into the dining room, and he found another two on the table. That makes eleven, and, with Auntie Jennison's, twelve…

'Wow, that's one more than last year.'

The rest of the day passed in a blur: school, presents, a small party, and a phone call from Becky; Mentor singing 'Happy birthday' and a visit from Mr Pomphrey.

'So have you enjoyed your birthday, Travis?' his dad enquired at bedtime.

'Wicked, Dad,' said Travis, 'absolutely wicked!'

'What was the best bit?'

'Well,' Travis scratched his head, 'I think it was Mentor singing "Happy birthday". It was nice, even if it was a bit of a shock; and of course, Auntie Jennison's scarf.' Travis was being crafty; he knew being nice about Auntie Jennison would earn him some brownie points.

'That's nice of you to say about Auntie Jennison's present, Travis. Now, what was the worst part?'

'Without a doubt, Dad, Alex's sister Kirsty turning up for my party – and she wouldn't leave me alone all the time she was here!'

'You won't mind that when you get older, Travis,' his dad said.

'Never ever! Girls? I don't think so, uh-uh!'

Christmas was looming on the horizon, and there were only three more days to the end of term. Travis was determined to get his homework out of the way as soon as term time finished – well, at least the history part.

'What's the project for the holiday then, sir?' he asked Mr Dalziel.

'You're a bit keen all of a sudden, aren't you, Travis?' said Mr Dalziel. 'Well, I don't suppose it matters if I tell you all now. I want an essay on the Great Fire of London… and Travis, more of an effort than Dunkirk, eh?'

Travis had managed to extend his visiting to fifteen minutes by now, but he thought it would take several trips to produce the essay. Travis decided to start that very evening. He told his mum and dad where he was going, and Mrs Travis said, 'Have a nice time dear,' just as if he was going to the cinema or the park. It seemed she had gotten quite used to things by now.

As soon as Travis ventured up the garden path towards the shed, Mentor spoke.

'Where are we off tonight then, Travis?'

'Well, I don't know about you, but it's 1666 for me,' said Travis.

'No need to be cheeky, Travis! You know what I mean.'

'Sorry, Mentor. I'm going to see the Great Fire of London. It's for a school essay.'

'Well, I can help you there then, Travis. You'll need platform 311 – it's at the back of Pudding Lane, where the fire started.'

'How do you know that, Mentor?'

Mentor chuckled. 'You don't think you're the only one I've had to guide, do you?'

Travis settled into the armchair: 12.45 a.m., 2nd September 1666. Platform 311. Travis pushed the 'go' button.

Travis emerged from Platform 311. The night was pitch black; he'd never seen as many stars, and so bright, with no street lights to lighten the night sky. Cool brisk east winds passed right through him which would fan the flames later. Far away, two cats were fighting.

Gradually his eyes became accustomed to the dark and he went around to the front of a row of houses and shops. Above one of the shops was the name, 'Thomas Farynor'. Travis remembered that this was the seat of the whole fire. As he stood watching, he heard a crackling noise, and through the downstairs window he could see flames quietly lapping at the window pane.

Within seconds rather than minutes the flames had spread upwards and outwards, and the lapping had become a roar. From within the house Travis could hear shouting and screaming. Then suddenly two men and two women were clambering through an upstairs window and starting to crawl along the rooftops to escape the flames.

From within the house Travis could hear more screaming and

a third female – a girl – appeared at the window. The quartet stopped, turned and called to the girl to follow them. She stood transfixed at the window, lacking the nerve to climb out, her face set with a look of terror.

Travis shouted, '*Get out, get out!*'

But of course she couldn't hear him. Quite suddenly the flames engulfed her, and in an instant she was gone.

Travis's watch alarm sounded. He didn't hesitate, but pushed the scarper button. Then he walked wearily back down the garden path, both fascinated and horrified at what he had just witnessed.

At 2 a.m. Travis woke up, screaming and crying. His mother was sitting on his bed, her arms around him.

'There, there, Travis. It's all right now, it was only a night-mare.'

Travis sobbed and cried. Eventually his mother settled him back down, but Travis spent a fitful night.

The next morning, before Travis was up, his mum rounded on her husband.

'Tom Travis,' she said, 'I need a word with you.'

Tom knew whenever she used his full name there was trouble ahead.

'You didn't hear a word from Travis last night, did you, Tom?'

'No, Mother, can't say I did.'

Travis's mum went on to tell him about Travis's nightmare.

'He's just too young for all this, Tom; you just don't know what it's doing to the boy. I want it to stop right now, I mean it!'

'Now you know full well, Barbara' – Tom never used her Christian name unless he was deadly serious, preferring to call her Mother – 'that you can say or do what you want, it can't be stopped, it's out of our hands. The only thing I can do is talk to the boy.'

'Do that then, Tom; but I'm not happy, not happy at all.'

'I'm not exactly happy myself, Mother,' he added.

Travis turned up for breakfast well after school had started, 'Oh, Mum, why didn't you wake me? I'm late for school now,' he complained.

'You needed your rest, Travis, and your dad's got something important to say to you, so don't go rushing about.'

Travis's dad came into the kitchen. 'How are you feeling this morning, son?' he asked.

'Fine, Dad, I'm just fine. I had a nightmare last night, but afterwards Mentor came and talked to me. I'll be all right now. Honest.'

'What did Mentor have to say for himself, then?' Tom enquired.

'Well, I can't remember all of it – at least I don't think I can – but I suppose it's all in there somewhere. I feel calm this morning, and I know I will be able to cope next time I see something horrible... well, I hope I can.'

Tom realised his son was growing up in a hurry.

Despite what he'd said at breakfast about feeling fine, Travis wasn't so sure, and decided to wait until after the Christmas festivities before he ventured into the shed again.

Monday, 22nd December dawned, more like a spring day than midwinter.

'What a lovely morning, Travis,' his mother remarked.

'Yes, Mum,' Travis replied, 'we'll probably get a lot of this now; you know, it's all due to global warming. This is all right for the short term but unfortunately the long-term implications are...'

Travis's mother was laughing. 'I only said it was a nice day, Travis, I didn't want a lecture on meteorology.'

Travis started to laugh, and just then his dad walked in. Tom winked at his wife and said in a rather stern voice, 'I'll stop your laughing, young Travis.'

'Why? What's up, Dad?' he asked.

'There's nothing up, but I'm driving up to fetch your Auntie Jennison today. Do you want to come?'

'Oh, Dad,' was all Travis could say.

Travis went round to see Alex later in the morning. He felt he had been rather neglecting him of late, and after all they'd been friends all their lives.

'Travis, just the man,' said Alex. 'I've decided I don't want to get in trouble when I go back to school, so I'm making a start on my homework. We could do it together, if you like...'

Travis jumped at the idea. 'I'm up for it, if you are.'

'Here, look what I've got from the Internet, Travis; it's all about the Great Fire of London.'

Travis started to read. He felt an inner calmness sweep over him as he read of the events that started the fire.

The account was so accurate, as Travis remembered it, that it was almost as if the author was there, as Travis had been.

'Who wrote this?' Travis asked casually.

'No idea,' Alex replied.

'A visitor,' Travis said out loud before he could stop himself.

'A *what*?' Alex asked.

'I said it sounds like something that A Visitor wrote… he's a journalist; haven't you ever heard of him?'

'Can't say that I have,' replied Alex.

'Dummy,' said Travis.

'Dummy yourself!' said Alex, and the wrestling match started.

Chapter Seven

'What time are you expecting Auntie Jennison, then, Travis?' Mr Pomphrey asked.

'About six, I think, Mr Pomphrey.'

'Now, you must promise me you'll bring Auntie Jennison round to meet me, won't you?'

'I don't know if you'd get on, Mr Pomphrey, and I don't know if she likes *Countdown*. In fact I'm pretty sure she doesn't,' Travis lied convincingly.

'Nonsense, Travis! It's the grand final tomorrow, and then it's not on again until after Christmas, so you must bring her around.'

'All right, Mr Pomphrey,' said Travis, 'you win!'

Travis heard his dad toot his car horn at about ten past six.

'Come on, Travis, they're here!' his mother called out.

Travis dutifully followed his mother out to the drive. The car doors swung open, clouds and clouds of cigarette smoke billowed out, and Travis's dad got out of the car looking as if a lie-down in a dark room would do him some good.

Then the dog from hell emerged, barking his head off, on the end of a lead about ten feet long. He was followed by Auntie Jennison holding the canary's cage aloft and at arm's length. The canary was already squawking and flapping all around his cage.

Oh no, thought Travis.

On top of her usual clothes, Auntie Jennison was wearing a huge, moth-eaten fur coat and sported a 1930s Indiana Jones-style dark brown Fedora hat. Travis noticed she still had her headscarf on underneath.

Travis glanced over disapprovingly at the sight of the fur coat.

'Come and take Scampi, Travis,' she said, 'and don't worry about the fur coat, the animals were dead about thirty years before I bought it.'

Travis's dad went around to the boot of the car; he dragged out a huge suitcase on wheels.

My God, how long is she staying? Travis wondered.

They all hurried into the house. Auntie Jennison was moaning and complaining all the time about the cold.

The warmest December day for thirty-odd years, and just listen to her, thought Travis.

Travis's mother took Auntie Jennison up to Becky's room, and Travis's dad struggled on behind with the suitcase.

'Travis!' his father called down the stairs, 'go out to the garage, would you? There's an electric fire right at the back, by my old motorbike – only your auntie's feeling the cold.'

'Hope she freezes to death,' Travis said quietly.

As soon as Travis brought the fire in, and before he could duck, Auntie Jennison grabbed him, lifted him right off the ground and as usual started to eat him.

The boy suffered in silence.

Travis and his dad went back downstairs while Mrs Travis settled Auntie Jennison in.

'You look all in, Dad; can I get you a drink?'

'Thanks, son, that would be great. A brandy and lemonade would be nice, and not too heavy on the lemonade.' He winked. 'If you know what I mean…'

'Dad?'

'Yes, son.'

'Dad, why didn't Auntie Jennison come by the platforms – after all, she is a visitor, isn't she?'

'Well, yes, she could have, but then there was Scampi and the canary, and they can't come by platform; and of course there's all her paraphernalia. But hang on, Travis, I've never told you that Auntie Jennison was a visitor before. How did you know?'

'I suppose Mentor must have mentioned it; I don't know.'

'Tom!' It was Mrs Travis calling. 'Put the kettle on, will you? Auntie Jennison would like a hot-water bottle and a cup of tea.'

'It's all right – I'll do it, Dad.'

'Thanks, Travis.'

At 5.30 the next morning, Travis was awakened by a crashing and banging coming from downstairs directly below his bedroom.

Sleepily, he wandered down to the dining room, and there was Auntie Jennison already dressed, standing on the dining room table. She had a claw hammer in one hand and a large four-inch nail in the other. Bits of plaster from the ceiling littered the table. An unlit cigarette was sticking out of her mouth.

The canary's cage was to one side on the dining room table; pieces of plaster had fallen into it and Charlie was trying to make a meal from them.

'Whatever are you doing, Auntie Jennison?' Travis asked.

'Oh, good morning, Travis! I'm just trying to make poor little Charlie feel at little bit at home, that's all.'

'But Auntie Jennison, it's half past five in the morning.'

'Yes, I am a little late getting up today, Travis; it must have been all that travelling yesterday.'

'Auntie Jennison, I don't think Dad will be very happy with all this mess.'

'Nonsense, boy,' she said. 'You must expect a little mess if you want to get a job done.'

Fortunately, before Auntie Jennison got carried away with the hammer again, Tom, woken up by the commotion, put in an appearance. Travis could see he was none too happy.

'Oh, here's your dad now, Travis. He can do it for me. Come on, Tom, hop up here, will you?'

Travis decided to leave while the going was good and wandered back up to bed.

Better have a pee before I lie down, he thought. Standing in front of the toilet, he noticed that Auntie Jennison had added her own personal touch. There, hanging on a furry twine loop over the top of the soft toilet roll, were the cut-up squares of the *Daily Mirror*.

Shaking his head, Travis went back to bed.

About a quarter to four that afternoon Travis attempted to sneak off to Mr Pomphrey's house.

'Where are you off to, Travis?' Auntie Jennison put in an appearance at just the wrong time.

'Oh, I'm going to see Mr Pomphrey next door,' he replied, and before he could stop himself he said, 'to watch *Countdo…*' his voice trailed away.

'I love *Countdown*! Never miss it; I'll just get my coat. I'm sure Mr whatever his name is won't mind.'

'Well, I don't really know. He can be a bit odd.' Travis was lying through his teeth.

Auntie Jennison wasn't even listening; she swept away and was back in next to no time. 'Come on then, Travis, let's go. We don't want to miss the beginning now, do we?'

My God, Travis thought, she looks just like a bag lady down on her luck.

Travis resigned himself and led the way.

Travis usually went in through Mr Pomphrey's kitchen door, but he thought that by going to the front Mr Pomphrey might not hear him and he could tell Auntie Jennison that he was out.

Very quietly, Travis knocked the door knocker.

'Not like that, boy!' said Auntie Jennison. 'Mind yourself – out of the way!'

Travis told Alex later that when she started banging it was like the drug squad on a bust.

Mr Pomphrey opened the front door. 'Come in, come in,' he said, and ushered them into the living room. 'Here, let me take your coat.' Mr Pomphrey took Auntie Jennison's coat into the hallway.

Upon his return, Travis said, 'Mr Pomphrey, this is Auntie Jennison; Auntie Jennison, meet Mr Pomphrey.'

Mr Pomphrey stepped forward. Auntie Jennison towered over him. He grasped her hand warmly and started to shake it, and Auntie Jennison immediately broke wind quite loudly. Travis hung his head, feeling quite mortified, but Mr Pomphrey seemed quite unabashed. 'Spoken like a true English rose, my dear,' he said. 'Wherever you be' – Auntie Jennison joined in – 'let the wind blow free… whether it be in church or chapel, let it rattle.'

Auntie Jennison added, 'It shows I've got a healthy gullet.'

They both started laughing, and poor Travis didn't know what to make of it all.

'Here, sit down here in front the fire,' said Mr Pomphrey. 'I'll turn it up for you – I've been told that you feel the cold.'

'Too kind,' said Auntie Jennison.

Mr Pomphrey turned the gas fire up full, turned to Auntie Jennison and said, 'Now, Auntie Jennison, Travis has told me how you feel the cold so I recommend Ginkgo Biloba tablets. You take just one every day. What they do is they increase the flow of blood to your extremities so you don't feel the cold as much, and another benefit is they improve your memory no end. Now, what did I do with them? Travis, be a dear, would you? I seemed to have mislaid them. Have a look round – there's a good boy. Now, Auntie Jennison, how would you like a nice cup of Earl Grey?'

'Oh, Mr Pomphrey, you're spoiling me.'

Mr Pomphrey disappeared into the kitchen. When he returned, instead of the usual mugs he normally drank from, he was carrying a silver tray with two bone china cups and saucers, a plate full of garibaldi biscuits and a glass of lemonade for Travis. He poured the tea and then said to Auntie Jennison, 'Shall I pull my chair over by you, Auntie Jennison?'

'Certainly, Mr Pomphrey, and you can call me just "Auntie" if you like.'

'Well, in that case, I would be honoured if you would call me Bill.'

Travis found it all a bit sickening.

'Bill, is it all right if I smoke?' Auntie Jennison asked.

'Of course it is. I don't smoke myself, but feel free. I'm afraid I haven't got an ashtray, though, Auntie.'

'It's all right Bill, I've brought my own.'

From her pinny pocket Auntie Jennison produced a huge brown plastic ashtray with the words 'Butcombe Bitter' printed around the outside. It was filthy dirty from cigarette ash and looked second-hand.

'Where did that come from, Auntie Jennison?' Travis asked. 'That isn't from our house, is it?'

'Well, actually,' said Auntie Jennison, 'I borrowed it. On the way here, your dad and I stopped in a pub, and I knew you wouldn't have any.'

'That was nice of the man to lend you an ashtray, wasn't it, Auntie Jennison?'

'Well, Travis, actually, he doesn't know yet,' replied Auntie Jennison.

'Oh, Auntie Jennison – you've stolen it!' Travis was mortified.

Mr Pomphrey started chuckling.

'Rubbish! Stupid boy, if we go back the same way I shall return it, and if not I shall put a stamp on it and post it. I've merely borrowed it for a short while, that's all.'

Travis didn't know whether to believe her or not.

With that, the signature music of *Countdown* started. Mr Pomphrey scurried around and found three pieces of paper. Auntie Jennison produced her own pencil and pen from her pinny pocket. That's not a pocket, thought Travis, that's a Tardis…

Auntie Jennison was amazing. She beat Mr Pomphrey and Travis out of sight, and the contestants on the programme as well. Travis and Mr Pomphrey started to congratulate her.

'I've got a confession to make,' she said. 'I might as well tell you – I cheated.'

'But that's impossible, Auntie Jennison,' Travis said. 'It's a live show; it's not like it's a repeat or anything like that, is it?'

Auntie Jennison winked broadly and said nothing. She touched the side her nose with her index finger, tapped it and began to cackle and laugh, blowing off all at the same time.

'Where's Auntie Jennison – is she still at Mr Pomphrey's?' Travis's mum asked on his return. Travis was still wiping his mouth from Auntie Jennison's parting kiss.

'Yes, Mum, you'd think they've known each other for years and years. In fact I think Mr Pomphrey's taken quite a shine to Auntie Jennison.'

Secretly, Travis felt a bit jealous; he'd be glad when Auntie Jennison went home.

Auntie Jennison and Mr Pomphrey went missing all day on Christmas Eve; Travis saw Auntie Jennison briefly at breakfast, and then that was it for the rest of the day. His mother didn't seem to know where they were, either; or if she did, she wasn't saying.

Auntie Jennison eventually came swanning in, just in time for tea.

The whole family took a double take of her. Gone was the moth-eaten fur coat. Instead, a full-length Burberry coat was draped over her shoulders. She was wearing a smart pair of black court shoes, and set on her head at a jaunty angle was a neat black hat with a small brim.

'We've been up to town,' she announced rather loftily. 'Oh, Barbara, dear,' she continued, 'would it be all right if Bill comes to Christmas lunch? I've told him you won't mind.'

Travis thought she looked quite posh, and she sounded it as well.

Travis's mum hesitated for a moment. 'Well, there's plenty for everybody, but I think you'll find that Mr Pomphrey usually goes to the British Legion for Christmas lunch.'

Auntie Jennison ignored her. 'Then it's all settled – good.'

Travis watched Auntie Jennison seat herself at the dining table. There was something different about her, somehow. Then it dawned on him: Auntie Jennison was wearing make-up – very discreetly – but make-up nevertheless.

Travis almost beat Auntie Jennison to the punch. On Christmas morning he came downstairs a little after six.

Auntie Jennison was already up, however, but only just; everyone else was still sleeping. He could hear Auntie Jennison singing away to herself in the kitchen. Leave your name on the way out, in the bin by the door, he thought. It was terrible. Under the Christmas tree were heaps of presents. He quietly went over and glanced down at them. Plenty with my name on, he thought. Better go out in the kitchen and see the old bat, I suppose.

'Hello, my love,' said Auntie Jennison, 'come here and have a nice kiss.'

Travis cautiously walked forward. *Whoosh*, she had him and he was being devoured yet again.

When she eventually finished with him and deposited him back on the floor, he said, 'Auntie Jennison, your cigarettes don't seem to smell too bad today, are you smoking different ones?'

'Well, actually, Travis, I haven't bothered with one yet today at all; maybe later.'

Travis studied her; the long black hairs growing from her facial warts had gone and she wasn't sucking a peppermint. In fact he'd been with her at least a minute and she hadn't blown off once. The truth suddenly hit Travis. She's in love, he thought; I'll need to warn Mr Pomphrey.

Becky and her husband arrived early, which pleased everybody, so by a little after seven thirty that morning, the whole family were sitting around the Christmas tree opening their respective presents. Travis's mum had bought something for Auntie Jennison on Travis's behalf, and she was busy opening it.

I hope it's a pair of gloves with three fingers on one hand and none on the other, he thought. In the event it was a rather smart-looking cameo brooch.

Auntie Jennison was overjoyed. Travis had another kissing, and for once it wasn't too bad; it wasn't too wet and there was no smell of tobacco or peppermint at all. I really will have to warn Mr Pomphrey, he reminded himself.

When all the presents had been opened, Auntie Jennison excused herself, left the room and returned a minute later with a smallish parcel and an envelope.

'Here you are, Travis. I'm sorry, I just haven't had the time to finish off a scarf for you, but perhaps you won't mind this instead.' All smiles, she held onto the envelope and handed Travis the parcel.

Travis eagerly ripped at the wrapping. Inside was a box, and inside that... '*Wow*!' he exclaimed. 'Auntie Jennison, I can't believe it! Look, Mum, look, Dad!' Travis was clutching a mobile phone.

'Auntie Jennison, you shouldn't have,' said his mother.

'Nonsense, Barbara... and here's a ten-pound top-up voucher from Mr Pomphrey.'

Auntie Jennison handed Travis the envelope. Before he realised what he was doing, Travis had launched himself at Auntie Jennison and was kissing and hugging her.

She's not so bad after all, he thought.

Mr Pomphrey turned up for lunch looking rather resplendent in a navy blue three-piece suit, which appeared quite new, complete with ribbons and medals from the war. He was wearing an immaculate white shirt, and his walrus moustache had been trimmed in a neat military style. Travis thanked him profusely for the phone top-up card, and they all sat down to eat their meal.

Travis's mum had made sure that Auntie Jennison and Mr Pomphrey sat together. Travis watched them intently and decided it was too late to warn Mr Pomphrey; he was as bad as Auntie Jennison.

As the Christmas holiday wore on, Auntie Jennison seemed more and more palatable; Scampi had given up chasing Travis, and Mr Pomphrey looked ten years younger.

When it was eventually time for Auntie Jennison to go home, Mr Pomphrey suggested that he kept Tom company and drove down with him. Tom said how nice it was of him to be so considerate (tongue firmly in cheek); he knew what the real reason was.

With the Christmas holidays almost over, Travis's thoughts turned to his homework again. He thought he might visit the Great Fire of London once more, and then he and Alex could finish their homework.

'Hello, Travis,' said Mentor, 'had a nice Christmas?'

'Oh, Mentor, don't be so daft – you know I have.'

'Only making polite conversation. Keep your shirt on!'

Travis decided it might be as well for his first trip after Christmas just to look at the fire from afar. The sight of the girl being engulfed by the flames was still fresh in his memory. He had read that Samuel Pepys, the diarist, had watched the fire from the Tower of London. He looked up the coordinates in the places book, set them and pushed the 'go' button.

Travis spotted Samuel Pepys right away. He was accompanied by a group of people and was waving a long ebony cane towards the distant flames. He was wearing a long, brown, silk coat and a brown wig, and a white cravat was drawn up tightly around his neck. In fact, he was just like the portrait Travis had seen of him. Travis sidled right up beside him and took in the scene. The houses on London Bridge were well alight, and the poor occupants were throwing their possessions into the water to try to save them; some were trying to escape the flames by boat. Away to his left, Travis could see people frantically demolishing houses to create a firebreak. The sky was both black and red at the same time. How long Travis stood there, he didn't know, but suddenly he was brought back to reality with the sound of his alarm. Travis decided enough was enough, and feeling a little disappointed that

Mr Pepys didn't appear to actually carry his diary with him, pressed the scarper button.

Alex came calling on Travis that evening, and by the time they had finished their homework together and swapped stories about Christmas it felt just like old times again.

Chapter Eight

Everything was back to normal in the Travis household. New Year had come and gone, and Travis was back at school. Travis's dad had learnt a new skill; he'd successfully artexed the ceiling that Auntie Jennison had spoilt, and Travis's mum had got rid of the last traces of Auntie Jennison's canary droppings.

It was just getting dark when Travis let himself in through Mr Pomphrey's back door (Travis had persuaded his dad to open up the hole in the fence again).

'Yoo-hoo, Mr Pomphrey,' Travis said, 'I'm here.'

'Come in, Travis, *Countdown*'s just starting.'

Travis hurried in; Mr Pomphrey had already poured Travis a glass of lemonade and had a saucer full of sweets on the arm of the chair.

Travis settled himself down and battle commenced. During the first commercial break Travis looked over and said to his host, 'If you don't mind me saying so, Mr Pomphrey, you don't seem to be quite with it today.'

'Yes, you're quite right. I've got a lot on my mind. Look, would you mind if I record the rest of *Countdown*? We can watch it later, but I really do need to talk to you, Travis. It's about Auntie Jennison.'

My God, thought Travis, perhaps he's going to marry her...

'Yes, that's fine by me,' he said.

Mr Pomphrey set the video recorder, then went over to the cupboard. When he came back, he was holding a litre bottle of brandy. He pushed it into Travis's hand.

'Oh, Mr Pomphrey, I'm not allowed.'

Mr Pomphrey chuckled. 'I don't want you to drink it – I just want you to have a good look at it.'

'Well, it's a bottle of brandy, Mr Pomphrey.'

'Yes,' Mr Pomphrey agreed, 'it's a bottle of brandy all right, but take a closer look at it.'

Travis carefully examined the bottle and gave a running commentary: 'Well, it's Martell's; it's got five stars here at the top of the label; it's all in French – there's no English writing at all and there's a white label over the cap with some numbers on.'

'So, Travis, what do you deduce from all that?'

'Here, steady on, Mr Pomphrey,' Travis said, 'I'm not Sherlock Holmes, you know!'

They both laughed.

'Well, think about it, Travis,' Mr Pomphrey said.

Travis looked puzzled and then said, 'I think this bottle was probably bought in France, because there's no English writing on it.'

'Exactly, my boy,' said Mr Pomphrey; he appeared to be growing quite excited. He took the brandy from Travis and put it back in the cupboard.

'Right then, Travis. Now I'd like you to look at these, please.'

From his jacket pocket, Mr Pomphrey produced two empty cigarette packets, one Benson and Hedges, the other Lambert and Butler. He showed them to Travis and said, 'I don't expect you to know anything about cigarette packets, so I'll explain about these.'

Travis interrupted. 'I know exactly what you're going to say, Mr Pomphrey; there's no government health warning on them.'

Mr Pomphrey grew more excited. 'So that means, Travis, that these cigarettes were bought abroad, doesn't it?'

'Yes that's right, Mr Pomphrey,' Travis agreed.

'And do you know where the brandy and cigarette packets came from, Travis?'

Travis felt his colours rising. He looked down at the floor.

'Auntie Jennison,' he mumbled.

'Yes, Travis – Auntie Jennison. So shall I tell you what I think?'

Mr Pomphrey didn't wait for Travis to answer but went on, 'I think that after I saw Auntie Jennison go into your shed on Christmas Eve, she went to France and bought brandy and cigarettes, because when I saw her coming back out of the shed she was holding a carrier bag. I think she's just like you – she's a visitor, that's what I think.' Mr Pomphrey looked quizzically at Travis.

All Travis could think to say was, 'Oh, Mr Pomphrey!'

'There's one thing that puzzles me, though, Travis. I know you visitors can go back, but how do you travel from place to place in the present?'

Travis thought there was no point in denying things, so he said, 'Well, I don't know much about it, except that I'm not allowed – it's too dangerous. But I know you travel platform to platform, or shed to shed, if you like.'

'Well,' said Mr Pomphrey, 'I don't want Auntie Jennison putting herself in danger for a bottle of brandy; I shall have to tell her off.'

'Perhaps it's not dangerous for her. I could ask Mentor about it, if you like.'

'Good idea, Travis, and the sooner the better. Can you speak to him now?'

'Erm, I've never tried when there's been anyone around before,' Travis replied. Then, feeling a little foolish, he whispered, 'Mentor...'

'Why are you whispering, Travis?' Mentor said.

'You're there then, Mentor?' Travis asked.

'I'm usually here, except when you're off on your travels.'

'Mr Pomphrey wants to know...'

'I heard him, Travis, I'm not deaf.'

'He heard you, Mr Pomphrey,' Travis said. 'Is it all right if I tell Mr Pomphrey everything, Mentor?'

'Well, it's highly irregular, but I suppose under the circumstances...' Mentor paused then went on, 'It's dangerous to travel in the present; there are all sorts of reasons. For instance, you could travel to another platform, step out into the open and be in the middle of a war, or a tornado, or you could walk into a couple of guard dogs; or if it was in America you could get shot for trespassing.'

Travis told Mr Pomphrey what Mentor had said.

'Do you think Mentor would mind if I asked him a question?' Mr Pomphrey enquired.

'Tell him to ask away,' Mentor answered.

Travis gave Mr Pomphrey the OK so he asked, 'Is there any safe way to travel platform to platform, Mentor? You see, I'd worry about Auntie Jennison if I thought she was endangering herself.'

Mentor replied, 'There's no absolutely safe way that you can do it. You see, you're as vulnerable as the next person when you're travelling in the present, but there are precautions you can take. Now, take Auntie Jennison; she would never just go platform to platform in the present. She would first visit five minutes in the past to make sure it was safe. Then of course she would always hold the scarper button in one hand, just in case.'

Travis told Mr Pomphrey what Mentor had said.

'She's rather crafty, isn't she, Mentor?' said Mr Pomphrey.

'Yes,' replied Mentor, 'and she's not the only one.' But of course Mr Pomphrey couldn't hear what he had said.

The next morning Travis and Alex were walking to school. 'Travis,' Alex said, 'you know my mum comes from Glasgow, don't you?'

'Oh, thank goodness for that! That explains it,' replied Travis, 'I thought she had an impediment in her speech.'

Alex gave him one almighty push and they both collapsed laughing.

'Well, I've got a job to understand her myself sometimes, and she's my mum. Travis, can you remember me telling you about my Nanna, up in Scotland?'

'Yes, she's the one who's not very well, isn't she?'

'Yes, and it looks like she's taken a turn for the worse, so we're all going up to see her this weekend.' Alex added, 'She lives on the bank of the loch, you know.'

'Coo, you might see the monster then,' said Travis.

'What monster?'

'Why the Loch Ness monster, of course, you dummy!'

'There's more than one loch in Scotland! She lives on the banks of Loch Lomond, not Loch Ness – so who's the dummy?'

'What you mean – they haven't got a monster as well?'

'Don't you know anything, Travis?'

'I do know one thing, Raincoat.'

'What's that then, Travis?'

'I know that you've got both your hands in your trouser pockets.'

'So what!'

'Well that means you've forgotten your school bag.'

'I'll catch you up!' shouted Alex, as he made a dash for his house.

'*Dummy!*' Travis shouted back.

The following Monday morning found Travis sitting on Alex's front wall waiting for him to go to school. He heard Alex's front door bang and Alex came shuffling up the path, his hands thrust deep into his pockets.

'Morning, Raincoat,' said Travis.

Alex mumbled something back that sounded like 'morning'. Travis looked around at him. His eyes were swollen and red and it was obvious he'd been crying.

Oh dear, thought Travis, his Nanna must have died. They walked on in silence, Travis pondering how to broach the subject. Suddenly he blurted out, 'How many Nannas have you got these days then, Raincoat?'

'Still the two,' Alex answered.

'Well, what's up then?'

'Nothing!'

They walked on towards school.

'Look, Alex,' said Travis seriously, 'I can see you've been crying. My dad said it's not babyish to cry when you're upset, and it's better than bottling it up. So tell me what's up.'

Given the go-ahead, Alex started to bawl. He'd just about finished when they got to the school gate. Travis and Alex found a quiet corner of the cloakroom and Alex started to tell Travis all that had happened in Scotland.

'Well, to start with, Travis, it's so far away you can't imagine. It's darker than here, the nights last for ever... and how cold is it? You couldn't see the loch for fog! There's nothing to do and no one to play with... it's horrible, and I hate it.'

Travis interrupted him. 'Well, it's all over now. You don't need to go back, do you?'

Alex immediately started to cry again, and through the tears he spluttered, 'We're going there to *live*.'

Travis didn't know what to say, so he just put his arm around Alex and gave him a hug.

After a while Travis suddenly had a thought. 'Listen, Raincoat, it's not so bad! I can come and visit you any time I want.'

'Look, thanks for trying to make me feel better, Travis, but you know that's impossible. Scotland's just too far away.'

'I'm telling you, I can visit you any time I want, any time.'

'So how are you going to do that then, Travis?'

'It's a secret; I just can't tell you.'

Alex immediately burst into tears again.

Travis got in from school at lunch time. 'Mum, Mum, guess what – Alex is going to live in Scotland and it's horrible there, it never gets light and you freeze to death – he said so,' Travis said excitedly.

'Now just calm down, Travis, and tell me all about it.'

Travis explained to his mum that with Alex's Nanna being very ill, Mrs Macintosh and her husband were going to sell up and move into Nanna's bungalow to look after her. Mr Macintosh would be going into partnership with his Scottish brother-in-law, and when Alex's Nanna eventually died the bungalow would belong to Mrs Macintosh so they wouldn't be coming back.

'The only good thing about it,' said Travis, 'is at least I won't have to see that horrible Kirsty any more.'

With that, the telephone in the hall started to ring. Travis's mum went to answer it, and some time later when she returned she said, 'You'll never guess who that was on the phone, Travis! Tell you what, we'll have twenty questions on who it was when I've dished up lunch.'

'Oh, yes please, Mum,' he said.

In Travis's house they often played the twenty questions game. If one of the family saw or spoke to someone they hadn't been in contact with for a long time, the others would try to guess who it was.

'I understand we're playing twenty questions then,' said Tom, as he picked up his knife and fork.

'Yes,' said Travis's mum, 'when you're ready.'

'Right then, was it – is it – a man?' Tom asked.

'No, and that's one question you've had.'

'So it was a woman,' said Travis.

'Yes, and that's two questions now.' Mrs Travis winked at Tom.

'Oh, Mum, that's not fair – you're always doing that.'

'All right then, that's only one question,' Mrs Travis said.

'It's Becky!' Travis shouted.

'No,' said Mrs Travis, 'and now that's two questions you've had.'

'Travis, don't waste questions like that. Ask sensible things, like about her age and her appearance. Anybody would think you've never played the game before,' Mr Travis said crossly.

Take the chill pill man, Travis thought, it's only a game; but he stayed quiet.

'All right,' Travis said, 'is she less than forty years old?'

'No,' said Mrs Travis.

'Is she under sixty?' Tom asked.

'No, and now that's four questions you've had.'

'Is it the lady in the off-licence?' Travis asked.

'No, and that's five; and anyway the lady in the off-licence is only my age.'

'Does she live near here?' Tom asked.

'No… six.'

'Oh, I give up! I can't think of anything else,' said Travis. 'It's a stupid game, anyway.'

Travis always thought it was a stupid game when he wasn't doing very well.

'If it wasn't for the fact you spoke to her on the phone, I'd say it was Auntie Jennison,' Travis said.

'Quite right, Travis,' said his mum, 'I don't know how you got there, but yes, you're right; it was Auntie Jennison.'

Travis jumped down from his chair, ran round the dining table punching the air and shouting, 'Yes, yes!'

'I thought you said it was a stupid game,' said Mrs Travis, smiling at her son.

Tom looked up. 'But Mother, Auntie Jennison hates phones,' he said.

'Well, she's says she's got one so that she can keep in touch with the family, especially as she's getting older now,' Mrs Travis said.

'What a load of old rubbish! She's got one so that she can speak to Mr Pomphrey,' said Travis, 'that's the real reason.'

'Out of the mouths of babes,' said Tom.

When Travis went to Mr Pomphrey's that afternoon, he was just in time to see him putting down the telephone.

'Hello, Travis,' he said. 'That was your Auntie Jennison; she's had the telephone put in, don't you know?'

'Really,' said Travis.

Four days later, a 'For Sale' sign appeared in the garden of Alex's house.

'I'm not staying in Scotland, you know, Travis. I'll run away,' said Alex.

'You'll get used to it,' said Travis, trying to pacify him.

'I won't be getting used to it,' said Alex, his voice rising, 'because I'm *not staying there*.'

Travis could tell the subject was now closed.

Later that day, Travis was round at Mr Pomphrey's house as usual.

'Travis, you didn't tell me that next door were moving… Mrs Macintosh hasn't said a word, either.'

'I thought you knew, Mr Pomphrey. I expect that Mrs Macintosh told you, but you just didn't understand her,' Travis said jokingly.

'Well, I must confess she can be a little difficult,' Mr Pomphrey admitted.

Travis went on to tell Mr Pomphrey the circumstances of the impending move.

'Alex will soon settle in up there,' said Mr Pomphrey.

'That's what I told him, but he says he'll run away.'

'Do you think so, Travis?'

'I wouldn't be surprised, Mr Pomphrey, I wouldn't be surprised at all.'

Chapter Nine

'Mum, Mum!' Travis called out.

'I'm here, dear,' Travis's mum called from the kitchen.

'Where's Dad?'

'He's out in the garden.'

'What's he doing out there? It's cold and it's getting dark.'

'I really don't know, dear. Why don't you go and see.'

Travis found his dad sitting on the old garden bench; his shoulders were slumped and rounded and his hands were clasped in front of him.

'Whatever are you doing out here, Dad?' said Travis. 'You'll freeze to death.'

'Just thinking, son, just thinking, that's all.' Tom put his arm around Travis and drew him onto the bench alongside him. 'It was going over in my mind. The night your grandfather disappeared – it's just like it was yesterday.'

'What was the name of the man he said he had unfinished business with Dad?'

'Ivan Roberts.'

Travis made an instant decision as his dad was talking; he'd pay his grandfather a visit, and see if he could help his dad. 'Dad, I'd like to visit and see for myself what happened the night Granddad went missing. Will you give me the coordinates please?'

'I can't see that it will do any harm. Yes, why not, all right.'

After tea, Travis armed himself with the coordinates and went off to the shed.

'Hello, Travis. Anything I can help you with tonight?'

'Oh, hello, Mentor. No, I think I'll be just fine, thank you.'

It seemed quite weird stepping back out of the shed. Travis immediately noticed there was no silver birch tree and there was a wide concrete path right up through the middle of the garden. To one side of the path was plain grass and to the other what appeared to be a vegetable patch with a few cabbages and some scruffy-looking Brussel sprouts. Without the pampas grass by the shed, and in full view, Travis could see his dad and his granddad sitting side by side on the bench.

Wow, this is weird, he thought.

As he watched, his granddad said something to Tom, got up and went into the house; Travis noticed the back door was painted the same bright green as Auntie Jennison's toilet door. After a while, he reappeared. He walked up to the shed door, turned, smiled at Tom, waved and then he was gone.

Travis studied his dad. He looks so young, and so much like me, he thought. And his grandfather looked like his dad did now.

Travis pushed the scarper button.

When he came back out of the shed, he didn't feel too bad at all, in fact not in the least bit tired. I must be getting more used to it, he thought.

Tom was sitting on the bench waiting for Travis. 'Well?' he asked.

'I can't say I saw anything out of the ordinary, Dad. You two were talking, then Granddad went into the house. What did he go in there for?'

'I really don't know. Perhaps he went for a pee or something.'

'Well, haven't you ever followed him to see?' Travis asked.

'I didn't really need to see my dad peeing, did I? He only did it the same as anyone else.'

'But perhaps he didn't go for a pee; perhaps there was another reason.'

Tom could see the sense in this and said, 'Look, the next time you go perhaps you'll follow him and see. I know it's grasping at straws, but there might just be something.'

'I'll go now, Dad,' said Travis. 'I'm not in the least bit tired, honest.'

'No, it's far too late and you've got school in the morning. I've waited twenty-five years; another day won't hurt.'

Next day Travis was up bright and early. He'd set his watch alarm and hurried to the shed.

Travis was already sitting at the kitchen table when his dad came in for breakfast.

'Peed the bed then, son?' He ruffled Travis's hair on his way to the kettle.

'No, I have not!' Travis answered indignantly. 'I went for a visit again, and sorry, Dad, but you were right. Granddad did only go to the toilet. I stood outside the bathroom door and waited for him until he came out, and then I followed him all the way to the shed.'

'Well, thanks for trying, Travis. I thought it was a bit of a long shot, but there you are.'

After breakfast was over, Travis gathered up his school books and went out to wait for Alex. One look at Alex's face told Travis that he was even more gripped by despair.

'Well, that's it, then Travis,' was his opening remark. 'Friday, and we're off.'

'Friday... but houses don't sell that quickly,' said Travis.

'I know, but it looks like we've had an offer. Nanna's taken a turn for the worse, and Mum says as it's big school in September – the quicker I get there, the better.'

'Oh!' was all Travis could muster up.

'I'm not staying there; Dad will still be in the house and I shall come back – you'll see.'

'Won't your mum let you stay here until the house is sold?'

'No, she's taking Kirsty and me on Friday.'

'You know I told you I could visit you whenever I wanted? Well, I wasn't joking. You had a mobile phone for Christmas – the same as me – so when I come up I can phone you and we can meet.'

'Just come to the house. Mum won't mind.'

'No, no one must know I'm there. No one – do you understand?'

'But why's that, Travis?'

'I can't tell you.'

'I know, Travis – it's another of your secrets!' said Alex, and stormed off in a huff.

The whole family turned out to see Alex off on Friday afternoon, Mr Pomphrey included. Alex and Travis both ended up in tears and Mrs Travis had to dab at her eyes with her handkerchief.

Travis had Alex's address written down and decided as soon as it was practically possible he would be off to Scotland.

Travis reckoned that Sunday morning would be a good time; he didn't want to lie to his parents about where he was going, so he thought he'd say nothing and just go.

Just after nine he started to sneak off towards the shed.

'Travis, Travis!' his dad was calling. 'Where are you off, then?'

'Nowhere, Dad.'

'Oh, for a moment there I thought you were off to the past again.'

'No, Dad, definitely not,' said Travis.

'Good! I need to talk to you; come back in the house, please.'

Travis followed his dad into the living room and settled cross-legged on the sofa.

'Travis, your mother will kill you putting your feet all over the furniture like that.'

Travis disengaged his feet and sat up.

'That's better,' said his dad. 'Now, you know that us visitors also have to make a living, don't you? Well, as you know, I've been tracing people's family trees for years, and being able to use the gift I've been very successful. Unfortunately for me, now that the gift's been passed on to you, things are a lot tougher. I come across dead ends that I just can't seem to get past. I suppose what I'm asking you, Travis, is, I wonder if you would be prepared to help out now and again?'

Travis couldn't believe his luck. It was the opportunity he'd been waiting for: he could do his dad's research and see Alex as well. 'Dad, the pleasure's all mine,' he said. 'When do I start?'

'Whenever you like, really, I've come to a dead end with a Scottish family by the name of Ross; I've managed to go back as far as 1751 but now the trail's gone cold.'

Scotland, thought Travis. Couldn't be better!

Tom continued, 'I'm doing it for an American family. I think if we could go back just one more generation they'd be happy.'

'Where in Scotland did the trail go cold, Dad?' Travis asked casually.

'Actually, it's quite near to where Alex has gone; it's a place called Georgetown. Listen, I'll give you all the details and you see what you can come up with, all right?'

'Sure thing, Dad,' said Travis, trying to hide his excitement. Within ten minutes he was on his way up the garden towards the shed.

'I know what you're up to, Travis,' said Mentor. 'Now, you know you're not allowed, and why.'

'Look, Mentor, I'm going to kill two birds with one stone, and it can't be wrong to want to see Alex, can it?'

'I know you want to see your friend, Travis, but it's dangerous to go platform-hopping...'

'Platform-hopping? Is that what you call it? Platform-hopping... oh yes, I like that.'

'I can't stop you, but take the same precautions as your Auntie Jennison does. Do you promise?'

'All right Mentor, just don't keep on.'

'Travis,' said Mentor, 'can I make a suggestion?'

'Oh, Mentor, what is it now?'

'Go back in the house and have a look in the atlas so at least you'll know where you're going. Remember, you've got to travel the same way as other people do when you're in the present.'

'OK, Mentor – you win.'

Travis went in and discovered it was only half an inch on the map from Georgetown to Luss, where Alex had gone. I can walk that, he thought.

Travis pushed the 'go' button and instantly found himself sitting in a wooden chair in the middle of what appeared to be a saloon bar from the Wild West. Not bad, Travis thought, but I'd rather have our Pullman coach. Mentor had warned him about different people's choice of transport.

Armed with his dad's information, Travis soon found what he was looking for in Georgetown. Dad will be over the moon with this, he thought. He quickly pushed the scarper button. 'Now,' he said aloud, 'now for the present – well, five minutes into the past, anyway.'

Travis set the time and pushed the 'go' button. Cautiously, he went out into the open air. Look at it, it's raining, he thought; it wasn't doing that just now in 1751.

The shed he'd emerged from was right by the side of a gate that led out to the road. Travis had a quick look round. No one about, no dogs, no nothing in fact. Looks pretty safe to me, he thought. Travis hit the scarper button, quickly reset the time for the present, and set off again.

Even more cautiously than before, he came into the open. It was raining hard and there was still no one around. He went quickly through the gate. Should have brought a coat, he thought. Just along the road was a bus stop. I wonder if I can get the bus to Luss? he asked himself. There was an elderly lady huddled up in the bus shelter.

'Excuse me,' said Travis, 'can I get the bus to Luss from here, please?'

The old lady looked at him. 'You're miles away from Luss, and even if there was a bus – which there isn't – you're standing on the wrong side of the road; but then you're not from round here, are you?' she asked.

'No, I'm here visiting, and I've got a bit lost,' said Travis.

'A bit lost! I should think you were; Luss is about twenty-five miles away in that direction,' she said, pointing her hand.

'Well is there a taxi office or something around here please? I've got money.'

'Straight up that road there,' the old lady said. 'Mind you, it's a wee bit of a walk.'

Things weren't going to plan. Travis was almost wet through and getting thoroughly fed up. He trudged off towards the taxi office. I must be losing my marbles, he thought, all I've got to do is find a platform that's nearer Luss. If Alex was here he'd call me a dummy. Travis had a quick look around, ducked into an alleyway and pushed his scarper button.

Sitting back in the Pullman, Travis quickly thumbed through the places book. No Luss. Oh no, he thought, I wonder where the nearest platform is? It's no good, I'll just have to ask Mentor. He slipped out of the Pullman.

'Are you there, Mentor?' he asked aloud.

'Yes, Travis, I was just starting to wonder where you were.'

'Mentor, there's no platform at Luss.'

'No, that's right. I know that.'

'Well then, why didn't you tell me?'

'Well, if you had asked me…'

'Oh, Mentor!'

'Look, Travis, I don't want to interfere, but if you go platform-hopping now, your dad will think there's something wrong. You've been in the shed for more than an hour.'

'Yes, Mentor, you're quite right. I can't argue with that. I'll try again after lunch.'

Travis went into the house; his dad had been reading the Sunday newspaper and hadn't noticed the time.

'Hello, son. How did you get on?'

Travis proudly showed his dad the missing names on the family tree.

'I'm impressed, Travis. Well done, lad,' Tom said.

'Dad, it was ever so strange when I got to the platform at Georgetown,' said Travis.

'What was strange about it?' his father asked.

'Well, it was like I was sitting in a Wild West saloon. There was even a piano in the corner and a pair of swinging doors.'

'That's because whichever visitor lives there can choose whatever they want. Because they're called platforms, most people use trains as their theme, but I have been to some where it's been aeroplanes, or even boats. H G Wells had his own idea of a time machine; it looked like a horse-drawn carriage without any wheels.'

'Was H G Wells a visitor then, Dad?'

'Yes, he was, all right – and a very good one at that. Do you know the strangest platform I ever saw?'

'No, Dad,' Travis replied.

'Believe it or not, once I found myself sitting in a dentist's chair, and there was even a drill overhead.'

They both laughed.

'Another thing that I want to ask you, Dad. What happens if two travellers wanted to use the same platform at the same time?'

'D'you know, I've never thought of that. I don't know – perhaps you'd better ask Mentor that one.'

'Dad, have you got any more work for me?' Travis asked hopefully.

'Yes, plenty; but I don't want you overdoing things, so no more for today.'

Travis was disappointed. His brain was already working over-time, trying to see how he could slip out again. The opportunity presented itself just after Sunday lunch. Travis's dad was busy finishing off the Ross family tree, and Mrs Travis was running up some new curtains on the dining room table. Travis quietly crept up the stairs and went into his bedroom, shutting the door behind him. He sat up on the bed and started to look at the map of Scotland in his atlas.

'Come on, Mentor,' he said, 'you're not being a bit of help!'

'That's because I don't want to be, Travis. You know very well you're not allowed.'

'Look, Mentor, I'm going anyway, with or without your help; so you might as well tell me the best platform.'

'Oh, very well,' said Mentor. 'From memory, Clydebank is the nearest to Alex's house, but that's still several miles away.'

'What's the platform number then, Mentor?'

'I don't know! I'm not brain of Britain, you know. You'll just have to look in the places book.'

Travis put on his overcoat, scarf, took all of his savings from his wardrobe and picked up his mobile phone.

'Now just be quiet, Mentor,' Travis said.

'They can't hear me anyway.'

'No, but I can.'

Travis crept down the stairs, let himself out through the front door, closing it quietly behind him, and cut along the side of Mr Pomphrey's house. He knew Mr Pomphrey would be having his afternoon siesta, so he wouldn't be seen. Then he cut back through the gap in the fence and into the shed. So far so good, he thought. Travis set the time, the same as he had that morning, pushed the 'go' button and he was there. Oh, a railway carriage! he thought. A bit like mine but nowhere near as posh... He climbed out of the carriage and went towards the outside.

Still raining, he thought. In fact he could see the street lights had already come on where it was so dark. The shed seemed to be at the edge of some disused ground. I suppose this could have been allotments at one time, he thought. Because of the heavy rain the streets seemed quite deserted. Suits me fine, he told himself, and pushed the scarper button.

Two minutes later, Travis was back, this time in the present.

Now it looks like I'm not too far away from the station, and there's sure to be a taxi there. Travis pondered whether he should phone Alex or hang on until he was nearer. He walked on through the driving rain, his coat done right up to the neck and his scarf tightly wrapped and pushed inside his coat. He was so intent on trying to spot the station that he was unaware of the car drawing alongside of him, or the sound of an electric window opening.

'Excuse me...'

Travis turned around. A man was looking across from his driving seat through the front passenger window of his car; he was smiling at Travis and waving an *A to Z* in his hand.

'Excuse me,' the man said again, all smiles, 'I'm totally lost. You couldn't help me, could you?'

'No, I'm sorry, sir, I don't live around here,' Travis replied.

'You're English – that's good,' said the man. 'So am I; that makes us friends.'

The man was very well spoken and friendly, and Travis immediately felt at ease.

'Where are you heading?' the man asked.

'I'm heading towards Luss, sir; well, at least I *think* I am.'

'What a coincidence! That's where I'm going. We'll be able to help each other out, then.' The man jumped out of his car and came round to the passenger side. Travis could see he was smartly dressed, and his black shoes were very shiny. Travis also noticed that he had two black eyebrows sitting like furry caterpillars above his deep-set eyes, a long straight nose, and his upper lip hardly existed at all. Opening the front passenger door and smiling, the man said, 'Come on, then! Hop in, before we both get wet right through.'

Just for a second Travis made as if to get in the car. Suddenly he remembered that ever since he was a small boy he had been told never to go with strangers. 'No, sorry sir, but I'm not allowed,' he said quickly.

'Come on, don't be so silly! I'm not going to bite you,' said the man, and grabbed Travis's arm. Travis tried to pull away but the man was too strong; he tried to reach the scarper button, but with

83

his coat and scarf in the way, it was impossible. Travis opened his mouth and tried to scream but no sound would come out. He was petrified. The man started to bundle him into the car.

'Stop that! Stop that! What do you think you're doing?'

A woman's shrill voice from behind Travis filled the dank wet air.

'*Police, police!*' she shouted. She came running at the man, her already opened umbrella waving threateningly in front of her. The man quickly let go of Travis's arm, bounded to his car, jumped in and in an instant he was gone.

Travis slid to the ground and started to sob.

The woman came over and crouched down by him. 'There, there,' she said, 'it's all right, laddie, you're safe now; it's all right, he's gone.'

The woman looked down at Travis. 'Well, I never did! Remember me?' she said. It was the lady Travis had seen that morning in Georgetown at the bus stop. 'It's all right; you're quite safe now,' she repeated. Then she helped Travis to his feet; he was still sobbing bitterly. 'It's certainly a small world; and I see you've managed to get yourself a coat, then. Come on, you come with me – I only live just there.' She pointed. 'We'll call the police.'

But the last thing Travis wanted was the police. He murmured, 'Thank you, thank you,' and ran off.

By the time Travis got near the station he had almost calmed down. He'd opened his coat slightly and his hand tightly clutched the scarper button. Just by the station he could see a taxi driver letting some drunken passengers out of his cab. He hurried towards him.

'Excuse me,' said Travis, 'are you for hire?'

The driver was a short man wearing a rather grand tartan turban. With a strong Glaswegian accent, he asked Travis, 'Where are ye going, laddie?'

'To Luss, please,' said Travis.

'Ha' ye any money?' the driver asked.

'Yes, plenty,' Travis answered. 'Look.' Travis produced five ten-pound notes from his pocket.

'How much ha' ye got there?' The driver's eyes lit up.

'I've got fifty pounds,' said Travis.

'Well, that's how much the fare is,' the driver said. 'Gie it here.'

'But fifty pounds…' said Travis. 'It's not that far!'

'Don't ye try to tell me how far it is! Are ye getting in or no? I dinna have all day.'

Reluctantly Travis climbed in the taxi. The back seat was absolutely filthy, the upholstery was ripped and the taxi stank of cigarettes, drink and stale vomit.

'Give us that money, then,' the driver said.

Travis handed over the money and sat back. The driver shot off like a maniac. With one hand he picked up his radio mike and shouted in Glaswegian or a foreign language at it (Travis couldn't tell which), and with the other – without any hands on the steering wheel – he changed an audio tape. Travis said, 'Excuse me, but you haven't put your taximeter on, and you're driving ever so fast.'

In reply the driver leant forward and turned his cassette player up as loud as it would go and jammed his foot harder on the accelerator pedal. Travis spent the next fifteen minutes hanging onto the door handle for grim death and clutching at the scarper button just in case they crashed. Suddenly they screeched to a halt. The driver didn't speak; he just indicated for Travis to get out. There in front of him was the sign saying 'Luss'.

Made it, he thought.

A line of cars came towards him and Travis had to wait while they passed. He then crossed over the road and headed towards Alex's house. It was still raining hard and Travis wanted to phone Alex but he was worried about getting his phone wet. Just along the road was a phone box. Travis went inside, had a quick look at the directions Alex had given him, and then got his phone out of his pocket.

<Sorry, caller, the cellphone you are calling may be switched off. Please try again later> the mechanical disjointed voice informed him.

What an idiot! Travis thought. He tried several times more and got the same result. Travis decided to walk up to the bungalow and approach it with caution, just in case Mrs Macintosh was about. The front of the bungalow was up a slight incline. Travis could see there were lights on in one of the front rooms, and as the curtains weren't properly closed. He could see Mrs Macintosh was sitting watching TV. Travis ran quickly up past the side of the house and around towards the back garden. Another light was showing; only this time the curtains were closed. Travis silently approached the window, but it was no good; he just couldn't see inside. Cautiously, he tapped the window softly and whispered, 'Alex, Alex.' He tapped again. 'Alex!' he called, a little louder. Suddenly the curtain came back.

Kirsty.

Travis pushed the scarper button.

Chapter Ten

Travis managed to get back inside his house without being seen. He ran up the stairs, hung his wet coat and scarf in his wardrobe, and went into the bathroom to dry off. Travis could hear the phone ringing in the hallway. His mother answered it but he couldn't hear what she was saying. Then she called up the stairs.

'Travis, you are up there, aren't you?'

Being careful that his mother didn't actually see him, he called out, 'Yes, Mum, what d'you want?'

'It's all right, Travis, it's nothing.'

Travis sat on his bed towelling his hair. 'You haven't been a lot of help, have you, Mentor?' he said.

'I can't interfere, human beings are free spirits... I can advise, but I can't dictate.'

'Weren't you worried, though, Mentor?'

'Yes, I was a little concerned; it would have been a complete waste of the last two years.'

'A little concerned, *a little concerned*! I nearly got killed back there! Haven't you got any soul, Mentor?'

'Of course I haven't, Travis. What a strange question.'

Travis's hair was nearly dry. 'I've got another question for you, Mentor; can two people go to a platform at the same time or through the door of the shed?'

'That's a very good question, but I don't think you'll even begin to understand the answer.'

'Try me – I'm not a dummy, you know.'

'Very well. It's all done with time-slip continuity. Basically, the moment your hand touches the shed door, you're locked into a five-dimensional thrust chamber. Once you push the "go" button, the acceleration of the reformer single unit is instantaneous, so you don't notice anything. This allows any other participant or participants to gain access at the optimum time without any load frequency; a thrust racer is always allocated to compensate for any variations caused by additional arrivals. OK so far, Travis?'

'My hair's dry now, Mentor. I'm going downstairs to see Mum.'

Travis ventured downstairs; his mother was still working on the curtains. 'All right, Mum?' he asked nonchalantly.

'Yes, Travis. You know, I've just had Mrs Macintosh on the phone.'

'How's Alex?' Travis asked.

'I didn't think to ask; she phoned up to see if you were here, because Kirsty has just told her mother that you were standing in her garden, not five minutes ago.'

Travis didn't answer.

His mother went on, 'Poor girl, it must be all that travelling, and the shock of moving; and of course, Travis, she really likes you. I expect she'll be seeing you in her dreams next.'

Travis went back up to his room and kept trying Alex's mobile, but with no success.

The next day, Mr Pomphrey was just settling down for a little siesta with the TV playing quietly in the background. His eyes were closed and he was just dozing off.

'Concerns are growing for a ten-year-old boy who has gone missing near Loch Lomond in Scotland. Alexander Macintosh, who only moved to the area…'

Mr Pomphrey was immediately awake.

The news bulletin continued. *'…last week, went missing sometime on Sunday afternoon; divers are currently searching the loch, as one theory is that he may well have fallen in. We now go over to our reporter, Angus Cameron, on the banks of Loch Lomond. What do we know about the boy, Angus?'*

'Apparently, the lad only moved up here from England last Friday. I understand he was reluctant to come and said he would run away. One theory is that he's trying to get back to where he came from; another theory is that as he doesn't know the area and he's fallen in the loch. As you can see behind me, the police divers are busy searching. The other possibility is of course that the lad's been abducted.'

'Thank you then, Angus, we'll return to that story when we have any more news.'

Mr Pomphrey turned off his TV and hurried next door to see Mr Macintosh. He was just in time to see Mr Macintosh's car disappear around the bend in the road. He then tapped on Mr Travis's door.

'Tom, have you seen the news?' he enquired.

'No, but I know what's happening, Mr Pomphrey. Mr Macintosh has been here, and he's gone to get a flight up to Glasgow to join his wife. He's asked us to keep a watch out for Alex in case he turns up here.'

'He told Travis he'd run away at the first opportunity,' said Mr Pomphrey.

'Yes, that's right, and if I know Alex, I'm sure he will.'

'Does Travis know yet?' Mr Pomphrey asked.

'No, we heard the news after he'd gone back to school.'

'Tell you what, Tom, send him round to see me when he gets home and I'll try to take his mind off things.'

When Travis arrived home from school, Mr and Mrs Travis sat him down and told him all about Alex.

'Why don't you go round Mr Pomphrey's, Travis?' his mum suggested, 'you always do after school.'

But before Travis could answer there was a knock at the door. It was Mr Pomphrey himself.

'Quick, Tom, put the TV on,' he said, 'they're about to go over to Loch Lomond.'

Up came the picture. The same reporter as before was standing by the side of the loch.

'*As you can just see behind me, the police frogmen have called off the search for the wee lad today. The light's almost gone. Earlier today a Mrs McCormack came forward and spoke of the attempted abduction of a boy on Sunday afternoon. The police have ruled out that it's the same boy, and say they are still keeping an open mind on what may have happened.*

'*I can now show you the interview I conducted with Mrs McCormack.*'

The picture switched to the reporter standing at the side of a road, facing an elderly lady. Travis recognised her immediately, and feeling himself going red he held his head down. No one noticed – they were too intent on watching the screen.

She told the reporter everything that Travis had remembered. She even recalled that Travis had no coat in Georgetown but was wearing one later. She described Travis so well that he couldn't believe he was going to get away with it. She said the man was driving a silver car and was tall.

The reporter asked how old the boy was. 'No more than eight,' she answered.

Travis was indignant. Eight, eight, he thought, what a cheek!

Tom looked up from the TV. 'That could almost have been you, Travis, except for the boy's age.'

Mr Pomphrey saved the day by saying, 'Travis, you'll just have to go and visit, and look for Alex.'

A stony silence filled the room. Mr Pomphrey realised what he had said. 'Oh, dear,' he added, mortified.

'What have you been saying, Travis?' Travis's dad looked livid.

Mr Pomphrey jumped in. 'It's all right, Tom, it's not his fault; honestly, he's never told me anything. It's a long story, and a question of putting two and two together. I suppose I've known for years, really, even before Travis was born. Years ago I saw your father go in the shed, then you, Travis, and now Auntie Jennison.'

'I don't know what to say – and all these years I thought that I've been so clever keeping the secret, and you knew all the time…'

'The secret's safe with me, never you fear, Tom.'

'I'm sure it is, I'm sure it is. Look, I don't want Travis to go rushing off to visit Scotland,' said Tom, 'he might see things he shouldn't. If he leaves it I know other visitors will visit, and find out the truth, especially as it's a young boy involved, and I expect they'll probably let the police know anonymously.'

Sure enough, by the six o'clock news someone had telephoned the police hotline and reported a ginger-headed boy getting into a silver car.

The caller said he went quite voluntarily and headed in a southerly direction. The newsreader asked on the police's behalf that the caller come forward, as the registration number he gave them belonged to a vicar in West Sussex, and it was obviously incorrect.

'He won't do that,' said Tom, 'he daren't; they'll start asking him too many awkward questions that he can't answer.'

'Then can I go, Dad? Alex is my friend, and I owe him that much.'

'All right. If, and I say *if*, we've heard no more by tomorrow night, you can go up to Alexandria and see what you can find out.'

'But that's in Africa,' said Travis. 'I'm going to Luss, not Africa!'

'Alexandria is in Scotland, and it's the nearest platform to Alex's house; it's only just a couple of minutes away.'

'But Mentor told me Clydebank was the nearest. Oh, Mentor...'

'Sorry, Travis, but I did say I was speaking from memory.'

'So I'm off to Alexandria then, Dad?'

'Like I said, if we've heard no more by tomorrow you can go.'

'Oh, thanks, Dad, thanks!' It was as if Tom had given Travis a ten-pound note.

The news about Alex was all around the school the next day, and Travis got fed up with trying to answer questions he didn't have the answers for. The day dragged on and the story of Alex slipped further and further down the news bulletins.

Travis came in from school. 'Any more news, Dad?'

'No, Travis, not a thing,' his father replied.

'That's it, then,' said Travis, 'I'm off.'

'Hang on! Just hold your horses for a minute, will you?'

'But Dad, you said I could go.'

'I'm not stopping you, Travis; I just want to talk to you first. Listen, Travis, you may well see something that could haunt you for the rest of your life. Mentor can't prepare you for watching something terrible happening to your best friend. I can ask Auntie Jennison to go for you. I know I said you could go and I'm not going back on my word, but please think about it very carefully.'

'Dad, I've *got* to go,' Travis said emphatically. 'As you just said, Alex is my best friend. I can't let him down, Dad. I'm going.'

'Come here and give me a hug, Travis; you're a foolish boy but I'm so proud of you.'

On Travis's fourth attempt, he got the timing exactly right and was just in time to see Alex sneaking out of the bungalow. He walked by the side of him, just like they were going to school. Travis looked at Alex. I've never seen him look so unhappy, he thought; Travis himself was close to tears. He kept a close eye on his watch. He knew that he'd wasted time trying to arrive at Alex's at the right time to see what had happened. They carried on along the road, the rain sheeting down. Alex was leaning into the strong wind and Travis couldn't be sure if it was rain or tears on his friend's face. Travis carried on studying his watch. It's no good, I'll have to leave it for now, he thought, and paying particular notice to the time, he pushed the scarper button.

'I'm back, Mum, Dad. Oh, hello, Mr Pomphrey,' said Travis.

'Come and sit down. You look exhausted, son,' Tom said.

'Yes, I've had it, Dad. I was there twenty-five minutes all together, but I think that's my limit.'

'Do you want anything, Travis?' his mother asked.

'No thank you, Mum, I'll be fine,' Travis replied, yawning.

Mr Pomphrey couldn't contain himself any longer. 'Did you find anything out, Travis?' he asked.

'Yes, Mr Pomphrey. Alex left home to run away all right. I saw him leave and I walked down the road with him; but because I wasted so much time hanging around waiting for him, we'd only gone a little way when I had to come back.'

'How far did you get, Travis?' his dad asked.

'Not far – not as far as school, probably as far as from here to the park.'

'That's not even a quarter of a mile,' Mr Pomphrey said. 'Travis?'

But Travis had already gone fast asleep, sitting up.

Travis's mother decided to keep him home from school the next day. She phoned in and told the school that Travis was a little off colour and he might not be back until Monday.

'What did you do that for, Mum?' Travis asked when he got up. 'I feel perfectly all right, I'm still just a bit tired, that's all.'

'Wouldn't you rather go to Scotland, Travis?' she asked.

'You know I would!'

'Well then…'

Some sixth sense had told Mrs Travis that after Travis's next visit he would need plenty of time to recover.

Chapter Eleven

Travis arrived back in the pouring rain within a couple of seconds of the time at which he'd left Alex. They walked on together. We're together but we're apart, thought Travis. Travis remembered when they were younger how they used to call themselves the Two Musketeers: 'One for both and both for one!' they used to chant.

Travis was aware of the bonnet of a silver car drawing slowly up beside them, and his heart started to pound.

'Excuse me.'

Alex looked around; it was a man's voice.

'I'm totally lost… can you help me?' He was waving an *A to Z* in his hand and leaning towards the passenger window.

'No, I'm sorry, I only got here last week,' said Alex.

The man was all smiles. 'Oh you're English, the same as me; that makes us friends,' he said.

By now Travis was screaming at the top of his voice, '*Don't get in the car, Alex, don't get in the car!*'

'Where are you heading?' the man asked.

'England,' Alex replied.

'*Alex, stay away from the car!*' Travis heard himself shouting.

'What a coincidence,' said the man, smiling, 'we can help each other out.'

Oh no, thought Travis.

The man hopped out of his car and ran to the passenger's side; he opened the front passenger door. 'Hop in – I'm not going to bite you,' the man said, smiling widely at Alex. 'Quick – hurry, before we both get drowned.'

'I'm not really allowed,' said Alex.

Yes, good boy, Travis thought.

'Don't you want to go to England then?' the man asked.

'Yes,' said Alex, 'more than anything else in the whole world.'

'Quickly then!'

Alex got in the front of the car; Travis slid into the back seat and they were off. They'd only gone a few hundred yards when Alex said, 'Stop the car! Stop the car! There's my friend there, trying to cross the road. He's come to see me; he's here!' His voice grew louder. '*Travis, Travis!*' he shouted.

There was Travis standing at the side of the road.

If only I'd been earlier, thought Travis.

'Please, mister, please stop the car.'

'I can't – this is what they call a clearway. You get in a lot of trouble if you stop on a clearway.'

Alex reached into his pocket and pulled out his mobile phone.

'What are you doing now?' the man asked crossly.

'I'm going to phone him.'

The man reached over and snatched the phone from Alex's hand. 'Don't you know you can't use a phone in this type of car? It interferes with the electronic ignition, and we'll never get to England if we break down.'

'Can I have my phone back, please, mister?'

'No, I'll hang onto it until you get out; you might be tempted to use it otherwise.'

'No, I won't, honest.'

'I said *no*.'

They continued along the road in silence.

Suddenly Alex looked up, 'I think I'll get out here please.'

'Can't stop here! I've already told you once,' the man said angrily.

'There's a lay-by coming up and you're allowed to pull in there if you want to.'

The man ignored the lay-by and drove straight on. Alex started looking around at the door handle. The man didn't say anything but Alex heard the loud clicking of the central locking coming on. Alex started to sob, quietly at first, then getting louder.

'Please stop, mister.'

Travis saw the man glance in his mirror and Travis looked around himself; there were no cars behind, or any in front. Travis watched as the man took his left hand off the steering wheel and clenched his fist.

'Do you know what? You're beginning to annoy me, you little shit!' he said.

The man's arm swung in a wide arc, and the heel of his fist caught Alex a sickening blow just below the bridge of his nose. Travis heard a crunch as Alex's nose shattered. Alex's eyes filled with tears; his nose was pumping blood. Desperately, he tried to release his seat belt.

'Oh, sorry, I am so sorry! What have I done?' the man said. He paused and passed Alex a handkerchief. 'Here, mop yourself up. I really am sorry.'

Alex groped for the handkerchief.

'Only joking,' the man said. 'Have some more!'

This time his arm shot out and he hit Alex with a straight left. It connected with his right ear, and Alex's eardrum ruptured. His head bounced off the window and blood started to trickle down his neck.

The man shrieked with laughter. 'Get under the dashboard!' he screamed. 'Get under *now*!'

He tried to push Alex to the floor but the seat belt was still done up. 'Undo your belt,' he ordered, 'undo it, I say!'

Alex fumbled with the seat belt and eventually released it. The man cuffed him across the back of the head and pushed him roughly to the floor.

'You dare move and you'll get some more – understand?'

Alex didn't answer.

The man cuffed him again. '*Understand*?' he asked again.

Alex whimpered, 'Yes.'

The man turned on the car radio and selected Classic FM. The strains of Vivaldi filled the car, but the man, apparently oblivious to the radio, started to sing, 'Today's the day the teddy bears have their picnic.' It was almost as if Alex was no longer there…

Travis sat in the back of the car, alternately watching Alex, the road signs and his alarm watch; all the while the tears were trickling down his cheeks. As soon as his alarm sounded he whispered, 'Goodbye, Alex,' and was gone.

Travis rushed out of the shed, tears streaming down his face. He ran into the house and threw himself on the sofa.

'There, there, Travis, it's all right now… you're home,' his mum said. 'Look at him, Tom, just look! This is all *your* fault – the boy should never have gone. I must have been mad agreeing with you.'

'He'll be all right in a minute,' said Tom.

'All right in a minute, all right in a minute? I doubt if he'll ever be right again. Just look at him, will you?' His mother's voice was growing shriller and shriller. 'My God, Tom Travis, where's all this time travelling going to end?'

'Calm down, Mother, you're upsetting the boy.'

'*I'm* upsetting him! *I'm* upsetting him?' His mother lunged forward and caught Tom across the face with the flat of her hand. 'You… you…'

She immediately collapsed on the sofa next to Travis and began to cry; Tom moved to comfort her and he put his hand on her shoulder.

'Get off me, Tom Travis; just get off me.' She cuddled Travis close, and Tom stood up and walked outside.

Tom was sitting on the garden bench. A whole two hours had passed since Travis had arrived back home. When he heard footsteps behind him he didn't need to look around.

'Here you are, Tom; I've brought you a drink – although you don't deserve it.'

'How's Travis?'

'Sleeping; he's on the sofa. Tom, he mustn't go anymore, ever.'

'Mother, you know that's not possible. It's what we do, it's why we're here! You can't stop the boy.'

'No, but we can stop him from going back to Scotland, can't we?'

'I don't think he'll want to go back, seeing the state he's in; but we must talk to him first.'

Travis slept all that day, through the night and most of the next day. When he eventually came down to the living room, Mr Pomphrey was sitting alone watching TV. He said, 'It's all right, Travis, you're not in the wrong house; I've sent your mum and dad to the pub for an hour; they've been fretting about you for almost two days, and I told them it would do them both good to get out for a while.'

'Oh, Mr Pomphrey, they had a terrible row! I've never seen Mum so angry – she hit Dad.'

'They're all right now, and that's the main thing; your mum was just worried about you, that's all.'

'I think… I think…' Travis hesitated.

'Take your time, Travis. Rome wasn't built in a day.'

'I think Alex is probably dead, Mr Pomphrey.'

'You do? What makes you think that?'

'I was there, Mr Pomphrey, it was awful…' His voice trailed away and he began to cry.

Mr Pomphrey put his arm round Travis's shoulders. 'That's it, let it all out! Get the lot out all in one go, that's what I always say.'

Travis cried bitterly for a good five minutes, while Mr Pomphrey watched in silence. 'Feeling better now, Travis?' he asked.

'Yes, thank you, Mr Pomphrey. I am, thank you.'

'Tell you what then, Travis, you go upstairs and have a nice wash, and you'll be presentable by the time your mum and dad get home.'

'A nice wash, Mr Pomphrey? There's no such thing!' Travis smiled and ran off upstairs.

By the time Mr and Mrs Travis came in, Travis was sitting on the sofa next to Mr Pomphrey, crossed-legged as usual, watching the television but with a faraway look in his eyes.

Mrs Travis was just about to say something about Travis's feet on the furniture when she thought better of it. Instead she greeted him cheerily. 'Hello! How are you two getting on, then?'

'Fine, thank you,' Travis said.

'In the pink,' replied Mr Pomphrey.

'Where's Dad?' Travis asked.

'He's walked up to the fish and chip shop; he thought we'd all have a treat.'

'Right then, I'll be off,' said Mr Pomphrey.

'You sit right there, Mr Pomphrey. Tom's getting you some as well; after all, you're like part of the family now, and it's the least we can do after you've looked after Travis for us.'

'Oh, Barbara, thank you so much! I do appreciate it.'

Tom brought in the fish and chips and they all tucked in, but Travis could only pick at his.

'Come on, son,' said Tom, 'you need to recharge your batteries, you know.'

'I'm sorry, Dad, but I'm just not hungry.'

'Look, Travis, we've deliberately not asked you anything about Scotland, but it might help to get it off your chest. Sometimes talking can ease the pain.'

'I can't talk about it tonight, Dad, maybe not tomorrow night, maybe never,' Travis said softly.

Travis's mum threw Tom a look and they finished their meal in silence.

'That was delicious. Thank you both very much,' Mr Pomphrey said. 'Can I make a suggestion?'

'Certainly,' said Tom, 'what have you got in mind?'

'I think Auntie Jennison might be of some help.'

'Great minds think alike,' replied Tom. 'I'll phone her right now.'

'If you wouldn't mind, Tom, I'll phone her myself. I haven't spoken to her for a couple of days.'

'Yes, of course; you can use our phone if you like,' Tom said.

'Oh, Tom, don't be so insensitive,' Mrs Travis said. 'I don't think Mr Pomphrey wants you around to hear what he's got to say to Auntie Jennison.'

'No, that's all right; I'd be pleased to use your phone, Barbara.'

'Do you want the number?' Tom asked.

'No, it's all right, I know it off by heart.'

Now there's a surprise, Travis thought.

Mr Pomphrey had only been speaking to Auntie Jennison for a few seconds when he came back into the living room shaking his head and chuckling away. 'She's going to phone me back. She says her hair's a mess, she hasn't got any make-up on and so she can't possibly talk to a gentleman caller looking like that!'

Even Travis had to smile.

Five minutes later, the shrill, urgent call of the phone made everybody jump.

'That could only be Auntie Jennison,' said Travis. 'When anybody else rings it's always a lot quieter.' It seemed Travis was regaining his sense of humour.

Mr Pomphrey took the whole call and came back in the living

room. 'I hope you don't mind not speaking to her, Tom, but when I said how upset Travis was she said she'd come by platform and be here in a couple of minutes.'

'I didn't realise that she knew that you know all about us,' Tom said. 'Was she surprised?'

'No, not in the least. She already knew… it looks as if she's been doing a little visiting of her own,' said Mr Pomphrey.

'No, Auntie Jennison isn't stupid.'

Barely a minute passed, and Auntie Jennison, looking like she'd been pulled through a hedge backwards, suddenly called from the kitchen.

'I'm here! Yoo-hoo, everybody!'

'Whatever's happened to you, Auntie Jennison?' Travis's mum asked.

'I fell over going up to the shed where the grass is so long, and I haven't been platform-hopping for a while, so I missed my footing in the dark.' Her wig was skew-whiff on her head, her hat skew-whiff on top of that, and she had an unlit broken cigarette in her mouth.

'Hello, Bill,' she said, the 'hello' lingering on her lips.

Mr Pomphrey stood up, walked over to Auntie Jennison, carefully took her hand, raised it to his mouth, kissed it and said, 'Enchanted.'

Travis thought it was all a bit disgusting.

'Do you like my new false teeth, Bill?' Auntie Jennison wrenched open her lips with both hands and stood there grinning at Mr Pomphrey.

'Very nice, Auntie,' said Mr Pomphrey.

Auntie Jennison whipped out her dentures and proudly showed them off, pushing them under everybody's nose. 'They cost an absolute fortune! You know, you'll never see a poor dentist.' Replacing them, Auntie Jennison rounded on Travis. 'Sit down there, Travis, my precious.'

Travis couldn't believe it; she hadn't tried to kiss him once!

'Now, I want everyone to be perfectly quiet.' Auntie Jennison sat facing Travis and gently placed one hand on each side of his temples; she closed her eyes and let out a deep sigh. No one dared to move; Mr Pomphrey felt a tickle in his throat but stifled the cough. The only sound was the grandmother clock ticking quietly away to itself in the corner.

For the first time in days Travis felt a serene calmness sweeping over him; the sensation seemed to come right from the ends of Auntie Jennison's fingers.

Auntie Jennison opened her eyes. 'Go to bed, Travis, my love,' she said. 'You will wake at ten tomorrow morning.'

Travis went around and kissed everybody, including Auntie Jennison. Then he said goodnight and disappeared up the stairs.

'I wish I could get him to do that,' said his mother.

'I got here just in time,' declared Auntie Jennison. 'The boy would have gone into shock tomorrow, and you could hardly tell the doctor what's what, could you? I must say, I'm very disappointed in Mentor; he hasn't looked after the boy at all well. The trouble is, he's got no feelings, no soul. No, you did the right thing. Thank you for getting Bill to phone me, Tom.'

'It was Mr Pomphrey's idea, actually, Auntie Jennison.'

'Oh, Bill, how thoughtful,' she said and smiled at him. 'Right, I shall need to treat Travis again tomorrow, and I shall have to see first-hand what happened in Scotland. Bill, you must come down to the cottage and stay; someone has to look after Scampi and Charlie.' She paused for a moment. 'The sleeping arrangements will be all above board; you shall have the spare room... and my bedroom door has an extremely secure bolt on it.'

Travis's parents smiled quietly to themselves.

Auntie Jennison continued. She sounded like a military field marshal organising a campaign. 'I shall be flitting about, first to take care of Travis, and then later in the week I shall go to Scotland. If the task proves time-consuming in Scotland, I shall need plenty of sleep. So prepare yourself for a long stay, Bill.'

'How long can you visit for, Auntie Jennison?' Tom asked.

'I have been known to do three hours, thirty-five minutes,' she said rather proudly.

'I've only ever managed two hours fifty myself,' Tom said.

'And who was it said that women were the weaker sex?' Auntie Jennison said triumphantly.

'What would happen if you stayed there until you fell asleep?' Mr Pomphrey asked.

'If you sleep you fall into a coma and there is no coming back; death follows shortly thereafter,' replied Auntie Jennison. 'Our guides drum it into us from the very beginning that *we must never overstay our visit.*'

'Has anyone ever died, Auntie?' Mr Pomphrey asked.

'Well, the book of records show if someone has disappeared, like Thomas did, but there would be no explanation as to the cause.'

'So it's possible that Thomas went to sleep and never woke up, then?' Mr Pomphrey asked.

'Yes, Bill, it's possible – but we just don't know,' Auntie Jennison said. She stood up and made towards the door. 'Right, I must go now; Scampi has to be fed and he'll be missing me.' She briefly put her field marshal's hat back on.

'Tom, I shall expect you to run Bill down to the cottage first thing tomorrow. As soon as you arrive, which should be by ten, I shall hop up here and see to Travis. As for you, Barbara, listen out for the boy. If in the unlikely event he wakes up in the night, you must phone me immediately. Do you all understand?'

'Yes, Auntie Jennison,' they all chorused meekly.

Auntie Jennison swept out of the back door and disappeared into the night.

Chapter Twelve

Not wishing to incur Auntie Jennison's wrath, Tom and Mr Pomphrey left for the cottage at seven the next day; but with the rush hour to contend with, they took a little over two hours and pulled up outside Auntie Jennison's just a bit after nine.

'Oh, it's beautiful, Tom,' said Mr Pomphrey, staring at the front of Auntie Jennison's cottage. 'Look at the Virginia creeper all over the walls.'

'Travis hates it; he says the biggest spiders in the world live in there. Look, Mr Pomphrey,' Tom said, 'Auntie Jennison's been on her own a long time and she's a bit, well, how can I say it? Well, things are a bit basic here…'

'In that case, Tom, I shall fit in very well.'

Before they got to the front door Auntie Jennison had it wide open, 'Come in, Tom, come in, Bill.'

Tom glanced around the inside. He couldn't believe the transformation. The hallway was light and airy, and there was a faint odour of fresh paint in the air. 'Auntie,' he said, 'what's been going on in here?'

'Do you like it, Tom?'

'Like it? It's absolutely fabulous!'

Tom told Barbara later it was like stepping into a show house. He couldn't believe it was the same place.

'I've had the builders and decorators working here for weeks. You see, I had a feeling I might be getting some company.'

'But you haven't said a word about it, Auntie Jennison, have you?'

'I don't have to tell you everything, Tom Travis!'

Auntie Jennison showed them into the living room, stood to one side and waved her arm, palm upward, at the décor. 'So what d'you think of this, Tom?' she asked.

'I don't know what to say, Auntie Jennison,' Tom replied.

'I do,' said Mr Pomphrey. 'It's very *un*basic!' He looked at Tom and laughed.

Guided tour completed, and all instructions to Mr Pomphrey regarding Scampi's requirements given, Auntie Jennison headed off up the garden and Tom went home in his car.

'Hello, Barbara dear, how did Travis sleep?' Auntie Jennison asked.

'I haven't heard a sound from him, Auntie Jennison,' Travis's mother replied.

'Good, good, it's a quarter to ten now so I'll give him until ten. Then, if it's all right with you, Barbara, I'll go up to see him.'

At ten o'clock Auntie Jennison bounded up the stairs two at a time and let herself into Travis's room. Look at him, sleeping like a baby, she thought. She went over to Travis's bed and, sitting down quietly on the edge, gazed down at Travis. She stretched her hands out to Travis's temples and again, just like the previous night, sat there silently with her own eyes closed.

Mrs Travis looked at the old grandmother clock. Ten thirty, she thought. I hope Travis is all right…

It was another twenty minutes before Auntie Jennison put in an appearance. 'I've taken as much from the boy as I can, Barbara. I think he'll be able to cope now. He's seen some terrible things, so I don't want you or Tom mentioning anything. When he's ready to tell you, he will, and I think you'll find that when he wakes up he'll be more like his old self.' She reached into her pinny pocket. 'Oh, look at me looking for a fag! I must be in a state.'

'Have you stopped completely, then, Auntie Jennison?'

'Almost,' came the reply. 'Listen, Barbara, I'm going now and I'll be in touch as soon as I get back.'

Travis lay on his back, gradually coming back into the real world; his immediate thoughts were of Alex. I wonder if he's all right, he asked himself, but then he already knew the answer.

Auntie Jennison's magic had worked well on Travis, putting Alex out of his mind. He wandered down the stairs. 'Hello, Mum! I'm absolutely starving.'

'Oh, Travis, that's the best thing I think I've ever heard you say!'

Mr Pomphrey was just putting Scampi's food into his dish as Auntie Jennison put in an appearance. 'Hello, Bill, I'm back,' she said.

'Hello, Auntie. How's Travis?' Mr Pomphrey had a worried look on his face.

'Sleeping like a baby when I left, but I know he'll be all right now.'

'Well, that's a relief.'

'Look, Bill, you know that I really am pleased to see you, but it's important that I go straight away and try to put an end to this whole sorry business. When I return I'm sure I'll sleep for a week, I don't know; but you're not to worry, and I'll see you when I get back. Help yourself to anything you want.'

Before Mr Pomphrey could answer, Auntie Jennison was out the door and gone. He felt a little peeved, but told himself it was all a matter of priorities, and at the moment in time he came well down on the list.

Despite Auntie Jennison telling Bill not to worry, he was on the phone to Barbara and Tom every few hours. After two days had gone by, he was saying, 'She might be in a coma, Tom… She could be dead, Barbara.'

On the sixth day, Mr Pomphrey was on the phone yet again. 'Tom, I'm telling you she might be dead!'

'You'll be dead when she gets the phone bill, Mr Pomphrey. She'll be back soon, stop worrying yourself.'

Secretly, Tom himself was growing concerned. He knew his own limitations and was gauging them against Auntie Jennison's. Six days was far too long to be gone. The most he had ever been asleep in the Pullman was four; it wasn't totally impossible that she'd ignored the waves of tiredness that would sweep over you and was lying in a coma somewhere, or could even be dead. Thoughts of his own father's disappearance once again filled his head, and he wondered if perhaps he'd overstayed on a visit. Every day Travis was asking for news. Mr Pomphrey was keeping on, and even the unflappable Barbara seemed tetchy. It was all becoming too much, and Tom, unable to visit himself any longer, felt totally helpless.

Travis came in from school. 'Any news, Dad?' he asked.

'No news is good news, son,' his dad answered, trying to sound confident.

'Oh, Dad, don't patronise me! I'm not a child any more, you know.'

'I'll give you "patronise"! Patronise, indeed! Come here, you!' Tom laughed and started to chase Travis around the house. Travis, shrieking with laughter, ran up to his bedroom, closely followed by his father. Travis collapsed in a heap on the bed.

'You're still not too big to tickle, you know! Patronise, indeed.' Tom tickled Travis and then collapsed on the bed beside him.

When Travis had got his breath, he said, 'Dad, do you think anything's happened to Auntie Jennison?'

'Your Auntie Jennison is what Mr Pomphrey would describe in military terms as "a seasoned campaigner". She's been round the block a few times, and a few times more. She'll turn up, never you fear; this is just a stroll in the park for her.' Tom uncrossed his fingers.

Auntie Jennison left Bill standing in the living room, gazing after her. She walked out of the house and across her flagstone yard up the three steps and on towards her shed. A push on the 'go' button, and soon she was emerging from the shed in Alexandria.

As Alex climbed into the front of the man's car, seven souls were already in the back. There was Travis, of course; Auntie Jennison; three visitors who had heard about Alex on the news; and two who were studying abductions long after the event. Gradually, one by one, they dropped out. Travis was first to leave, closely followed by one of the students. Then there was quite a gap, and after some two hours and forty-seven minutes into the journey, Auntie Jennison found herself sitting alone. Not that she was aware of it, mind you. Four hours and five minutes, and Auntie Jennison, almost in a state of unconsciousness, finally pushed the scarper button.

One hundred and seventy-three hours after Auntie Jennison had set off she started to stir. Apart from a raging thirst, which she quickly cured by drinking some spring water she always kept in her carriage for such emergencies, she felt none the worse for her ordeal. She climbed down from her carriage and started back towards the house.

Mr and Mrs Travis were waiting in the garden, as were Travis, Mr Pomphrey and Scampi, when she emerged from the shed. The moment they saw Auntie Jennison, a huge cheer went up and they all gathered around her, applauding.

It was Tom who spoke first. 'You had us all worried there, Auntie Jennison,' he said.

'I did four hours and five minutes, you know! Four hours and five minutes – I can hardly believe it myself.'

They all went into the house. Auntie Jennison lit up a cigarette, a thing they hadn't seen her do for quite a while. She beckoned for them all to sit down and then she started.

'I'm afraid it's all bad news. After I got in the car I saw what happened to poor Alex and I sat there for just over two hours watching the road signs and praying the man would stop driving…'

Mr Pomphrey interrupted. 'Why did you want him to stop the car, Auntie?' he asked.

'Well, you can leave the car whenever you want, but even a visitor can't get back in a car that is doing seventy miles an hour.'

'Ah!' Mr Pomphrey exclaimed.

'Anyway, after about two and quarter hours, the man looked straight in the driving mirror, and if I didn't know better I could have sworn he could see me. Then he said aloud, "I don't know how many of you are left back there, but I won't be stopping for a couple of hours yet, so you just as well scarper now." Then he started laughing like a lunatic. We drove on and he glanced at his watch. We'd been going a good three hours by then, and he looked in the mirror again. "Anyone left back there?" he said. "I doubt it, but I have to be sure, don't I?" He didn't speak again, and then I just had to leave. I think I only made it just in time. But I really did want to find out what happened to that poor little soul.'

'I think you were very brave, Auntie Jennison,' said Travis.

'Hear, hear,' chorused the others.

'You know what we're dealing with here, don't you?' Auntie Jennison said.

'A visitor,' Tom replied and grimaced.

'Yes, Tom, a visitor – a *bad* visitor – almost impossible to catch.'

Once everybody was convinced that Auntie Jennison was over her ordeal, they decided to head for home, with the exception of Mr Pomphrey, who said he'd like to spend some time with her.

'Don't worry about me,' he said. 'I can get the train back. It's a pity Auntie Jennison can't put me in a carrier bag, though, and then we could both platform-hop!'

Auntie Jennison and Mr Pomphrey stood at the front gate of the cottage and waved goodbye to the Travises.

'Come on then, Auntie, let's have a nice cup of Earl Grey. There's something I want to talk to you about,' said Mr Pomphrey.

Mr and Mrs Travis and Travis waved to Auntie Jennison and Mr Pomphrey as they drove away.

'Dad,' said Travis, 'do you think we'll ever find out what happened to Alex?'

'Well, I think your Auntie Jennison is right when she says it's a visitor who's taken Alex, and it will be very difficult indeed to track him down. You see, he's got the advantage all the time – and of course, the scarper button. I'm sorry to have to say this, Travis, but you're just going to have to do your best to get Alex out of your mind.'

'I'll never do that, Dad – never.' Travis sat in silence for a while and then, hanging his head, he said, 'I've got a confession to make. I know you're going to be very angry but I can't bottle it up any longer.'

'I wondered how long it would take,' Mr Travis said.

'What, you mean you know?'

'Yes, Travis, we all know. You went platform-hopping, didn't you?'

'Yes, Dad.' Travis hung his head in shame.

'I'm glad you decided to come clean. At first I thought about punishing you, but I know I would have done exactly the same thing in your shoes, and anyway I think the scare you had was punishment enough. Auntie Jennison said the same man who had Alex had tried to take you.'

'How do you know that, Dad?'

'Auntie Jennison went visiting and saw you.'

'Coo! The crafty old thing!'

'You started it.'

And for the first time in days they all laughed.

Back at Auntie Jennison's, Mr Pomphrey was arranging the teacups. 'I'll pour,' he said.

'Right, then, what is it you would like to talk about, Bill?'

'I don't really know how to say this without upsetting you, Auntie,' he hesitated and then went on. 'Well, the thing is, I'd like to think we've grown into quite good friends over the last few weeks, and I can see over that time you've, well, sorta *changed*. I think what I'm trying to say is that, well, I… I…' He hesitated again. 'I prefer you just the way you were! There, it's said now.'

'I must confess, it's all been a bit of a strain,' said Auntie Jennison, looking quite relieved.

'I really don't mind what you look like, Auntie. It's what's inside that matters to me, and I find your little quirks quite amusing. And as for the cigarettes, they don't bother me at all.'

'In that case, Bill' – she took out her false teeth and put them to one side – 'you don't know what a relief that is!'

Chapter Thirteen

Over the next few weeks, things returned to more or less normal in the Travis household. Not a day went by, though, when Travis didn't spare a thought for Alex, and they all watched the news just in case of any new developments. There was a reconstruction on *Crimewatch*, and Mr and Mrs Mackintosh were interviewed at length, but in the event there was no more news of Alex's disappearance. Travis had continued to help his dad with the family trees and his mother was totally dedicated to the garden now that spring was finally here. A 'Sold' sign had finally gone up in Alex's house, although there was no sign of anyone new moving in.

'I really think it's about time we all went on a family trip,' announced Mr Travis. 'Next week's half-term, and if we don't go now, Mother will be saying she's too busy with the bedding plants. Isn't that so, Mother?'

'Quite right, Tom. What did you have in mind?'

'I thought a few days in Cornwall might be nice.'

'Oh yes, Tom, that would be lovely,' Mrs Travis said.

'Oh Mum, Dad, can Mr Pomphrey and Auntie Jennison come – and Becky as well?'

'Here, steady on, Travis! You'll want Uncle Tom Cobley and all to come, the way you're going on.'

'I don't see any reason why not, Tom,' Mrs Travis said. 'But what's all this, Travis – you wanting Auntie Jennison to come along? Suddenly realised she's not so bad after all, have you?'

Travis shuffled his feet. 'Something like that,' he said quietly.

'Sorry, Travis, didn't quite catch that. Speak up,' his dad said.

'You heard!'

Mr and Mrs Travis started laughing, and Travis joined in.

Travis came in from school on Thursday afternoon, excited at the thought of the Cornwall trip.

'Talk of the devil,' said Mrs Travis. 'I was just saying to your dad, Travis, Becky and her husband can't make it this time. They're going up to Bradford for a wedding party. Mr Pomphrey is spending a few days with Auntie Jennison, so it's just the three of us.'

'Oh, that's a shame, Mum; I was really looking forward to seeing everybody together. It would have been just like it was at Christmas.'

'Actually, Travis, Auntie Jennison did say she might platform-hop and pay us a flying visit.'

'A flying visit, eh! What, she's bought a broomstick now, has she?'

'Don't be so cheeky, Travis.'

'Sorry, Mum.'

With suitcases packed, Saturday morning, a little after nine, found Tom getting the car out of the garage for the 150-mile drive to Cornwall. Knowing what Travis was like about long car journeys, Mrs Travis had been sworn to secrecy about the distance and likely duration.

On the way to Cornwall, Travis counted a massive five Eddies to his mum's one. His dad said he had to concentrate on the motorway too much and only scored one as well. Travis decided the real reason was that neither of them was any good at it. As usual, Travis thought they were never going to get there, and by the time they got to Plymouth he was sound asleep. He was still fast asleep as Tom passed a sign which said 'Polperro 1 mile' and he only stirred when Tom stopped the car outside a bed and breakfast in the middle of the village.

After unpacking, they all decided to go exploring and set off towards the harbour. The tide was out and all the boats were stranded high and dry on the sand. Everywhere all over the harbour were swans, seagulls and ducks foraging among the sand for anything edible. The noise of the seagulls was horrendous and Travis clapped his hands over his ears; he decided there were at least two million of them. They wandered along to a little shop towards the end of the harbour wall, where the smell of Cornish pasties was wafting out of the shop invitingly.

'Come on then, Mother,' Tom said, 'let's sit on the wall and have a pasty each, shall we?'

'You only brought me for my purse, Tom Travis,' Mrs Travis said.

'Not true, not true! There's your sparkling personality as well as your purse.'

Mrs Travis kicked him gently on the leg. They wandered on along and found a spot on the harbour wall and all sat in a row munching away at their pasties.

'It's no good, Tom,' Mrs Travis said, 'I can't sit here any longer – my bum's making buttons. Look, there's a bench along there.'

They all moved along to the bench. Running along the wooden top rail was a faded brass plaque, and as they settled down on the bench, Travis read it out. *'In loving memory of Trevor Bains, born 10th of August 1936, died 16th of September 1978, R.I.P.* I wonder what that's all about,' he said.

'I expect he was a fisherman who got lost at sea, Travis. They often do that in places like this,' his dad replied. 'Hang on, Travis, what was the date you said he died?'

Travis repeated the date.

'Well, I never! There's a coincidence,' Tom said. 'That's the same day as your granddad went missing.'

After the pasties they decided to go for a walk up along the cliff path. The climb up the steep steps past the funny little cottages had them all breathless.

'Not such a good idea this,' Tom said, 'that pasty's hanging a bit heavy. If ever we get to the top we'll have to see if there's anywhere to have a sit down.'

'Trouble is, you see, Dad,' Travis said, 'you're getting fat.'

'Not too fat to catch you, young man!'

But he was. As they came to the top of the climb the fresh wind coming off the sea hit them.

'Wow! Look at the waves down there, Mum, Dad,' Travis said.

'Not too close to the edge, Travis, do be careful,' Mrs Travis said.

Travis gingerly crept towards the edge. 'Wow! That must be at least a thousand feet down there.'

'Well, I don't know how far it is, but it's certainly a long way. Now come back here, please.'

They came to a little hut on the cliff path and sat on the bench inside. After they'd spent some time getting their breath and admiring the sea views, Travis asked, 'What are we going to do now? I'm getting bored…'

'Yes, I think I've recovered enough for the journey down,' his dad said. 'How about you, Mother?'

'Yes, I'm fine now. Travis, how would you like to go and see the model village next?'

'Wow!' Travis replied. 'Yes please. Wicked!'

Early evening found the family sitting in a dark corner of the Noughts and Crosses pub. Travis thought it was quite exciting as he'd never actually been in a pub before. The man behind the bar had told Tom as long as the little boy behaved himself it would be all right. Little boy indeed, Travis thought.

A television was playing in the corner; there was no sound, just the subtitles. A fruit machine stood alone in the corner, its lights flashing, trying to entice people to part with their money. Some background music was coming out of the loudspeakers on the wall; Travis thought they should be called 'soft speakers' because you could hardly hear anything at all. A lady wearing a white apron was wandering around holding up a dish, looking exasperated and calling out, 'Who ordered a portion of peas?' Everyone ignored her.

Travis looked up. He could see someone peering through the grimy window into the pub. 'Dad, look – it's Auntie Jennison,' he said, pointing.

'I'll go and fetch her, Travis; older ladies can be funny about walking in a pub on their own.'

Travis's dad escorted Auntie Jennison in. Oh my God, Travis thought, she looks just like a bag lady again.

'Hello, Barbara, hello, Travis, my little sweetheart! Tom, I'll have a gin and orange; I don't want any of that ice stuff in it though, and you'd better make it a large one. Oh, and Tom, I need more cigarettes. Get me a couple of packets at least.'

'Whatever you say, Auntie Jennison,' Tom said.

'How's Mr Pomphrey?' Travis asked.

'Oh, Bill… Yes, he's just fine,' said Auntie Jennison. She reached into her pinny pocket and produced three lighters and four different packets of cigarettes. 'Ooh look,' she said, 'that's rather a nice ashtray.' And she dragged it closer.

'I thought you didn't smoke now, Auntie Jennison?' Travis asked.

'Only occasionally, Travis, my love; now come over here and give your old Auntie a kiss.'

Back to normal, Travis thought.

'Right then, what have you all been up to?' Auntie Jennison asked, stuffing a peppermint into her mouth. With peppermint on board, it was only a matter of time; and sure enough, Auntie Jennison looked up and said, 'There goes another one! Shows I've got a healthy gullet.' Thankfully, it was one of her inaudible ones.

Travis's mum gave Auntie Jennison an account of the day's events, and then the adults started their usual small talk. Travis knew he would have to sit quietly because Auntie Jennison wouldn't have it any other way.

After a while, Travis looked at his mum and asked her, 'Is it all right if I go down to the harbour on my own, Mum?'

'Providing you're careful. The tide's in now, and don't be gone too long.'

'Thanks, Mum, see you all later.'

'Don't I get a kiss before you go, my precious?' Auntie Jennison asked, puckering up her lips.

Travis went out through the door wiping his mouth and ran along towards the quay. The fishermen were unloading their little fishing boats and taking the fish to a long shed by the side of the water. Although it was beginning to get dark, the seagulls were still looking for any fish that might get dropped or discarded, and the noise they were making was as bad as before. Travis sat on the same bench as he had that afternoon with his mum and dad. He looked again at the brass plaque. 'Trevor Bains,' he said aloud. 'Trevor Bains...' he repeated.

It was then that the penny dropped. Travis ran back to the Noughts and Crosses as fast as his little legs would carry him. He bounded down the three steps into the bar and ran across to where his parents were sitting. The man behind the bar looked disapprovingly over the top of the glass he was polishing, first at Travis, then at his parents.

'For goodness sake, Travis, where's the fire?' his dad asked.

'Where's Auntie Jennison, Dad?'

'She had to go, but she said to say goodbye.'

'You've developed a sudden interest in Auntie Jennison, haven't you, Travis?' his mother enquired.

Travis decided to say nothing about what he thought he knew until he'd spoken to Auntie Jennison. 'Just wondered where she was, that's all,' he replied. He suddenly noticed it wasn't only Auntie Jennison that was missing; the ashtray on the table had disappeared as well.

The next morning, the seagulls had the Travis family awake before it was barely light, and the din was unimaginable. Travis dressed, went outside and switched on his mobile phone. Making sure he was all alone, he punched in Auntie Jennison's number. Nothing! Oh no, he thought, no signal… it must be all those hills.

After breakfast Travis asked his parents if he could go exploring on his own.

'Yes,' said his mum, 'but mind what you're doing, and we'll meet you in the Noughts and Crosses at midday.'

Travis felt really grown-up, allowed out exploring and meeting his parents in the pub. Wait till I tell Ale… I can't tell him though, can I? he thought.

Travis walked down past the pub. The streets were almost deserted. Of course, he thought, it's Sunday for one thing, and out of season for another. There was a little shop almost opposite the pub, and above it a sign said 'HARBOUR TRADING'. Travis thought it a very strange sign. How could you trade one harbour for another? After all, they were all fixed in place, weren't they?

There was a tall thin man just letting himself into the shop. He saw Travis and said, 'Sorry, lad, I'm not open today. I'm just doing some stocktaking.'

Travis said the first thing that came into his head. 'Actually, sir, I was hoping for some information. You see, we're doing a project at school—'

'A project, eh?' the man interrupted. 'Yes, fine, what do you want to know?'

It seemed 'project' was the magic word. Travis decided he'd

have to remember that. 'Well, I was wondering, sir,' he continued, 'about the man's name on the bench by the harbour.'

'Which one? There's about half a dozen, to my knowledge.'

'Trevor Bains,' Travis replied.

'Oh yes – that's the chap that got murdered. Well, everyone *said* he was murdered. They found his body just along from here, you know.' He pointed towards the harbour. 'Had a hole right through him, they said; seems he was shot. I didn't live here at the time; it's years ago now. You'll need to talk to some of the older residents; I don't really know that much about it.'

Travis thanked the man and walked on towards the harbour. An old man with tanned, leathery skin and wearing a cap was sitting right on the quayside. He was sucking on his pipe and running his fishing net through his hands, studying it intently.

'Excuse me, sir,' Travis said very politely, 'I was wondering if you could help me.' He remembered the magic words. 'You see, we're doing...' He hesitated. 'We're doing a project at school.'

'Certainly, young man! What d'you want to know?' the old man replied, putting the fishing net down.

Travis asked him what he could tell him about Trevor Bains.

The old man removed the pipe from his mouth. 'Trevor Bains? Yes, I knew him personally.' Travis was getting excited as the old man continued. 'He was always well turned out, seemed to have money to burn. He'd come in the pub and buy everybody in there a drink. He'd go missing for a while, and then he'd be back. No one knew where he lived or what he did for a living; there were some people, mind, who thought he was mixed up in drugs or something – and that's why he got murdered.'

'Did they ever catch anybody?' Travis asked.

'No, they didn't have a clue,' the old fisherman said. 'They say he had a hole right through him you could put your fist through. To tell you the truth, I didn't really like him; he was the sort that would have the sugar out of your tea. Mind, to be fair, I was as bad as the rest. I'd take all the drink he wanted to buy, but I didn't like him. No, he had a nasty streak. I can remember one night in the pub someone stepped on his foot; he always wore patent leather shoes, and very expensive-looking. Anyway, like I said, someone stepped on one of them. It was terrible. He head-butted the man, and then he got the poor fellow on the floor and gave him a good kicking. It took five of them to stop him; he was like an animal. The poor chap was in a terrible mess. Of course, it was a bit of a dilemma for the landlord, as Trevor used to spend so much money in his pub…'

'Could you show me where they found him?' Travis interrupted.

'Hang on, young fella, I haven't finished yet!' The old man paused and relit his pipe. 'Anyway, he used to spend so much money in the pub the landlord barred the other chap. But the landlord didn't last long after that; this is only a small place and the word soon went round. People just stopped going in there. Now, what was it you wanted to see?'

The old man took Travis along past the harbour wall towards the sea and then he pointed. 'Right there, it was, right there that they found the body.'

'What – at the bottom of those steps?' Travis asked.

'Yes, right there.'

Travis thanked the old man and started back along the quay.

'Hang on, young fella,' the old man called out, 'I just had a thought, it might pay you to look in the Museum of Smuggling. There's a section in there about the only murder in Polperro. Hey, and good luck with your project.'

Travis ran round the back of the harbour to the museum. It's Sunday, he thought, and it's out of season. Sure enough, the sign said, 'Open 10 a.m. to 6 p.m., March to October'. That's it, then, thought Travis pessimistically, I've had it…

Just after midday, Travis, with the air of an adult, nonchalantly strolled into the bar of the Noughts and Crosses, just as if he'd been doing it all his life. The man behind the bar looked at him disapprovingly; Travis put his head down and scuttled over to where his parents were sitting.

'What have you been up to, then, Travis?' his dad asked.

'Oh, I've been down by the harbour and I had a chat with one of the fishermen. Dad, when are we going to go home?'

'Don't you like it here, then, Travis?' his mother asked.

'Oh yes, it's a beautiful place, but there's not much to do for a ten-year-old, is there?'

'Well, funny enough, Travis, your mum and I thought exactly the same thing. What would you like to do?'

'I think I'd like to go and see Auntie Jennison,' Travis answered.

Travis's parents stared at each other.

'Did I hear you right, Travis? Now let's get this straight,' said his dad. 'You. Travis Travis, being of sound mind, want to leave here and go and see your favourite Auntie Jennison... is that correct?' Tom winked at Travis's mother.

'Yes, that's right,' Travis said.

'I'm speechless!' said his dad.

'Me too!' his mum exclaimed.

Travis thought some explanation might be in order. 'I wanted to see the difference in her place, now it's been done up, really,' he explained lamely.

'What? You taking an interest in Auntie Jennison's decorations after the state your room gets into? I don't think so,' said his dad. 'What's the real reason, Travis?'

'Dad, you'll just have to trust me.' Travis bit his lip.

'All right, son,' he replied, 'we'll leave in the morning.'

'Thanks, Dad, thanks, Mum!' Travis was all smiles. 'I promise I will tell you when I can. Oh, Dad,' he added, 'what's "patent" shoes?'

'They're patent leather shoes; they're the kind of shoes they wear for ballroom dancing, and they're very shiny.'

'Thanks, Dad.'

'What d'you make of all that then, Tom?' Travis's mum asked when they were alone. 'What can he be up to?'

'No idea, Mother, but we'll get it out of Auntie Jennison anyway,' said Tom.

Chapter Fourteen

The next day wouldn't come quickly enough for Travis; he was up long before his parents, so he wandered down the narrow streets to the museum just on the off chance that someone might be there, but it was all locked up and deserted. Then after breakfast they all set off for Auntie Jennison's, Travis checking the miles on the road signs at every opportunity.

'Dad, I've had an idea,' Travis said. 'There's no need for you to come to Auntie Jennison's with me. I could platform-hop straight from home.'

'Nice try, Travis,' said his dad, 'but you know we don't like you platform-hopping – it's too dangerous.'

'But Dad, Auntie Jennison's is quite safe; nothing can happen there.'

'Well, I don't think it would hurt, Tom,' Travis's mum said, 'and it would save Travis dying of boredom on the journey.'

'We'll see,' Tom said.

'Thanks, Dad,' Travis said.

'I haven't said yes yet, Travis,' said Tom.

'No, course you haven't, Dad.'

Travis leant forward and nudged his mother over the seat and they both started laughing. The rest of the journey home passed in slow motion to Travis; even playing spot the Eddie had lost its appeal. But as usual Travis won all hands down with three, while Barbara scored one and Tom didn't get any. 'I think, sometimes,' Travis said, 'that you two only humour me because I'm a child.'

No sooner had they arrived at the front door of their house than Travis said, 'Right, I'm off then.'

'Just hold on, young man, hold your horses,' his dad said. 'I'm going to phone Auntie Jennison first to make sure everything's all right and you should be having something to eat. Also, saying hello to Mr Pomphrey might not be a bad idea.'

'Mr Pomphrey's already at Auntie Jennison's, Dad, and I'm not in the least bit hungry, so can I go now, please?'

'Not before I've spoken to Auntie Jennison.'

Travis ran down Auntie Jennison's garden as fast as he could go. He didn't even notice that the wilderness was no more, that the outside toilet had gone, or that there were new decorations in Auntie Jennison's passageway. 'Auntie Jennison, Auntie Jennison!' he called out.

'In here, Travis.' Auntie Jennison's voice came from the living room. 'Come in, sweetheart.'

'*Wow*! Cool!' Travis exclaimed. 'Auntie Jennison, this looks really nice.' Even Travis couldn't fail to be impressed by the makeover. Mr Pomphrey, all smiles, was sitting in the chair by the new gas fire looking like he'd lived there all his life. Travis wasn't too sure he approved.

'Come here, Travis,' said Auntie Jennison. She scooped him up and gave him a good slobbering; the overpowering combination of the smell of peppermint and cigarettes was back. 'I know what you're thinking, Travis, but it's the only little vice I've got.'

That – and ashtrays, Travis thought.

'Hello, Travis,' Mr Pomphrey said. 'Did you enjoy yourself in Cornwall?'

Before Travis could answer, Auntie Jennison chipped in, 'Come and sit down here with me, Travis.' She patted the settee by her side, and Scampi, suddenly thinking his name was 'Travis', took Travis's seat. Gently, Travis lifted him down: not a growl!

'Let me just light up a fag, and you can tell us all about it,' said Auntie Jennison. She reached into her pinny pocket and produced a packet of Woodbines and a lighter; she stuffed a cigarette into her mouth and at the same time produced a peppermint with bits of fluff on it. She popped the fluffy peppermint into her mouth and continued, 'Here you are, Travis, this one's for you.' With that, she produced an equally fluffy peppermint from her pocket.

'No, thank you, Auntie Jennison,' Travis said sweetly. 'Mum says too many sweets are bad for your teeth.'

'Please yourself, then, Travis, but they keep you regular.' As if to prove the point, she blew off loudly. 'Right, just let me light up.' She sucked on her fag and peppermint simultaneously. 'Bill just loves the smell of Woodbines, don't you, Bill? It reminds him of the war.'

Mr Pomphrey sat there grinning like a Cheshire cat, nodding his head in approval.

'Be a love, Travis, my angel,' said Auntie Jennison, 'and fetch me an ashtray from the sideboard.'

Travis walked over to the sideboard, and there on the top was the ashtray with 'Butcombe Bitter' on it. Sitting to the side was the one from the Noughts and Crosses. Travis decided to say nothing.

'Right then, Travis, tell us all about Cornwall,' Auntie Jennison said.

Travis quickly sketched over the more mundane aspects of the trip and then he got to the bit that was burning holes in him. 'Auntie Jennison, I want you to look in the records, please.'

'Do you indeed!' Auntie Jennison replied. 'And what am I looking for, pray?'

'Trevor Bains,' Travis said excitedly. 'If I'm right, I think Trevor Bains is the key to Granddad's disappearance.'

Mr Pomphrey leaned forwards in his chair. 'Who's this Trevor Bains then, Travis?' he enquired.

'Well, Mr Pomphrey, I think Trevor Bains is Ivan Roberts – that's the man Granddad said he had unfinished business with; I think they're one and the same person.'

'And what makes you think that, then?' Mr Pomphrey asked.

'Well, I think I've got Richard Whitley to thank, actually. You see, Trevor Bains in an anagram of Ivan Roberts.'

'Well, I never! What a clever boy,' Mr Pomphrey said.

'Auntie Jennison, was my granddad any good at *Countdown*?'

Auntie Jennison chuckled. 'There wasn't any *Countdown* when he was around. That was so long ago that Richard Whitley actually had his own hair!' They all roared with laughter. 'Actually, Travis, your granddad was very good at crosswords, and sums as well.'

Auntie Jennison stood up, stubbed out her cigarette, produced the huge records room key from her pocket and announced, 'This way!' Then she marched off towards the records room with Travis and Mr Pomphrey trailing on behind.

Auntie Jennison unlocked the door and went straight to the bookshelves on the left-hand side of the room. 'Now let me see,' she said, 'A to C.' She picked up a smallish blue book and thumbed through it. The suspense was killing Travis. She replaced the book and walked to the bookshelves on the other side of the room.

'Well, Auntie?' Travis looked at her imploringly.

'Patience, Travis, patience! I've only just started,' she replied, looking along the bookshelves, murmuring all the while.

'Come on, come on,' Travis was muttering under his breath.

'Mmm!' Auntie Jennison exclaimed.

'What is it, Auntie Jennison?' Travis was almost bursting.

'Ah! Here we are.' Auntie Jennison lifted an enormous book off the shelf and placed it on the desk. 'Now let me see.'

She opened the book and flicked the pages over, then carefully and slowly (too slowly for Travis) she started to work her way through. Pointing with her index finger, she read out, 'Babage, Backhouse, Bagley, Bailey, Bannerman... no Bains here, Travis.' She looked up at Travis, paused, peered at Travis's disappointed face, and then added, 'Only kidding, Travis!'

'Oh! Auntie Jennison, is he there, is he really really there?'

'Yes, Travis, here we are: Bains, Trevor, born 10th August 1936, Polperro, Cornwall; first called, 5th April 1956; active, 31st May 1959, from platform 106; died 16th September 1978 – there!'

'I must go straight to Cornwall, right this minute, Auntie Jennison,' Travis declared.

'Yes, and I'm coming as well,' said Auntie Jennison. 'I shall go back to 16th September 1978, because I can stay longer than you, and anyway it might be a bit grisly. And as for you, you will go back to earlier today.'

'Why earlier today, Auntie Jennison?' Travis asked.

'So that you can go in the museum, of course!'

'Oh, yes. Well then, can we go now, Auntie Jennison?'

'Yes, come on, Travis! Let's strike while the iron's hot. Bill, if Tom or Barbara telephones, tell them I've taken Travis out somewhere.'

'Where shall I say, Auntie?'

'Oh, use your imagination! Say the pub, or something,' Auntie Jennison replied.

Like a whirlwind, as usual, she locked the records room door, and, with a 'See you later, Bill; come on, Travis, hurry up,' she was gone.

Auntie Jennison emerged from platform 106 at twilight; she carefully picked her way along the side of what appeared to be an electricity substation and came to a three-foot-high rusty wrought-iron gate. She hooked her skirt up and vaulted over the gate like a twenty-year-old, just for the fun of it, although she could have passed straight through. In front of her was a steep set of stone steps. 'Chapel Steps' was inscribed on a small wooden sign, hanging crookedly on the wall opposite. She started to make her way down the steps. Passing the entrance to the Blue Peter pub, she noticed right at the bottom of the steps and in front of her a telephone box. She sat on the bottom step and waited.

Travis passed by the electric substation and went straight through the gate. He ran down the steps and checked his watch: half past seven; everyone should have gone home by now. He half floated and half ran all the way around to The Warren, the street where the museum was to be found. Oh, that's good, he thought, no one around. He started chuckling to himself, suddenly realising no one could see him anyway. He walked straight through the front door. Inside, it was almost pitch black, and instinctively he looked for the light switch. Oh, no, he thought, I can't turn it on, and I should have set the coordinates for earlier! What a dummy! And his thoughts turned to Alex. Making his way through the gloom, Travis searched for the section about the Polperro murder. Gradually his eyes became accustomed to the dark, and there, right in the corner, he saw what he was looking for.

Auntie Jennison looked at her watch: ten thirty. The full moon made up for the lack of street lighting, and the strains of the pub singer in the Blue Peter was floating along on the night air. Auntie Jennison joined in just to while away the time. Hurried footsteps was the first thing she was aware of; then she heard a loud groan. Looking over her shoulder, she could see by the light of the street lights right at her eye level a pair of shiny shoes, wringing wet through, with splashes of blood over the toes; and she noticed that the bottom of the man's trousers were wet as well. She glanced up and the first thing she noticed was the man's eyebrows. They were black and thick in contrast to his salt and pepper hair, and there, clutching at his chest, was Trevor Bains, blood oozing between his fingers. He staggered towards the telephone box but his legs gave out, and almost in slow motion he sank to the ground and was no more. Auntie Jennison, ignoring him completely, looked at her watch and pushed the scarper button.

Travis peered at the headline in the local paper. It said, 'MURDER IN POLPERRO?' The print underneath was small, and Travis's time was running out. He could just make out, 'Police are mystified.' Disappointed, he pushed the scarper button.

Auntie Jennison reset the coordinates and this time emerged from the platform just two minutes before she had seen Trevor Bains. She stood waiting by the rusty gate. This time she didn't have long to wait; suddenly the platform door shot open and Trevor Bains came lurching through. His long legs easily passed over the gate and he started down the steps. The blood he was trying to stop leaking out started to run through his fingers, then onto his clothes, and on down to his shoes. He staggered down the stairs and Auntie Jennison watched him die for the second time. Auntie Jennison started back up the steps; there was no sign of any blood, but a trail of wet footprints led all the way back to the rusty gate. Happy with what she'd seen, she pushed the scarper button.

'Come on! Sit down, Travis, and tell me what you've found out,' said Mr Pomphrey.

'Not a lot, Mr Pomphrey; it was too dark to see much. I hope Auntie Jennison had better luck than I did. Did Mum or Dad phone?'

'No, I haven't spoken to a living soul, Travis.'

They sat waiting for what seemed like for ever, as far as Travis was concerned, and then they heard the familiar, 'Yoo-hoo, I'm back!'

In came Auntie Jennison. She flopped into a chair, pulled out her cigarettes and lit one up. Travis didn't need any bidding; he went straight over and fetched her an ashtray, while off went Mr Pomphrey into the kitchen to make a cup of tea.

'Right then, Travis, tell me what you know while Bill makes the tea. I expect you've already told him, and then I can tell you both what I saw afterwards.'

Travis told Auntie Jennison what little he had found out, and how disappointed he was. With that, Mr Pomphrey came in, poured out the tea and handed Travis a glass of Coke. Auntie Jennison lit up another cigarette, a completely different brand this time. She fished in her pocket for a fluffy peppermint and then she began.

'Well, I don't know about you, Travis, but don't you think that Trevor Bains's choice of platform was a bit strange?'

Mr Pomphrey interrupted. 'What was it like, Auntie?' he asked.

'The only way I can describe it is to say it was like a medieval dungeon, complete with chains, shackles – and it even had a rack. Would you agree with that, Travis?'

'Yes, I would, Auntie Jennison,' Travis answered.

Auntie Jennison went on to tell them all about what she'd seen, and her assumption about the blood; and then she added, 'I think he was trying to get to the phone box to get help. But listen here, I realised tonight what a lucky escape you had in Scotland. You see, Travis, it was Trevor Bains who tried to get you in his car. And it was the same Trevor Bains who killed poor little Alex. He looked about fourteen or fifteen years older just now, but it was the same man all right. Same shiny shoes, same eyebrows, same cruel mouth…'

Mr Pomphrey's mouth dropped open. 'But – but – if he died in 1978, how could he try to kidnap Travis and kill Alex?'

'Because, Bill, Mr Trevor Bains, as well as being a visitor, was a player too.'

'I just don't understand what you mean, Auntie,' Mr Pomphrey said.

'Do you want to explain it to him, Travis?'

'Yes, if you like, Auntie Jennison,' Travis said. 'Besides going to the past and being able to platform-hop, most visitors can go into the future; but not all can, and some just don't want to.'

'Why don't they, Travis?' Mr Pomphrey asked.

'The thing is, Mr Pomphrey, the future is like the present. It can be a dangerous place. Some people just aren't brave enough to go, although the future is where you can make a real difference with good and evil.'

'Can you go to the future, Travis?'

'I may be able to when Mentor tells me I can.'

'Yes,' said Auntie Jennison, 'I've been meaning to have a word with that Mentor.'

'Tell her I've gone out,' a voice inside Travis's head said.

'So what you're saying then, Travis, is that Trevor Bains is a visitor, but when he's a player he becomes Ivan Roberts,' Mr Pomphrey put in.

'Was a player, Mr Pomphrey,' said Travis. 'Although he died in 1978, you see, he came to the present *before* he was killed.'

'I think I understand, Travis,' said Mr Pomphrey. 'So, does that mean other people could still suffer under the hand of Trevor... I mean, Ivan Roberts?'

'Yes, because it's already done in his future.'

'It certainly takes some understanding,' Mr Pomphrey commenced.

'Yes, that's one of the reasons it takes a long time between being called and being active,' Auntie Jennison said.

'But none of this brings us any nearer to a connection with your granddad, does it, Travis?' Mr Pomphrey observed.

'Not exactly, Mr Pomphrey, but at least we know that the Ivan Roberts who Granddad had unfinished business with was the same man as Trevor Bains, and just like Granddad, he was a visitor.'

'Was your granddad a player as well, Travis?' Mr Pomphrey asked.

Travis looked at Auntie Jennison quizzically.

'Yes, and as I remember it, he did more playing than visiting,' Auntie Jennison replied, on Travis's behalf.

'Let me get this right then,' Mr Pomphrey said. 'So when Trevor Bains, or call him Ivan Roberts if you like, died, he had just left the platform because he got as far as the bottom of the steps; so he was either shot in his present or his future.'

'That's exactly right, Bill,' Auntie Jennison said. 'What we need to do now is find out which it was and where.'

Auntie Jennison's telephone interrupted the conversation and she went to answer it. 'That's your dad on the phone, Travis, to speak to you,' she said. 'I've told him nothing, mind.'

Travis went out to the hall and spoke to his father for a few minutes. When he returned, he said, 'We're like three conspirators – or like the Three Musketeers!'

'One for all and all for one,' Mr Pomphrey said.

Travis thought of Alex.

Chapter Fifteen

Half-term holidays were soon over, and Travis settled back into school routine. His mother seemed to be spending more and more time in the garden and Travis was still helping his dad with researching family trees, but Ivan Roberts and Alex stayed uppermost in his mind. Mr Pomphrey seemed to be spending more and more time with Auntie Jennison, and nothing seemed to be progressing towards finding out any more about his granddad. Travis phoned Auntie Jennison at regular intervals but no one could come up with anything new. Becky came to stay one weekend, which broke things up, but by the following Monday afternoon, Travis was back to feeling down in the doldrums. Then, he had an idea.

'Dad, could I go and see Auntie Jennison again by platform-hopping? Please, Dad.'

'I'd love to know what this fascination is with Auntie Jennison all of a sudden, Travis,' his dad said. 'Well, providing your school work's up together, and providing it's all right with your mum and Auntie Jennison, you can go at the weekend.'

'Oh, Dad, I've got the most cool and the bestest dad in the whole wide universe!'

'Yes, I know, Travis; and you're only saying that because it's true.'

As usual, Travis couldn't get through the door of Auntie Jennison's quick enough. 'Auntie Jennison, Auntie Jennison, I'm here!' he called, steeling himself for the onslaught.

'Travis, my little cherub, my angel!' Auntie Jennison grabbed Travis, squeezed the life out of him and commenced her ritual greeting. After smothering Travis with kisses, she said, 'Bill's not here yet, Travis, so we'll sit down and have a nice chat.'

Auntie Jennison settled herself down in the chair, and before she could say anything, Travis whipped out a packet of peppermints from his pocket and proffered one to his host. 'Here, Auntie Jennison, have one of mine for a change.' Travis had been careful to get Auntie Jennison's favourites, so he knew she wouldn't refuse.

'How kind, Travis, thank you – and they're my favourites too!'

Travis was delighted; he took one for himself and sat there sucking the unfluffy peppermint with relish. 'Auntie Jennison,' he began, 'I've been thinking, we don't seem to be getting anywhere, so I was wondering if another trip to Polperro might help?'

'I think you're grasping at straws, Travis, but I don't suppose it would hurt,' said Auntie Jennison. 'There goes another one!'

'Something put Granddad on the track of Ivan Roberts, Auntie Jennison, and I think the answer is somewhere in Polperro. Did Granddad ever go there on holiday, perhaps? You know, years ago…?'

Auntie Jennison looked thoughtful and then said, 'I seem to recall him going to Cornwall when he got married to your grandmother first of all, or perhaps it was later on; I don't know, you'll have to ask your dad that one.'

'Wouldn't that be in the records books, Auntie Jennison?'

'Well, the date of your grandfather's marriage to your grandmother would be, but that wouldn't tell us anything.'

'Perhaps they went on honeymoon there?'

'Perhaps. I don't know, it's all a long time ago now.'

'Can we try, Auntie Jennison? Can we try, please?'

'Look, Travis, we've really nothing to go on,' Auntie Jennison replied. 'I'll tell you what I'll do…' A pause, then, 'There goes another one! I'll phone your dad and ask him if he can remember going to Cornwall as a boy, or anything.'

'Won't he want to know why you want to know, Auntie Jennison?'

'Most probably, but I shan't tell him. I don't want him building his hopes up.'

She went off into the hall. Travis played around with Scampi on the floor; the dog seemed quite well disposed to Travis these days. Auntie Jennison returned after quite some time with a thoughtful look on her face.

'Your dad's no fool, Travis. In the end I had to tell him that it was about your granddad's disappearance.'

'What did he say, Auntie Jennison?' Travis asked.

'I'm afraid he got quite excited at the thought of finding out something new, but when I told him it was just another avenue we were exploring, he didn't seem too happy; so I had to tell him that that was all I was prepared to say for now.'

'Did he know if Granddad ever went to Polperro?'

'Yes, that was where your dad got the idea of going,' Auntie Jennison replied. 'He remembered going there when he was a boy on several occasions. Apparently they used to stay with a lady called Mrs Evans, a widow, who would look after your dad while your grandfather and grandmother went out in the evenings.' She paused. 'There goes another one! I asked him how old he would have been then, but he said he couldn't remember when they first started going there. He did tell me of one thing that he could remember happening, though, and he thought he was probably about eight or nine at the time.'

'And what was that, Auntie Jennison?'

'He said that one morning when he got up he could see his dad had a plaster over his eye; his dad said that he'd fallen over the night before after leaving the Blue Peter. I found that strange, because your granddad hardly drank and was as sure-footed as a mountain goat!'

'D'you think that there's something in that, Auntie Jennison?'

'I don't really know, but it might be worth trying to track down this Mrs Evans, if she's still alive. Your dad said she lived up a steep hill.'

'It's all steep hills down there, Auntie Jennison. I wouldn't want to be a postman,' said Travis. 'When can I get going?'

'Not I, Travis, we; I'm going as well. It's another four weeks to Easter, so we can't wait until your school holidays, so don't tell your dad. But we'll platform-hop down there, then you can go to the museum and I can see if I can find Mrs Evans.'

'What about Mr Pomphrey, Auntie Jennison?' Travis asked.

'Someone's got to look after Scampi,' she replied.

All on purpose, Mr Pomphrey's train ran late and Auntie Jennison and Travis were left kicking their heels until mid-afternoon. Auntie Jennison seemed as impatient as Travis to get going, and when Mr Pomphrey eventually arrived, Travis was on pins waiting for the off. Auntie Jennison herself was finding it very difficult not to be rude and just go rushing off immediately.

Mr Pomphrey, unaware of what had taken place, was full of all sorts of questions. 'Auntie,' he said, 'all this time travelling is very fascinating, you know. I've been wondering, are there any famous time travellers?'

Auntie Jennison looked at Travis. 'Look, Bill, Travis and I think we might well be on to something, and we need to go to Polperro right away. When we get back we'll have a nice cup of tea and I'll tell you all about visiting and playing. As for you asking about famous ones, Harry Houdini springs to mind. Now Bill, we really have to go.'

'Harry Houdini, eh? OK, Auntie, have a good trip.'

Auntie Jennison went first and waited for Travis just outside the rusty gate on Chapel Steps. The gate was even rustier now and one hinge appeared to be broken. They walked down Chapel Steps together, and then Travis went off towards the museum while Auntie Jennison made for the post office.

Travis paid his pound to the lady on the door of the museum and went straight to the section on the Polperro murder. There were a few pictures of where the police assumed the murder took place, a couple of photographs of where the body was found, some newspaper cuttings and a printed card giving dates and general background.

Travis read the newspaper cuttings:

The body of a man found late on Saturday night at the bottom of Chapel Steps in Polperro by customers from the Blue Peter pub has been identified as that of Trevor Bains. Police sources say he appears to have been shot at that locality, and police are appealing for any witnesses to come forward.

Mr Bains, formerly from Polperro, is thought to live abroad and police are anxious to contact any relatives or anyone who can give any information.

Most of the cuttings said the same thing, except the last one, dated three weeks after the murder, which said:

The police are convinced from the post-mortem examination that the weapon used was of a high calibre, from the size of the entry and the exit wounds. However, despite an exhaustive search of the area, so far no bullet or bullet case has been found. It appears that Mr Bains had been shot once in the upper back, and the round had passed right through him. Police are looking into the possibility that it could be a gangland killing or revenge-motivated attack.

Travis was reasonably pleased with what he had found and wandered back out into the bright spring sunshine. The air was fresh and crisp coming off the sea and the seagulls were making their usual racket. As Travis walked round the back of the harbour, he noticed the old man who had told him about the museum.

'Hello, sir,' Travis said, 'remember me?'

The old man peered at Travis. 'Ah yes, you're the lad who did the project. How did it go?'

'Very well, thank you, sir,' Travis replied, and then he added convincingly, 'I got top marks – thanks to you, sir.'

'Well done! Glad to hear it, young man,' the old man said.

'I was wondering, sir, you were so helpful before, I was wondering...'

'Not another project!'

'Yes,' Travis lied. 'You see, we're doing a project on, um, we're doing a project on the old families of Polperro...'

'Well, well, well! What will these schoolteachers think up next?' The old man shook his head. 'All right, what can I do for you?'

Travis never knew why he asked the next question, but suddenly he heard himself saying, 'Before I ask you about this project, sir, there's one other thing I wanted to know about the murder... if you can help me?'

'And what is it you want to know?'

'Well, I don't suppose you can remember when the fight in the pub was?'

'Yes, I remember the day and the date. That's not bad for a man of my age, is it? I bet you can't guess how old I am,' he said. Then he added rather proudly, without waiting for an answer,

'I'm eighty-four years young – well, all bar the shouting.'

Travis wasn't silly. 'Really, sir, eighty-four? I don't believe it; you're kidding me. I thought you were about seventy.' Travis knew it wasn't just old ladies who boasted about their age, but he could never understand why most of their lives they'd hide their ages, and then when they got old they wanted to tell the world.

The old man stuck his chest out, 'Yes, and I did my bit.'

'What – in the army, sir?' Travis asked.

'Army, army? The Senior Service, son!' And he gave Travis a naval salute. 'Now, what was it you were asking?'

Travis reminded him.

'Oh yes, the fight. It was on 18th July 1970.'

'Are you sure about that, sir? Travis asked.

'I'll say,' said the old man. 'It was my fiftieth birthday – but what's that got to do with the murder?'

'Oh, just tying up loose ends, that's all,' Travis lied. 'Now, about these families?'

'Well, this is a very small port, and there are only a few old family names in the place. Let me see, there's the Blatchford family, and then there's the Trelawny family and then the Teglios – they came from Italy, you know. Here, wait a minute! Shouldn't you be writing all this down?'

'Well, the teacher said we should concentrate on only one family, and I was waiting until you got to a name that I liked… for instance, Evans.'

'Can't say I ever heard of them. Now, where was I? Ah yes, now there's the Jolliffs, the Quillers and the Reed family.'

Travis realised he was getting nowhere, but he didn't want to be rude to the old man so he said, 'The Reed family. Yes, tell me about them, please. That sounds like an interesting name.'

The old man caught hold of Travis's arm. 'Just walk along here with me, will you, and I'll show you something.'

They walked past the wooden bench that was inscribed with Trevor Bains's name, and a few yards farther along came to a similar bench. It too had a brass plaque.

'Read what it says on there,' said the old man.

Travis read aloud, *Justin Reed, tragically lost at sea, 10th of August 1965, aged eight. Our little boy now swims with the mermaids for ever.'*

'Strange thing,' the old man said, 'they never found the body. Anything round here that falls in the sea always turns up eventually – anything at all – but that poor little mite didn't.'

'Thank you, sir,' Travis said, 'you've been most helpful.'

'Hang on, son, I've only just started. There's a lot to tell about the Reeds, you know.'

Travis thought quickly. 'I'm really sorry, sir, but I've suddenly realised I'm supposed to meet my aunt, and she'll worry if I'm late.'

'All right, son, and good luck with this project.'

'Project?' Travis said. 'Oh yes, thank you, sir.'

Travis walked away. He didn't know where to find Auntie Jennison as they hadn't made any proper arrangements about meeting up, such was their rush to get to Polperro, so Travis decided to head towards the Noughts and Crosses and hang around there on the off chance she'd turn up. He looked cautiously through the grimy windows of the pub but there was no sign of Auntie Jennison. Then suddenly, from about fifty yards up the road, he heard, 'Yoo-hoo, Travis! Yoo-hoo, here I am! Yoo-hoo!'

Embarrass me – why not? thought Travis.

Auntie Jennison came bounding down the street. 'Everything all right, my little sweetie?'

My God, she really does look like a bag lady, thought Travis. 'Yes, fine. I'd love a glass of lemonade or something, Auntie Jennison.' Anything to get her off the street, he thought.

Auntie Jennison whisked Travis into the Noughts and Crosses, sat him in a corner and went over to the bar and got some drinks. Then she sat herself down, dragged over a rather nice-looking dark blue cut glass ashtray, pulled out her fags and lit up.

The man from behind the bar came over to the table, and without a word rather pointedly took the glass ashtray and replaced it with a dirty yellow plastic one with part of one side missing.

Oh dear, thought Travis.

'Come on then, Travis,' Auntie Jennison said, glancing disapprovingly at the man, 'spill the beans, as they say.'

Travis told her all about the museum and about his conversation with the old man.

'That's interesting about the little boy, though, isn't it, Travis?'

'Yes, but it's not much help to us, Auntie Jennison, is it?'

'But the man said that everything always gets washed back up from the sea, didn't he?'

'Yes, that's what he said, but for once it didn't… I don't know what you're driving at, Auntie Jennison.'

'Well, they only *assumed* that he had fallen in the sea and drowned. What if Trevor Bains had taken him? After all, he had to start at some time in his murderous ways.'

'Auntie Jennison, you're a genius!' Travis said.

Chapter Sixteen

'So that's about it, Bill.'

Auntie Jennison and Travis had arrived back and were sitting around the fire with Mr Pomphrey. She went on, 'And what with the post office being closed, and then all the time it took me to find out that Mrs Evans had died, my trip was a complete waste of time, really.'

'So what's the plan now, you two?' Mr Pomphrey asked.

'Tomorrow, Travis will go to find out more about Justin Reed, and I will go to the fight in the pub,' Auntie Jennison announced.

'Auntie, just before you went off with Travis, you said you'd tell me all about some famous visitors.'

'Quite right, Bill. Well, I've already mentioned Harry Houdini; then there's that other fellow – you know, the one who walked through the Great Wall of China. Not much in that, and not all that clever; there's a platform on each side, you know. Then of course there was Merlin in the court of King Arthur, and Leonardo da Vinci—'

'Then there was Jack the Ripper,' Travis interrupted, 'and Nostradamus, and old Mother Shipton.'

'Quite right, Travis, but I suppose the most famous of all, Bill, is someone you'll have never heard of, or are ever likely to—'

Mr Pomphrey interrupted. 'Who can that be then, Auntie?'

'Tell him, Travis,' Auntie Jennison ordered.

'It was Bobby Luke Clayton, Mr Pomphrey,' Travis said.

Mr Pomphrey looked totally blank.

'Told you he wouldn't know, Travis,' said Auntie Jennison in rather a superior manner.

'Bobby Luke Clayton was the man who shot J F Kennedy, Mr Pomphrey,' Travis said.

'But… but,' Mr Pomphrey spluttered.

'Bit of a shock, isn't it? And do you know, Mr Pomphrey, that I had to sit and listen to Mr Dalziel in school telling me it was Lee

Harvey Oswald! I was just itching to put him right.'

'He wouldn't have listened to you anyway, Travis,' Auntie Jennison remarked.

'You see, Mr Pomphrey, Bobby Luke came from Mississippi, and he didn't like the way that President Kennedy had handled the Cuban missile crisis; he thought that President Kennedy had brought the world to the edge of a nuclear war, which I suppose he had. He didn't like it because President Kennedy was the first Catholic president of the USA, or the fact that he treated black people equally and fairly; so on 22nd November 1963, he shot him. It was him on the grassy knoll; that's where he did it from. He did the deed, pushed his scarper button, and then he was gone.'

'So he was a visitor gone wrong, and then he left Lee Harvey Oswald to face the music,' Mr Pomphrey said. 'That's awful! Was he ever caught?'

'I'm very proud to say it was my grandfather who tracked him down. You see, that's what he did, my granddad: he was a tracker.'

'And a very good one at that,' Auntie Jennison said.

'So what happened once he had tracked him down, Travis?' Mr Pomphrey asked.

'I don't know, Mr Pomphrey,' Travis replied.

Mr Pomphrey glanced at Auntie Jennison, but the look on her face told him not to pursue the subject any farther.

The next morning, Travis, at Auntie Jennison's request, was taking Scampi for a walk.

'Morning, Travis,' said Mentor, 'how are you today?'

'I'm fine, Mentor. I haven't heard much from you lately.'

'No, you don't seem to need me these days. It seems that Auntie Jennison has taken over.'

'I do believe you're jealous, Mentor.'

'Not in the least – even if I could have or understand such an emotion! You know you're not allowed to platform-hop, and Auntie Jennison's been encouraging you. I just don't approve, that's all.'

'Well, I won't be platform-hopping today. I'm off visiting Polperro to track down Justin Reed.'

'I think you'll waste a lot of time because you don't even know where he lives, do you?'

'Any suggestions then, Mentor?'

'Yes, you should go down there and talk to the old man again. He'd know the address.'

'What, like platform-hop, you mean?'

'Um, um, yes… well, that's the best bet, if you were allowed.'

'Oh, shut up, Mentor, will you?'

When Travis got back inside the house he found Mr Pomphrey sitting at the dining room table. On his head he was wearing what appeared to be a knitted woollen hat.

'Whatever's that you've got on your head, Mr Pomphrey?' Travis asked.

'D'you like it, Travis?' Mr Pomphrey replied, turning his head from side to side. 'Auntie Jennison knitted it.'

'But it's got a hole in it. Can I see?'

Mr Pomphrey took off the hat and handed it to Travis. 'Look, Mr Pomphrey, it's got a hole here and another… This isn't a hat, it's a tea cosy!'

'So it might be, but it's very smart. Just look at the bright-coloured stripes. And it keeps my head warm; in future I shall wear it at all times when I'm in the house.'

He's going as mad as Auntie Jennison, Travis thought.

'Ah, you're back then, Travis. Good morning, Bill. I see you're wearing your hat – and very smart, if I may say so.' Auntie Jennison followed her voice into the dining room.

'Auntie Jennison, it's got holes in it!' Travis said.

'They're not holes, silly boy, they're ventilation slits! You don't want Bill's head to overheat, do you?'

Auntie Jennison and Mr Pomphrey sat beaming at each other. They've both lost the plot, thought Travis. 'Auntie Jennison,' he said, 'I think it might be an idea if I platform-hop today and see if I can find the old man. It could save some time because he's sure to know where the Reed family lived.'

'What a good idea! Travis, you are a clever boy,' Auntie Jennison beamed.

'Actually, it was Mentor who thought of it,' said Travis.

'Are we talking about the same Mentor who doesn't approve of you platform-hopping?'

'Yes, the very same, Auntie Jennison.'

'Mmm,' Auntie Jennison said.

'Old bat!' Mentor exclaimed.

Travis walked carefully down Chapel Steps. There was drizzle in the air and a sea mist was shrouding the town; the steps were slimy and slippery underfoot. I wonder if the old boy will be around in this weather, Travis thought. A quick look around the harbour proved fruitless; a few intrepid day trippers were taking some photos, and two seagulls were squabbling over a starfish. Travis walked along past the Noughts and Crosses and peered through the window.

'Who are you looking for then, my lad?' said a voice behind him. It was the old man. 'Who's in there that you're interested in?'

'Actually, sir, I was looking for you,' said Travis.

'Well, you won't find me in the pub at this time of day. What, d'you think I'm an old alcoholic?'

Travis felt his colours coming up.

'Only joking, young man. How's your project coming along?'

'Oh yes, the project,' Travis said. 'That's what I wanted to see you about; I was wondering if you could tell me where the Reeds live?'

'*Lived*, not live; there's no one left there now. It's the first pale blue painted cottage on the left-hand side as you go up Landaviddy Lane. You can't miss it, but there's nothing to see. I can tell you what you want to know; in fact, I can save you a lot of trouble.'

'That's ever so kind of you, sir, but I really wanted to see the cottage so I could pick up on the atmosphere of all those years ago.'

'How old are you, young fella?'

'I'm ten, sir,' Travis replied.

'Ten, eh? Only ten! You're very grown-up for ten! Atmosphere, indeed… Take a tip from me. You're obviously a very clever young man. If you listen at school, when you grow up you could be just like me. Join the navy, and that way you could travel all around the world. Just imagine all those places you could visit!'

'Yes, that's a nice idea, sir; I think I'd like to do some visiting,' Travis said, smiling. He thanked the old man and made to walk up Landaviddy Lane, but as soon as he was out of sight and he could see there was no one around he pushed the scarper button.

Travis set the coordinates for 10th August 1965, platform 106, and pushed 'go'. Half floating, half running, he started up Landaviddy Lane. Further and further he went up the hill, but there was no sign of a blue cottage; all the houses were either natural stone or a uniform white colour. What a dummy I am, Travis thought, this is nearly forty years ago, and all the houses are bound to be different now. He made his way back down the lane. I suppose I'll just have to platform-hop and see the old man again, he thought. As he was almost at the bottom of the lane, he saw a small boy coming out the front door of a cottage. A woman appeared in the doorway behind him.

'Try to be as quick as you can, Justin,' she said.

'OK, Mum, I'll run all the way.'

Off went Justin with Travis in hot pursuit. They raced off down Landaviddy Lane and around the corner towards the old Saxon bridge, avoiding the crowds of tourists ambling along. It was the shiny shoes Travis spotted first, followed by the eyebrows; Travis felt the hair on the back of his neck bristle. *Trevor Bains*, he thought, he's younger, but it's definitely him!

Trevor Bains reached out and grabbed the boy's arm as he went past. 'Not so fast, my friend. Why are you in such a hurry?'

'I'm on an errand for Mummy to get some shopping, and she said to be quick.'

'Well, I'm a plain-clothes policeman, and I can't have you youngsters running around the town, can I?'

'A policeman? I didn't know; I'm sorry, mister.'

Travis couldn't believe it. With all these people around, it looked like Trevor Bains was about to kidnap the child.

'All right, off you go – but walk, all right?'

'Yes, mister.'

Justin walked away. Trevor Bains sat himself down on a bench, and Travis just knew that he was just waiting for his opportunity. Travis, looking anxiously at his watch, waited with Trevor Bains.

He didn't have long to wait. Skidding around the corner came Justin.

'I thought I told you to walk!'

'Oh, sorry mister, I was in a hurry.'

'Now that's twice in one day. I think you had better come along to the new police station with me...'

'Please, mister!' Justin started to cry. 'Please let me go.'

'Right, stop your crying, and I'll tell you what I'm prepared to do. You take your shopping home to your mum and then tell her you're going out to play. I'm sure she doesn't want a policeman coming round knocking on her door. Then you come up to the new police station at the top of Chapel Steps and my sergeant will give you a caution. Do you know what that means?'

'No, mister, I don't,' Justin sobbed.

'It means he will tell you off, and if you promise not to do it again, that will be that. Now, dry your eyes, and off you go – and not a word to anybody, mind.'

Travis's alarm rang on his watch. He knew he'd seen enough, and pushed the scarper button.

Travis walked back into Auntie Jennison's living room. Scampi came over and wagged his tail excitedly. Travis picked him up and started to make a fuss of him. 'Where is everybody?' he asked the dog.

Travis went through to the dining room; Mr Pomphrey was sitting at the dining room table, dressed in his three-piece suit with his tea cosy on his head. He was sucking one of Auntie Jennison's peppermints.

'Hello, Travis. Guess what! Auntie Jennison's going to knit a bobble for my hat.'

'I can't wait,' Travis remarked.

'So how did you fare then, Travis?' Mr Pomphrey asked.

'Well, I saw Trevor Bains trying to kidnap Justin Reed, and I'm sure that he went on to do so, but my time was running out and I'd seen enough. Anyway, Mr Pomphrey, I take it Auntie Jennison's not been back yet?'

'No, no sign of her so far. I was wondering about something, Travis. Are all platforms like garden sheds?'

'In England most of them are, Mr Pomphrey, because they blend into the background; but you couldn't have a garden shed in the middle of, say, Manhattan, could you?'

'Yes, I see what you mean. And you couldn't have one in the middle of Marrakech, either,' Mr Pomphrey said.

'Or Moscow, Mr Pomphrey.'

'Or Monte Carlo, Travis.'

'How about Montevideo, then, Mr Pomphrey? Your turn.'

'Melbourne.'

'Madagascar.'

'Morandava.'

'Morandava? You're kidding, Mr Pomphrey, aren't you?'

'Am I, Travis?' Mr Pomphrey replied.

'Yoo-hoo, I'm back!' As usual, Auntie Jennison collapsed in the nearest chair and pulled out her cigarettes. 'Lots to tell everybody,' she announced.

'I'll go and make some tea, Auntie, and then we can hear all about how you got on,' Mr Pomphrey said.

Mr Pomphrey disappeared into the kitchen, and Travis told Auntie Jennison his news. Then when they were all ready, Auntie Jennison started her story.

'So I came down over Chapel Steps and went straight along to the pub – there was quite a crowd in there, but there was no sign of Trevor Bains. I had a good look round; they certainly had a nicer class of ashtray in there in those days.'

Travis shook his head and groaned inwardly.

'What time was all this then, Auntie?' Mr Pomphrey asked.

Auntie Jennison continued, 'It was nine o'clock. At first I thought I was too early, and then I heard someone ask the landlord if the man who Trevor Bains assaulted had had to go to hospital.'

'And had he?' Mr Pomphrey asked.

'Yes; he had to have five stitches above his eyebrow. Anyway, the conversation in the pub turned to Trevor Bains. It seems he was something of a mystery man. Everybody knew him but nobody knew anything about him.'

'So when did it happen then, Auntie Jennison?' Travis asked.

'That's neither here nor there, Travis,' Auntie Jennison replied, 'because all of a sudden Granddad and Grandma Travis walked in the pub. They certainly were a handsome couple, Travis.'

'I thought you said Granddad didn't drink, Auntie Jennison?'

'No, I said he hardly ever drank, but he would have the odd shandy now and again. Anyway, I decided to stay with them and see if anything happened. They only had the one drink and then they went for a stroll along towards the harbour.'

'What happened next, Auntie Jennison?'

'I'm coming to that. I heard your granddad say to your grandma about going for a walk up along the cliffs. They made for Chapel Steps and I followed on just behind. As we got to the corner of Chapel Steps a man came hurtling round the corner and hit your grandmother right off her feet; he was going so fast he went straight through me as well. "Get out the way, you stupid cow!" he shouted at her. Granddad was livid. "You need teaching some manners!" he said.' A long pause followed, then Auntie Jennison said, 'There goes another one! Well, the man was a lot taller than Granddad; he came back and as quick as a flash headbutted him. Granddad reeled back, shook his head, and quietly said to the man, "Is that the best you can do?" His fists came up, but the man took off back up Chapel Steps like a rocket, so Granddad chased after him. The man's long legs outran those of your granddad's, and he went out of sight by the electricity substation; then he was gone.'

'No prize for guessing where he went, or who the man was, Auntie Jennison,' Travis said.

'Yes, you're right, Travis. It was Trevor Bains.'

'He must have pushed his scarper button, Auntie,' said Mr Pomphrey.

'Yes, Bill, and I think that was how Travis's granddad first found out that Trevor Bains was a visitor gone wrong,' Auntie Jennison replied.

'I don't want to put a damper on things,' said Mr Pomphrey, 'but although we've got all this information now, it still doesn't bring us any closer to finding Travis's granddad.'

As if in reply, Auntie Jennison broke wind.

Chapter Seventeen

'Only two weeks to Easter, Travis! Twenty questions on who's coming to stay, if you like.'

'Oh, Mum, I'm not really in the mood for twenty questions. Why don't you just tell me?'

'Travis, this isn't like you! Whatever's the matter?'

'Nothing, Mum. So who's coming for Easter?' Travis said, sounding totally disinterested.

'Becky and Mark; she says she's got some news to tell us.'

'Oh, that's nice. I'm going round Mr Pomphrey's now for *Countdown* – all right, Mum?'

'Yes, all right dear. Off you go.'

Travis let himself in Mr Pomphrey's back door, called out and went into the living room. Mr Pomphrey had the paper and pencils ready, and there were sweets, lemonade and tea. The television was all warmed up and already tuned to Channel Four.

Mr Pomphrey was sitting in his chair. He beamed at Travis and said, 'What d'you think then, Travis?'

'What do I think about what, Mr Pomphrey?'

Mr Pomphrey turned his head from side to side.

'Whatever's that on your tea cosy, Mr Pomphrey?' Travis asked.

'How many times, Travis… it's not a tea cosy, it's a *hat*! In fact, now it's a bobble hat.'

'But Mr Pomphrey, bobbles are round. That one's oval, and there's bits hanging out of it.'

'Nothing a pair of scissors won't put right, Travis,' Mr Pomphrey declared. 'Anyway, shush now, it's just starting.'

When *Countdown* had finished Mr Pomphrey looked across at Travis, took his tea cosy off, scratched his head and said, 'Look, Travis, you don't need to say anything. I know what the problem is, but you must realise it's the same for me, for Auntie Jennison, and especially for your dad.'

'I just feel so helpless, Mr Pomphrey; I just don't know what to do.'

'Tell me something, Travis. How many platforms are there?'

'I really don't know. I've got no idea, Mr Pomphrey.'

'Can you find out?'

'Yes, that's easy. You see, there are two books in the carriage. One's the places book and the other is the platform book; the information on numbers is in the platform book.'

'Can't you ask Mentor?'

'I don't expect he knows.'

'Of course I know,' said Mentor, inside Travis's head. 'There are seven hundred and sixty-two in the UK.'

'Seven hundred and sixty-two,' repeated Travis.

'All right, thank you, Mentor,' Mr Pomphrey said.

'What is it, Mr Pomphrey?' Travis asked.

'Oh, it was just a thought; never mind.' He paused. 'Can you tell me something else, Travis?'

'Mr Pomphrey, you're getting as bad as Alex is... was.' His voice faltered and his face dropped.

Mr Pomphrey ignored him and went on. 'Can you tell me, if there aren't any such things as ghosts, who is it that people see dressed up in medieval costumes?'

'They are players, Mr Pomphrey; they've travelled from their present into their future – which of course is our present. Look, I'm sorry, Mr Pomphrey, but I shall have to go. I've got an awful lot of homework to get through. I'll see you tomorrow, and thank you for the lemonade and sweets.'

'All right, Travis, we'll carry on the conversation next time.'

Travis's mum was in the kitchen as usual and Travis was sitting at the dining room table, finishing off his homework; Travis could hear his mum and dad talking, but he wasn't really listening.

'Tom,' said Mrs Travis, 'you'll have to have a look at the overflow on the flush; the water's running all down the wall out the back.'

'Don't worry, I've already had a word with Becky on the phone and Mark is going to fix it when they arrive. No point in having a plumber for a son-in-law if you don't make use of him.'

Mrs Travis started to laugh.

'What's so funny about that then, Mother?' Tom asked.

'No, I wasn't laughing at that; I was laughing at your dad's idea of plumbing.'

Mr Travis started to giggle. 'Yes, in some of his ways he could be just like Auntie Jennison, couldn't he?'

Travis could hear his parents laughing, so he came wandering in from the dining room and said, 'What's that about plumbing?'

'Your mum and I were just laughing at Granddad's little peculiarity when it came to the toilet, Travis, that's all.'

'Peculiarity – what peculiarity's that then, Dad?' Travis asked.

'Well, when these houses were first built, the toilets all had flushes which were called "high-level"; the cistern was almost up to the ceiling. Gradually, as the years went on, most people replaced their cisterns with the ones like you see these days. My dad decided that you couldn't flush a toilet properly unless there were copious amounts of water, so he replaced the original cistern with an even bigger one. You had to pull the chain four or five times to make it work, and then it sounded just like the Niagara Falls.'

Mr and Mrs Travis started laughing again.

'Yes,' said Travis's dad, 'you could hear it all over the house! There was no sneaking off for a quiet pee in those days.'

'So what happened to it, Dad?' Travis asked.

'As soon as we could afford it, we changed it for the one we've got now, and it looks like this one's on its last legs.'

Travis went back to his homework with his dad's words going around and around in his mind: *Sounded just like the Niagara Falls*, that's what Dad said, Travis thought. 'Mentor,' he said under his breath, 'can you remember the exact coordinates for when Granddad disappeared?'

'Of course I can, Travis,' Mentor replied.

Travis ripped off a small piece of paper from his scrap pad. Fire away, Mentor, he thought. Travis silently left the dining table, gathered up his school books and noiselessly went through to the hallway; he put his books in his school bag, slipped out of the front door and went along the side of the house. Armed with the coordinates that Mentor had given him, he went to the shed.

145

Travis came out of the shed, and there was his granddad sitting with his dad on the rustic bench, just like before. Travis watched as Thomas Travis got up and went into the house. Travis overtook him on the stairs and whipped into the bathroom before him. He sat on the edge of the bath and waited. He could see what his parents meant about the cistern; it ran almost the full width of the ceiling.

Travis's granddad came in and climbed up onto the toilet seat; he reached up to the top of the cistern and felt about with his hand. When he brought his arm down, he was holding the most enormous revolver that Travis had ever seen.

He reached up again and this time retrieved a shoulder holster and ammunition. Dexterously, he fitted the holster under his jacket, loaded the revolver and slid the weapon in place. My God! He's done that a few times before, Travis thought. He watched as his granddad left the bathroom, then Travis pushed his scarper button.

Back in the Pullman, Travis decided to make a quick trip to Auntie Jennison's.

'Auntie Jennison!' he called out, as he came through the passage.

'I'd know that voice anywhere,' said Auntie Jennison. 'To what do I owe the pleasure?' She encircled Travis with her arms and gave him her usual peppermint- and tobacco-flavoured greeting. 'Come and sit down, Travis, and bring me an ashtray, please.'

Travis went over to the sideboard. Oh no, he thought, not another one! He picked up the cut glass, dark blue ashtray and waved it under Auntie Jennison's nose. 'Where did this come from, Auntie Jennison?' he asked.

'No idea, Travis; I'm getting a bit forgetful. I've probably had it for years.'

Travis decided he was wasting his time. 'Look, I mustn't stop long, Auntie Jennison, but I've found out that the night Granddad disappeared, he was tooled up.'

'Tooled up, tooled up? Whatever are you talking about, Travis?'

'Oh, Auntie Jennison, don't you know anything? That's what they say in films. Granddad was carrying a gun!'

'What sort of gun was it, Travis – a rifle?'

'No, Auntie Jennison. I think Granddad had been watching too many of those old "Dirty Harry" films; I'm sure it was a magnum that he had.'

'Yes, I've seen those films. It's called a .44 magnum; it's the most powerful handgun in the world – well, at least that's what Dirty Harry said. What else was it he said, Travis? Wasn't it something about making his week?'

'*Day*, actually, Auntie Jennison.'

'Look, Travis, I've been thinking. Your dad's been very patient, he doesn't ask questions, and I know I said not to build his hopes up, but I think now is the time that we tell him everything. You never know, some of it might make some sense to him, and there might just be something we've missed.'

'But what about the platform-hopping, Auntie Jennison?'

'Well, naturally we'll leave that bit out.'

Travis confronted his dad as soon as he got back home.

'So that's it, Dad, now you've got the whole story.'

'I don't know what to say, Travis; you've got further in the time since you've been visiting than I have in twenty-five years.'

'It wasn't just me, Dad! Mr Pomphrey and Auntie Jennison played just as much a part in it, if not more than I did; and anyway, Dad, we still don't know what happened, do we?'

'I still think you're very clever, Travis.'

'Dad, perhaps this is why I've been called early.'

'Yes, Travis, perhaps it is, perhaps it is.'

Chapter Eighteen

Becky and her husband Mark arrived in the early evening, the day before Good Friday. Becky sat the whole family down and said, 'I've got an announcement to make. Travis, how do you feel about becoming an uncle?'

'But I'm not old enough! I'm only ten,' Travis said. 'And anyway, I haven't got enough money to stump up for birthday and Christmas presents, cards and things. No – sorry, Becky, can't be done; you'd better forget all about the idea and wait until I'm a bit older.'

They all roared with laughter; Travis looked completely baffled.

'I think, Dad,' said Becky, 'it's time you had a little chat with my brother...'

The next morning they all braved the Good Friday traffic and headed off down the motorway for a day out in Weston-super-Mare. Travis hated the journey, especially as now he could platform-hop. All his thoughts of Alex, Granddad and Trevor Bains faded as Travis enjoyed, first, a ride along the sands on the donkeys, then candyfloss, and, after that, all the attractions of the pier. A ride on the big wheel and then on to the Castle of Doom, which Travis found a bit tame after all his experiences. It was fish and chips for lunch, and then a trip to the helicopter museum, which fascinated all the male members of the family, while the females looked on politely, trying not to appear too bored. A little after five o'clock, on the way back home, ten-year-old Travis Travis, tired but happy, fell asleep in the back of his dad's car.

Easter sped by, and it didn't seem like two minutes before the family were waving goodbye to Becky and Mark. Travis's thoughts almost immediately returned to his granddad's disappearance. He mulled over in his head everything he knew so far, but whichever way his mind turned, it came up blank.

Travis went into Mr Pomphrey's after the first day back at

school; Mr Pomphrey was sitting in his chair, his face wreathed in smiles like a Cheshire cat. 'Come in, my boy, come in. Don't worry about *Countdown* for now, Travis, I'm recording it,' he said.

'You're looking rather pleased with yourself, Mr Pomphrey,' said Travis.

'I've got some news for you, young man; you'll be only the third person in the world to know.'

'What is it, Mr Pomphrey?' Travis asked.

'Auntie Jennison has kindly consented to become my wife.' Mr Pomphrey beamed all the more.

'Oh, Mr Pomphrey, I'm so happy for you.'

'Yes, Travis, and we want you to be best man.'

'Best man? But Mr Pomphrey, I'm only ten!' protested Travis.

'Well, by the time we get married, Travis, you'll be at least fourteen.'

Travis looked at him, bewildered.

'I know what you're thinking Travis, but you can't go rushing into a lifelong commitment. That's the trouble with people these days; marry in haste, repent at leisure.'

'But Mr Pomphrey, you're...'

'Yes, I know how old I am, but Auntie Jennison assures me that I'll be around for a long time yet, and she said I've got a good few years left in me. She went and had a look in the future. Travis, I've got a question for you.'

'Oh, Mr Pomphrey – I'm going to start calling you Alex! Questions, questions, questions!'

'I was wondering... when visitors go bad, how do they get rich?'

'It's usually the thought of the easy money that makes them go bad in the first place. Some only use their talents to get rich; they put nothing back into society, and then you never hear of them again. Others get rich and do things like Trevor Bains has done.

'There's various ways of going about it, but you need to play and not visit. A trip to the future can give you racing results, football results, the ups and downs of stocks and shares, and of course you could win the National Lottery, but that would draw too much attention to yourself.'

'So then, Travis, if you could go to the future at the right time the chances are you could find Trevor Bains – or should I say, Ivan the Terrible – because he would be rich and famous.'

'Not necessarily, Mr Pomphrey. The problem is, for a start we don't know when in the future he is, and we don't know where; and if he's clever he won't be famous because he won't draw attention to himself.'

Mr Pomphrey picked up a piece of paper and read from it. 'You could try 22nd May 2018 at about three in the afternoon and see if he's there.'

'I don't understand you, Mr Pomphrey,' Travis said.

'Hang on, Travis, I'll explain in a minute. Now, can you remember Mentor saying there were seven hundred and sixty-two platforms?'

'Yes, that's right – seven hundred and sixty-two.'

'But what else did he say?'

'I said in the UK,' Mentor answered.

'The UK, Mr Pomphrey; Mentor just told me.'

'But how about the rest of the world?' Mr Pomphrey asked.

'Thousands,' Mentor said.

'There's thousands, Mr Pomphrey.'

'Would there be as many as two thousand, seven hundred and seventy-two?' Mr Pomphrey asked.

'Oh yes, even I know that,' Travis said.

'Are there as many as fifty thousand?'

'No, not as many as that, Mr Pomphrey. What are you getting at?' Travis looked puzzled.

Mr Pomphrey's smile widened even more. 'Could you ask Mentor if he knows where platform two thousand seven hundred and seventy-two is situated?'

Mentor replied, 'I can't remember all of them, Travis, you'll need to look in the book.'

'I'll have to go and look in the book, Mr Pomphrey – if that's OK?'

'If you wouldn't mind, Travis. I might be wrong, but at least it's worth a try.'

'But where have these dates, times and the platform number come from, Mr Pomphrey?'

Mr Pomphrey tapped the side of his head. 'From inside here,

Travis,' he replied. 'You see, numbers are to me what words are to you. I've worked it out using the names Trevor Bains and Ivan Roberts.'

'How did you do it, Mr Pomphrey?' Travis asked.

Mr Pomphrey laughed. 'That's a little conundrum for you to puzzle when you feel like it. Maybe I'll tell you one day, or maybe I won't.'

'Oh, don't tease, Mr Pomphrey! Tell me, please.'

'I might have it all wrong, Travis, so we'll leave it at that for now.'

Travis couldn't get to the shed quick enough; it seemed that at last something was happening again. He picked up the platforms book and started to thumb through it. Here we are, he thought: platform 2772 Bidart, Aquitaine, France. Latitude, 43 degrees 27 minutes North. Longitude, 1 degree 35 minutes West.

He ran back into Mr Pomphrey's. 'Mr Pomphrey, Mr Pomphrey, it's in France! The platform's in France.'

'France, eh!' Mr Pomphrey said. 'I'll phone Auntie Jennison and tell her the news. I suppose you're too excited to bother with *Countdown* now, Travis?'

'Yes... Shall we give it a miss for today, Mr Pomphrey?'

Mr Pomphrey went off to the telephone while Travis sat in the armchair, his mind poring over all the possibilities. After what seemed like an age, Mr Pomphrey came back in the room.

'Auntie Jennison said she'd like to come straight over now, but Charlie's lying on the bottom of his cage and doesn't seem too well.'

'You know Auntie Jennison, Mr Pomphrey; I expect the canary's dead. I'll platform-hop and go and see.'

'Auntie Jennison, I'm here!' Travis called from the passage.

'In here, Travis, my love. Take a look at my Charlie, would you? I don't think he's very well.'

Travis reached inside the cage and picked up the canary. 'How long has he been like this, Auntie Jennison?' he asked.

'He's been off his food for about three weeks now, Travis.'

'Yes, but how long has he been lying on the bottom of his cage?'

'About a week or so.'

'Auntie Jennison, just look at him! He's as stiff as a board.'

'Perhaps he's just cold. Can't you put him by the fire or something... perhaps pop him in the oven?'

She's raving, Travis thought.

'Perhaps we could try paracetamol, Travis?'

'Auntie Jennison, I don't know quite how to tell you this, but Charlie is dead.'

'Are you sure, Travis?'

'Auntie Jennison – just take a look at him, will you.'

Auntie Jennison peered at Charlie and turned him over and over on Travis's outstretched hand. She poked him with her finger and then said, 'Oh well, put him in the pedal bin. I'll just have to get another one.'

Totally round the bend, Travis thought; she's as mad as a March hare.

'Let me have a fag and you can give me an update, Travis.' All thoughts of Charlie had gone from Auntie Jennison's mind.

Travis went back through everything that he and Mr Pomphrey had talked about. Then Auntie Jennison said, 'It looks like you'll be a player sooner than later, Travis, providing it's all right with Mentor.' She paused and then said, 'I'm afraid you'll be on your own in the future. You see, my playing days are over. I went forward the other day on a personal matter—'

Travis interrupted her. 'I know, Auntie Jennison, and I understand congratulations are in order.'

'Yes, has Mr Pomphrey told you about us?'

'Yes, Auntie Jennison, and I'm really happy for both of you.'

'Oh, Travis!' Auntie Jennison lunged at him and made a proper meal of him, cuddling, cooing and kissing.

When Travis had recovered, he said, 'Why can't you be a player any more then, Auntie Jennison?'

'I was lucky to get back, Travis, I had terrible chest pains. You see, I'm getting old and everything's wearing out; but don't you dare say a word to Bill, you hear! The doctor said that it was all down to smoking.' Auntie Jennison chuckled and tapped the side of her nose with her finger. 'But we know differently, don't we?'

'Look, Auntie Jennison, I don't think we should say anything to Mum or Dad about me playing. Perhaps it would be better to let them think that you're still doing it; they'll only worry if they think it's me.'

'That's a bit sneaky, Travis, but the alternative is they'll probably forbid you to go. You know, it can be very dangerous, Travis; but you're a sensible boy, and we both know it must be done. Now, I think you had better go on home and we can both have a good think about how to go about it. I'll ring you tomorrow after I've been out and bought a new Charlie.'

Chapter Nineteen

Travis waited for Auntie Jennison's phone call, and when the phone eventually rang in the evening, he said, 'It's all right, Mum, I'll answer it.'

He went out into the hallway and shut the living room door behind him. 'Hello? Oh, hello, Auntie Jennison.'

Auntie Jennison answered, 'Hello, Travis, my very special boy. I wish I was there so I could give my special boy a special kiss.'

I'm glad you're not, Travis thought. 'Yes, I'm disappointed that you're not,' he said.

'I've been giving things some thought, Travis, and I can't see how you can go off to the future for hours on end without Tom and Barbara worrying and becoming suspicious, so you'll need to come down here to stay – and Bill as well.'

Crafty old thing, Travis thought. Any excuse to see Mr Pomphrey...

Auntie Jennison continued, 'When are your next school holidays, Travis?'

'We've got a few days off for May Day, but that's ages away, Auntie Jennison,' Travis said.

'Don't be ridiculous, Travis; we're over halfway through April now.'

'But Auntie Jennison, I want to get started.'

'Course you do, Travis, my love, but prudence and patience. Now, I'll talk to you soon. Kiss, kiss!' And she was gone.

Travis tried desperately to settle into his normal routine. The only consolation for the long wait until the next holiday was his afternoon visits to Mr Pomphrey. They'd spend hours talking and plotting; however, their fellow conspirator, Auntie Jennison, was conspicuous by her absence.

'Not like Auntie to be missing for so long,' said Mr Pomphrey. 'Perhaps she's off visiting, or playing.'

'Maybe, Mr Pomphrey.' Travis was saying nothing.

'Travis, could I ask you a question?'

'Mr Pomphrey, I've said before, you ask more questions than Alex ever did.' Travis was finding it easier to talk about Alex now. 'What is it you want to know this time?'

'Well, I was wondering, why can't you go to the same time in the future more than once?'

'I think the best way I can explain it, Mr Pomphrey, is like this. Think of the moment in time where we are, right at this minute, and think of it as a stationary point. Now imagine that time is like a moving walkway; it never stops. We can go back as many times as we like, we can hop on and off the walkway, because the past is finished with, and going back is only like seeing the same film in the cinema at different times of the week. All right so far, Mr Pomphrey?'

'Yes, I can understand that part all right, Travis, thank you.'

'Right then, Mr Pomphrey, now when you go into the future, you become part of it. It's not a film, it's real. That's why it can be dangerous, d'you see?'

'So far so good, Travis,' Mr Pomphrey said.

'Now, imagine jumping back on the walkway, only this time it's, say, twenty years in the future: you're now really part of it. Time will move on with you as part of that time, and when you come back you will have aged by the same amount of time as you've been gone. Now, say you come back after a year; well, you can't go back to twenty years in the future again, because you've already been there once; you can only go twenty-one years into the future or beyond – you see?'

'Yes, I'm still with it, Travis.'

'I'm not sure I am, Mr Pomphrey,' said Travis and smiled. 'So if you tried to go to the same point as before, nothing will happen. You can't go there twice, d'you see?'

'Yes, I understand that, Travis. But what if you went into the future by, say, just one week; in a week's time, could you bump into yourself just arriving from now?'

'Wow! I'm impressed, Mr Pomphrey. Not many people would have thought of that. Theoretically you could, but we're pro-grammed – if that's the right word – by our guides to avoid getting into that kind of situation.'

'What would happen if you did meet yourself, Travis?'

'Apparently it's only ever happened three times, Mr Pomphrey; Auntie Jennison was telling me all about it. One of her record books is called *The Book of Madness*. It's all in there.'

'I'd like to see that book, Travis.'

'Why don't you ask Auntie Jennison? You could read for yourself what happened.'

'Yes, I think I will, but just for now, Travis. You tell me what happens.'

'Apparently, Mr Pomphrey, it's like a drug more powerful than heroin or crack cocaine. You see, once you meet yourself, you get a mutual attraction to yourself, and that attraction is stronger than anything else in the world, because you have the same ideas, the same views on things and stuff. There's no escape, it's like a powerful magnet.'

'A bit like a narcissus thing, then, Travis?'

'Exactly, Mr Pomphrey. The problem is that, after a short while, one of you develops into Mr Squeaky Clean while the other you develops into Mr Very Nasty. Actually, Mr Pomphrey, it's the original form of schizophrenia.'

'So what happens to you, Travis?'

'Madness, Mr Pomphrey; it's as simple as that. In one of the three cases they killed each other. I don't know about the other two.'

'I'll ask Auntie,' Mr Pomphrey said.

And then, as if right on cue, they heard someone calling. 'Yoo-hoo! Yoo-hoo everybody!' And in came Auntie Jennison.

'How did you get here then, Auntie Jennison?' Travis asked.

'How d'you think, stupid boy!' Auntie Jennison grabbed Travis, encircled him with her arms and whispered in his ear, 'I caught the bus.' She then proceeded to devour him whole. When she eventually finished she put him down and said, 'Hello, Bill, you're looking especially smart today, if I may say so.'

'Hello, Auntie, and you're looking even more beautiful than ever,' said Mr Pomphrey, sticking his chest out.

Yuck! Travis thought.

'Look, Travis, the love of my life, how would you like to pop round and tell Tom and Barbara I'm here, and tell them I'll be round later. Oh, and tell your dad to pop down to the bus station and pick up my suitcase – I sent it on separately – there's a love.' She winked at him. 'I need to talk to Bill about the wedding.'

'Does that mean you're staying then, Auntie Jennison?'

'Of course I'm staying, stupid boy! Why else would I bring a suitcase?'

'Auntie, you can stay here if you like,' Mr Pomphrey said.

'Don't be so ridiculous, Bill! Now I'm a bride-to-be, I couldn't possibly. People would talk, and I've got my reputation to think of.'

'Auntie,' said Mr Pomphrey, 'where are Scampi and Charlie?'

'Yes, well, the new Charlie's right off his food. I don't think he's settled in very well. He was having a rest on the bottom of his cage when I left, and I didn't have the heart to disturb him. I've left him plenty of water, mind you.'

'Auntie Jennison,' said Travis, 'I don't suppose Scampi's off his food as well, by any chance?'

'It's funny you should say that, Travis,' said Auntie Jennison, 'he hasn't come out of his basket now for a few days, even when I call him. D'you think he needs the vet?'

'Tell you what, Auntie Jennison, I'll pop round and see Mum and Dad then I'll platform-hop and go and have a look at Scampi for you.'

'Oh Bill, did you hear that? What a treasure that boy is! Isn't he wonderful? Come here, my darling…'

But Travis was already halfway through the door.

Sure enough, when Travis got to Auntie Jennison's, both Scampi and the new Charlie were a memory. It was almost dark when Travis had finished digging the grave. I don't know how Auntie Jennison will take this, he thought, she's had the dog for years. He carefully covered the dead animals with soil then stood over the grave and said aloud, not knowing much about funerals, 'For what you are about to receive, Lord, I hope you are truly grateful… ashes to ashes, dust to dust, halleluiah. Amen.'

'Hello, Mum, where are Dad and Auntie Jennison?' Travis asked.

'Your dad's gone to the station to pick up Auntie Jennison's things, and Auntie Jennison must still be with Mr Pomphrey,' his mum answered.

157

'Scampi's dead, Mum, and so is the bird. I've buried both of them.'

'Oh, what a shame! And you're a good boy for burying them, Travis, but didn't you mind?' his mum asked.

'No, I've seen too many things already to worry about a dead dog and a canary, Mum,' Travis answered.

'Yes, you have, haven't you, Travis? And I can't say as I like it. Do you want me to break the news to Auntie Jennison?'

'No, it's all right, Mum, I'll tell her.'

'Are you sure, dear?'

'Yes, Mum, honestly. I'll go straight round to Mr Pomphrey's now.'

Travis ambled slowly towards Mr Pomphrey's back door. He was beginning to wish he'd let his mother break the news.

'Auntie Jennison, Mr Pomphrey, I'm back.'

'Come on in, then, Travis,' said Mr Pomphrey. 'What news?'

'Not good, I'm afraid, Mr Pomphrey. Auntie Jennison, the thing is…'

'I know, Travis,' Auntie Jennison chimed in, 'Charlie's gone to the great aviary in the sky; I shan't be buying another bird at that shop – it didn't last ten minutes. I shall take it back next week and demand a full refund.'

'Auntie Jennison, I buried it,' said Travis.

'Well then, we'll just have to dig it up again, won't we? Now you're not going to tell me you've buried Scampi as well, are you, Travis?'

'Yes, I'm really sorry, Auntie Jennison, but when I got there Scampi was already dead.'

'Oh well, dogs don't last for ever. Now pass me that ashtray, would you, Travis? This one's full up.'

She's totally barmy, thought Travis. Then he said aloud, 'Mr Pomphrey, I've been thinking. You know you came up with that date and platform number… well, that date can't be Ivan Roberts's starting point, because I've met him and he took Alex. I think his starting point must be a lot earlier.'

'I see what you mean, Travis, but I still think the date I gave you must have some significance,' he said.

'I'll tell you both what I think, shall I?' said Auntie Jennison. 'I think it's time for a cup of tea and a nice Benson and Hedges.'

'Oh, Auntie Jennison, I thought you were going to come out with some gem of wisdom,' said Travis.

'I might,' said Auntie Jennison, 'when I've had some suitable refreshment. You know, Bill, a small sandwich wouldn't be wasted.'

'I can take a hint,' said Mr Pomphrey, and he disappeared into the kitchen.

When Mr Pomphrey returned, Auntie Jennison lit a leisurely cigarette, popped a peppermint into her mouth, took a bite on her sandwich and stared at the ceiling.

'Come on, Auntie Jennison,' said Travis. 'What do you think?'

'Don't rush me, Travis... there goes another one... I think that Trevor Bains started by killing Justin Reed, and he took him to another platform in the present, or the same platform sometime in the future. I think that either the date or the platform number that Bill has come up with is crucial to all of this.'

'Yes, but, Auntie,' said Mr Pomphrey, 'it could be the same platform in the present or a different one in the future.'

'Yes, of course, you're quite right, Bill. What a clever man,' said Auntie Jennison. 'Isn't he clever, Travis? So you'll need to check out both possibilities.'

'Auntie Jennison, if he took Justin Reed to another platform in the present and it's not platform 2772, we're in trouble.'

'If I can make a suggestion,' said Mr Pomphrey, 'why doesn't Travis visit platform 2772 and get some idea of the place? You never know, there might be a clue or two there.'

'Splendid, Bill! Did you hear that, Travis? What a marvellous man you are, Bill Pomphrey. Now, off you go, Travis, there's no time like the present to go back to the past.'

'I'd love to go now, Auntie Jennison, but I think Mum and Dad wouldn't be too pleased. It's getting late now; I'll go tomorrow.'

'What a sensible child you are, Travis! Isn't he sensible, Bill? Very well; now come here and give your auntie a big kiss, and then go and tell Tom and Barbara that I'll be there shortly.'

For the second time that evening, Travis was obliged to undergo Auntie Jennison's manifestations of love.

Chapter Twenty

'You're home early from school, Travis.'

'Yes, Mum. Teacher said I knew everything there was to know and I could go home.'

'Right! Now let's have the real reason, Travis?'

'There's a power cut and all the computers have gone down.'

'Haven't they heard of good old-fashioned pen and paper?'

'That's exactly what I told them, Mum, but they insisted I went home – and it would have been rude of me to argue, wouldn't it?'

They both started laughing. 'I'll give you another good laugh if you want, Travis,' said his mum. 'Take a look out of the kitchen window.'

Travis looked out of the window, and there on the lawn were Mr Pomphrey and Auntie Jennison playing football! Auntie Jennison was in goal; two rolled-up coats marked the goalposts. She had her long skirt tucked up into the legs of her knee-length bloomers, and was diving athletically to save the goals – with a pipe hanging out of her mouth. Mr Pomphrey, sleeves rolled up and minus coat and waistcoat, was doing his best to blast the ball past Auntie Jennison. Travis could hear them whooping and laughing through the double glazing.

'Just look at them!' said Travis. 'How old are they? I suppose I'd better go and join in.'

'Hello, Travis,' said Auntie Jennison, 'don't wear yourself out with too much football. Remember, you're off to visit platform 2772 later on.'

'Never mind me, Auntie Jennison; I thought you were supposed to be taking things easy.'

'I'm only in goal, Travis, and that's not energetic at all.'

'I think I'll go now, Auntie Jennison, then I'll be back in time for *Countdown*. I'll slip away and Mum will probably think I'm still with you.'

'*Bonne chance*, Travis,' said Mr Pomphrey.

'I didn't know you could speak French, Mr Pomphrey,' Travis said.

'*Un peu*,' Mr Pomphrey replied, laughing.

'Off to France, Travis?' Mentor said.

'*Oui*,' replied Travis.

'Very clever,' Mentor remarked.

Travis arrived at platform 2772. The inside was done out like a fisherman's cottage; the walls were adorned with nets, corks, a lobster pot and some starfish. He got to the doorway and he appeared to be in the middle of a dense thicket composed solely of tall clumps of bamboo, gently swaying in the breeze. Far away, he could hear surf pounding on a shore, and from the platform door he could see a narrow path. He started along it and found it wound towards a single-storey house with a large sloping roof. It had a stone-built chimney which ran right up the outside wall, not unlike the ones Travis had seen in pictures of Swiss chalets.

Travis passed the front door and found himself in a narrow lane which climbed away in front of him. Towards the end of the lane he could see the road petering out into a rough track. He got to the end of the road and started along the track when suddenly he was on a cliff top. The waves were coming in from an angry sea, thick and fast, and hammering on the rocks below; he could see by the way the track fell away that the sea had claimed anything beyond a long time ago.

Travis went back past the house and came to the other end of the lane. '*Avenue de la Grande Plage*' it said on the sign facing him; the road ran to his left and his right. Eenie, meenie, minie, mo, he thought, and turned to the right. A couple of rather splendid rooftops came into view, and as he got nearer he could see tall white walls surrounding a row of large properties, with ornate wrought-iron gates. He passed slowly by each house in turn, looking at the nameplates, until he came to last but one in the road. Travis's watch alarm went off and he pushed his scarper button.

'I'm recording *Countdown* for you Travis,' Mr Pomphrey said, 'you seem to have been gone a long time.'

'Yes, I'm feeling rather pleased with myself actually, Mr Pomphrey. You see, I've done three-quarters of an hour today, and although I do feel tired I'm still OK.'

'Three-quarters of an hour, eh, Travis?' said Auntie Jennison. 'That calls for a rewarding kiss! Come on, you know you like it.'

'Yes, Auntie Jennison,' said Travis, and submitted.

'So I've kept the best bit till last,' Travis said, after he had told them of his visit to Bidart. 'The very last house I looked at had a tall white wall all the way around it and solid gates you just couldn't see through. I noticed lots of weeds and litter along the bottom of the gates; they hadn't been opened for a long time. I read the nameplate on the entryphone, and then my time was up.'

'Travis, don't tease – what was the name?' Auntie Jennison asked.

'Ivan Roberts, Auntie Jennison, it was Ivan Roberts.'

Mr Pomphrey and Auntie Jennison started applauding and cheering.

'What a result, Travis!' Mr Pomphrey said. 'So it looks from all the weeds and stuff that the place is empty, then.'

'Yes, so I'm going back for another look tomorrow,' Travis said.

'How far did you go back today, Travis?' Auntie Jennison asked.

'Only to earlier on, just before midday, Auntie Jennison,' Travis replied.

'In that case, tomorrow, go back six months,' Auntie Jennison told him. 'We need to know when Ivan Roberts lived there.'

After school the next day, Travis, without any thoughts of *Countdown* or anything else for that matter, rushed off to the shed and on to Bidart.

He swiftly went along past the tall white wall and focused his eyes on the ground under the gate: no weeds; clean and tidy.

Travis could feel the excitement mounting inside him by the second; he passed straight through the wall and along the shimmering white granite drive the other side. He glanced around, and there to one side was the biggest swimming pool you could imagine. A youngish man was sunning himself on a sun lounger. Travis went over to him. He looks just like a girl, Travis thought, with his long, curly eyelashes, dark wavy hair and a very slim build.

Travis turned and went towards the house. In the kitchen doorway stood another man who could have been the first one's twin; he called over to the first man, 'You'll be in trouble lying there if Ivan catches you.'

Yes, Travis thought, he's certainly alive, but he must be out.

Travis slipped back out of the gate and saw a car just along the road with its bonnet up. It must be broken down, Travis thought. He could see a man looking into the engine compartment, but as Travis looked more carefully he realised the man was really watching the house. Curiosity got the better of him and he went towards the car. My God, it's Granddad! he thought. And there was Thomas Travis leaning on the car with his magnum strategically placed across the top of the engine.

'What happened then, Travis?' Mr Pomphrey asked. 'Did he shoot him?'

'As I watched, Mr Pomphrey, a Mercedes Benz, black and shiny and ever so big and posh, came around the corner. Granddad stepped out from behind the bonnet of his car and he raised his gun...'

'Did he fire, Travis?'

'No, the car careered into the wall. Granddad rushed over with his gun raised and I followed on, but when we looked inside, the car was empty.'

'He pushed the scarper button just in time, then, Travis.'

'Yes, certainly looks like it, Mr Pomphrey.'

'Well, at least we know where he was six months ago, and that your granddad was on his trail, don't we?'

'Yes, that's right, Mr Pomphrey. I think tomorrow that I'll have a look at what was happening, say, three months ago at his house. Who knows, Granddad might have caught up with him by then! But where's Auntie Jennison, Mr Pomphrey?'

'She decided to back home, Travis. She said she had things to do, but she left her instructions.' Mr Pomphrey began to chuckle.

'I bet she did, Mr Pomphrey, if I know Auntie Jennison,' Travis giggled.

'Yes, you're to – and I quote – "phone me punctually at seven every evening and give me an update".' Mr Pomphrey stood up and saluted.

Travis stood up and saluted as well, and they both started laughing.

Travis visited the next day, the day after and the day after that.

'We've come to the place called stop, Mr Pomphrey,' Travis said, 'there's been no sign of Granddad or Ivan Roberts since the day that I saw Granddad. The house was shut up soon afterwards and the two pretty-looking boys packed up and left. I think it's time to go to the future now.'

'So you think you're ready for the future, Travis.'

'Mentor said so, Mr Pomphrey.'

'And when d'you intend to go there, Travis?'

'Not until next week when the school holidays start. Oh, and by the way, I like the new addition to your tea cosy!'

'How many times do I have to tell you it's *not* a tea cosy – and the addition, as you call it, happens to be my regimental badge! Auntie found it in an antique shop in town.'

'Well, I must say it adds a certain something to it, Mr Pomphrey.'

'Oh, thank you, Travis. Listen, I'll get Auntie Jennison to speak to your parents, and we can go down for a visit next week. Then you can go from Auntie Jennison's.'

'Travis, Travis, are you there, dear?' his mum called up the stairs. 'Auntie Jennison's been on the phone; she wants Mr Pomphrey to go down to visit her next week, but because they're "betrothed", as she calls it, she won't hear of it unless there's a chaperone! I've never heard anything like it; she wanted you to go with Mr Pomphrey, but I told her you wouldn't be interested. She seemed quite upset, so I told her that at least I would ask you.'

'Oh, Mum, you know I can't stand it for ten minutes at Auntie Jennison's, but if it's for Mr Pomphrey's sake, I suppose I'll just have to go.'

'No, don't worry about it, Travis, I'll explain to Mr Pomphrey.'

Travis did some quick thinking. 'Mum, has Auntie Jennison got a new dog yet?'

'Not to my knowledge, Travis, why?'

'I was just thinking, if she was going to get a new puppy, I wouldn't mind going down there. It would be fun picking one out.'

'All right, Travis, I'll give her a ring back and we'll see.'

I deserve an Oscar, Travis told himself.

Chapter Twenty-one

'But I don't even *want* another dog, Travis,' Auntie Jennison said crossly. 'I don't know why you said such a thing; you can be such a stupid boy at times.'

'It was the only thing I could think of, Auntie Jennison, otherwise I'd still be stuck at home... so perhaps you could have a kitten instead, Auntie Jennison?'

'Have you taken leave of your senses, Travis Travis? Cats and canaries don't mix!'

'What are you calling the new canary, Auntie Jennison?'

'Well, I've given it a lot of thought. I toyed with several names but I finally came up with the name Charlie.'

'Oh, that's nice, Auntie Jennison.' Totally shot away, Travis thought.

'Anyway, put all that to one side. You haven't said a proper hello to me yet. Come here, my perfect angel!' Auntie Jennison gave Travis a good smothering and then said, 'Right, we must draw up a battle campaign.'

'I'm all for that,' said Mr Pomphrey.

'Now listen to me, Travis, this is your first time into the future and I want you to promise me you won't stay too long,' said Auntie Jennison. 'We shall be worrying about you all the time you're gone, so even if there's something really interesting happening you know you can always carry on where you left off... and anyway it's getting on towards lunch time.'

'All right, Auntie Jennison, I promise.'

Travis said his goodbyes and started up the three steps towards Auntie Jennison's shed. The wilderness was gradually returning to its original condition.

'So this is it then, Travis. Now, you're quite clear about the way it all works, aren't you?'

'I think so, Mentor. You can only go to the same forward point in time once – that's called the setting-off point, and then

166

when you're there, time starts ticking away from that spot. However long you stay you age by the same rate as you do here, and you can't go back to your setting-off point again, but you can push the scarper button and come back here. That's right, isn't it?'

'That's right,' said Mentor.

'Mr Pomphrey gave me the date that Trevor Bains went to, didn't he? I could start there.'

'It will pay you to start a lot earlier than that, Travis. Now listen, I want you to always be aware that what you are embarking on is the most dangerous thing you will ever do. You're in a strange environment, at a different time, and you're all alone. Promise me you'll be extra careful, Travis.'

'Mentor, I do believe you're worrying about me!'

'Nothing of the sort,' Mentor replied, 'I don't understand worry.'

'Anyway, Mentor,' Travis said, 'any last minute advice?'

'Yes, make sure you come back safe and sound.'

'That's nice of you, Mentor; you have got feelings after all.'

'No, it's not that, Travis. At the moment I haven't got anyone else to guide.'

'You're a hard man, Mentor,' Travis said, and walked the rest of the way to the shed, shaking his head and laughing.

'You humans are a strange lot,' Mentor said.

Travis walked into the shed and for the first time ever when he came to the point where the corridor split he turned to the right. It was much like the left, he thought; the similarity didn't end there, either. As Travis reached the end of the corridor he could see everything was identical to the other platform in Auntie Jennison's shed.

'Oh, Mentor,' he said a little disappointedly, 'I thought it might all be different; are my platforms at home identical as well?'

'Yes, they are, Travis, but you can have whatever you want in your own shed. When it comes to that I'm just like a genie.'

'Yes, but I only get one wish.'

'No, two.'

'Two?' Travis asked.

'Yes,' replied Mentor, 'you can choose two different platforms if you want.'

'I already knew that, Mentor. I thought I was in for a treat.'

'You don't want much, Travis Travis, do you? How many other ten-year-olds do you know who can go time travelling?'

'Point taken, Mentor,' said Travis and climbed into Auntie Jennison's carriage.

Now what was it Mentor said? Don't make your setting-off point too far in the future, Travis thought. I know – I'll just go into the future by just one day, and I'll go to Polperro.

Travis had cagily walked past the substation and out through the rusty gate; the sun was a lot higher in the sky than the last time he had been there and felt quite warm on his face. He walked past the fish and chip shop, stopped and walked back. Why not? he asked himself. Travis went in and bought three pieces of fish and some chips. He whipped around the corner and pushed the scarper button.

'Auntie Jennison, Mr Pomphrey, fish and chips for lunch!' Travis called out.

'You weren't long, Travis! Did you change your mind and go to the fish and chip shop instead?' Mr Pomphrey asked.

'I hope it's fresh, Travis,' said Auntie Jennison. 'I can't stand it if it's not fresh; you know how delicate my stomach is.'

Travis waited, and sure enough Auntie Jennison obliged...

'Auntie Jennison, it's so fresh it hasn't even been caught yet.' He lifted the bag so they could see 'Polperro fish and chip shop' printed on the side.

Mr Pomphrey and Auntie Jennison gave Travis a standing ovation.

Auntie Jennison put down her knife and fork and looked at Travis. 'So you're now officially a player, Travis,' she said, wiping her mouth. 'I must say, that was delicious.'

'It's a long way to send the boy on an errand, Auntie Jennison, isn't it?' said Mr Pomphrey, with a twinkle in his eye.

'Oh, I don't know, Bill. Perhaps we'll try authentic curry from Bombay tomorrow – that's if it isn't too much trouble, Travis?'

'My pleasure, Auntie Jennison.'

They all started laughing. Auntie Jennison broke into the

laughter with, 'Travis, I don't want to spoil the fun, but I think we need to make a plan for tomorrow.'

'Tomorrow? Auntie Jennison, I was going again this afternoon.'

'No, I don't think so, Travis. I know it's not tiring like visiting, but it all needs careful consideration.'

'All right, Auntie Jennison, you win,' said Travis.

'I've been wondering,' said Mr Pomphrey, 'I know if you go to 2018 it's only fourteen years away, but what if the fashions are different? You'll stick out like a sore thumb.'

'If I go to Bidart, Mr Pomphrey, I could wear shorts. After all, it should be quite warm as it'll be the end of May. And then I wouldn't look silly, would I?'

'Good thinking, Travis,' Auntie Jennison said. 'One problem with that, though: suppose it's tipping down with rain?'

'I'll just take pot luck; after all, it will only take a minute to get a coat or a brolly.'

Travis opened the platform door at Bidart just a few inches. Very, very cagily, he peered around the old timbers. The sun was shining, and Travis could hear the roar of the sea. There was an elderly man standing in the garden about ten feet away; his back was facing Travis. Travis stood absolutely still, and the man moved away towards the house. Perhaps he's a visitor as well, Travis thought, and if he is and he sees me it won't matter anyway. Travis decided he wouldn't take the chance so he stood in the shed doorway and patiently waited. After a few minutes the old man disappeared into the house. Travis, not wanting to go past the front door, cut across the garden straight through a vegetable patch and out into the lane.

He made straight for Ivan Roberts's house. As it came into view, Travis could see the front gates were standing wide open, and as he watched a shiny black Mercedes swept noiselessly into the drive. The gates closed behind it.

If only I was invisible now, thought Travis, or could walk through the wall! What to do? He'd never faced this situation before and was in a quandary. He didn't want to leave the spot in case he missed something, but on the other hand if Ivan Roberts came out he could be in a lot of trouble. The problem was taken out of his hands, however, when the electric gates swung open and silently the Mercedes swept out into the lane. Travis pressed himself against the wall and the Mercedes carried on past. That was stupid of me, he thought, what if Ivan Roberts was in the car? What if he saw me? Travis started to panic. Not all it's cracked up to be, this time travelling, he thought.

Travis started to shake. He ran back along the road and headed up the lane to the cliff top. Sitting up there on the cliff, staring out to sea, he gradually calmed down; I really will have to be more careful, he thought. Travis was determined not to go back to Auntie Jennison and Mr Pomphrey until he had something to tell them, so after a while he went back along the lane again and out onto the main road. How can I get close enough without being seen? he asked himself. He could see the electric gates were now closed, but to go any nearer would be foolish.

A delivery van turned the corner and pulled up almost opposite Ivan Roberts's house. Travis could just make out the word '*Pain*' on the side of the van. *Bread*, Travis thought, it's the bread delivery man. A short little man wearing a dark blue beret on his head climbed out of the van and went around to the back. He opened the doors and reappeared carrying a large basket full up with French sticks. Whistling away, he crossed the road to Ivan Roberts's house.

Travis seized his chance. Running silently for all he was worth, he got to the van and hid behind the opened doors. From his position Travis could just see past the delivery man to the electric gates. The man pushed the button on the entryphone and spoke into it. Almost immediately, the gates started to swing open. Still whistling, the man went inside and started to walk along the granite drive. Travis broke cover, ran across the road and stared at the nameplate on the gate; then, as quickly as he had run across the road, he ran back and hid behind the van doors.

The delivery man returned, but this time he had someone with him, and they walked straight over to the van. Travis could feel his heart starting to pound. He couldn't quite see past the delivery man to see who he was with, and then suddenly he came into Travis's view. One look was enough; Travis pushed the scarper button.

Mr Pomphrey wiped the curry sauce from around his mouth. 'Travis, that was excellent – wasn't it, Auntie?'

'It certainly was, Bill, but I didn't really expect you to go to Bombay, you know, Travis.'

'I didn't, Auntie Jennison. I got it from Tandoori Nights in the High Street – but I had you two going, didn't I?'

'Oh Travis, you are a caution! Isn't he a caution, Bill?'

'He certainly is! So all in all, the trip to platform 2772 in the year 2018 was all a waste of your time, Travis,' said Mr Pomphrey. 'Frankly, I must say I am very disappointed. I really thought I was onto something. Are you sure there was no sign of Ivan Roberts?'

'No, I'm sure, Mr Pomphrey; I don't think he ever went to Bidart in 2018. I think Ivan Roberts died shortly after I saw Granddad in Bidart. Never mind, at least we've eliminated that possibility, and we can move on to something else.'

'Yes, but what, Travis – but what?'

'I think,' said Auntie Jennison, 'that you could still be right about the date, Bill. After all, you were right about the platform number. Ivan Roberts did live there at one time. I think we need to look at another locality at the same time.'

'But Auntie Jennison, haven't you forgotten I can never go back to that time now?' Travis said.

'Not that precise time, no, but quite near it. You weren't that long in Bidart, were you?'

'No, not that long, Auntie Jennison.'

'We all need to put our thinking caps on,' she declared.

They all sat quietly around the dining room table except for Auntie Jennison, who was puffing away on her cigarettes, crunching peppermints and occasionally blowing off. Even the newish canary seemed to have joined in the self-inflicted silence. Auntie Jennison's clock on the wall boomed out the hour.

'How long have we all been sitting here?' Mr Pomphrey looked at his pocket watch.

'Too long,' said Auntie Jennison. 'Come on, you lot, it's no good moping around! Anyone for football?'

'Oh, Auntie Jennison – not football!' Travis said.

'All right then, tell you what – let's go in town and buy a puppy.'

'Wow!' Travis exclaimed. 'Double wow.'

Travis didn't like the man in the pet shop. He didn't offer to show them any puppies, and he asked Auntie Jennison all sorts of questions, including how old she was. 'It's for a lifetime, you know, owning a dog,' he said, 'and if you don't mind me saying so, madam, I think you're a trifle... what shall we say... rather *advanced in years* for that commitment.'

Travis watched as Auntie Jennison started to bristle. Oh dear, he thought. Mr Pomphrey wasn't looking any too pleased either. Travis was surprised at Auntie Jennison's reply. She looked the man up and down and said, 'Well done – you've passed the first test with flying colours. Always assess the suitability of the customer first.'

'Excuse me, madam, but who exactly are you?'

'The council never announces the arrival of a secret shopper. That would be foolish in the extreme. Now, lead on, let's have a good look at your stock.'

The man's attitude suddenly started to change but he said defensively, 'We don't actually allow customers in the kennel area; we prefer to bring the puppies out here.'

'But I'm not a customer, am I?' said Auntie Jennison. She poked the man with her umbrella. 'Lead on, I say, lead on.'

The man took them through to the back of the shop, mumbling all the time about excusing the mess. 'Here you are, sir, madam.'

The din was horrendous. As soon as the puppies saw company coming, they started whining, barking and scratching at their cages.

Auntie Jennison had a good look around and then beckoned for the man to go back out into the shop. 'This won't do, it won't do at all,' she said.

'What's the problem?' said the man, grovelling. 'I've never had any trouble before – all the animals are well fed and treated properly.'

'EEC ruling 72798/1,' Auntie Jennison declared. 'That's the problem: size of cages. They are just too small for the amount of dogs you've got in them.'

'Oh dear, I'm sorry, I didn't know...'

'Ignorance of the law is no excuse, so I'm afraid you're in a lot of trouble. This carries a hefty fine,' Auntie Jennison said, shaking her head.

Travis sensed that she was moving in for the kill.

'Is there nothing you can do?' the man pleaded.

'I sincerely hope and trust you're not attempting to bribe a council employee…' Auntie Jennison said.

'Oh no, madam! Heavens above, the very idea. But if there was just something…'

'Well…' Auntie Jennison paused for a long while; she rubbed her hand over her chin. Then she said, 'Umm, you seem like a nice man. I don't want to get you in trouble if I can help it, so I'll tell you what I'm prepared to do. I'll give you one week to look up the legislation on cage sizes and get things sorted out; I can't say fairer than that, can I? But I'm afraid there's an immediate problem with your King Charles spaniels. They're more over-crowded than any of them.'

'Well, no, there aren't any more in that cage,' the man retorted.

'If you're going to argue…' Auntie Jennison looked daggers at him.

'No, no arguments. I tell you what, you came in for a puppy – why don't you have one of the spaniels?'

'I didn't come in for a puppy at all! I told you I'm just a secret shopper, but perhaps my nephew here would like one. It's his birthday next week, you know. How about it, Travis?'

My birthday isn't until December, Travis thought, but he tried to look excited and said, 'Oh, yes please, Auntie Jennison, I'd love a puppy.'

'They're rather expensive, though, aren't they?' Auntie Jennison remarked.

'To you, madam, there would be no charge at all.'

Travis was playing with the new puppy on the floor; Mr Pomphrey was sitting in an armchair, chortling away. 'I've never heard anything like it,' he said. 'Did you see his face, Travis, when Auntie Jennison came out with the EEC ruling? What was the number again, Auntie?'

'I don't know, I just made it up. Anyway, serves him right. What a nasty, seedy, horrible little man. Did you notice his whining voice? And did you notice all those horrible nicotine stains on his fingers? And the cheek of him mentioning a lady's age, indeed!'

'I suppose you're going to call the new puppy Scampi, then, Auntie Jennison?' Travis asked.

'Whatever gave you that idea, Travis? Haven't you any sense? I wouldn't dream of calling him by the same name – that would be boring. I've already had one dog called Scampi, and I certainly don't want another. No, the dog must be called something else. The dog, after all's said and done, is yours. Yes, true, it will live here, but it's your dog so you must name him.'

'Can I, Auntie Jennison? Can I really?'

'Choose away, Travis, but choose carefully.'

Travis carried on playing with the pup and after a little while looked up and said, 'I shall call him Alex.'

'Splendid, Travis! Absolutely splendid,' said Mr Pomphrey.

Travis suddenly got up and went across to the sideboard. He came back to Auntie Jennison and held out his hand. In it was an ashtray. 'Auntie Jennison,' he said, 'this is the ashtray from the pet shop; it was on the counter.'

'I know that, Travis, and I sincerely hope you don't think I stole it!'

'Well, how *did* you come by it then, Auntie Jennison?'

'The nice man offered it to me when you were busy looking at that parrot he had in the corner.'

'Auntie Jennison, there weren't any parrots,' Travis replied.

'Well, whatever they were… Now, you'll have to excuse me, I need the toilet. Lunch is playing havoc with my digestive system.' To make the point, she blew off loudly and was gone.

'She did steal that ashtray though, Mr Pomphrey, didn't she?' Travis said, looking at Mr Pomphrey.

'Nobody's perfect, Travis. Remember that, nobody's perfect,' he replied.

Chapter Twenty-two

'Why are you wearing a rose in your tea cosy, Mr Pomphrey?' asked Travis.

'Travis, how many more times – it's a *hat*.'

'Couldn't we call it a bobble cosy, then, Mr Pomphrey?'

'Yes, all right, it's my bobble cosy from now on; the reason for the rose is that it's 1st August today, and today's the day the regiment celebrates. It's called the Minden rose and it goes back right to 1759. It commemorates our victory at the battle of Minden, and the whole regiment wears the rose today. Anyway, to change the subject, are you looking forward to going to big school then, Travis?' Mr Pomphrey asked. 'Is it a bit harrowing going up a year early? And how did your dad talk the authorities into it?'

'I am looking forward to it, Mr Pomphrey, but I must admit I'm facing it with more than a little trepidation,' Travis replied. 'I think Dad has some sort of influence over the headmaster. Actually, Mr Pomphrey, Dad blackmailed him; but the thing was, as Dad said, there was no point in staying there another year, when I'm ready to move up.'

'Blackmailed him? What – Tom Travis? He wouldn't do a thing like that, would he?' Mr Pomphrey asked.

'Well, it was for the best. Dad said my education was of para- mount importance and took precedence over the headmaster's…'

'Trepidation… just now, paramount… precedence,' Mr Pomphrey said. 'My God, Travis, you're certainly growing up.'

'Mr Pomphrey,' said Travis, 'you know when they found the body of Trevor Bains, can you remember Auntie Jennison saying that his shoes and the bottom of his trousers were soaked?'

'Yes, that's right.'

'Well, do you think that's of any significance to what went on?'

'Um, I see what you mean. I think that if we could find out what the police made of it, it might be useful,' Mr Pomphrey replied.

'Perhaps if I went back to the museum in Polperro, I might have missed something.'

'What, you mean platform-hop? You'll be in trouble, mind, if Tom or Barbara find out.'

'Mr Pomphrey, I'd be in trouble if they knew I was a player, but we're not going to tell them, are we?'

Travis wasted his time at the museum. The newspaper cuttings revealed nothing new, and soon he felt down in the dumps and no nearer the truth about his grandfather's disappearance, so he decided to call it a day. However, there were so many people milling around that Travis found it impossible to find a quiet corner where he could push his scarper button.

As he walked towards Chapel Steps he spotted the old fisherman who had told him all about the murder.

'Hello, sir,' said Travis, 'nice to see you again.'

'Hello, young man. Fancy seeing you again. I suppose you're on another of your projects,' said the old man, chuckling.

'Actually, sir, I'm back on the old one – you know, about the murder. You see, Teacher was so impressed with the information you came up with that he decided to extend the project.'

'I don't see what you mean, "extend it". No one was ever caught, and there's not much more to tell.'

'How about the water on his shoes and his trousers?' Travis asked. 'Was there ever any mention of that?'

'You certainly do your homework, young man! I'd completely forgotten about the water. It was odd, but the water on his shoes and in his socks was sea water; it was almost like he'd been dunked in the sea, like you would with a biscuit in tea.'

Travis could feel the excitement rising. He couldn't think what the significance of the old man's comment was, but he instinctively knew it was of some importance. I must get back to Mr Pomphrey and Auntie Jennison and see what they make of it, he thought.

Travis didn't want to appear rude to the old man, so he stayed chatting with him, every now and again looking at his watch.

'I suppose you're keeping your eye on the time because you've got to meet your aunt again?' the old man asked.

Travis seized the opportunity. 'Yes, I'm ever so sorry, sir,' he said, 'but I do have to rush off.'

'You youngsters,' said the old man, 'always in a hurry!'

Travis ran all the way down Auntie Jennison's garden, shouting, 'Auntie Jennison, Mr Pomphrey!'

'Steady on, Travis,' said Mr Pomphrey. 'Auntie's in the dining room. Come on through, and let's have all your news.'

'Come here, my little darling, have a nice peppermint and an even nicer kiss,' said Auntie Jennison. Travis steeled himself for the inevitable onslaught.

'So that's about it,' he said in a while.

'I don't see why you're so excited, Travis,' Mr Pomphrey said.

'I know exactly why,' said Auntie Jennison. 'Don't you see, Bill, the sea water on Ivan Roberts's trousers means that he must have been shot near or in the sea.'

'He could have been paddling when your granddad caught up with him, Travis.'

'Oh yes, Mr Pomphrey, everybody goes for a paddle with their shoes and socks on,' said Travis, and started to laugh.

Auntie Jennison joined in laughing, blowing off at the same time. 'Perhaps he washed his hair with a hat on as well,' she said.

'I think you two are taking the mickey,' said Mr Pomphrey, and joined in the laughter.

When they had all calmed down Mr Pomphrey said, 'You need to eliminate all the other platforms now, Travis, until you find the right one.'

'That's impossible – it could take for ever, Mr Pomphrey,' Travis said.

'Yes, but where do you go when you're in trouble? I know if it was me, I'd head for home,' Mr Pomphrey said.

'You mean Polperro, Mr Pomphrey?' Travis asked.

'Well, yes... familiar surroundings. He probably felt safe there.'

'What an excellent thought! I think you could be right, Bill,' said Auntie Jennison. 'Next stop for you, Travis – Polperro!'

The next morning, Travis, Auntie Jennison and Mr Pomphrey sat around working out the best time for Travis to go to Polperro.

'I think you should try three or four weeks after 22nd May 2018, Travis,' said Auntie Jennison, 'things might have happened and perhaps there would be something in the newspapers – you never know.'

'All right, Auntie Jennison, then that's what I'll do,' he said.

Travis started to back towards the door; he knew what was coming next.

'Travis, don't I get a nice kiss before you go?' Auntie Jennison held both her arms out.

'Morning, Travis,' said Mentor, 'I almost felt like she was smothering me as well.'

'Yes, I don't think I'll ever get used to it,' Travis said, wiping away at his mouth.

'Would you like me to do something about the platform while you're gone?'

'Such as?' Travis asked.

'How about a makeover?'

'You've been watching too much of Mum's poo TV, Mentor.'

'Well, to be honest, I feel a bit, what shall I say… *redundant* these days.'

'But I didn't think you had any feelings, Mentor.'

'No, of course I haven't. Now, you'd better be going.'

Travis had taken the precaution of taking both a coat, hat, shorts and a plain red T-shirt. As Mr Pomphrey had pointed out to him, his West Life T-shirt could look a bit out of place in fourteen years' time. Travis tentatively looked out of the platform door. He could see that there were more weeds than the last time he had been there. He could feel the warmth of the sun and the sky was a pale blue. He slipped into his shorts and T-shirt and started down over Chapel Steps.

A large crowd of people were gathered along the harbour side, all looking out at the water.

Travis spotted a figure sitting alone on a bench. It couldn't be, could it? he asked himself; but yes, it was the old fisherman. He was sitting hunched up and carrying a white cane. He must be over ninety, Travis thought, and still going. Travis approached cautiously; he could see the old man's sightless eyes peering out to sea, the same as the other people. His hand holding the white cane had a slight tremor and Travis could see a wheelchair positioned by the side of the bench.

'Hello, sir,' Travis said, trying to make his voice sound like it had broken.

The old man cocked his ear towards Travis. 'Who's that there?' he asked.

'Remember me?' Travis asked gruffly.

'Yes, I certainly do! I might be getting old, but I'm not losing my mind. I think you must have caught a summer cold since I was talking to you last week,' the old man replied.

'Last week?' Travis didn't understand.

'Yes, last week. It was just last week when you were asking about the murder.'

The penny dropped. 'Oh yes,' said Travis, 'last week, of course.'

'You youngsters! You can't remember from one week to the next, can you? I don't know how you'll manage when you're my age; I bet you can't guess how old I am.'

'No sir,' replied Travis. 'About seventy-five?'

The old man chuckled. 'What is it you youngsters say? *I wish!*'

'Anyway, sir, what's going on here?'

'Have you been away or something?' the old man asked. 'It's all the bodies.'

'Yes sir,' replied Travis. 'I've – I've been away with my parents, and I only came back today. What d'you mean, sir, all the bodies?'

'It's been in all the newspapers all over the country and on TV... You must have seen it.'

'I've been to France, actually, sir,' Travis said, 'so I haven't seen anything at all.'

'Help me into my wheelchair then, young man, and you can push me home; it's only up the hill a little way. Then you can read all about it. I've got all the newspapers at home. I can't read them anymore, but the newsagent's such a nice man I don't like to cancel them.'

Travis helped the old man into his wheelchair and started to push him through the gathering throng.

'There's another one!' Travis heard someone shout.

'Did you hear that, sir?' Travis said to the old man.

'I'm blind, not deaf, you know! Now, where exactly are you taking me?'

'Home.'

'Oh yes – all right, then.'

Travis got the old man to his front door and tried to help him to his feet.

'No need to help – I'm quite capable, thank you.'

Only ten minutes ago he wanted a hand, Travis thought.

'What are you coming in for?' the old man asked.

'You remember, sir,' Travis said, 'I'm doing a project and you're going to let me have the newspapers.'

'Yes, that's it – a project. Well, come in, come in. Don't just stand there.'

Travis walked into the cottage; behind the door was a pile of newspapers on the floor standing about two feet high.

'How long have you been blind for, sir?' Travis asked.

'I don't know,' said the old man, 'must be a few weeks now.'

Travis gathered up as many of the newspapers as he could carry, thanked the old man and made to leave.

'Young man, before you go, tell me, what's your name?'

'It's Travis, sir.'

'You will come and see me again then, won't you, young Terry?'

'Yes sir, thank you, sir,' said Travis. Terry indeed, he thought.

He hurried back towards the harbour. More and more people had gathered and Travis could see an ambulance, several strange-looking police cars and a helicopter hovering overhead. A television crew were standing around smoking and looking bored. The weight of the newspapers was beginning to tell on Travis's arms and he decided to get back to Auntie Jennison's. The only problem was trying to find somewhere quiet.

Quickly he made his way back to the old man's house; the old man was standing in his doorway, craning his neck to hear the hovering helicopter. Travis stood silently beside him and waited for his chance. Before long, leaning on the wall for support, the old man inched his way out of the doorway and along his front wall. Travis slipped past him, and once in the safety of the cottage he pushed his scarper button.

Chapter Twenty-three

Travis staggered into Auntie Jennison's under the weight of the newspapers.

'Here comes the paper boy, Auntie,' Mr Pomphrey said.

'My, you've been busy, Travis! Now just put those down and come and have a cuddle,' Auntie Jennison commanded.

Travis told them all about the old man and the excitement at the harbour. Then, splitting the newspapers into three piles, they started to go through them.

'This is no way to go about it,' Mr Pomphrey said. 'What we need to do is find the nearest to 22nd May and start from there with just one pile.'

'Oh, you are clever, Bill,' said Auntie Jennison. 'I wish I'd thought of that.'

'Logical thought in the services, Auntie,' Mr Pomphrey replied, tapping the side of his head, 'logical thought.'

They sat there beaming at each other.

It wasn't until they came to 4th June's newspaper that they hit the jackpot.

'Wow, look at this!' said Travis, and he started to read aloud. *'The body of a young boy, washed up in Polperro harbour yesterday, has so far not been identified. A post-mortem is to be held later today and police are anxious for any information to help identify the child.'*

'Look at this!' said Mr Pomphrey excitedly. 'This is from the *Sun*, from the sixth. *England beat Australia by eight wickets in pre-Ashes warm-up.'*

'Oh, Mr Pomphrey,' Travis said, 'and I thought you'd found something important.'

'That is important, Travis,' Mr Pomphrey said, 'but this is more important. *Dental records have been used to identify the remains of a boy recovered from Polperro harbour in Cornwall. The deceased has been named as eight-year-old Justin Reed. Justin Reed disappeared forty years ago…'*

'No, it wasn't,' Travis interrupted.

'Bear in mind this is the *Sun* I'm reading,' Mr Pomphrey said. 'I'll continue: *Justin Reed disappeared forty years ago from Polperro. Initial results from the post-mortem are inconclusive. Police sources say the body has only been in the water for about two weeks; they are working on a theory that it has been refrigerated for the last fifty years.*'

'Look at this, you two!' said Auntie Jennison. 'This is from the sixth. *Three more bodies in harbour* – so the headline says. I'll read on. *Another three bodies of so far unidentified young boys have been washed up in Polperro harbour, now bringing the tally to four. So far the only body identified is that of Justin Reed, who disappeared on 10th of August 1965. The body has been taken for further examination as the cause of death so far is unknown. Police were working on the theory that the body, which is in an excellent state of preservation, has been refrigerated for the past fifty-three years; however, a government pathologist, who we understand has examined the body, has dismissed this theory as poppycock. He said the only way the body would be so well preserved is by using Cryonics, a system of preserving body tissue, and even then there would be ice crystal formation causing ice damage, and there was no such damage on the body.*' Auntie Jennison scanned the next few lines. 'He goes on to say that in his opinion the body was in the water for a maximum of three weeks, and before that he had no idea of where it had been, and he was mystified.'

Travis held up a copy of the *Sun*. 'Look at this, everybody,' he said.

BODY COUNT IN HARBOUR REACHES TWELVE.

'What day's that for, Travis?' Auntie Jennison asked.

Travis looked at the date line. 'It's for 8th June, Auntie Jennison,' he replied.

'Your granddad was dealing with an evil force, Travis. Twelve bodies indeed! I wonder how many more there'll be. I've never subscribed to his preferred method of dealing with these people, but on this occasion I think execution was the only answer.'

'You mean Granddad was a sort of executioner, Auntie Jennison?' Travis asked.

'Yes, Travis, I'm sorry to say he was. He was a visitor, player, tracker and executioner – that's what he did.'

'How many people did he execute, Auntie Jennison?'

'Too many, Travis, as far as I'm concerned. We could never agree on that.' And as if to show her disdain, Auntie Jennison broke wind.

'Oh dear!' Mr Pomphrey said. 'This is from the eleventh: *Body toll now sixteen.*'

'This is all very harrowing. I think we should break off for a cup of tea, Bill, what do you say?' Auntie Jennison enquired.

'A nice cup of Earl Grey, Auntie, and a Coke for Travis, perhaps?'

'Splendid, Bill.' Auntie Jennison reached into her pinny pocket. Travis, who had been sitting like a coiled spring, leapt into action.

'Here you are, Auntie Jennison, have one of my peppermints,' he offered. No fluffy peppermint for me this time, he thought.

'Travis, you are such a sweetie, generous to a fault. Thank you.' Auntie Jennison reached back in her pinny pocket. 'Here you are, my darling, I insist you have one of mine in return.'

Travis reached out for the offensive-looking mint with the intention of trying to palm it, but Auntie Jennison said, 'Open wide,' and popped it in his mouth.

Mr Pomphrey came back in with the tea tray and said to Travis, 'You haven't said anything about my appearance today, have you?'

'Is there something different about your bobble cosy, Mr Pomphrey?' Travis asked.

'No, look farther down.'

Travis looked Mr Pomphrey up and down. 'Oh yes, I see, Auntie Jennison's been knitting again.'

'It took me for ever, but I think you must agree Bill looks rather splendid in his... shall we call them, *bobble slippers.*'

'Yes, wonderful, Auntie Jennison, absolutely wonderful...'

'You don't think one bobble looks bigger than the other, Travis, do you?'

'No, Auntie Jennison, they're both perfect.'

With the tea things put away, they returned to looking through the papers.

'I hate to say this, Travis, but you'll need to go back. This is the last one and it's dated the thirteenth.' Auntie Jennison folded the newspaper and put it to one side. 'Well, we're up to seventeen bodies now. It's got to be the worst ever… all those poor souls.'

'Yes, Auntie Jennison, and there's still no sign of Alex.'

'Look, Travis,' said Auntie Jennison, 'you really should pop home and see Tom and Barbara.'

'Yes, I know that, Auntie Jennison; but things are warming up and I'd love to take Dad home some real news.'

'Right then, Travis, tell you what: one more trip, and then home no matter what the outcome, agreed?'

'Agreed, Auntie Jennison.'

After a powwow, they decided between them that Travis should go a further week into the future and they settled on 20th June, arranging for him to get there earlier in the day before too many sightseers were about.

Travis made his way around the harbour looking for the old man at a little after nine o'clock. I'm too early, he thought, I'd best go to his house. Travis walked up to the front door. He could see the door was slightly ajar. He tapped softly on it, then slightly louder, and gave it an exploratory push; the door creaked and then swung slightly open. A man in a dark suit and a black tie towered over him.

'Sorry to disturb you, sir,' said Travis. 'I was looking for the old… I was looking for the—'

The man stopped him. 'Who did you say you're looking for?'

'I'm looking for the elderly gentleman who lives here.'

'Oh yes? And what do you want him for, then?' the man asked.

'He was helping me with a project I was doing at school,' Travis replied glibly.

'Oh, right, then you had better come in,' the man said. 'How long ago was this, when you were talking to him last?'

'Just last week.'

'Last Wednesday, perhaps?' the man asked.

'Yes, that's it,' Travis said, 'yes, definitely Wednesday. And he told me to be sure to come back to see him today.'

Before he could move, the man had grabbed him by the T-shirt. His hand grasped Travis's scarper button through the material.

Travis raised his hands, but the man was cutting off his escape.

'*Liar*!' the man shouted. 'My father didn't even know what day of the week it was!' He pushed Travis to the floor and with his free hand punched him in the left eye.

Travis's eyebrow split and the blood oozed down his face; his left eye immediately began to swell and close. The man punched him again, this time lower down on the side of his face. Travis had never been hit so hard.

'*Call the police*!' the man shouted towards the kitchen. '*I've got one of them!*'

'Beat an old man up, would you? You and your mates, rob an old man?' He cuffed Travis in the side of the head, still hanging onto his T-shirt. 'For your information, my father *died* in hospital after you finished with him. Now it's your turn!'

The man swung at Travis again, but Travis managed to take the blow on his upper arm, which immediately went dead. He punched Travis in the stomach and all the wind and any fight he had left deserted him.

'The police are on their way, John.' A middle-aged woman appeared from the kitchen. 'Stop it, John, stop it! You'll kill him!' she screamed.

'Yeah – with any luck,' said the man. He stood up and released Travis, who slumped sideways on the floor. The man stood back and aimed a kick at Travis, which landed on his upper thigh. He aimed again, and this one landed in the small of Travis's back; yet another kick caught the back of his head.

'Stop it, John, for God's sake – stop!' The woman grabbed at the man's arm. 'Go outside and wait for the police. I'll get something for his face.'

The woman pushed the man through the front door and ran back into the kitchen; Travis seized the opportunity and was gone.

'What did the other fella look like then, Travis?'

'Oh, very funny, Mentor, ha ha!'

'Don't try to move, Travis. I'll summon Auntie Jennison,' Mentor said.

'Can you do that, Mentor?'

'Oh yes. Stay there.'

Auntie Jennison and Mr Pomphrey came running up the garden towards the shed.

'My poor lamb, whatever has happened to you?' Auntie Jennison said.

'I've been beaten up, Auntie Jennison.' Travis started to whimper.

'There, there, my darling, you lie still a moment. Bill, go into the house. Move the dining room table so I can get to the chaise longue, then go into the kitchen and get a washing-up bowl. Half fill it with cold water, let the cold tap run for a while, then add some ice cubes from the freezer... and I shall need a towel as well.' Auntie Jennison fished into her pinny pocket and produced the record room key. 'I want you to go into the record room and open the top right-hand drawer of the desk. Inside, you will find the following all in white oval containers: Temple Tincture, Cut Closer, Rib Repairer and Bruise Balsam. Bring them to the dining room. You lie still, Travis, while Bill gets things organised.'

Mr Pomphrey hurried away indoors. Auntie Jennison stayed cooing and clucking over Travis, then she bent over and, as she had been doing all Travis's life, swept him up effortlessly up into her arms and carried him into the dining room. She carefully put Travis onto the chaise longue, perched herself alongside him and said, 'There are healers Travis, and there are healers; but I am *the* healer. Don't fret – no noise now, Bill – this will hurt, Travis, but it's one hurt and over.'

Auntie Jennison looked Travis over. 'We'll start with your thigh, Travis.'

Auntie Jennison opened the Bruise Balsam, took a small smear of the almost colourless contents on her index finger, and massaged it into her hands. She clamped her hands on each side of the huge mark forming on Travis's leg and closed her eyes.

'Feel anything, Travis?' she asked.

'Yes, Auntie Jennison, it's getting warm,' Travis answered. Gradually the warmth grew, at first gently, then it began to gain momentum. Suddenly it was hot, and just as quickly it became unbearable. Travis and Auntie Jennison screamed out at the same time.

She plunged her hands into the freezing water, which bubbled and seethed. Steam started to rise from it. Travis looked up at Auntie Jennison; her face was dripping with sweat. She took her hands from the water and wiped her hands and her face.

'How does that feel, Travis?' she asked.

Travis flexed his leg backwards and forwards. 'Wow, Auntie Jennison, that's cosmic!' he answered.

Auntie Jennison repeated the treatment all over Travis's body until only the gash over his eyebrow was left.

'Travis, I'm afraid you'll have a scar there even when I've finished,' she said. 'But never mind, I expect the girls will find you even more handsome!'

Travis gave no answer, but somehow the thought of girls didn't seem quite so bad these days.

Auntie Jennison took a corner of the towel and put it in the now warm water. She carefully dabbed the blood away from the gash. 'This is going to sting, Travis, so get ready.' She took a small amount of the Cut Closer and ran her finger along each side of the gash, then quickly squeezed the gash together.

'Count with me, Travis, up to fifteen. Come on, count!'

They both counted aloud; and all the while Travis could feel the pain in his head fading away.

'There you are, my dear,' Auntie Jennison said. 'A spot of Temple Tincture and you'll be almost as good as new.'

Thirty minutes later, Travis was sipping a Coke and relating to Auntie Jennison and Mr Pomphrey all that had happened to him in Polperro, feeling very little the worse for his ordeal.

'Let me look at your eye now, please, Travis,' Auntie Jennison said.

Travis obediently went over and stood in front of her.

'Yes, you'll do! The swelling's almost gone and the scar... well, you can hardly see it.'

'Thank you ever so much, Auntie Jennison,' said Travis, and before he realised he was doing it, he had both arms around Auntie Jennison's neck and was kissing her.

Chapter Twenty-four

'While you've been gone, Travis, I've been doing some calculations,' Mr Pomphrey said. 'I've been looking at how frequently these poor children's bodies have been turning up, and the assumptions I made about when Trevor Bains – or should I say Ivan Roberts – started disposing of them. I think that what happened was this Ivan Roberts went forward to 2018, as I said in the first place. I think I've got the date right but the time could be a bit out. You see, I think he waited until it got dark or even later, and then put them in the sea; the fact that his shoes were wet seems proof of that.

'So if my calculations are right, I think your granddad must have shot him on or about 19th June 2018.'

'The only thing about that, Bill,' said Auntie Jennison, 'is that we don't know how many children there are involved. It could be well into July, or even August.'

'Yes, I know what you're saying, Auntie, but the way I've been looking at it is based on how much time it took to dispose of each one and how many years his killing spree lasted.'

'So if I go and have a look at 18th June first, Mr Pomphrey, and go from there, you think I'll be about right.'

'Travis Travis,' Auntie Jennison said, 'you're not going anywhere at all until you've seen your mum and dad and rested up a bit.'

'Oh, Auntie Jennison!'

'No arguments!' Auntie Jennison gave Travis one of her looks, and Travis meekly nodded his head.

He dutifully platform-hopped home just in time for tea.

'What have you been up to, Travis?' his mother asked.

'How do you mean, Mum?' Travis responded innocently.

'Come here – and don't give me that innocent look.' She caught hold of Travis's face in both hands and gently inclined it up towards her. 'What's this mark?'

'I fell out of a tree, Mum, and cut my eyebrow. Auntie Jennison had to use Cut Closer on it.'

'Look at me, Travis,' said his mother. 'No, I don't believe you, but I suppose it's better not to ask.'

At that point Travis's dad came in. 'Hello, son! What news from Auntie Jennison's?'

Travis's mother answered on Travis's behalf. 'He's been time travelling again, Tom, and this time he's been hurt.'

'Is this true, Travis?'

'Yes, Dad,' Travis replied lamely.

'I knew it,' Mrs Travis said, 'I just knew it.'

'I think we'd all better sit down and you can tell us what's been going on – and no lies, Travis, do you hear?' His mum sounded none too pleased.

Travis told his parents everything that had happened so far, but was economical with the truth when it came to the part about the beating he had taken.

When he had finished, his mum looked up and said, 'I know I can't stop you, Travis, but I love you more than anything else, and if anything happened to you I don't know how I'd cope, so please, please be careful.'

'Travis, I'm so pleased with the progress that you've made trying to find Granddad,' said Mr Travis, 'but if you feel it's too much and too much worry for your mum, and you want to stop, I will understand.'

'Mum, Dad, you both know I can't stop. It's why I'm here! I start again first thing tomorrow.'

'How old are you next birthday, Travis?' his dad asked.

'Eleven.'

'Eleven going on thirty more like. Come here and give us a hug.'

The next morning couldn't come soon enough, but nevertheless Travis enjoyed an evening with his parents. His mother declined to watch any poo TV, and instead they sat around playing Trivial Pursuit and Scrabble, which of course Travis won.

'I just had a thought, Travis,' his mother said. 'You've left Auntie Jennison and Mr Pomphrey un-chaperoned this evening.'

'Yes, and you know what she said about being betrothed,' added his dad, giggling.

'Actually,' Travis said, 'she asked me to sleep there tonight and to be back by nine thirty sharp; she said she couldn't have anybody getting the wrong idea.'

Precisely at nine thirty, Travis walked into Auntie Jennison's living room; it didn't do to keep Auntie Jennison waiting. The puppy was fast asleep on her lap, so Travis approached, feeling quite safe, as he knew she wouldn't disturb the puppy to assault Travis.

'I just said to Bill, it's almost nine thirty, Travis. How's Tom and Barbara?'

'They're just fine, Auntie Jennison, but I'm afraid Mum's worrying herself silly about me,' Travis replied, stroking the pup's head.

'No doubt we all worry about you. I'm sorry, but Barbara and your dad will just have to get used to it. Anyway, Travis, do you want anything to eat before bedtime? I think an early night is called for.'

'No thank you, Auntie Jennison, the quicker I get to bed, the quicker tomorrow will be here.'

'Tell you what, Travis,' Mr Pomphrey said, 'how about I get us all a nice cup of cocoa?'

'Splendid, Bill,' Auntie Jennison said, 'absolutely splendid – and a small sandwich and some pickles wouldn't go amiss.'

Despite the cocoa, Travis tossed and turned most of the night, and when it eventually got light he decided not to wait any longer but to set off there and then for Polperro. I'm so early, he thought, even Auntie Jennison hasn't got up yet. Outside, the dawn air was chill; he watched as his breath funnelled upwards into the still air; he could see a couple of stars still hanging around for the last of the night sky. A few birds were starting to twitter, warming up for the dawn chorus.

'Am I too early for you, Mentor?' he said aloud. 'Are you still asleep?'

'Sleep is a luxury reserved for you humans,' Mentor answered.

'Don't you ever rest then, Mentor?'

'I wouldn't know what to do.'

'Well, when you rest you don't actually do anything.'

'That's a strange concept and I've never been able to understand it. If you humans were immortal I could, but as you're finite I just can't.'

'See you later, Mentor.'

'Yes, Travis, you take ca—'

Travis set the time and the coordinates. He planned to arrive in Polperro and buy himself a newspaper. Down he went over Chapel Steps around the back of the harbour, and soon found himself a little breathless, leaning on the counter of the paper shop. '*Daily Mail*, please,' he said to the newsagent.

The man was engrossed in his own newspaper, which he had opened right across the counter. He pointed lazily in the general direction of the corner of the shop. Travis walked over, picked up the paper and returned to the counter, fishing out a pound coin as he did so.

The man hardly looked up but held out his hand for the money. He turned towards the till, turned back and put the pound coin on his newspaper in front of Travis.

'What's this then?' he asked.

'A pound coin, sir,' Travis replied.

'I can see what it is. Are you trying it on, or something?' The man was growing angry.

'I-I don't know what you mean, sir,' Travis stammered.

'These haven't been any good for ten years now. Where did you get it from? I hear the old boy up the road collected old coins… You're not one of the robbers, are you?' The man started to come round from behind the counter.

Travis didn't hesitate. He ran as fast as he could straight out the shop and towards the harbour. He could hear the man running behind shouting, '*Stop, thief! Stop him!*'

Travis kept going, but the man seemed to be gaining. Travis launched himself off the harbour wall straight into the sea. Just as the water closed over him he pushed the scarper button.

Wrapped in a blanket back in Auntie Jennison's living room, Travis told Auntie Jennison and Mr Pomphrey what had happened. Mr Pomphrey went over to the pile of newspapers and said, 'Look here! Look at the top of the paper – it says, "Price 60c". You'll need some of the new money, whatever it's called, Travis, or else you'll be in trouble all the time.'

'Oh dear, how silly of me,' Auntie Jennison said. 'I should have checked. You two, stay there and I'll go and have a look and see if it's in the records. You go and have a nice bath, Travis, and find some dry clothes. I don't know how long it will take.'

'But Auntie Jennison, I've already had one bath this morning – in the sea,' Travis protested.

Auntie Jennison said nothing but just looked.

'On my way, Auntie Jennison,' Travis said.

Travis was back from his bath in less than ten minutes. 'That didn't take long,' Mr Pomphrey observed.

'I'm not that keen on water, Mr Pomphrey,' Travis said.

'No, I don't know anyone your age who is. Auntie Jennison's not back yet, Travis, so can I get you anything?'

'Yes please, Mr Pomphrey. Could I have a glass of Coke? I can still taste the sea water in my mouth.'

Travis was drinking his Coke and Mr Pomphrey sipping a cup of tea when Auntie Jennison came back in the room, clutching a writing pad in her hand.

'Sit there, Auntie, and I'll pour you a nice cuppa,' Mr Pomphrey said.

Auntie Jennison looked at Travis and nodded towards Mr Pomphrey. 'Irreplaceable,' she remarked, and Travis smiled in approval.

'Right, this is what we're looking for. It took some finding, but apparently the currency will be replaced in the year 2007, in February,' Auntie Jennison was reading from her writing pad. 'Originally we were going to join the Euro, but it was stopped, and then when Mr Blair became president of Europe he introduced the Blairo; it is divided up into 100 Cottoes, so the price on the newspaper refers to 60 Cottoes, not 60 cents.'

'President of Europe indeed!' said Mr Pomphrey disparagingly. 'I wonder how he wangled that?'

'Where did they get the name "Cottoe" from, Auntie Jennison?' Travis asked.

Auntie Jennison looked at the writing pad again. 'Ah yes, here it is, the Cottoe is named after his deputy. So there you are, Travis – and we'll need to get some Blairoes for you.'

'That's not going to be easy, Auntie,' Mr Pomphrey said.

'We'll have to put our thinking caps on,' said Auntie Jennison.

'Or our thinking cosies,' Travis said, smiling.

Travis set off for Polperro again mid-morning; Mr Pomphrey had meticulously written down all the times that Travis had been there, so hopefully there would be no chance of bumping into the newsagent or the old man's son. Travis held the paper with the times written on it up in front of him while he punched in the coordinates.

This time when he emerged from the platform it was ten at night and was barely dark. Travis had made a plan of his own; he had decided to hide somewhere and see if he could spot Ivan Roberts.

He went down almost to the bottom of Chapel Steps and climbed over a low wall. Sitting there in the gloom, he waited, trying not to think of any spiders that might be sharing his hiding place.

Every now and again he'd look at his watch. The time dragged on and on. At pub kicking-out time, he heard the bell sounding, then several minutes later voices and footsteps; but no sign of his quarry. Travis sat in the dark. Two o'clock, his watch told him, then three; then four, and it was already starting to get light. Reluctantly, he decided to call it a night.

Sitting back in the Pullman, Travis mulled things over and over in his mind. 'I'm going wrong somewhere,' he said aloud, 'I know what to do; I must hide right opposite the platform so I can see Ivan Roberts if he comes out.'

Travis reset the coordinates, this time for the next night... a little later too, he thought to himself.

It was ten thirty; Travis went straight to the wall right opposite the platform entrance by the old rusty gate. He climbed over and crouched down along the bottom of the wall, not quite touching it for fear of spiders. Then, with one hand on his scarper button, he waited. The pub closed for the night and he heard the voices of the revellers as they made their way home, then silence. Travis carefully altered his position to a more comfortable one.

He felt he must have dozed off, for suddenly he heard the rusty gate that led to the platform creak. Travis held his breath; he daren't look up but peered at his watch in the gloom instead. He heard footsteps slowly climbing the steps, then nothing.

Cautiously he straightened up; Chapel Steps were deserted, completely empty. Travis sat back down alone in the dark. He was about to push the scarper button when he heard the gate creak again. The same slow footsteps sounded again, climbing away from him up the steps. Travis clutched his scarper button and straightened up. Just going out of sight into the darkness he could see a tall man carrying something that looked heavy. Travis checked the time and pushed the scarper button.

Mr Pomphrey was sitting up to the dining room table surrounded by pieces of paper, assorted pens and pencils and a calculator. A pencil was protruding from one of the slits in his bobble cosy.

'What exactly are...?'

'Hush, Travis,' Mr Pomphrey said, putting his index finger to his lips, 'I've nearly finished.' He carried on scribbling away.

'There!' he exclaimed triumphantly. 'It's worse than any of us could ever have thought. I think there's at least twenty-three bodies, but I think the most important thing is, Travis, if my calculations are right then I know the date and time your granddad finally caught up with Ivan Roberts.'

'Hear that, Travis?' Auntie Jennison said. 'I'm marrying a genius, a veritable genius! Bill, you're wonderful.'

'Steady on, Auntie. I could be wrong, you know,' Mr Pomphrey said.

'Nonsense, Bill, impossible,' Auntie Jennison retorted. 'Now, I think that calls for a celebration. All up the pub for a pub lunch, and then tomorrow, Travis, you can resume your quest.'

'Auntie Jennison, I'd really like to go today. I'm all for going to the pub – it makes me feel quite grown-up – and then perhaps I could go this afternoon.'

'We'll see, Travis; now, let me think, which pub shall we have lunch in?'

'The nearest one, Auntie Jennison. You know – the Star,' Travis suggested.

'No, definitely not the Star, Travis. You see, the man in the Star and I had a bit of a misunderstanding, I don't go in there any more.'

'Well, how about the next one along the road? What's it called, Mr Pomphrey?'

'That's the Duke of Essex. No, Travis, Auntie Jennison can't go in that one either, I'm afraid.' Mr Pomphrey offered no explanation.

'Where *can* we go then, Auntie Jennison?' Travis asked.

Auntie Jennison began stroking her chin. 'Let me see... the Rose and Crown; no, I had a difference in there. The Anchor; no, the man's very offensive. The King's Arms; no, I don't think so. The Old Crown; no, definitely not.' She paused. 'I know – that one where they don't allow smoking. What's it called, Bill?'

'The Freshers,' Mr Pomphrey replied.

'That's it, then. The Freshers it is.'

Chapter Twenty-five

Next morning Travis was sitting in the Pullman coach, looking at Mr Pomphrey's piece of paper. Eagerly, he punched in the coordinates, and with the fingers of his right hand firmly crossed and held aloft, he pushed the 'go' button.

He climbed right to the top of Chapel Steps until the pathway ended and went on towards the cliff top across the rough scrubland. The stars were twinkling and he could hear the sea pounding below. Travis looked to his left and right, searching for a suitable hiding place. With his eyes gradually growing accustomed to the dark, he spotted two rocks side by side with a crevice running between them. Travis hurried over to check them out. He was not disappointed; the rocks provided excellent cover, and he was still able to get a good view of the way back to Chapel Steps and the cliff top. Towards the back of the rocks there were even more, and Travis thought that, if necessary, he could always effect an escape by that route.

Travis settled himself between the rocks and started his vigil, every now and again glancing at his watch. The darkness seemed to close in on him and the shadows started to play strange tricks with his mind. As the time ticked on, Travis was making himself more and more nervous. Before long he was starting to shake, his legs twitched uncontrollably and his hands were wet through with sweat. If only I'd brought a drink, he thought. His mouth was as dry as a bone and his tongue felt twice its usual size.

In an instant, all was forgotten. There, emerging from the dark, strode Ivan Roberts, carrying what looked like a sack in front of him. He was so close Travis could hear him panting. He must see me, Travis thought. He loomed over Travis, right beside his hiding place, and then he was gone towards the cliff top.

Travis watched as he lifted the sack as high as he could and threw it over the cliff. Ivan Roberts turned and sauntered back towards Travis; he was softly whistling 'The teddy bears' picnic'. Travis saw him lift his hand to his chest, and suddenly Ivan Roberts was gone.

Travis sat there, panting, shaking and sweating, but before he had time to compose himself he heard voices, then quiet laughter, then silence.

Straining his ears, Travis leant forward from his hiding place. More footsteps. He could just make out the figure of a man, skirting around to the rocks on the other side of the rough ground. It wasn't Ivan Roberts; this man was shorter. Then he too was gone.

More silence, then out of the gloom he heard someone coming. And there was Ivan Roberts again, carrying yet another bundle; it looked like a sack – just the same as before. He passed close by Travis's hiding place once again and walked to the cliff top. Travis could see a shoe and part of a leg sticking out of the side of the sack. Then, as Ivan Roberts lifted up the bundle, Travis heard a gunshot, and as he watched, Ivan Roberts pitched forward over the cliff top.

The bullet from the gun passed right through him and buried itself deep in Alex's already lifeless body. The force of it knocked Ivan Roberts straight off the cliff top and he did a complete somersault, but as his feet entered the sea he managed to push his scarper button.

There, standing in the open, a gun still smoking in his hand, was Travis's granddad. '*Gotcha!*' Travis heard him say. Travis's granddad went quickly to the cliff top and looked over. He turned and slowly started to walk towards Travis, the gun now held loosely in his hand.

Travis was about to break cover, but as he was about to move he saw a purple blue light streaking towards his granddad. A bright flash lit him up and he fell. Then he lay there motionless on the ground. It looked for all the world as if Travis's granddad had been struck down by lightning.

'These new stun guns certainly are the business.' Travis now knew whose voices he had heard. 'Get that gun away from him in case he comes round.'

Travis could see two policemen standing over his granddad

shining torches on him. 'Look at this – it's a magnum, and it looks brand new,' one of the policemen said. 'And look at his funny clothes! He looks like he's been to a Seventies theme night somewhere.'

'Here, Luke, what's that he's got around his neck?'

'He must be a medallion man!' They both started laughing.

'Bet that's worth a bit. Get it off him, Pete.'

Travis watched as, first, one policeman then the other tried to relieve Granddad of his scarper button.

'Go and get the cutters out of the APV, Luke, and you might as well drive it along here so we can have more light.'

One of the policemen disappeared into the dark; the other was still frantically tugging away at the scarper button. Silently a strange-looking vehicle approached, no wheels, no sound – wow, Travis thought.

'Let's have some light over here, Luke.' Two huge spotlights suddenly lit up the scene and Travis cowered down lower in his hiding place.

'Get the bigger cutters, Luke; these won't even look at it.'

Luke obeyed and the two policemen toiled away at the chain around Granddad's neck.

Travis heard the cutters come together with a snapping sound. 'Got it!' Travis heard one of them cry, and he watched while the two policemen examined the scarper button in the huge spot-lights.

'This should fetch a few nice Blairoes; proper little medallion man, isn't he?'

Travis watched as one of the policemen laughed and pocketed the scarper button.

Travis's granddad started to moan. 'Finish him off, Luke, and let's spare the court the trouble. Resisting arrest, isn't he!' They both started to laugh again.

'You give him a few whacks with your nightstick first, Pete. Make it look like he was having a go, then I'll do the business.'

Pete duly obliged and produced his telescopic nightstick. Deliberately and callously he started to beat Travis's granddad around the legs and arms. Travis had seen enough. He came out from behind the rocks and approached the two policemen.

'What's going on here?' he asked.

'Clear off!' Luke said. 'Police business – and anyway you should be home in bed.'

'Why are you hitting that man, Officer 5006?' Travis had spotted the number on the policeman's shoulder.

'Resisting arrest... Now scarper, before we nick you too,' Luke said.

Travis stood his ground. 'What are you going to do with him?' he asked.

'How many more times! *Sling your hook.*'

Travis didn't budge. The copper called Pete whispered something to his colleague; Travis could only catch the odd word now and again. Ignoring Travis completely, they handcuffed the still unconscious body of Travis's granddad and unceremoniously dumped him in the back of their vehicle.

'So where are you taking him now, Officer 5006?' Travis asked.

'Where d'you think? Now clear off!'

The police APV slid silently away along the cliff top, gathering momentum at an amazing rate, and soon it was gone. Travis was left with just his scarper button for company.

As he opened Auntie Jennison's shed door, the heat from the sun hit him like a furnace. He squinted up at the sky: not a cloud; a couple of wispy vapour trails were the only interruption to the pale blue canvas.

Travis ran down towards the house. Mr Pomphrey and Auntie Jennison was making the most of the weather. Mr Pomphrey, in his suit but minus his tie, was sitting in an old striped canvas deckchair with a white handkerchief knotted at the four corners on his head. His shirt collar was folded out over his jacket. With his trousers rolled up, his feet were in a bowl of water and his bobble slippers neatly set to one side.

Auntie Jennison made no concessions for the heat and had a blanket over her knees; an ashtray sat on each side of her on the ground and a fag was hanging out of her mouth. Travis noticed another fag burning away in one of the ashtrays. She was wearing the most enormous sunglasses Travis had ever seen, and she was totally preoccupied knitting something that resembled a pair of gloves. Alex the puppy was curled up fast asleep under Auntie Jennison's deckchair.

'Hello, Auntie Jennison, Mr Pomphrey – I'm back.'

The puppy immediately came to life and ran to Travis to be made a fuss of. Auntie Jennison jumped up and let the knitting slide off her lap with all the stitches coming away from the needles.

'Oh, Auntie Jennison, your knitting! I'm sorry I startled you,' Travis said.

'Never mind the knitting; I was doing it all wrong anyway. Now come here, Mr Perfect.' Auntie Jennison cuddled and cooed over Travis with a certain warmth that even he was surprised at. Then she said, 'Bill, I'm sure Travis is gasping for something to drink.'

'Yes, of course. You sit here, Travis, and I'll make us all a drink – that's if you want one as well, Auntie?'

'Oh well, I wasn't going to bother, but as you're offering, all right then, Bill… and Bill, I'm a bit peckish… perhaps a cake or two.'

Crafty old fox, thought Travis.

'No telling Auntie Jennison anything till I get back,' Mr Pomphrey said, drying his feet. 'I don't want to miss anything.'

It took Travis the best part of the rest of the morning to tell them what had happened. Mr Pomphrey continually interrupted, asking questions that Travis had no answers for, like, 'Do they have a death penalty?' and, 'What does APV stand for?'

'When I was hiding by the rocks, Auntie Jennison, and Ivan Roberts walked past me, I could feel the evil coming out of him! It was horrible. I thought he might see me… I was so frightened.' Travis started to sob.

'There, there, my pretty,' said Auntie Jennison, placing her hands on each side of Travis's face. 'Close your eyes, Travis,' she ordered. Travis felt waves of calmness sweeping through him. 'There, there,' she repeated.

Auntie Jennison kept hold of Travis for a good few minutes; Travis was quite content to stay by her. After a while she looked down at him and said, 'You should be all right now, Travis, am I right?'

'Yes, I'm fine now, Auntie Jennison. Thank you... and to be honest, I'm feeling rather peckish.'

Mr Pomphrey looked at his pocket watch. 'Is that really the time?' he asked himself. 'Tell you what, you two sit here, and I'll go and rustle up some lunch.'

'No, Bill. Just like yesterday, we've got to celebrate Travis's successful day. Let's all go to the pub – but not the same one as yesterday.'

'But Auntie Jennison,' Travis said, 'you said what a splendid meal it was yesterday, didn't you?'

'Yes, I know that, Travis, but there weren't any ash... There was nowhere to have a smoke, and anyway Mr Pomphrey's beer looked cloudy to me.'

'There was nothing wrong with it, Auntie,' said Mr Pomphrey, winking at Travis.

'Yes there was, I tell you! And anyway I had a dirty glass; I can't stand it when the glasses are dirty.'

'Well, why didn't you say something about it yesterday, then, Auntie Jennison?' Travis asked, and winked back at Mr Pomphrey.

'I'm far too polite,' Auntie Jennison answered. 'No, I must insist, a different pub's called for.'

They all ended up at the Mason's Arms, a good twenty-minute walk away, and it seemed it was the only pub on the route that Auntie Jennison was allowed in. All through the meal, Travis watched Auntie Jennison like a hawk; she behaved impeccably, not going near an ashtray once.

He watched her as they sat in the pub garden afterwards, and he even watched her as she threaded her way between the tables to go to the ladies. She seems to be cured, Travis thought; after all, there are only so many ashtrays anybody needs.

About three in the afternoon Auntie Jennison asked the man in the pub to call a taxi for them, which he quickly did. 'What a nice man! Isn't he a nice man?' Auntie Jennison remarked.

When they all arrived back at Auntie Jennison's, Charlie the canary and Alex the pup chorused a greeting. Auntie Jennison flopped into a chair.

'That was excellent,' she declared. 'What a lovely meal, and such a nice man, and he wouldn't even let me pay for the phone call for the taxi. We must go there again.' She reached into her pinny and produced three packets of cigarettes and two lighters.

'Here, let me get you an ashtray, Auntie Jennison,' Travis offered.

'No need, Travis, but thank you.' Auntie Jennison reached into her pinny pocket. 'I seem to have one here. My word, I wonder where that could have come from…'

Chapter Twenty-six

'Alpha papa victor six to control.'

'Yes, yes, go ahead, alpha papa victor six.'

'Returning to base, one, I C one male, restrained and in custody, firearm incident, request daylight search coastline, sector five.'

'Affirmative, alpha papa victor six.'

'Could be something in this for us, Luke. We could do with a bit of recognition.'

'You can say that again – we're not exactly flavour of the month, are we?'

'When that bloke's body turns up on the tide, Luke, the boss will be all sweetness and light. In the meantime we can go to Looe tomorrow and flog the tomfoolery.'

By the time they got back to the police station, Thomas Travis had regained consciousness. Handcuffed, and not realising his scarper button was sitting in the policeman's pocket, he bided his time.

'Come on, you – out!' The two policemen bundled Thomas in through the back door of the police station.

'Right, what have we got here?' the duty sergeant asked.

'Name?' He looked inquiringly at Thomas.

'Could you take these handcuffs off, please, they're rather tight,' Thomas asked politely.

The duty sergeant leant over the desk towards Thomas. 'Name?' he repeated more loudly.

'I'll tell you who I am once you get these things off me.'

The duty sergeant shook his head. 'Looks like we've got an awkward one here, boys. Explain to him where he's going wrong, will you?'

Luke turned towards Thomas and punched him in the stomach. Thomas sank to his knees, all the breath knocked out of him. The two policemen then dragged him back up to his feet.

'Name?'

'It's Travis, Thomas Travis,' Thomas gasped.

'There, that's better! It wasn't difficult, was it?' The duty sergeant was grinning at him.

'Address?'

Thomas was quicker thinking this time. 'No fixed abode,' he replied.

'Why are you wearing those funny clothes?'

'I'm a Seventies freak, sir.'

'Ah! Learning some manners, are we? You're a freak all right, my son, and you're in a lot of trouble. You got anything to say?'

Thomas decided not to ask for the cuffs to be removed again. Instead he replied, 'Yes, I'd like to see a solicitor, please.'

The three policemen roared with laughter. 'I'll bet you would!' said the duty sergeant, 'and I'd like to win the lottery, but it won't happen. Put him in the cells for now, and we'll see what turns up in the morning. And get that gun down to ballistics… oh, and boys, be gentle with him.' The duty sergeant started laughing.

Thomas was escorted down a long corridor, his arms and legs aching from the beating he had received. Say nothing, he thought, and you'll be out of here as soon as their backs are turned. They took off his cuffs and roughly threw him into the cell; Luke gave him a parting kick just for good measure. The cell door slammed behind him and Thomas reached for his scarper button. Through the viewing hatch of the cell came a voice. 'Looking for this, perhaps?'

Thomas looked around. Luke was dangling the scarper button in front of him, just in view, but just out of arm's reach. The viewing hatch slammed shut and Thomas could hear their footsteps and laughter echoing and receding down the corridor into the distance.

Next morning Luke and Pete parked their APV right where they shouldn't on the side of Fore Street in Looe, and ignoring the black looks of the traffic warden, arrogantly sauntered across the road to the doorway of Jacob Goldberg's pawnshop.

The quaint old brass bell jangled as the two walked into the shop. A long counter ran down the back of it and above, a square wire mesh extended to the ceiling. There was a serving hatch, bolted shut, and at one end of the counter a stout door which led to the back of the shop. The only object on the customer's side of the counter was a large grandfather clock which almost touched the ceiling; it was too big to pass through the door.

Mr Goldberg, grey-haired, with spectacles perched right on the end of his long nose, and wearing a faded brown suit with a matching tie, stood hunched behind the counter. He saw the two policemen come through the door and his face dropped. 'What do you two want? How many times are you coming in my shop?' he said with a thick Jewish accent. 'Nothing I have here is stolen, never you find anything, yet you still come back! Why for you waste my time?'

'Open the hatch, we've got something for you,' Luke said.

Mr Goldberg reluctantly pulled the bolts and swung the hatch open. Luke delved in his pocket and placed the scarper button on the counter in front of Mr Goldberg. He picked it up by the chain, examined it and said, 'Look, it's broken. So why would I be wanting broken jewellery?'

'Have a proper look at it, old man,' Pete said aggressively.

Mr Goldberg took an eyepiece from his pocket, removed his glasses and peered at the scarper button. 'Worthless dreck, no good at all,' he declared, and threw the scarper button down on the counter.

'What d'you mean, worthless?' Luke said. 'Take another look at it – it's gold.'

'Looking at it I can be doing all day,' Mr Goldberg said. 'It won't turn it into gold. I tell you true, it's not worth anything.'

'We were hoping it was worth at least, what shall we say, Pete? One hundred Blairoes.'

'It's not worth one! Are you mad?'

'He's calling us mad, Luke. I don't like that – let's turn his shop over.'

'No, no, please don't do anything to my shop!' Mr Goldberg started to plead. 'Here – I give twenty Blairoes, and you go.'

'Twenty? The figure we had in mind was a hundred, wasn't it, Pete?'

'Listen, I give fifty, I have no more,' Mr Goldberg said. 'Times are hard, business is not what it was.'

'Give me the fifty then, old man,' Luke demanded.

Mr Goldberg opened his till and counted out fifty Blairoes onto the counter. Luke picked the money up and greedily stuffed it in his pocket. 'Right then, that's my fifty! Now give Pete his fifty.'

Mr Goldberg knew it would be no good to argue and counted out another fifty Blairoes.

'Make out a receipt for the jewellery. We wouldn't want anybody to think it wasn't all legal now, would we?' Pete said, chuckling.

Mr Goldberg shakily wrote out the receipt and handed it to Luke. The two policemen walked to the door of the shop.

'A pleasure as always, Mr Goldberg,' Luke said. 'You take care now.' And they both swaggered out of the shop laughing.

Mr Goldberg looked at the scarper button again, picked it up, made to throw it in the bin, changed his mind, opened a drawer in the counter and popped it inside instead.

Two weeks went by, and as Luke and Pete returned to the station for their meal break, the duty sergeant approached them and said, 'The inspector wants to see you two about that shooting a couple of weeks ago.'

'Wonder what he wants?' Pete asked.

'I expect we're in for a commendation,' Luke answered.

'Just get in there, you pair of dreamers!' the duty sergeant said.

'Come in, you two, there's been a development with that shooting in Polperro. Are you absolutely sure it was a man you saw go over the edge of the cliff?'

'Yes sir,' they chorused simultaneously.

'No doubt in either of your minds?'

'None, sir,' Luke answered. Pete shook his head.

'Well, they've recovered a body from Polperro harbour early today and early indications are that this...' the inspector hesitated and looked down at his paperwork... 'this Thomas Travis's gun was the murder weapon all right; but the body isn't that of a man.'

'What are you getting at, sir?' Luke asked.

'The body they recovered is a boy about ten or eleven years old.'

Luke and Pete stood looking at each other in absolute bewilderment.

'I know what I saw sir,' Luke said.

'Listen,' the inspector said, 'it was a dark night, the adrenalin was pumping, the gunshot, the confusion, the boy was quite tall... you could have been mistaken. The thing is, chaps, you may well have caught this serial murderer that we've been after, and this could mean a commendation for you two.'

Pete looked up. 'Yes, it was dark, and it was all over in an instant; I suppose it could have been a boy.'

'It's all coming back to me now, sir,' Luke said. 'I heard a boy's voice shout "No!" just before I heard the gunshot.'

'Why didn't you mention this before?' the inspector asked, 'there's nothing about it in your report.'

'I thought it was just the sound of the sea playing tricks with my hearing before, that's why I didn't mention it,' Luke replied.

'So it was a boy we heard, then,' Pete piped up. 'Yes, it's all coming back to me as well.'

'This' – the inspector looked at his paperwork again – 'this Thomas Travis... once we get the result of the post-mortem, we'll fast-track him under the new system and he should be sentenced by the end of next week. OK you two, just write out a new report putting in the bit about the boy shouting, and we're home and dry.'

Pete and Luke, feeling well pleased with themselves, sauntered down the corridor to the mess room. 'Here come the conquering heroes!' someone called across mockingly.

'Jealousy, jealousy, you're all jealous!' Luke retorted. He and Pete sat at a separate table. No one in the station could stand the sight of either of them; someone had once called them 'Old Nick's Nickers', and the name had stuck.

A week to the day later, Thomas Travis, his hands and feet shackled, found himself shuffling into Number One Court at Exeter Assizes.

He glanced around; the public gallery was full to overflowing, and reporters were sitting all in a row, their pencils poised above their notepads. There was no jury in evidence, just several people, all wearing wigs, talking frantically in the well of the court.

Thomas Travis was led to a box on the left-hand side of the court where two burly-looking guards were already waiting for his arrival. He was bundled into the box and a hand on each of his shoulders forced him down onto a seat.

'All rise!' No sooner had Thomas settled than he found himself being dragged back up into an upright position. Three elderly judges walked slowly to their throne-like seats at one end of the court. One was hobbling on a stick, and it looked from his ruddy complexion and grimace that an extreme bout of gout was bothering him.

The three bowed to the assembled court and the court bowed back; there was a clattering of seats, then silence.

The judge with the stick, who was sitting between the other two judges, looked at Thomas and growled, 'Do you understand the fast-track system of justice?'

'No, sir,' Thomas replied.

'Call the judge *M'lud*,' a voice whispered in his ear.

'No, M'lud,' Thomas repeated.

'Hasn't anyone explained anything to the defendant?' The judge sounded exasperated and grumpy. The well of the court broke into excited chatter.

'*Silence!*' the court usher called out. '*Silence in court!*'

'When a new system is inaugurated there's always likely to be teething troubles,' the judge continued. 'But really... All right, we'll adjourn for fifteen minutes. Take him to the cells and explain everything to him.'

Thomas was bundled unceremoniously down a flight of stairs to the room that passed for a cell. It was barely six feet by four, dark and smelling of stale urine.

Thomas could hear high heel shoes clip-clopping along the corridor and a female voice telling the guard to let her in the cell.

'Not very nice in here, is it, Mr Travis?' A girl in her mid-twenties stood in front of Thomas. 'I'm here on behalf of the court to tell you the procedures.'

'I haven't even had a solicitor to speak to,' Thomas said. 'Are you going to represent me?'

'Where have you been, Mr Travis? This is fast track. When the defendant has no defence, then the evidence is read out and sentence passed, simple as that.'

'But there's no jury!' Thomas protested. He was grasping at straws.

'Look, Mr Travis, I can't tell you anything you want to hear. All you can do is go back up there and hope Mr Justice Richmond's gout isn't playing him up too much today.'

'The evidence is quite clear in this case,' Mr Justice Richmond was just summing up. 'We've heard from the two brave police officers how they heard the poor unfortunate boy screaming; we've heard how the defendant shot the boy down in cold blood...' Things weren't looking good for Thomas... 'and how the two officers, after a tremendous struggle, managed, without any thought for their own personal safety, to arrest the defendant – and I commend them for that.' Mr Justice Richmond paused, groaned and moved his foot to a more comfortable position. 'We have heard how the bullet that killed the boy came from the defendant's gun. Although the post-mortem was inconclusive, owing to the time the body was in the sea, there is no doubt in my mind that the defendant shot and killed the boy. As for the other bodies washed up in Polperro harbour, there is no evidence to connect the defendant with any of the other crimes, but enquiries continue and may well do so.'

Thomas was dragged to his feet.

'Have you anything to say to the court before I sentence you?' The judge stared icily at Thomas.

'No, M'lud.' Thomas looked straight back at Mr Justice Richmond.

'No remorse!' He shook his head from side to side.

The three judges whispered to each other for a few seconds and then Mr Justice Richmond looked at Thomas and said, 'Thomas Travis, you have been found guilty of the most heinous crime of murder. You took a young boy, with his life in front of him, and for your own evil ends ended it. It's at times like this I wish the death penalty was an option for me; you have shown no regret, no shame at all for your crime. I shall sentence you to the maximum I can under fast track. You will go to prison for a minimum of fifty years, with no leave of appeal and no parole. Take him down!'

Just as well he only had gout in the one foot, Thomas thought ironically. Chained to a prison officer, he was led out into the bright sunlight and into the back of a waiting van.

'Who's a lucky boy then?' the prison officer said. It was the first time he had said anything. 'I can think of worse places to spend the next fifty years.'

'Why, where are you taking me?' Thomas asked.

'The new nick – built it especially for the likes of you. It's called Samson.'

'Samson?' Thomas asked quizzically.

'Knew you wouldn't know, but I'm sure you can remember all the fuss with the Prince of Wales when they decided to build a prison in the Scilly Isles.'

'Oh yes,' Thomas replied, not wanting to give anything away.

'Listen, my name's Prison Officer Harding. We're going to be together for a long time, so while there's no one around you can call me Mike, OK?'

'Mike, I didn't kill that little boy,' Thomas said.

'They all say that! I wish I had a Blairo for every time I've heard that one.'

'Honestly,' Thomas said.

'Well, I've been watching you in court, and you don't come across as a child killer, and I've dealt with a few in my time. No, there's something different about you, can't put my finger on it, but something... I wouldn't even bother talking to you ordinarily; but like I said, there's something – just something.' Prison Officer Harding settled back in his seat and terminated the conversation by closing his eyes.

Thomas Travis watched through the tiny window while the van sped through the country lanes. Then he too closed his eyes and drifted off to sleep.

The vehicle came to an abrupt halt and brought Thomas back to reality.

'Here we are,' said Mike Harding. 'Helicopter next – have you ever been in a helicopter, Prisoner 501?'

Thomas suddenly thought, I'm just a number now.

'You wouldn't believe the sort of transport I'm used to,' he said.

Mike Harding ignored him and Thomas, still in chains, was

led to the waiting helicopter. Once inside and seated between another two prison officers, the chains were removed from Thomas's legs and arms. He sat rubbing away at where they had chafed him. 'Thank you so much,' he said.

'Just following the regulations. You never know when you might have to swim travelling in one of these things. Can't have you drowning and cheating the system of the next fifty years!' one of the officers said.

Fifty years, Thomas thought, fifty years...

After what seemed a short flight, the helicopter touched down, the doors were opened and Thomas took his first look at Samson Island. Not a tree, he thought; gorse, bracken, some clumps of Livingstone daisies and precious little else. The chains were put back around his legs and wrists by Prison Officer Harding and he hobbled to a waiting van. 'Only a few hundred yards to go now,' Harding said.

The van rounded a bend and abruptly pulled up. 'Here we are – home sweet home,' said Harding.

Thomas looked around him: no bars, no barbed wire and no high walls: just a complex of new-looking granite buildings, all single-storeyed, with grey slate roofs.

'Right, you'll be straight in for induction, then you'll see the governor, understood?'

'Yes, Officer Harding.'

Thomas was led into a room where he was finally relieved of his chains; he then had to suffer the indignity of a strip-search, and then was wheeled in front of the doctor.

'You've probably noticed there are no apparent preventative means of trying to stop you escaping from here, but don't even let the thought cross your mind,' the doctor said. 'You see this?' He held up what appeared to be a minute piece of plastic. 'It's a chip; it goes under your skin, and we know where you are all the time. If you try to remove it and it comes in contact with the air, the alarm sounds. Now come over here; you won't feel a thing.'

After the doctor, Thomas was fitted out in his prison garb, tracksuit bottoms, shorts and thick and thin tops, boxers, socks and vests. He was given a pair of heavy boots and a pair of trainers. Then off to the hairdresser. More like a sheep shearer,

Thomas thought, and then it was the governor.

Officer Harding ushered Thomas into the governor's office, closed the door, and Thomas and the governor were alone. They stood on each side of the governor's desk and surveyed each other.

The governor seemed to be quite a lot younger than Thomas, mid-thirties or thereabouts. He was tall and had an open face; his eyes were set far apart and a smile flickered around the corners of his mouth. Thomas noticed his hands looked like a workman's – not at all what you'd expect.

The governor didn't miss a trick. 'See, you're looking at my hands – come to that later. Do sit down.' He spoke in a clipped, cultured voice and he gestured towards a chair in the corner.

'No, bring it up here, don't want to shout.' He beckoned for Thomas to bring his seat closer. 'That's better. Welcome to Samson Island. It's not much, but with some all-round effort it will be. You'll notice we've cut all your hair off; symbolic thing, you know. Like Samson in the Bible, you've lost all your dignity, just as he lost his strength; and as it grows again so will a new you. Should make you a better man for it. You're one of only fifty-five prisoners here at this moment; there will be more to follow when the place is up and running properly. Knuckle down, shoulder to the wheel and all that and the time will fly by. All the prisoners who are here are here for good; there are no records kept on the island and no one here will know why you are here. I advise you not to tell anyone you've killed a child; better to say it was your mother you killed than that, do you understand?'

'Yes sir, but I didn't kill a child.'

'You will address me as "Governor", and as far as the law is concerned, you are a guilty man serving his sentence. Now where was I... oh yes, you will be expected to work, and the choices are limited. As you can see by my hands, it's every man to the pumps for my latest idea. Do you like gardening?'

Thomas, sensing that gardening seemed a better bet than sewing mailbags, working in a machine shop or anything else, said, 'Love it, Governor, I absolutely love it.'

'Splendid fellow! Going to get along really well, I can tell; never wrong, you know. We're going to have a walled garden out there.' He pointed over his shoulder. 'Course, we need to build the wall first, and what does a wall need? Lots of granite – and that's where you come in! So, first thing tomorrow, it's off to the quarry for you to start digging it out.'

Chapter Twenty-seven

'I've had a long chat with Tom and Barbara today, Travis,' Auntie Jennison said. 'Big school's looming on the horizon, and your mum and dad need to take you shopping for your uniform, so you and Bill will be going back home tomorrow. I've brought your dad up to date, but I've been careful to leave out the bits where you've been in a scrape.'

'Auntie Jennison, we're so close now.'

She gave Travis one of her looks. 'Home tomorrow,' she repeated.

Travis shrugged his shoulders.

Big school came as a shock to Travis. He had only a few friends from junior school. Everyone seemed to tower over him, and some of the pupils looked like men. He noticed that two or three of them even had moustaches. The older boys and girls seemed to have modified their uniforms into a more fashionable style, and the playground was teeming with what seemed a boisterous, noisy, unruly mob. Travis felt threatened and just wanted to go home.

Six weeks later, just coming up to half-term, Travis had settled into becoming one of the unruly mob and felt quite at ease in his new environment. By mutual consent with his parents, Auntie Jennison and Mr Pomphrey, Travis had shelved all time travelling until half-term; but with the prospect of searching out his Granddad Travis, he was getting the itch.

'Becky's coming up to visit, Travis,' his mum said.

'When's that, Mum?' Travis asked.

'Well, half-term of course, silly.'

'Shan't be here, but say hello for me,' Travis replied.

'Oh yes you will, young man! You hardly ever see your sister, and the baby's due soon.'

'Well, I'll see her when she's had it then, won't I?'

'I'm not standing here arguing with you, Travis Travis; you'll do as I say!'

He went off in a sulk.

Becky waddled in for half-term. Travis looked at her in amazement and said, 'Coo, look how fat you are!'

'Don't be so rude, Travis,' said his dad.

'It's all right, Dad; he's quite right. The doctor says I'm carrying far too much weight.'

'Perhaps you've got twins in there, Becky?' said Travis, pointing at her stomach.

'I see you've had a word with him, Dad,' Becky said.

'Yes, I know all about it now, thank you, Becky. Mind, I don't think I like the sound of it very much. Have you had a scan?'

'Well yes, as a matter of fact I have. Why d'you ask?'

'Perhaps it *is* twins – after all, you are huge,' Travis said, prodding his sister's stomach gently.

'No, it's definitely not twins, Travis! They're not stupid at the hospital – they're doing scans all the time.'

'I still think it's twins…'

Travis's dad looked at his son but Travis avoided his eyes. 'Here, can you spare me a few minutes?' his dad asked, 'and we can leave the women to have a natter in peace.'

Travis's dad put his arm around Travis's shoulder and guided him into the dining room.

'You promised not to go time travelling until half-term, didn't you, Travis?'

'But I haven't been. Honest, Dad.'

'Well, what was all that about in there just now?'

'I don't know what you mean, Dad,' Travis said innocently.

'Yes, you do, my lad – about twins! I'm not stupid, Travis.'

'Oh, that.'

'Yes, *that.*'

'Can you remember just after Becky went home at Easter, you sat me down and explained things to me?'

'Yes.'

'I went and had a look, not long after I started playing; she is having twins, Dad – a boy and a girl – and they will be born a bit early.'

'Hang on, son,' his dad interrupted. 'I don't want to hear any more; I've heard too much already.'

'Look, Dad, I know there won't be any babies yet. If I stay at home tomorrow, can I go down to Auntie Jennison the day after? Half-term is only for a week.'

'I'll have to think of something to tell Becky…'

'Thanks, Dad!' Travis gave his father a hug and ran off to the telephone.

'I'll be down tomorrow, then, Auntie Jennison … How's Alex? … See you tomorrow then, Auntie Jennison, bye.'

Travis's dad persuaded Mr Pomphrey (not that he needed any persuasion) to accompany Travis to visit Auntie Jennison's, and they set off for the train at midday.

'I've never heard anything so ridiculous,' Becky said to her mother, 'chaperone indeed! She's quite mad, you know.'

'I've told you all before,' Mrs Travis said, 'she's just a little eccentric, that's all.'

The puppy went round and round in circles when Travis and Mr Pomphrey put in an appearance, and they could both hear Charlie squawking from the dining room. 'Everyone's pleased to see you,' Auntie Jennison said; she proffered her cheek to Mr Pomphrey and then made a lunge at Travis.

'Hang on, Auntie Jennison,' Travis said, 'I've got something for you.' He reached into his pocket. 'Here you are, Auntie Jennison.'

'Oh, Travis, thank you – it's exquisite! Look, Bill, look at what Travis has brought me! Look, Alex.'

She bent down and showed the puppy the small silver ashtray she held in her hand. Alex duly obliged by barking and running round and round again. 'He likes it, Travis, and so do I. Now come here…'

Oh dear, Travis thought.

After a late tea, Mr Pomphrey, Auntie Jennison and Travis sat down to discuss their next move.

'Now we need to find out two things,' Auntie Jennison announced. 'First, where's Thomas's scarper button, and second, where's Thomas?'

'I think, Auntie,' said Mr Pomphrey, 'that Travis needs to concentrate on the scarper button first. After all, it's the only way of bringing Thomas back, as far as we know.'

'Marvellous, absolutely marvellous! Good thinking, Bill.' Auntie Jennison looked approvingly at Mr Pomphrey. 'What a brain… don't you think so, Travis?'

'Yes, Auntie Jennison, I do, so I'll concentrate on Granddad's scarper button then,' Travis replied.

'Yes, that's settled then, Travis. The scarper button it is,' Auntie Jennison said. 'Now, what do you suppose the two policemen did with it?'

'*Sold it*,' Mr Pomphrey and Travis chorused simultaneously.

'Exactly!' Auntie Jennison said. 'A second-hand shop or perhaps a pawnshop.'

'Or a jeweller's,' Mr Pomphrey said.

'Or a jeweller's,' Auntie Jennison repeated.

'There can't be that many near Polperro, can there, Auntie Jennison?' Travis asked hopefully.

'Wouldn't have thought so. I don't think there would be anything in Polperro – mostly gift shops,' Auntie Jennison replied. 'Better to try somewhere else close by, I think.'

'Perhaps Looe or Plymouth, Travis,' Mr Pomphrey suggested.

'Travis, nip out to the platform and have a look in the book, will you, sweetheart?' Auntie Jennison asked.

Travis went out to the shed and found a platform quite close by in Looe; he was sorely tempted to go there and then, but he knew that upsetting Auntie Jennison didn't pay, so reluctantly he went back into the house.

'Here we are, Auntie Jennison,' he said, 'platform 400, Looe, Cornwall. I'll get straight down there.'

'Travis, you'll need money, you know,' Auntie Jennison said. 'Somehow you'll need to get some Blairoes.'

Mr Pomphrey fished in his waistcoat pocket. 'Here, Travis, these should fetch something.' Travis looked and Mr Pomphrey was holding his hand open. On his palm were his war medals.

'I couldn't, Mr Pomphrey, I just couldn't.'

'Take my gold watch then, Travis, you'll need something to barter with.'

Reluctantly, Travis took hold of Mr Pomphrey's gold watch and chain and slipped it into his pocket. 'I'll only part with this as a last resort, Mr Pomphrey,' he said.

'If that's all it takes to see good old Thomas again, it'll be well worth it,' Mr Pomphrey said.

'Auntie Jennison, Mr Pomphrey,' Travis said, 'I know it's getting late, but could I go and have a quick look at platform 400, please.'

'Set your alarm for one hour – not a minute more, Travis; by then it will be bedtime,' said Auntie Jennison.

Travis was out through the back door before you could say knife.

'Hello, Travis,' Mentor said, 'I'm coming with you today, and you know what that means, don't you?'

'Yes, I know, Mentor. It means you'll soon be moving on to somebody else.'

'You don't sound very pleased, Travis; after all, it means you can manage without me.'

'I don't expect you to understand this, Mentor, but I really will miss you,' Travis replied.

'Yes, you're right there, Travis, I don't understand. I suppose we'd better get on.'

Extremely cautiously, Travis gingerly opened platform 400's door. Standing right in front of him was a man. 'Hello,' he said. Travis slowly raised his hand to his scarper button. 'Don't be afraid… you're a visitor, right?'

Travis nodded his head; he looked the man up and down. He was about twenty-four or five, chubby, with rounded cheeks, thick, pouting lips and carefully groomed, wavy fair hair. He looks like his mum had dressed him ready to come out, Travis thought. The man slowly undid a button on his shirt, and Travis could see a scarper button.

'Yes, it's all right, I'm a visitor as well,' the man said. He spoke with a soft voice. Up north, Travis thought, they'd call him a 'soft lad'.

'What's your name?' the man asked, with a slight lisp. Without waiting for a reply, he said, 'I'm Christopher Higgins, but you can call me Chrissie, everybody calls me Chrissie… What's your name?'

'I'm Travis – pleased to meet you.' Travis stuck his hand out in a grown-up fashion.

'Yes, and I'm pleased to meet you, Travis,' he said, pumping Travis's hand up and down. 'Tell me, what's your guide's name?'

'It's Mentor,' Travis replied.

'Mine's Hector. Hang on, he's just saying he remembers Mentor. Hector says hello.'

'Not Hopeless Hector – he's useless, thick as a plank! Travis, let's go, let's get out of here. Quick, press the scarper button,' Mentor said inside Travis's head.

'Mentor said hello as well, Chrissie,' Travis answered.

'You can't be visiting, or else I wouldn't be able to see you, so that means you must be platform-hopping. You're a bit young for that… you'll be in trouble if you get caught.'

'Actually,' Travis said proudly, sticking his chest out, 'I'm a player.'

'A *player*! I don't believe it. I'm impressed. How old are you?'

'I'm ten and eleven-twelfths.'

'That's amazing, and there's me – I've only been visiting for six months.'

'Yes, but look what a divvy guide he's got.'

Travis ignored Mentor and went on, 'You might be some use to me, actually…'

'Mind what you say to him, Travis, he sounds like he's as stupid as his guide is.'

'Anything I can do, anything at all – I like helping people,' Chrissie said. 'What time slot are you from, and what are you actually doing here?'

'Don't tell him anything, Travis.' Mentor raised his voice inside Travis's head.

'I'm from 2004 and I'm doing… I'm doing a project – it's on the Polperro bodies.'

'A *project*… how strange. I don't really understand.'

Travis tapped the side of his nose knowingly. 'Can't say too much, you understand.'

'Yes, of course, I shouldn't pry,' Chrissie said. 'Now, how do you want me to help?'

'I need newspapers to know what happened to my... to the man who committed the murder... and I need a list of all the jewellers, second-hand shops and pawnbrokers in a twenty-mile radius of here. Can you do that for me?'

'Easy! The man, I've suddenly thought – you know his name is Travis, same as yours. Hardly any relation, though, eh? Not to a murderer; he was fast-tracked!'

'Fast-tracked? What d'you mean?' Travis asked.

'It's the new justice system. Some people think it's crazy. There's no trial really, you're just guilty and that's that. He got fifty years and no parole. Still, he deserved it.'

'Where would they have taken him? What prison is he in?'

'Could be anywhere. Since they've started the new system it seems half the country's building new prisons and the other half are in them!' He started laughing. 'I know I shouldn't laugh, but the world's gone mad.'

'Look,' Travis said, 'I haven't got much time at the moment...'

'That's a good one,' Chrissie said, 'a time traveller with no time!' He started laughing again.

'If I come back tomorrow, or at some time to suit you, can you see what you can find out for me?'

'Tomorrow then, same time, if you promise me one thing?'

'What's that?'

'Can I watch you disappear?'

'I'm back, Auntie Jennison! I'm back, Mr Pomphrey!'

'You weren't even gone an hour, Travis. That's a good boy – any news?' Auntie Jennison asked.

'*Tell her you've met a right couple of divvies, Travis,*' Mentor said.

'I came out of the platform in Looe, Auntie Jennison, and bumped straight into another visitor; it was a bit of luck really. I've asked him to do some donkey work for me, and I'm going back tomorrow to get the results.'

'Splendid news, Travis; we can all sleep well tonight.'

'Auntie, Travis, I've been thinking,' Mr Pomphrey said. 'Wouldn't it be easier if you just took a trip into the future and had a look to see if your granddad ever turns up?'

'I'll answer that one, Bill,' Auntie Jennison said. 'Although Travis knows the answer only too well, don't you, Travis?'

Travis could feel himself going red. 'Dad told you then, Auntie Jennison?'

'Yes, he did, Travis, and the only reason you weren't in a lot of trouble was because in the first place you had only started playing, and in the second place, that imbecile Mentor didn't warn you!'

Mentor stayed very quiet.

'I don't understand, Auntie.' Mr Pomphrey sounded puzzled.

'It's like this, Bill, you are not allowed to pry into anything to do with your immediate family or yourself. For instance, in Travis's case he went to have a look at Becky at the end of her pregnancy. What if she had died?'

'But hang on, Auntie, didn't you have a look and come back and tell me I had still got a good few years left yet?'

'Sorry, can't stop! Those beans are playing havoc with me.' Auntie Jennison rushed out, blowing off loudly.

Chapter Twenty-eight

'Hello, Travis, you're punctual,' said Chrissie. 'I like punctual. I'm a very punctual person myself, and if everybody were punctual a lot more, things would get done. That's a lot of the trouble in this world, you know: no self-discipline. No one cares any more, no one is punctual any more… well, not many people, anyway.'

Travis had been in Chrissie's company for less than thirty seconds and already he was beginning to feel annoyed. 'Anything for me, Chrissie?' he asked sharply.

Chrissie produced a list of shops from his pocket and some newspaper cuttings. 'Here you are, Travis; and this is ever so exciting, you know, nothing exciting ever happens to me.'

'What – you're a visitor and nothing exciting ever happens? Isn't being a visitor enough?'

'I'd like to be a player like you one day, Travis. Now, that *would* be exciting.'

'You never know, Chrissie, you never know,' Travis replied.

'I think Hector and Chrissie are well matched,' Mentor said, 'just like a pair of pumpkins at Halloween: nothing inside their heads, scraped right out.'

Travis tried hard to keep a straight face. 'Thank you for all your trouble, Chrissie,' he said.

'No, no trouble at all. Is there anything else I can do – anything at all? You've only got to say the word; just say the word.'

'Tell you what, Chrissie, if there's anything anytime, I'll come and knock on your door, all right?'

'I'll be waiting, Travis. Just one thing; can I watch you disappear again?'

'Chrissie, you don't know what pleasure it gives me.'

Travis sat in the carriage studying the list of shops. He must have been up all night sorting this lot out, he thought; the newspaper cuttings would have to wait until later. The list went on and on, right as far as Plymouth in one direction and Truro in the other. Travis made his mind up: I suppose I'll just have to go back and see Chrissie, he thought.

'I'm back,' Travis said.

'But you've only just gone – that's amazing!' Chrissie said.

'It's not amazing at all. You're a visitor – you know how it all works,' said Travis.

'Yes, of course, I wasn't thinking. Sorry.'

'*You need a brain to think*,' Mentor said.

'I need to know something else, if you could help…' Travis began.

'Anything, I've told you before, anything.'

'The two policemen, the ones who arrested my namesake – I need to know the extent of their district. You know their beat?'

'My uncle's a policeman. I can ask him if you like.'

'*Be careful, Travis*,' said Mentor, '*he's bound to say the wrong thing.*'

Travis decided to throw caution to the winds. 'Yes, I need to know, but it's important that you don't mention me.'

'You can trust me. After all, I'm a visitor, aren't I?'

'Same time tomorrow, OK?' Travis said.

'Yes, that's fine. One thing…'

'Yes, I know,' said Travis. 'Watch!'

'Right on time! I knew I could rely on you, Travis,' said Chrissie. 'What have you been doing since I saw you yesterday?'

'Chrissie, what planet are you on?' Travis said, growing exasperated. 'It's tomorrow for you, but all I did was reset the coordinates.'

'Of course… you must think I'm really stupid, Travis.'

'*Go on, Travis, tell him! Go on, I double dare you!*' Mentor said.

'No, I don't think you're stupid, Chrissie.'

'*You little liar*,' Mentor said.

'Right, what have you found out then, Chrissie?'

'I asked my uncle and he said they only go as far as Looe and Liskeard.'

'You didn't mention me, did you?'

'Only in passing.'

'Oh, Chrissie! I asked you not to say anything.'

'*Told you he was stupid, Travis,*' Mentor said.

'I only said you wanted to be a policeman and you wondered how far you had to go, that's all.'

'Is that all you said? Well, thank you then, Chrissie, I really have to go now; but if I need you, I'll be back.'

'That was in a film, wasn't it, Travis?'

'What was?'

'I'll be back.'

'If you say so, Chrissie. Bye now.'

'Travis?'

'I know.'

Travis pushed the button. Sitting in the carriage, he tried working out the best time to go back to Looe, hopefully avoiding bumping into Chrissie. In the end, it was 'eenie, meenie, minie, mo'. Travis crossed his fingers and pushed the 'go' button. He eased the platform door open, and a quick look around confirmed that he was alone. Behind the platform was a low fence, and Travis could see a roadway beyond. He climbed the fence and put as much distance between the platform and himself as he could. A little breathless, he slowed down to a more leisurely pace and started towards the first shop on his list.

One look at the place told Travis he was wasting his time and he took his pencil and crossed it off the list. He trudged around for a good hour and there were only two left to go by the time he came to Mr Goldberg's shop.

The door creaked and the old brass bell jangled as Travis walked in the shop. Mr Goldberg was standing behind his wire mesh. He looked over the top of his spectacles and beamed at Travis; he liked children. 'Hello, my son,' he said, 'what is it I can be doing for you?'

Travis produced Mr Pomphrey's gold watch and chain from his pocket and dangled it in front of Mr Goldberg's face. 'I want to sell this, please sir,' Travis replied.

Mr Goldberg opened the wire mesh hatch and held his hand out. Travis reluctantly gave him the watch, and the pawnbroker turned the watch over and over in his hand.

'A fine piece, this. Where did you get it from?'

'A friend of mine gave it to me,' said Travis.

Mr Goldberg felt around in his pockets and produced a small pocket knife with an ivory handle; he opened the knife and revealed a very thin blade.

'What are you going to do, sir?' Travis asked, looking worried.

'Having a look inside. It's all right, the blade is so thin there will be no damage. Who did you say gave you the timepiece?' Mr Goldberg asked.

'Mr Pomphrey,' Travis replied.

Mr Goldberg went through his pockets again. 'What have I done with my eyepiece?' He looked along the counter and on the floor. Mr Goldberg opened the drawer set in his counter and started to look inside. 'Look at the mess in here! One day I am cleaning it out.'

Travis watched disinterestedly as Mr Goldberg produced first an old pair of scissors, a spectacle case, several pieces of paper, a couple of paper clips and some rubber bands. He carried on rummaging around inside the drawer. Two pens, a stapling machine, some old receipts, a scarper button, a roll of Scotch tape appeared... and, eventually, his eyepiece.

Travis's eyes almost popped right out of his head, for there, sitting on the counter, was his granddad's scarper button; he fought to contain his excitement.

'Who did you say gave you this?' Mr Goldberg asked.

'Mr Pomphrey,' Travis heard himself saying; it was almost like he was in a dream.

Mr Goldberg had the back of the watch open and was peering inside. 'What is his Christian name?'

'It's Bill, sir,' Travis replied, still in a trance.

Mr Goldberg could see through the eyepiece that the grime around the edge of the watch meant that it hadn't been opened for a long time. There inside he could see inscribed: *To William Pomphrey, from all his colleagues. July 1988.*

'This Bill Pomphrey, very old he must be; the date on the watch is 1988.'

'Yes sir, he's very very old,' Travis replied.

'He must be a good friend to you; do you know how much this watch is worth?'

'He's my bestest friend in the whole world since Alex died,' Travis said sadly.

'Who was Alex?' Mr Goldberg asked.

'He got—' Travis hesitated; no need to say too much, he thought. 'Run over and killed.'

'Oh, I am sorry. Here, don't look so sad. I cheer you up – do you like tricks? I show you a trick with this watch.'

From under the counter Mr Goldberg produced a small red box covered in red velvet. He opened the lid on the top and popped the watch inside and then he shut the lid. Then he got another red box, identical to the first one from under the counter and placed it on the counter a little way from the first box. He opened the lid and invited Travis to look inside; Travis could see it was completely empty.

From inside his jacket he produced a conjurer's wand, made a few passes over both boxes, and with a flourish opened the first box. It was empty. With a flourish he held out the other box to Travis. Travis opened it, and sure enough inside was Mr Pomphrey's watch.

'Wow, that's really good, sir! I didn't see how you did that.' Travis was impressed.

'Now, about this watch. I can let you have twelve hundred Blairoes for it, and I rob myself.' Mr Goldberg had his business head back on.

'If you let me have the... the piece of jewellery on the counter,' Travis said, 'you can keep the watch.'

'I keep the watch, no, but the jewellery is broken. It's worthless. A businessman I am, but I don't rob children.' Mr Goldberg shook his head.

'I really need the jewellery, sir, you see...' Travis broke off and undid his shirt, showing Mr Goldberg his scarper button. 'That one on the counter belonged to my grandfather. If you look, it's the same as mine, it's a family thing.'

'Well, well I never,' said Mr Goldberg, handing Travis the scarper button. 'Take it and keep it, I want nothing for it.'

'Can I have the watch back, sir? You see, I don't need to sell it now,' said Travis.

'Is the price no good? I can go another hundred, but no more, you understand.'

'No, it's not the money, sir; honestly, I've changed my mind, that's all.'

Mr Goldberg reluctantly took one last look at Mr Pomphrey's watch, and Travis slipped it safely in his pocket with the scarper button. Feeling very relieved, he said to Mr Goldberg, 'I'm something of a conjuror myself, sir. Would you like to see a trick that I promise you will baffle you for the rest of your life?'

'This I must see,' Mr Goldberg replied.

'Come and stand round this side of the counter, sir, and face me.'

Mr Goldberg undid the heavy door at the side of the counter and approached Travis.

'All right, just there, that will do fine,' said Travis. 'Now please notice, I have nothing up my sleeves.' He pulled his sleeves up in a theatrical way. 'Now you can see there's no way I can reach your brass bell.' Travis stretched himself to show it was out of reach. 'So if I leave the shop, the bell is bound to ring, agreed?'

'Agreed,' said Mr Goldberg.

'Also, there is no way I can open or close the front door without it squeaking.' Travis opened and shut the door to demonstrate.

'Yes, yes,' Mr Goldberg said.

'I want you to turn your back to me, sir, and as soon as you hear me say goodbye, turn around slowly, all right?'

'Agreed, shall I turn away now?' Mr Goldberg asked.

'Yes, that's it – hold it right there, sir. Goodbye.'

'I would have loved to have seen his face after you disappeared, Travis,' said Mr Pomphrey, chuckling.

'I bet he went and looked inside his grandfather clock,' Auntie Jennison cackled.

'I can just see him stood opening and closing the front door and trying to stop his bell ringing!' Mr Pomphrey chuckled away. 'Anyway, no more suspense, Travis. Let's see the scarper button,' he demanded.

With a flourish, Travis produced the scarper button and Mr Pomphrey's watch from his pocket. 'Here's your watch back, Mr Pomphrey,' Travis said. 'I'm glad I didn't have to part with it.'

Mr Pomphrey grasped the watch and held it lovingly to his chest. He put the chain through his waistcoat buttonhole, placed the watch back in his waistcoat pocket and patted it. 'I never thought I'd see it again, Travis; that watch means such a lot to me.'

Auntie Jennison sat looking at Mr Pomphrey. 'Take a good look at that man, Travis, and hold this moment in your heart. This isn't a man – he's a saint.'

Double yuck, fingers down the throat! thought Travis.

Auntie Jennison picked up the scarper button. 'Look, you can see where it's been cut from Thomas's neck,' she said.

'Let me see, Auntie.' Mr Pomphrey took the scarper button and held the broken chain up to the light. 'Yes, look here, you can see where it's been cut with something. You know, I've never held a scarper button before; it's strange, but for metal it feels quite warm.'

'I've never noticed that before, have you, Travis?' Auntie Jennison asked.

'No, never, Auntie Jennison,' Travis replied.

'Such an observant man – isn't he observant, Travis? He doesn't miss a trick.' Auntie Jennison sat there gleaming.

For the second time that day Travis thought, *Yuck*. He said, 'I nearly forgot in all the excitement... Chrissie gave me a load of newspaper cuttings. They're out in the shed. I'll go out and fetch them.'

Auntie Jennison, Mr Pomphrey and Travis sat round in silence passing the newspaper cuttings to each other; all you could hear was the rustle of paper and the occasional noise from Auntie Jennison.

'Fifty years – that's terrible!' Mr Pomphrey declared. 'No jury, no real evidence, what sort of system is that?'

'At least we know they took him to Samson. That's a start, anyway,' said Auntie Jennison.

'Can you go and get him before he's done too much of his sentence, Travis?' Mr Pomphrey asked.

"Fraid not, Mr Pomphrey,' Travis said, shaking his head. 'You see, I can't bring him back until the same length of time has elapsed there as has here since he disappeared. We need to know where he is in the year…' Travis hesitated.

'2043, Travis,' said Mr Pomphrey.

'Wasn't that quick, Travis. Wasn't Bill quick there? You were quick, Bill.'

Oh no, Travis thought, she's beginning to sound just like Chrissie.

'Anyway, I know you're flushed with success, Travis,' Auntie Jennison said, 'but I'm afraid you've got to think about school, and you really must see Becky before she goes back. I suggest that you, Bill and I – not forgetting Alex – jump on the coach and get going. I'll leave Charlie enough food and water for a couple of days. All right?'

Auntie Jennison had made her mind up, so there was no arguing. She phoned for the times of the coaches and they set off up the road to the coach stop.

'Mr Pomphrey, you've still got your bobble cosy on,' Travis remarked.

'I know I have, Travis,' said Mr Pomphrey. 'I'm not getting old and forgetful, if that's what you think. It's just more comfortable than an ordinary hat, that's all.'

'So that's why you're wearing your bobble slippers as well, is it, Bill?'

Auntie Jennison, blowing off all the time, and Travis both fell about laughing.

Auntie Jennison had messed up the coach times and they ended up having to get a connection, and of course it was all 'that stupid man on the phone's fault', as far as Auntie Jennison was concerned.

'Well, Auntie Jennison, it looks like we've got an hour and a half to kill,' Travis said.

'Yes, come on, there's a pub over there. Bill, run over and see if they let children and dogs in.'

Mr Pomphrey came back out of the pub and beckoned to Auntie Jennison and Travis. They went inside and found a corner table almost hidden from the bar area. Travis heard Auntie

Jennison let out a contented sigh and she settled herself so that she had a full view of the bar.

'Oh look, Travis,' she said her eyes lighting up, 'what a lovely green ashtray!'

Oh dear, Travis thought, she's on a mission.

'Right then, Auntie, Travis – what can I get you?' Mr Pomphrey asked.

'Bill, I feel quite overcome,' Auntie Jennison said. 'It's that stupid man on the phone – he's put me all on edge... I'd better have a brandy; make it a big one and put some port in it, there's a dear, and twenty cigarettes from the machine. I appear to only have about sixty-odd here.'

Mr Pomphrey never batted an eyelid. 'Travis, what can I get you?'

'A lemonade will be fine, thank you, Mr Pomphrey,' Travis replied. He was determined that this time he'd guard every ashtray in the pub if need be.

Auntie Jennison sat sipping her drink and sucking the life out of her cigarette, Travis watching her every move.

'Right, I need the toilet,' Auntie Jennison announced.

'Me too,' added Travis. 'Come on, Auntie Jennison, we'll go and find them together.'

'Lead on then, Travis, lead on,' Auntie Jennison said.

Travis walked slowly in front of her, keeping one eye to her all the time until they reached the toilets. The gents' door was right next to the ladies'. Travis watched Auntie Jennison go into the ladies and he whipped into the gents, stood behind the door for a few seconds and then re-emerged and leant against the wall, waiting for Auntie Jennison. She duly emerged and they made their way back to the table.

'Come on, you two,' said Mr Pomphrey, looking at his pocket watch, 'ten minutes before the coach leaves.'

Travis again watched Auntie Jennison and stayed right beside her as they left the pub. He glanced back the table they had occupied, and the dark green glass ashtray Auntie Jennison had been using was still there. Mission accomplished, Travis thought.

Auntie Jennison and Mr Pomphrey started to cross the road, with Travis just behind, when suddenly Auntie Jennison stopped in her tracks. 'It's no good,' she said, 'I'll have to go back – I seem to have left my brolly behind.'

Quick as a flash, Travis replied, 'You never had a brolly with you, Auntie Jennison.'

'Oh no, of course not,' she said. 'How silly of me!'

Travis strutted along feeling rather pleased with himself.

They were so late by the time they got to Travis's house that Becky, who was now absolutely humongously huge (as Travis had put it), and her husband, were just about to leave.

Once Becky saw Auntie Jennison and Travis, the coats came back off and they all sat down. Travis was itching to show his father the scarper button, but he resigned himself to making small talk until Becky decided to go.

Auntie Jennison settled herself down, and as usual from her pinny pocket produced her now four packets of cigarettes and three lighters.

Travis sprang up confidently. 'All right, Auntie Jennison,' he said, 'don't get up, I'll fetch you an ashtray.'

Auntie Jennison reached into her pinny pocket again and produced a dark green glass ashtray. 'No need, Travis, my sweet, no need…'

Chapter Twenty-nine

Thomas Travis stood at the doorway of his new home. The governor never referred to 'cells'; true, there was a lock on the door, but Thomas had been given a key and he was free to come and go from his room at will.

Thomas surveyed the room. It was surprisingly large; the top half of the walls painted in a soft, tasteful yellow, the bottom in a calming green. A bed was placed against the wall on one side of the room and a desk-type table and chair along the other. A small cubicle revealed a toilet, shower and a small washbasin. Not bad, Thomas thought.

The prison governor believed relieving the inmates, or 'Samsons' as he preferred to call them, of their freedom was punishment enough; no need to treat them like animals.

Thomas walked into the room, pushed the door together and flopped down on the bed, staring at the ceiling. His thoughts strayed to his loved ones forty years away. He knew in his heart that Sarah, his wife, would never cope without him; he only hoped young Tom could be a strength to her. Come on, Thomas, he told himself, snap out of it. He got up and turned towards the door. Pinned on the back of the door was a notice which read:

> Welcome to Samson Island. You are now a Samson. Escape from here is impossible, and attempting escape is punished by banishment to a high security prison or the use of deadly force, whichever is deemed appropriate.
>
> The aim of this establishment, ultimately, is to be self-sufficient and need no Government funding whatsoever; therefore during your stay with us you will work a forty-hour week. This establishment will be run as a business; your input is valuable and will be sought on a regular basis.
>
> Ultimately there will be two hundred and fifty Samsons living together here, hopefully in harmony. Violent or unreasonable conduct will be punished by either of the above methods, which-

ever is deemed appropriate. The governor is available to you, at any reasonable time, to discuss any problems you may encounter, or indeed for any other matters.

This is your home now; make the most of your stay.

Thomas found it difficult to believe he was reading a prison notice, not that he had any experience along those lines. Sounds more like holiday camp, he thought, and then he remembered he was off to the quarry the following day.

In the event, Thomas only stayed hewing out granite for three weeks. Younger, stronger and fitter Samsons were arriving at Samson Island and Thomas was moved to actually helping to construct the wall for the enclosed garden. Every day Thomas seemed to gain a new skill, and quite soon he was actually shoulder to shoulder laying stone with the governor.

The wall itself was quite impressive. The north-facing structure stood some ten metres high; Thomas soon found that no one remembered feet and inches. The base of the wall was a metre and a half wide and tapered on the outside to meet the vertical inside wall. At the top, the wall measured half a meter across and was finished with a solid granite coping stone. The opposite wall was much lower, to let in as much winter light as possible, and the two other walls rose gradually to meet the north wall. By the time the wall had its topping out ceremony, Thomas had already celebrated the first anniversary of his incarceration.

The area the wall enclosed was three-quarters of an acre, and a news film crew from the mainland came to feature it on local television.

The one thing that Samson Island was short of, besides trees, was topsoil for the new garden, and Thomas had often puzzled where it would come from. He'd asked the governor on more than one occasion and always got the same answer: 'Shouldn't be a problem.'

One Saturday morning, shortly after the wall was finished, Officer Harding knocked on Thomas's open door. 'Governor would like to see you, Thomas, in his office, if you please.'

Thomas lightly tapped the governor's door.

'Come.'

'You wanted to see me, Governor.'

'Do sit down, Thomas. Always on about the topsoil. Well, got a job for you, need someone to supervise. Go and get your chip removed, then report to Harding. Cut along then, there's a good chap.'

Thomas had hardly got his bum on the chair when he was standing back in the corridor trying to take it all in. He went along to the doctor's office and then on to find Officer Harding.

'What's going on, Mike?' Thomas asked.

'The governor's taking a chance on you, Thomas. You're to go to the mainland, no chip, only me with you, and organise the shipments of topsoil; it's an opportunity you'll only get once.'

'Come off it, Mike,' Thomas said, 'we both know you don't need a prisoner to organise shipments of topsoil. What's it all about?'

'You're nobody's fool, are you, Thomas?' Mike replied. 'The truth is that the governor's been getting a lot of stick from his bosses recently over his softly-softly methods, and he needs some ammunition—'

'Like, look at this model prisoner!' Thomas interrupted. 'We can send him off Samson, and he likes it so much he can't wait to come back... Is that it? How do you know I won't run away?'

'I don't think you've anywhere to run, Thomas.'

'That's very perceptive of you, Mike, very perceptive indeed.'

Five years later, the prison authorities had changed their view of the governor of Samson, and prisons all around the country were adopting his methods. The walled garden had become a valuable asset to the economy of the prison, and the addition of an orangery a couple of years later, and several hothouses, suggested by Thomas, had put him in the governor's good books. Thomas had spent every available spare minute in the prison library learning all he could about horticulture, and he used his time in the garden putting that knowledge into practice.

As head gardener of Samson, Thomas enjoyed his position. Resigning himself to spending the rest of his life there, he decided to make the best of a bad job. Thomas as head gardener was now invited to the monthly planning meetings which influenced the whole economy of the prison. Seven years into Thomas's sentence, the governor was speaking at the monthly meeting.

'Gentlemen, I think congratulations all round are in order. Last month's figures, now in, show machine shop profits up an additional five per cent; the call centre, two new contracts and three per cent increase in profit; and as usual Thomas here has done wonders with our diets. Thomas's suggestion for our own fishing vessel is being investigated and I have high hopes in that direction.

'You all know my aim is to run Samson as a business. Have to tell you, though, I've taken things as far as we can, and without fresh ideas the dream can't be realised. Close to the target, but tantalisingly, it's just over the horizon.

'On another note we now have thirty-one Samsons unchipped, Thomas here of course being the first. Can't imagine how we forgot to chip you when you came back from shore leave that time…'

'Hardly *leave* though, was it, Governor?' Thomas retorted.

The governor ignored him and went on. 'Must have fresh ideas… under pressure from above, you know. Well, if that's it, all dismissed.'

Thomas mulled over what the governor had said over the following weeks; the governor's dream had become Thomas's dream as well. Then, one day, out of the blue, Thomas said to him, 'I think we should consider opening the gardens to the public, Governor. That would be a first-rate source of revenue.'

'Lot of dangerous men here, Thomas. Don't know about that one.'

'Like me, you mean, Governor?' Thomas started laughing.

The governor looked at Thomas pensively; he said not a word, turned on his heel and was gone. He's a strange one, that one, Thomas thought.

Later that day Thomas watched as the governor paced around the garden, deep in thought. Later still, he was marching around with a clipboard in one hand and a tape measure in the other, mumbling inaudibly to himself.

A few weeks later, the governor, accompanied by two men in immaculate suits and an equally well-dressed woman, turned up in the walled garden. Thomas thought how ridiculous they looked, all sporting brand new safety helmets, and fluorescent jackets – the governor included.

'Thomas – over here, a moment of your time.'

Thomas obediently went over to where the governor and his guests were standing. 'Yes, Governor,' he said, acknowledging the others with a nod of his head.

'Pods, Thomas. What d'you think of pods?'

'Not quite with you, Governor,' Thomas said.

'Pods, man... Eden Project and all that.' Thomas was completely stumped. 'Talk to you later, cut along.'

By the time Thomas was called into the governor's office he had been to the prison library, had looked up all the information on the Eden Project and felt quite confident to talk to the governor about it.

'Made me look a bit of a fool back there, Thomas, don't you know?' the governor said. 'All the world like you'd never heard of the Eden Project! Been thinking about your idea. Visitors to the establishment and all that, cracking idea; like it, like it a lot. That's what the fuss was all about this morning, Thomas. I've got funding for pods – artificial sunlight, marvellous for the winter blues, you know. We should be open for business in two years and in profit in seven. Here, take this lot, read, digest and come and see me tomorrow.' He handed Thomas an enormous folder bulging with papers.

Thomas walked out of the governor's office in a daze; the gardens almost ran themselves, with his team of six, and this was something he could really get his teeth into. He never thought he could feel so elated at being confined in a prison.

The next two years flew by, and Thomas and the governor stood side by side surveying the almost finished project.

'It's a shame we've had to build the wall, Governor,' Thomas said, 'quite ironic, really... building a wall to keep people out!'

'Can't have them getting in without paying, Thomas. Quite a trip across from Tresco and Bryher, but they'll do anything to save paying, some of them. TV crew coming tomorrow, Thomas. I'm going to show you off; as usual, you've done a splendid job, well done.'

The new pods lifted the morale of the whole population of Samson, while the rest of the country was freezing in the dead of winter. The usually dank cold weather was banished to the other side of the metal and plastic, and with the artificial sun shining down it seemed everybody suddenly wanted to be gardeners. The governor, as usual, had everything sorted out, and the strict rotas enforced for occupying the pods worked like clockwork. Sure enough, almost seven years to the day after the pods were started, the prison turned a profit.

Thomas was standing down at the new jetty watching the two liberty boats, *Samson* and *Delilah*, unloading the latest visitors when the governor came up behind him.

'Heard you wanted to see me, Thomas,' said the governor, looking quizzically at him.

Thomas looked around at the governor and started to laugh and laugh. The governor didn't know what was going on but joined in all the same, and soon they were laughing like a pair of hyenas. The visitors filed up past the two of them looking bewildered and wondering, could this really be a prison?

Eventually, Thomas and the governor settled and composed themselves. 'Share the joke then, Thomas, there's a good fellow.'

'Just wondering which one of us was the governor, that's all!' At this they both started laughing again. 'Why I wanted to see you, Governor,' Thomas said, still chuckling, 'is because I've had another idea. There's just room for a shop over there.' Thomas pointed to an area quite near the jetty. We could sell some produce, handicrafts, postcards, mementoes and that sort of thing.'

No one on the island was in the least bit surprised when, two years later, the New Year's Honours List came out, and, there, for all to see, was the prison governor's name. He was to be awarded an OBE.

'You know, Thomas,' the governor said, 'this is your award really. Wish there was something I could do to repay you, but can't let you out, I'm afraid.' He smiled.

'Do you really mean that, Governor – that you'd like to do something for me?' Thomas asked.

'Well within the realms of possibility,' the governor answered.

'I'd like a bath and a proper cistern,' Thomas said.

'A bath, whatever for? No one bathes; lying in your own dirty water… Where would you find a bath anyway, these days? Ridiculous idea! And what's a – that other thing you said – what's that?'

Thomas got special dispensation and went off to visit Cornwall's reclamation yards, where he found a tatty-looking old corner bath and a huge cast iron cistern; he returned to Samson and awaited his purchases.

Mike Harding tapped on Thomas's door. 'I think you're losing your grip, Thomas.'

'How d'you mean, Mike?' Thomas asked.

'Down on the jetty there's a right old load of rubbish, waiting for you!'

Far from the other inmates feeling jealous of Thomas's bath and cistern, as he had feared, they all found it amusing that he wanted to lie in hot water for hours on end – and as for the noise the cistern made, one of the prison comedians would impersonate the noise every time he saw Thomas, much to the amusement of everybody, Thomas included.

Thomas had now been a guest at Samson for more years than he cared to remember, when one morning, whistling away, he strolled along to the governor's office with a sheath of papers in his hand. The door to the governor's office was wide open and just inside was the figure of Officer Harding, ashen-faced and shaking. He stood slumped against the wall with his weapon drawn and pointing vaguely in the direction of the corner of the room. As Thomas walked in, the whole scene opened up before him. The governor's chair was upturned on the floor and there were papers everywhere. In the corner at the far side of the room was the governor with a knife held at his throat. He'd been taken hostage.

Thomas recognised his assailant instantly – a nasty piece of work by the name of Scrivens. Scrivens had one of the governor's arms twisted behind his back and was standing behind his captive almost out of sight; Thomas could only just see the side of Scrivens's face; the point of the knife was being pushed firmly into the governor's neck.

Thomas looked at Mike Harding. 'Give me your weapon, Officer Harding,' he said quietly but authoritatively. Without a word, Mike Harding handed the weapon to Thomas. Thomas turned and faced the governor and Scrivens. 'Let the governor go,' he demanded.

In answer, Scrivens pushed the knife harder into the governor's neck and growled. Thomas watched as a thin trail of blood trickled down and started to soak into the governor's white shirt collar.

'Final warning, Scrivens!' Thomas said.

Scrivens snarled, and in one movement Thomas raised the weapon with his arm outstretched and fired. A needle-thin beam of bluey purple light hissed past the governor's cheek and found its target. The knife hit the floor with a clatter and the governor lurched to one side against the window sill.

Scrivens hit the floor and lay there twitching; Thomas walked slowly towards him turning the weapon sideways in his hand. Scrivens, the governor and Mike Harding heard the *click*, *click*, *click*, as Thomas slid the indicator gauge from mild stun to full kill. Thomas looked down at Scrivens; the man's eyes were wide open, and although unable to move, he stared in dumb terror at Thomas. Thomas bent at the knees slightly, held the weapon against Scrivens's brow and squeezed the trigger. A crackling like distant fireworks echoed around the room, Scrivens twitched once more and was a memory.

'*Gotcha*,' Thomas said.

Still ashen-faced and shaking, Mike Harding came over and knelt down besides Scrivens. After searching for a pulse, he looked up and said, 'My God, Thomas, you've killed him!'

'No, Mike, I've executed him,' Thomas replied. He calmly handed back the weapon to its owner and then he went over to the governor. He picked up his chair and gently lowered him into it.

'Let me have a look at you, Governor,' he said. He inspected the governor's neck and smiled. 'It's just a scratch; you'll live. Actually, Governor, I came in to discuss the surplus of begonias, but I suppose it can wait under the circumstances...'

Two days later, a knock came on Thomas's door. 'Can I come in, Thomas?'

'Course you can, Mike. Here, you sit in the chair.'

Thomas hoisted himself onto his bed and sat cross-legged with his back against the wall. 'Can I get you anything, or shall we ring for room service?' They both chuckled.

'I've come to see you, Thomas, even before I've been to see the governor; first of all, I want to thank you for the other day – you saved both our lives. In all my years in the prison service I've never been so scared! I thought we were both goners, and it's because of that that I've decided to retire. I've already done nearly five years more than I needed to, and I shall be sixty next month, so before my luck runs out I'm calling it a day.'

Thomas sat in a stunned silence, staring at the floor; eventually he looked up and said, 'I really don't know what to say, Mike.'

'There's nothing to say, Thomas. You could wish me luck for the future.'

'That goes without saying, Mike, you know that.'

'I need to ask you something, though, Thomas, and I won't rest until I know the answer. In my heart I know you didn't kill that child; but you are a killer, aren't you?'

Thomas hesitated and then said, 'Yes, you're right. I'm an executioner.'

'What d'you mean – you were a hit man?'

'No, certainly not. I never killed anyone for money. It's more of a moral thing. If they deserved to die, I executed them.'

'You mean you were judge, jury and executioner too?'

'Yes, exactly that.'

'So who gave you the right to decide whether or not someone had to die?'

'Oh Mike, Mike, you sound just like my Auntie Jennison!'

'Auntie Jennison?' Mike asked.

'Auntie Jennison is – was – a relative of mine, and we argued the point about what I did till the cows came home; we could never agree about that.'

'You mean, this auntie of yours knew all about what you did?'

'Oh yes, she knows, I mean *knew*, everything.'

'You've never mentioned having any family before, Thomas. Is she still alive?'

'She was over eighty when I came here, Mike,' Thomas started to chuckle.

'Share the joke then, Thomas,' Mike said.

'No, I was just thinking about Auntie Jennison and her idiosyncrasies, that's all.'

'How d'you mean, Thomas, idiosyncrasies?'

'Auntie Jennison smoked as many cigarettes in a day as she could manage, ate peppermints continually and repeatedly broke wind.'

'She sounds quite a character, this auntie of yours,' Mike said.

'You're not wrong, believe you me!' Thomas started chuckling again.

'Anyway, Thomas, changing the subject completely, the other reason for my visit.' Mike lowered his voice conspiratorially. 'The word is, you're in for a free pardon.'

'A free pardon? My whole life is here, Mike! I'm knocking on a bit myself; where would I go? What would I do? I don't want it, Mike, I don't want it. Now, if you don't mind…'

Thomas turned his head toward the wall, and a dejected Mike Harding left the room, quietly closing the door behind him.

Chapter Thirty

The excitement was mounting in the Travis household. Becky had gone into hospital, Travis's mother had gone with her as a birthing partner, Auntie Jennison had come to stay and they were all just waiting for the word. Of course, Travis already knew what was what, but he had to keep his counsel.

'Can I go and see Mr Pomphrey for a while, Dad?' Travis asked.

'Yes, all right son, if it's all right with him. But if he's busy, mind you come straight back.'

'And Travis,' Auntie Jennison said, 'let Bill know that I'll be round to see him as soon as there's any news.'

Travis knew that wouldn't be for a while, but he said nothing and skipped out.

'Hello, Mr Pomphrey... a message from Auntie Jennison, and is it all right if I stay a while?'

'Course it is, Travis. Here, have a sweet.' Mr Pomphrey handed Travis a sweet – no fluff, no bits on it.

'Thanks, Mr Pomphrey,' Travis said. 'Auntie Jennison says she'll be round later on.'

'All those newspaper cuttings we went through, Travis, and we still really don't know where Thomas ended up.'

'At least we know where he began his prison sentence, though, Mr Pomphrey. It's a starting point.'

'I've worked out the exact date you need to rescue him, Travis, allowing for leap years and all, the very date—'

Travis interrupted, 'That was very good of you, Mr Pomphrey, but there was no need. You see, providing it's over twenty-five years, any day will do.'

'All that work, Travis, and it took me all of five minutes!' said Mr Pomphrey, chuckling. 'Now, I've got something to show you. It doesn't mean anything to me like my watch or medals do, and you can take it to exchange for Blairoes next time you go.'

Mr Pomphrey reached into his waistcoat pocket and produced a small rosewood snuff box. He handed it to Travis. 'Open it, Travis,' he said.

Travis opened the snuffbox; inside, folded carefully, was an old white £5 note.

'I've never seen one of these before, Mr Pomphrey. Is it very old?' asked Travis, unfolding the note.

'If you look at it, Travis, you will see it is from 1938. Together with the snuffbox you should get quite a bit of money. You may need some clothes, for a start; perhaps Auntie Jennison can find out what fashions are like in 2043.'

'Are you sure about this, Mr Pomphrey?' Travis asked.

'I told you they mean nothing to me, nothing at all. Take them.'

'Thank you very much, Mr Pomphrey.'

Travis folded up the £5 note, carefully replaced it in the snuff-box and put it in his pocket. Then he looked at his watch and said, 'I'd better go round home, now, Mr Pomphrey – the phone's about to ring.'

Sure enough, as Travis walked into his home, he could hear his dad talking excitedly to his mum. Travis's dad beckoned for him to go into the living room. Auntie Jennison was sitting on the couch with Alex sitting up on her lap; as soon as the pup saw Travis he jumped down and ran to him. Travis got down on the floor and was playing with the dog when his dad walked in.

'That was Barbara on the phone,' he announced. 'Becky had a little boy, six pounds, one ounce, at five thirty this afternoon… and thirty-five minutes later, a little girl: five pounds ten ounces.'

'Phew, no wonder she was huge!' said Travis.

'When can we see her, Tom?' Auntie Jennison enquired.

'We can all go down tomorrow if you like, Auntie Jennison, and we can make a day of it,' Travis's dad replied.

'Splendid! Travis, off you go round to see Bill. Tell him the news, ask him to put his coat on and to come round – and be sure to bring plenty of money with him.'

'Why, what's happening now, Auntie Jennison?' Travis asked.

'We're off to the pub to wet the babies' heads – that's what!'

Before Travis went around to Mr Pomphrey's house, he sneaked off up to his bedroom. He had a plan.

As usual, Auntie Jennison had chosen a table to sit at, hidden out of sight of the serving area of the bar. Her eyes lit up when she saw the ashtray on the table. Although plastic, it was bright red and bore the logo, 'Watsons', repeated right around the outside.

'Pass me the ashtray, please, Bill,' she said.

Travis watched as she picked it up to examine it, murmured to it and then placed it squarely in front of herself.

'Nice ashtray, Auntie Jennison,' Travis remarked.

'Very nice, Travis, very nice indeed,' Auntie Jennison replied, fondling it.

Travis got up and made his way to the bar. The man standing behind it was a big man, not unlike Mr Pomphrey, and was all smiles.

'What can I get for you then, young man?' he asked.

Travis immediately liked him: 'young man'… Travis was flattered. He reached into his pocket and produced a £5 note. 'My auntie, over there, sir, has took a shine to one of your ashtrays, and I was wondering if I could buy one from you as a present for her. I've got five pounds.'

'What a nice thought! Five pounds, eh? Well, these ashtrays, the brewery provide them, you see, so they don't cost me a penny. Tell you what, you put your money back in your pocket and I'll go and fetch you a new one from out the back.'

The man returned with a brown paper bag in his hand. 'Here you are, young man,' he said, 'compliments of the management. You know, some people wouldn't ask – they'd just take one.'

'Just take one…' Travis repeated. 'Thank you very much, sir.'

Travis rejoined the family at their table. 'I've got a present for you, Auntie Jennison, look.'

'Oh, Travis, what is it?' She peered inside the bag. 'Oh Travis,' she said, 'that's wonderful! Thank you, my love.'

Travis stayed out of arm's reach on his side of the table. 'The man behind the bar gave it to me, Auntie Jennison,' he said.

'How kind – what a nice man! Isn't that kind?' Auntie Jennison leant back and carried on puffing away at her fag.

'Oh, I did enjoy that,' she said, when they got home. 'That was a good idea of yours, Tom, to go out and wet the babies' heads.'

Travis was well pleased with himself. Cured her at last, he thought. He went off to bed thinking about the snuffbox and the white £5 note. Then, making a mental note to ask Auntie Jennison about the currency in the year 2043, he drifted off to sleep.

Next morning, Mr Travis, Travis, Auntie Jennison and Mr Pomphrey set off for the journey to the hospital where Becky was staying. The conversation all the way down revolved around what Travis should or should not do, and much speculation as to the whereabouts of Thomas Travis. For once, Travis thought, the journey seemed to whisk by.

Becky was sitting up in bed looking radiant and just as fat, as Travis felt he just had to tell her; the two tiny babies were in a separate room, and Travis and Mr Pomphrey were the last to go in and see them.

'I wonder if either of them will be visitors, Travis?' Mr Pomphrey asked.

'No way of telling, Mr Pomphrey,' Travis replied.

'I just thought there just might be—'

'Something like 666 on their heads or something?' Travis put in, and they both started laughing.

'I do like their names, though, Travis – Thomas and Sarah, after their great-grandparents.'

'Yes, I like them too; but you know, Mr Pomphrey, I don't feel any different now that I'm an uncle. I thought there might be some difference at least.'

'The difference will come when you get to nurse them, Travis, you'll see.'

The Travis family said their goodbyes and piled into Tom's car. After the return journey, they all arrived home tired but elated. Auntie Jennison decided on staying until the next morning, and the arrangement was that Mr Travis would then drive her home with Mr Pomphrey to keep him company, and then Travis and Mr Pomphrey would go down to see her at the weekend.

Eventually the weekend arrived, and Mr Pomphrey and Travis turned up at Auntie Jennison's in time for Saturday lunch.

'Guess what I've cooked for you, Travis,' said Auntie Jennison, 'it's your favourite. I asked Barbara how you like it, so wash your hands and sit up to the table – you too, Bill.'

Travis was almost frightened to sample Auntie Jennison's attempt at corned beef, jacket potatoes and curried beans. No one could do it like his mum and he knew what Auntie Jennison's idea of knitting gloves was. He sat there gloomily looking at the plate.

'Oh yes, I nearly forgot,' said Auntie Jennison, 'brown sauce.'

She went to the cupboard and came back with a new bottle and put it in front of Travis.

'Thank you, Auntie Jennison,' said Travis. He shook the bottle, undid the lid and carefully let the sauce drizzle onto his food.

'Well, go on, then!' Auntie Jennison had her head almost on Travis's plate. 'Try it.'

Tentatively, Travis lifted the fork to his mouth. Just as he was about to pop the first mouthful in, his eyes strayed to the mantelpiece above the fire opposite him. At each end was an ashtray, bright red in colour, sporting the logo 'Watsons'.

Auntie Jennison had followed Travis's eyes. 'Don't you think they look absolutely splendid, Travis?' she asked.

Travis had eaten the first three mouthfuls of his meal before he even realised that he had done so.

'Well, not too much garlic, is there? I'm not used to garlic.' Auntie Jennison looked inquiringly at Travis.

'Hang on, Auntie Jennison,' Travis said, 'I'm still sampling.'

He concentrated on the job in hand.

'Well?' Auntie Jennison asked again.

'Fabulous, Auntie Jennison, absolutely fabulous! It's better than Mum's.' And Travis meant it too; Auntie Jennison had hidden talents. He knew what he'd be eating at Auntie Jennison's in future.

When the meal was over, while Mr Pomphrey was busy washing the dishes, Travis played with Alex. Auntie Jennison had disappeared into the records room.

'Come and sit down, you two,' she ordered upon her return. 'I've had a look. Those Blairoes never lasted long; they've gone back to pounds, shillings and pence.'

'That's good,' said Mr Pomphrey, 'never did like the decimal currency.'

'It's a bit different this time, though, Bill. There's ten pennies to a shilling and ten shillings to a pound.'

'Sounds like a foreign language to me,' said Travis.

'You'll soon get the hang of it, Travis,' Mr Pomphrey said.

'Right, first thing you need to do then, Travis, is to get yourself some LSD,' said Auntie Jennison.

'What for? That's a drug, isn't it?'

Auntie Jennison and Mr Pomphrey both started laughing. 'Explain it to him, Bill,' she said.

Travis thought his best bet would be to try his luck at the same pawnshop in Looe, setting his time for 2042, to give himself plenty of leeway; he emerged cautiously from platform 400. He could see a bald-headed man standing a little way up the garden with his back to him.

'*Bet that's Chrissie, the divvy.*' Mentor couldn't help himself.

Don't be so cruel, Mentor, Travis thought.

'*Don't talk to him, Travis, or you'll be sorry.*'

The man turned. He looked just like he'd stepped out of the Seventies, platform shoes, flared trousers, a colourful fitted shirt with a huge collar and a droopy long moustache.

What do you look like? Travis thought.

'Chrissie, is that you?' he called out.

'I know you, don't I?' Chrissie said.

'Yes, I'm Travis… Travis, remember?'

'Yes, of course. Well, you said you'd be back. Remember, "I'll be back" – but it certainly has taken you a long time. It must be over twenty years; you haven't grown much, have you?'

'*Travis, let's get out of here,*' Mentor said. '*He's worse than he was the last time!*'

Travis ignored Mentor and said, 'Chrissie, I need a favour. Is what you're wearing fashionable these days?'

'I'll say! Cost me an arm and a leg, this lot.'

'I need some clothes so I can fit in without standing out in a crowd, understand?'

'What are you up to then, Travis?' Chrissie asked.

'Now you know I can't say, Chrissie. Can you help me or not? I can pay you after I've sold some things.'

'Yes, of course I can help you. Give me the sizes and I'll have you kitted out just like me.'

'*This I must see*,' Mentor said.

'OK, but don't go overboard, Chrissie. I don't want to look like a clown.'

'You don't think I look like a clown though, do you, Travis?' Chrissie looked crestfallen.

'*Go on, Travis, tell him*,' Mentor said.

'No, of course not, Chrissie. I'll get all my sizes written down… same time tomorrow?'

'Yes, no problem. One thing, Travis, before you go…'

'You want to see me disappear, yes?'

'How did you know that?'

With 'divvy' ringing inside his head, Travis pushed the scarper button.

Travis went back to Auntie Jennison's. She armed herself with a tape measure, and Mr Pomphrey got a writing pad and pen, and they started to chart Travis's sizes.

'These measurements will come in very handy, Travis,' Auntie Jennison said. 'It's your birthday very shortly and I may well buy you something to wear. I think you're getting far too old for toys now.'

Travis didn't answer; he didn't even want to think about what Auntie Jennison might buy. The pairs of gloves over the years were enough.

Travis took the measurements to Chrissie, Mentor declining to accompany him, and everything was set for Travis to pick up his new outfit – the very next day for Chrissie, or just after lunch, in Travis's case.

'Are you coming with me this time, Mentor?' Travis asked.

'Too right, Travis! Wouldn't miss it for the world – I want to have a good laugh.'

'Don't be horrible, Mentor, I'll look all right.'

But he didn't, and Mentor was still laughing as Travis walked back down Auntie Jennison's garden, still wearing his new togs.

'Come and let's have a look at you, Travis!' Auntie Jennison said. 'Give us a twirl.'

'Oh, Auntie Jennison,' Travis said, 'I look terrible.'

'I think you look very nice, Travis,' Mr Pomphrey said.

That's good coming from the man who wears a tea cosy on his head, Travis thought.

'Very fetching, Travis, very fetching indeed. I think you look a proper dandy,' Auntie Jennison declared.

'Seems the only thing that isn't right about my appearance, although as far as I'm concerned there's nothing right about it, is my hair. Apparently it's far too short.'

'I've got an old wig you could borrow, Travis,' Auntie Jennison suggested.

'I don't think so, Auntie Jennison, but thanks anyway.'

'It will soon grow, Travis,' Mr Pomphrey said. 'You'll just have to wait a while before you go back.'

'I can't do that, Mr Pomphrey, I don't think I'll get arrested or anything just because my hair's too short. Oh, and by the way, Auntie Jennison, Mentor told me I won't be seeing him for much longer.'

'You can't see him now, Travis,' Mr Pomphrey said, chuckling.

'Don't be pedantic, Mr Pomphrey, please,' Travis said.

'Hark, Bill! "Pedantic", if you please,' Auntie Jennison said. 'Don't make me laugh, Travis, those beans we had at lunch time are beginning to work.'

Any excuse, Travis thought.

'No more Mentor, eh?' Auntie Jennison said. 'Good job as far as I'm concerned. That one, he's lost his touch; time he called it a day. He reminds me of that other one... now, what was his name... oh yes, I remember: "Hopeless Hector".'

Mentor was mumbling profanities inside Travis's head. Travis looked up and announced, 'Tomorrow I'll go and see about getting some money, short hair or no short hair.'

'I didn't like what Auntie Jennison said about me yesterday, Travis.'

'I thought it was a little unfair as well, Mentor, but hang on – I didn't think you had any feelings.'

'I think I've been around you humans so long, some of it is beginning to rub off. I'm saying goodbye to you today, Travis. You don't need me any more, and I'll tell you this, providing it doesn't make you too big-headed: you're the best pupil I've ever had.'

'It's really nice of you to say that, Mentor – even better than Auntie Jennison?'

'Yes, even better than her. I'm only saying it because it's true, Travis, you are the best. Listen, when you go into the platform today that's the last time you'll hear from me, I've already got my new pupil, so before I go, do you want your platform altered in any way?'

Travis opened the shed door and paused in the doorway.

'I don't want any alterations, thank you, I like the platform just the way it is; but Mentor, can't you stay with me? I'm so close to Granddad now; don't you want to know how it all turns out?'

Mentor started chuckling. 'Don't you think I don't already know, Travis Travis? Goodbye.'

In that instant, Travis knew Mentor had gone for ever, and Travis's whispered goodbye went unheard. He felt suddenly alone, and waves of sadness swept over him. I can't go time travelling today, I can't do it, he thought.

'Forgot something, Travis?' Auntie Jennison asked. 'Come here, my sweetheart, what's wrong?'

'Oh, Auntie Jennison – it's Mentor. He's gone.' Travis started to sob.

'There, there, my pretty. He wouldn't cry for you like that,' Auntie Jennison said, cuddling Travis close to her.

'I'm sorry, Auntie Jennison, but I can't go anywhere today. I'm just too upset, it's like Mentor has died,' said Travis, and burst into tears.

'I understand. We'll put everything on hold. You're back to school tomorrow, so let's leave things as they are until next weekend.'

Through the tears, Travis spluttered, 'Yes, Auntie Jennison, I'd like to do that.'

'Tell you what, Travis, I know how to cheer you up. We'll have a day out and go for a nice pub lunch!' Auntie Jennison's eyes started to sparkle.

Oh no, Travis thought.

Chapter Thirty-one

In the event, Becky and Mark, plus the twins came to visit the next weekend, and Travis was told in no uncertain terms he wouldn't be going anywhere until Becky had gone back home. Travis had the opportunity of nursing the babies, and he found to his surprise that he actually enjoyed it; he now realised what Mr Pomphrey had meant.

The following weekend, Travis made his mind up to go to the pawnshop in Looe, and with his hair still too short, but dressed in his flares, he emerged warily from platform 400 in the year 2042. He'd chosen June, so that he'd at least have some summer sun. The rain was teeming down. Just my luck, he thought; I can always go back and choose a different day. No, I'm here now, and with this rain, there's less chance of bumping into Chrissie…

By the time he got to the pawnshop the rain had eased off to a fine drizzle and all the indications were that the sun would soon be coming out.

Too late for Travis. He stood in the shop doorway doing his best impression of a drowned rat. He pushed the shop door open; the familiar ding-a-ling of the brass bell greeted him, but unlike before the door refused to squeak. The shop looked much as he'd remembered it, except the grandfather clock was missing and the wire grill had been replaced by a much more substantial-looking one. The door at the side of the counter had been replaced as well, and that too looked more like the entrance to a fortress than to the back of a shop.

The whole shop had had a lick of paint, and some newish-looking lamps shone brightly overhead.

Behind the counter stood a man. He looked like a younger version of the old man Travis had dealt with before. His clothes looked similar to the ones that Chrissie wore, but not as colourful. He too sported a long droopy moustache and had collar-length hair.

Travis could see he was fiddling with something in front of him on the top of the counter. As the doorbell rang, the man looked up, and Travis could tell by his smile that he was looking at the old man's son.

'You look like you've swum the English Channel,' the man said, 'hang on there a minute.'

He disappeared into the back of the shop and reappeared with a towel; he opened the hatch above the counter and passed the towel to Travis.

'Thank you very much, sir,' said Travis, and started towelling his hair.

'Not much there to dry, is there?'

Travis ignored the remark.

'Do you like magic?' the man asked.

Travis handed the towel back. 'Yes, sir, absolutely love it.'

'My dad was quite a magician,' the man said. 'See this box here, he showed me this trick years ago, when I was a young man.'

Travis looked. It was the same box, though the red velvet had faded and the box looked a little tired. The man proceeded with the trick and Travis was suitably impressed at the end of it.

'You think that was good? Well, Dad used to go on and on about a trick he saw in the shop right here. It was done by a young boy. Dad said the boy disappeared, just like that! There used to be an old grandfather clock over there in the corner, and Dad thought at first the boy was in there, but he wasn't; he pondered for years how the boy had done it. Then, one night – just after supper it was – he said he'd exhausted all the possibilities, and the only explanation left was that the boy was a time traveller.'

'A time traveller... really?' Travis said.

'Yes, for a while we thought the old man was going senile, but in every other respect he was perfectly all right. Then the day before he died he came running into the back room' – the man pointed towards the back of the shop – 'shouting at the top of his voice that he had been right all the time. I never saw him look so happy.'

'You said he died the next day, sir?' Travis was horrified. 'Was it something to do with the boy?'

'Oh no, the silly old fool was playing around with an electric plug and electrocuted himself. Bless him, he was always messing around with the electrics – that's why I've had all the wiring replaced.' He gestured towards the overhead lamps.

'So how was it that he knew he was right, sir?' Travis asked.

'He said the boy came back to see him; he said he did the trick again and that the boy let him hold his arm while he did it.'

'You don't believe that really happened, though, do you, sir?' Travis asked.

'Believe it or not, I do! You see, he was totally compos mentis, if you know what I mean?'

'Yes sir, I know,' Travis said. He knew what he had to do. 'So how long ago did all this happen?' he asked, trying to sound casual.

'I can tell you exactly. He died on Bonfire Night, 2025. Anyway... enough of that. What can I do for you?' the man said.

Travis produced the snuffbox and the white £5 note from his pocket. 'Before you ask, sir, these items were given to me by Mr Pomphrey.'

'Mr Pomphrey must like you very much. This is a fine example of an old English note,' the man said, examining it. 'The snuffbox, though, isn't really worth that much. You see, no one seems to be interested in anything to do with tobacco any more.' He looked sideways at Travis. 'How do you value them yourself?' he asked.

Travis was immediately stumped; he knew about the currency but knew nothing of the values. 'I haven't really thought about it, sir,' he replied.

'I can offer you, what shall we say...' the man paused. 'I can give you eighty pounds for the lot.'

'Eighty pounds?' Travis repeated.

'Perhaps I could stretch a little more; shall we say ninety?'

'I think I'll take them away and think about it, sir, if you don't mind.'

'You strike a hard bargain, don't you?' the man said.

'Not really, sir. I don't wish to appear to be rude, but I need to ask somebody first.'

Travis knew that Chrissie would know what ninety pounds

would buy. He reached over the counter to pick up the £5 note and the snuffbox.

'Tell you what,' the man said, 'save you coming back – I'll give you a full one hundred pounds. How's that?'

Travis realised that this person was not the kind man his father was. 'The figure I had in mind actually, sir, was one hundred and fifty.' Travis could hardly believe what he was saying.

'One hundred and fifty?' replied the man. 'I've got to make a living, you know! Let's say one hundred and ten.'

Travis was beginning to enjoy himself. 'One forty.'

'One twenty, and not a penny more,' the man said.

Travis didn't waiver. 'One thirty, and not a penny less!' Travis said.

'Meet me halfway,' said the man, 'one hundred and twenty-five.'

'OK,' Travis said.

'Done!' said the man, and pumped Travis's hand up and down.

Travis left the shop, and fifteen minutes later was on the way back down the road on 4th November 2025. A gang of youths on the other side of the street wolf-whistled and shouted as Travis passed by. Travis realised he was still dressed for 2042. 'I'm a trend-setter,' he shouted back, 'you'll all look like this in a few years' time.'

Travis pushed open the door to the pawnshop; the now familiar sound of the brass bell greeted him, as did the squeaky door. The old man was standing behind the counter, and as soon as he saw Travis his face started to open up into a smile.

'Can I help you, young sir?' he asked.

'Don't you remember me?' Travis approached the counter and the old man peered at him over the top of his spectacles.

'You're the boy with the trick, I tell you true, I work it out! Listen, you come in my shop, somehow you know I have the broken jewellery, but it not broken jewellery, it something special. I am thinking, you must have it, right?' Travis nodded in agreement. 'I knew, I knew! First I look everywhere when you gone, I even look in the clock; then I think and I think for years, I am thinking you are from another planet. Then no, then I think about your clothes, a little old-fashioned, your politeness, not like the children of today. Then I have it: you are from a different time! Please, I must know – am I right?'

'Yes, sir, you're right, I'm from the year 2004.'

'I knew it, I just knew it!'

'Would you like to see me disappear again, sir?'

'Very much, so very much.'

'Come around the counter then, sir.'

The old man was through the door and standing in front of Travis like a shot. 'Catch hold of my wrist, sir, and face me,' said Travis. He held out his arm and the old man did as he'd been told.

'Are you ready?' Travis asked.

'I am, I am,' the old man replied excitedly.

'Goodbye, sir,' said Travis, and he pushed the scarper button.

Travis hurried to Mr Pomphrey's house to show him the money he'd got from the pawnshop.

'This looks more like Monopoly money than the real thing, Travis,' Mr Pomphrey said. 'What's one of these worth in today's money?' He held up a pound note.

'That's the problem, Mr Pomphrey,' Travis said, 'I've no real idea of values, so I'll have to be ever so careful when I go back. Where's Auntie Jennison, Mr Pomphrey?'

'I'm not allowed to say, other than she's gone out with your mum and dad.'

'They haven't gone shopping by any chance, have they?' Travis asked.

Mr Pomphrey looked at Travis and just smiled.

'It's my birthday next week, Mr Pomphrey, and putting two and two together…'

'Sometimes, you know, Travis, two and two don't make four.'

'Yoo-hoo, I'm back!' came a shout from the back door. Auntie Jennison came into the house laden with parcels. 'I've managed to get Travis…' Her voice trailed away.

'I think they make four this time, Mr Pomphrey.'

'Travis, I need an urgent word with Bill,' Auntie Jennison said.

'Take Alex into the garden, and when I've finished Bill will come and find you.'

'Come on, Alex, I know when we're not wanted…'

Travis went out into the garden and threw a ball for Alex, who, infuriatingly for Travis, didn't seem to want to let it go again. Just as Travis was getting fed up with the game Mr Pomphrey put in an appearance.

'Come on, Travis, you can come back in now,' he said.

Travis, Alex and Mr Pomphrey went back into Mr Pomphrey's living room; Auntie Jennison was sitting drawing away at her cigarette, and looking like a little girl who'd done something extremely naughty.

'Hello, Travis, my gorgeous! Come and sit by your old auntie. What would you like for your birthday, if you could have whatever you wanted?' she asked.

'That's easy, Auntie Jennison,' Travis replied. 'I'd like to get Granddad back.'

'Did you hear that, Bill? Is it any wonder that I love this child so much?' Auntie Jennison grabbed Travis, lifted him bodily off the floor and, cuddling him, smothered him with kisses.

I wish I'd said I wanted a scarf now, Travis thought. Auntie Jennison eventually released Travis and sat him in his seat, saying, 'You know, Travis, I won't be able to do that much longer – you're getting far too heavy and far too grown-up!'

There is a God, Travis thought.

'What's the plan, Travis?' Mr Pomphrey asked. 'Have you got one yet?'

'Yes and no, Mr Pomphrey. I think I must start at Samson Island; unfortunately the nearest platform's miles away, so I really just don't know what to think.'

'It could take some time for you to even get to Samson Island, Travis,' Auntie Jennison said. 'And I think if it turned out you were away from home overnight your mother would go frantic. Better to wait until the weekend after your birthday, then you and Bill can come down to the cottage. Your mum will then have no idea how long you'll be gone, and what she doesn't know she can't fret about.'

Mr Pomphrey nodded his head in approval. 'Leaving it until

then is a good idea, Travis. It gives you the opportunity to go visiting, have a look at the platform and the surrounding area, and find the best way to get to Samson Island.'

'You know, Travis, Bill should have been a visitor himself. You really are so clever Bill, so clever! Isn't he clever, Travis?'

Here we go again, Travis thought.

It wasn't long before Travis decided to visit platform 106. He set the time for just a few days earlier and set off. When he arrived, he found that the platform had a nautical theme and it fascinated Travis. It was done out like the bridge of a luxury liner from before the Second World War; Travis absorbed his new surround-ings, and for a brief few seconds he completely forgot the purpose of his trip. Remembering that visiting had its limitations, he quickly went out into the open air. He was totally bewildered as he surveyed his surroundings: no gardens, no houses; in fact, no nothing. He appeared to be in the corner of a field. A tall hedge ran along behind the shed and beyond that he could hear the faint roar of traffic. Sounds like the motorway, he thought, I don't like this one bit; miles from anywhere, no transport… no, I don't like it at all. He decided to go home.

'Mr Pomphrey, you've come up trumps again,' Travis said. 'So it's twenty-two miles to the airport at Land's End, and I can do it by bus – that's great.'

'There's one thing, though, Travis. Perhaps there won't be any buses in 2043.'

'Well, there's bound to be buses, but I don't care if I've got to walk it, Mr Pomphrey. I'm going to get there.'

Travis had to go to school on his birthday. He'd pleaded with his mum and dad to be allowed to stay at home, but they were having none of it; although he never minded helping giving the bumps to anyone else, he wasn't too keen on it himself. Unlike junior school, his classmates were bigger and stronger, and Travis swore they threw him up until he touched the ceiling!

When Travis left for school, the postman hadn't been, al-though Travis had waited until the last possible minute before leaving himself; so when it came to lunch time Travis was out of the school gate and along the road as fast as he could go. Breathless and excited, he arrived at home, 'I'm home,' he called out, 'any post for me?'

Travis's mum and dad were already sitting up to the dining room table.

'Post for you – whatever gave you that idea?' his dad said.

'Oh Dad, don't tease, you know it's my birthday.' Travis started looking around.

'Birthday? What, today?' His dad winked at Travis's mum.

'Oh, for goodness' sake, Tom Travis,' she said, 'it's Travis who's eleven today, not you – although sometimes I'm not too sure!'

With a sigh, Tom Travis reached under the table and produced a sheaf of envelopes.

'Wow! Look at this lot,' exclaimed Travis. Excitedly, he tore at the envelopes and placed the cards all over the table, then he went back through the envelopes giving each one a good shake in turn to make sure there was no money inside.

'You'll be getting your presents when you come home this afternoon, Travis,' his dad said, 'there is a reason for that, and I'll tell you then.'

'Oh, Dad!' Travis complained.

'You'll understand why later and that's that.'

If Travis had hurried home for lunch, it was nothing to the frantic dash he made at teatime. He let himself in the house and called out, 'I'm home!' That's funny, he thought, where is everybody? 'Hello… anyone home?' he called again.

Travis went through into the living room; no one about. He thought he'd try the kitchen.

'Surprise, surprise!' the family chorused. They were all jammed in the kitchen: Travis's mum and dad, Becky, minus the twins and Mark, Auntie Jennison and Mr Pomphrey were all waiting for him. Spontaneously, the strains of 'Happy birthday to you' broke out, and when the singing died down Travis's dad made him go into the living room, where Mr Pomphrey produced one of Auntie Jennison's scarves and blindfolded Travis.

'Can you see anything at all, Travis?' Mr Pomphrey asked, waving both hands in front of Travis's eyes.

'Not a thing, Mr Pomphrey.'

'Good,' Mr Pomphrey sat him down on the sofa; Travis could hear all sorts of busy noises going on, accompanied by Auntie Jennison's own brand of home-grown noises.

Lots of giggling and whispering followed. 'Can I look yet?' Travis asked.

'Almost ready, Travis,' his dad replied.

Suddenly the blindfold was whisked off and Travis sat there blinking, his eyes growing accustomed to the light.

'Wow! Oh, fab!'

'Is it all right, Travis?' his mum asked.

'All right, all right?' he repeated. 'It's not just all right, it's wonderful.'

'What about the colour?' Auntie Jennison asked.

'Yes, yes, I love blue.'

'It's metallic blue, actually, Travis,' his dad said.

'Can I try it now, please?' Travis couldn't wait to get going.

'Not right away, Travis. I couldn't say anything at lunch time, but you need to open your other presents first. You'll see why in a minute.'

Travis enthusiastically tore at the wrapping on the other presents, reading the tags and thanking everybody as he did so.

'Now you can understand what I meant, can't you, Travis?' his dad said.

'Yes, Dad,' Travis said, putting the safety helmet on his head.

'Don't just sit there, Bill. Help Travis with the elbow protectors,' Auntie Jennison ordered.

Mr Pomphrey sprang into life and soon Travis was kitted out.

'Off you go, Travis, but not for too long – we're having a birthday tea,' his mother said, 'and it will be dark soon.'

Proudly, Travis wheeled his mountain bike out through the living room towards the front door.

'I'll have my birthday kiss when you come back, Travis,' Auntie Jennison said, puckering up her lips.

'All right, Auntie Jennison,' Travis replied, 'see you all later.'

Mr Pomphrey had given Travis a chain with a combination lock in order to lock his bike up; unfortunately, he'd lost the code for the combination when he was wrapping it up, and when

Travis came in from his bike ride poor old Mr Pomphrey was really upset.

'I'm so sorry, I've looked and looked through all the rubbish, I've looked everywhere and I just can't find it. You might just as well throw it away and I'll buy you another one.'

Travis started to laugh. 'When did you wrap it up, Mr Pomphrey?'

'Yesterday, after I finished lunch… why?'

Travis started laughing again and skipped out to the kitchen.

Ten minutes later he reappeared.

'You'd better have a good explanation for this, Travis, we've all been waiting to start tea,' said his dad, sounding quite cross.

'The combination, Mr Pomphrey, the combination is tucked in a hole in your bobble cosy.'

'Ventilation slot, Travis!' Auntie Jennison gave Travis one of her looks.

Mr Pomphrey took his bobble cosy off, and sure enough there was the code. 'How did you know that, Travis?' he said.

'Being a time…' Travis suddenly realised Becky was present… 'I think I'd better be quiet,' he said.

'Travis has been practising all sorts of conjuring tricks, haven't you, Travis?' Auntie Jennison said, coming to the rescue. 'He does a good one with mind-reading, don't you, Travis?' She looked hard at him.

'Yes, Auntie Jennison,' he replied.

'Is that the one you just did on Bill?' She looked hard at him again.

'Yes, Auntie Jennison.'

'Oh,' Becky said, 'can you do the same one for me?'

'Course he can,' Auntie Jennison replied on Travis's behalf, 'straight after tea – and I'll have my birthday kiss all at the same time.' She looked at Travis and winked.

After another rendition of 'Happy birthday' and the cutting of the birthday cake, all the tea dishes were cleared away and Auntie Jennison said, 'Right, Travis, birthday kisses time!'

While she was smothering Travis she was busy whispering in his ear.

'Come on then, Travis, let's see this trick,' Becky said.

'Certainly, Becky, we'll do it just like I did it with Mr Pomphrey. You pretend to mislay something, but of course you must hide it. Then I go out into the kitchen for a while and tune my mental thoughts into yours, and when I come back I'll find whatever it is you've lost, OK?'

Travis disappeared into the kitchen and Becky took a comb and a bunch of keys from her handbag. She hid the comb under the sofa and the keys behind the television.

It was only a short time before Travis was back. He looked at Becky and said, 'I think there are two objects gone missing, am I right, Becky?'

'Yes, but how did you know that?'

'Because I do. Now, is one of these objects made of plastic and the other made of metal?'

'Travis, how can you know that? I know – you've got an accomplice in the room!'

'No, Becky, the only person who's telling me where the objects are is you. Now, tell me what the metal object is?'

'It's a bunch of keys.'

'And the plastic?'

'A comb.'

Travis placed both his hands to his temples, closed his eyes and said, 'Yes, the keys are behind the telly, and the comb is under the sofa.'

Applause broke out and Travis took a bow.

'That was absolutely fantastic, Travis! I didn't know you could do anything like that,' Becky said.

'I can disappear as well, Becky.'

Auntie Jennison shot Travis a look that said everything.

'Well, actually, I'm still practising that one and I haven't got it quite right yet.'

'Perhaps you'll be able to show us it at Christmas, Travis?' Becky suggested.

'If I've got it right by then, I will, Becky,' Travis replied.

A little after seven, Travis's dad and mum drove Becky home, leaving Travis in Auntie Jennison and Mr Pomphrey's care.

'You nearly let the cat out the bag earlier, didn't you, Travis?' Mr Pomphrey smiled.

'Auntie Jennison rescued me though, Mr Pomphrey, but I expect I'll be in trouble with Dad, won't I, Auntie Jennison?'

'No, it's all right, Travis. I had a quiet word with him, and I told him for one thing it's your birthday and for another you're only eleven,' said Auntie Jennison. 'And I believe that that deserves a nice kiss, don't you?'

Chapter Thirty-two

'The governor asked if you could spare him a few minutes, Thomas.'

'Hello, Mike, haven't seen you all week. How did the house hunting go?'

'Yes, fine, it looks like we're all fixed up, Thomas. Just a matter of waiting now.'

'You really are serious about this retirement, then, Mike?'

'Never been more serious about anything in my life. I've had it, Thomas. There's only a couple of things I'll miss here and one of them, Thomas, is you.'

'Nice of you to say that, Mike.'

'When your pardon comes through you must come and visit; we're moving to Wiltshire.'

'Still on about that pardon! I was having a good day until you mentioned that, Mike.'

'Come on then, there's a good chap. We mustn't keep the governor waiting.'

'Got to do this all official today, Thomas,' Mike said as they approached the governor's office.

Thomas was marched into the governor's presence; a photographer and a reporter were standing to one side and two official-looking types to the other.

Mike Harding came smartly to attention, 'Thomas Travis, Prisoner 501, with escort, reporting, sir,' he said.

'Yes, thank you, Officer Harding.' The governor had what appeared to be a parchment document rolled up in his right hand. 'Thomas Travis, it gives me the greatest of pleasure to present you with this document, which contains the king's pardon. You are now a free man; your debt to society has been paid.'

The governor stepped from behind his desk, handed Thomas the pardon, and warmly shook his hand. Thomas looked at Mike Harding, who was almost in tears. The photographer snapped hurriedly away and the reporter asked Thomas what were his reactions. Thomas mumbled something suitable and wished that the whole affair would swiftly come to an end.

Eventually everyone left, and at Thomas's request he and the governor were left alone together at last.

'Governor, I've got something to say,' Thomas said.

'Hang on, Thomas; I've got something to say as well. In the first place you will no longer address me as "Governor"; from now on I'm plain Jeremy. Now, I'm not stupid, Thomas, I know what's what. Spoken to Harding, don't you know? Everything's sorted out, you can stay on here, on a proper wage, the business can stand it, and then when you retire you can please yourself what you do. Now it's your turn.'

'Thank you, Gov… Jeremy, thank you very much!'

Thomas Travis, feeling on top of the world, walked back along the corridor to his own office. Waiting outside was Mike Harding; he stared at Thomas.

'Well?'

'Well what?' Thomas asked.

'Pleased?'

'Mildly.'

'Mildly – you're kidding me!'

'Yes.'

'Come here, you!' And, whooping and hollering like a couple of school kids, Mike Harding chased Thomas along the corridor.

It felt quite strange for Thomas to receive an invitation for Mike Harding's leaving party, and even stranger just to walk in the Prison Officers' Club without anyone batting an eyelid. He walked up to the bar.

'What can I get you, Thomas? Whisky, brandy, gin perhaps?' Mike was in the chair.

'Actually I don't really drink, Mike, but as this is a special occasion, I'll let you choose.'

Three gin and tonics later, Thomas, feeling extremely squiffy, sat himself down next to Mike.

'Excuse me if I slur my words, Mike, I don't drink usually… We've become good friends over the years, and our paths probably won't cross again, so there's something I've got to tell you.'

'Hold on a minute, Thomas. Before you say anything else, our paths *will* cross, because now you're a free man you can come up to Wiltshire and visit us; and anyway look what I've bought you.' Mike reached into his pocket. 'Here, take this, regard it as a little going-away present.'

'Very nice, a vid phone! What can I say, Mike?'

'Well, "thank you" would suffice,' Mike answered. 'My number's already programmed in, so you've no excuses not to keep in touch.'

'Thanks, Mike, I will come up to visit.'

'Now what was it you wanted to say?'

'Oh nothing… you've said it all, really.'

As things turned out, Thomas, although constantly in touch with Mike, didn't seem to make the journey to Wiltshire; there always seemed to be some barrier in his way. Mike told his wife that he felt Thomas, although so sure of himself in most ways, was frightened to leave Samson Island.

Then, out of the blue, at one of the monthly meetings at the prison, the governor announced, 'Gentlemen, the establishment has come a long way in twenty-five years… lots of water under the bridge and all that, time for new blood. Leaving at the end of next month – simple as that – sorry to go, but my work here is finished. Time to retire – call it a day.'

No one moved or uttered a sound. The various people around the table had different thoughts. What's the new governor going to be like? Will he run things the same? Thomas thought. What will happen to me?

Eventually someone spoke. 'I think I can speak for everyone here, Governor, when I say we'll all miss you.'

A resounding 'Hear, hear!' went around the table.

The rest of the meeting went by with the governor trying his best to reassure every one of the new governor's intentions. 'Spoke to the new fellow on the phone, you know. Sounds progressive, young and enthusiastic… should fit in very well.'

Thomas wasn't so sure. After all, he himself was coming up to retirement age, and once Jeremy left, where would he stand? It was with this in mind he went to see the governor.

'Jeremy, can you spare me a few minutes?' he asked.

'All the time you need, Thomas,' the governor replied.

'Frankly, I'm worried. You know I've been here twenty-five years, and I'm due to retire soon; will the new governor throw me out?'

'He's not obliged to keep you, Thomas, but he'd be a fool to let you go. You know as much about this place as I do, probably more.'

'But there are no guarantees, are there, Jeremy?'

'No, none, I'm afraid. I certainly will be speaking for you, but that's all I can do.' Thomas's shoulders sagged and a look of sadness came over his face. 'Look, Thomas, it's not the end of the world, you know. There is life beyond Samson. Listen, go and see Mike Harding... take a break.'

Thomas went back to his office and phoned Mike. 'Mike, how are you?'

'I'm fine, Thomas, but what's up with you?'

'Had some bad news, Mike. The governor's retiring.' His voice faltered. 'I don't know what's going to happen to me.'

'You'll be all right, Thomas, just you wait and see. Listen, why don't you come up here for a few days?'

'The governor suggested that, Mike; if it's all right with you, I'll take you up on your offer.'

'Leave it all to me. I'll fix the travel arrangements and I can pick you up from Bath Spa Station when you get here. You've never even been on the EMS, have you?'

'I suppose it would be quite an adventure for me.'

'Yes, that's the spirit! You can get the heli to Penzance, link to Plymouth and EMS on to Bristol, and then the link to Bath. I'll arrange it all as soon as I've stopped talking to you and before you change your mind.'

When Thomas put the vid phone down, he realised what a cosseted existence he had led for the last twenty-five years. The very thought of leaving Samson caused waves of panic to sweep through him. Are you a man or a mouse? he asked himself. Squeak up, he thought, and he smiled to himself...

Within three days Thomas was looking at the travel tickets on his desk, representing a far different system from the one he used the last time he travelled anywhere in 1978. With a book of vouchers, universal for each form of transport, he had only to tear off the correct amount for each stage of the journey and hand them in. With a certain amount of trepidation, he went into the governor's office, bade him farewell and walked down to the helipad.

The twenty-eight miles across the water soon went by, and smack on time the link train pulled away from the side of the Penzance helipad for the first stage of the journey to Plymouth. The link train was to be the slowest part of the journey, as there were five stops along the way.

The link train announcement came over the loudspeaker. 'Next stop, Camborne, three minutes' duration.' Thomas settled back in his seat and watched as the countryside unfolded before him. The train noiselessly slid into Camborne Station, where the solitary figure of a young lad stood on the opposite platform, waiting for his train. He looks a bit young to be out on his own, Thomas thought.

After three minutes, the train was gathering momentum again and Thomas found it hard to comprehend the speed that it was capable of. The journey to Plymouth was soon a memory and Thomas boarded the EMS train.

Shaped like a bullet, and seemingly hanging over each side of a central rail, the train had ten coaches, each eighty feet long. A bit different to the old Pullman, he thought, but not as quick; he smiled to himself.

Not as quick as the Pullman, but pretty impressive, he had to admit. The announcement came through: 'Welcome to the Electro Magnetic System of travel. Your estimated time of arrival at Bristol Temple Meads today is eleven sixteen.' Thomas looked at his watch: ten forty.

A faint humming noise passed through the carriage and the whole train rose up from the central rail. Then there was silence, and the train smoothly and readily started to accelerate.

Thomas had barely enough time to engage his fellow passengers in conversation before the train was slowing down again at Bristol Temple Meads.

The link train to Bath took a mere ten minutes, and as Thomas walked along the platform at Bath Spa he was pleased to see Mike was waiting for him.

Thomas's stay with Mike, scheduled to last a few days, stretched on to a week and then two, and it was only after Thomas had phoned the governor that he decided it was time to leave.

'You don't have to go back, you know, Thomas. You are, after all, a free man now.'

'No, I must go back, Mike. The new governor has arrived at Samson and I want to know where I stand. Besides, from what the governor said, things are getting in a bit of a mess without me.'

'Nobody's indispensable, you know, Thomas.'

'Nobody except me, Mike!'

Thomas nervously walked along the corridor to the governor's office. Jeremy was standing beside his desk and the new governor was sitting in the chair behind it. One glance told Thomas who was in charge.

Jeremy's whole face lit up when he saw Thomas. 'Thank the Lord you're back, Thomas. Terrible mess, you know.'

'Yes, thank you, I'll deal with this if you don't mind,' the new governor cut in.

Thomas had the feeling there and then that he and the new man just weren't going to get along.

'Leave you to it, then,' Jeremy said, and with a glance and a smile at Thomas, he left the office.

'Right then, former prisoner Travis, I've been looking at the way things are run around here and I don't like the laid-back attitude everyone seems to have.'

'We turn in a profit every year,' Thomas said.

'We turn in a profit, *Governor*. You will call me Governor.'

'Well, Governor, as you rightly said, I am a former prisoner, so I will be grateful if you call me Mr Travis, in future.' Thomas was starting to bristle.

'As you wish. But frankly, I don't see much of a future here for you, Mr Travis. You have one month after your sixty-fifth birthday to leave Samson. That's all; close the door behind you.'

A stunned Thomas went along to his office. Sitting behind his desk was Jeremy. 'I've even lost my office, then, Jeremy, have I?'

'Of course not, Thomas! Just keeping the seat warm for you.' Jeremy got up and ushered Thomas into his seat. 'Listen, I did all

I could, but he's adamant, you've got to go. The whole place has gone downhill in the two weeks you've been gone; the man's a fool. Never thought I'd say this, Thomas, but I can't leave quick enough.'

'I had such a good time up at Mike's, and I've come back to this,' Thomas said despondently.

'Spoke to Harding after you left him, Thomas; he's coming down for my leaving bash. Perhaps you could get something sorted out, up his neck of the woods...'

'Maybe, Jeremy, but there's one thing for sure: I won't be seeing my time out here.'

Chapter Thirty-three

'Now then, Travis, have you got everything?'

'Yes, Mr Pomphrey, I think so,' Travis replied.

'Wars aren't won on "I think so", Travis! Now, let's go through the checklist.'

'Oh, for goodness' sake, Bill, leave the boy alone!' Auntie Jennison said snappily. 'You've checked and double-checked and even triple-checked everything.'

'Can't be too organised, Auntie,' Mr Pomphrey replied.

Auntie Jennison ignored Mr Pomphrey and said, 'Right, come and say a special goodbye to your old auntie – and be careful.'

'Yes, and come and give me a hug as well.' Mr Pomphrey put his arms out.

Goodbyes said, and Travis, hoping he was fully equipped, walked up Auntie Jennison's garden to the shed.

He couldn't have picked a better day to go to platform 106 – the sun was warm and the sky was stippled with just a few clouds high up.

As before, there was no one around. Some trees were missing and the remaining ones seemed a lot bigger, but this time there was something different: no traffic noise. Travis stood and listened. There was just the sound of birds singing and a bee buzzing.

Travis climbed over an old rustic gate and dropped down into a lane on the other side; he started to walk towards where he had heard the sound of traffic on his previous visit.

He'd been walking for about five minutes when he saw two boys about the same age as himself walking towards him. 'Hello,' he called out as they got closer, 'I'm afraid I've got a bit lost.'

'Where are you heading?' the older of the two boys asked.

'I'm looking for the motorway,' Travis replied.

'Motorway? They did away with the motorway when they put the link in.'

'I'm not from around here,' Travis said.

'You must be from Mars then,' said the same boy. 'They did away with all the motorways years ago.'

'I've got to get to Penzance,' Travis said.

'You'll need to get on the link then.' The younger boy spoke for the first time.

'What's the link?' Travis asked. 'Is it a coach?'

'He is from Mars,' the older boy said, laughing. 'The link's a train, you dummy.' Travis suddenly thought of Alex.

Travis took a deep breath. 'All right, so I'm a dummy. Where can I find the link, please?'

'At Camborne Station, of course.' Both boys pointed along the road.

'Thanks, then,' Travis said.

'Before you go, tell me something,' the elder boy said. 'Is your hair so short because you've had head lice?'

'No, it's because where I come from everybody's hair is like this.'

'You do come from Mars, then!' one said, and both boys ran off laughing.

Travis carried on along the road, and there in the distance he could see what appeared to be an elevated roadway. As he got nearer he could tell that that was where the motorway used to be. He kept going, walking adjacent to the old motorway, until at first a few houses came into view; then, further along the road, he knew he was approaching the town centre. He noticed that there were very few cars, and the ones he saw made no noise and seemed to float along on a cushion of air.

Travis spotted the sign for the link station and walked towards the ticket office; there was no queue and not many people about.

'Yes, what can I do for you, son?' The man in the ticket office looked inquiringly at Travis.

'I'd like to go to Penzance, sir,' Travis answered.

'Central or heli?' the man asked.

'Um, heli please.'

'Vouchers or credits?'

'Well, I've got cash, if that's all right?'

'Cash, well there's a novelty! Don't get much of that these

days. Let me see,' the man looked at a sheet. 'How old are you? Under ten, am I right?'

Travis was fuming, but as he didn't know the value of his money nodded his head in agreement.

'Single or return?'

'A single, sir, please.'

'Three pounds exactly, if you please.'

Travis fumbled with the unfamiliar money and eventually gave the man a £5 note; he took his change with a thank you and enquired how long he would have to wait.

'The same as you do for any link anywhere,' the man replied.

Travis walked on through to the link platform and stood waiting. Another train slid silently in on the opposite side of the station, and Travis watched disinterestedly until the train silently pulled away again. Travis's train came gliding into Camborne Station and Travis noticed he had the whole carriage almost to himself, which suited him fine. Conversation was the last thing he wanted with anyone, and keeping himself to himself seemed the best choice. Travis watched as the countryside hurtled past the window, and after only ten minutes he saw the overhead sign flashing, 'Next stop Penzance Central'.

Three minutes later the train was off again. It seemed to Travis that as soon as it gained speed it was slowing down again and sure enough the sign flashed again: 'Terminus Penzance Heli.'

Travis alighted from the train and went through the exit doors. Although he had been to the helicopter museum he was amazed at the sheer size of the helicopters he could see parked up a little way away on the tarmac. From what he could make out there appeared to be three separate queues for tickets. Over the first desk it said, 'Samson Island'; Travis didn't look any farther. He joined the queue and fished a handful of notes from his pocket. A youngish girl sat at the desk and an older man stood at her side.

'Can I have a ticket to Samson, please, miss?' Travis asked.

'Yes… VO first, though, please,' the girl responded.

'VO?' Travis's face was a complete blank.

'Your Visitor's Order, son,' the man chipped in.

'Um, my auntie's got it,' Travis lied. 'She told me to go on ahead.'

'I'm sorry but you'll have to wait until your aunt gets here,' the girl said kindly. 'I don't expect she'll be too long.'

Travis mumbled a thank you and went towards the exit. On the left-hand side he could see the gents' toilet, so feeling totally cheesed off, he whipped inside the first cubicle and pushed the scarper button.

If Travis felt cheesed off when he left Penzance, it was nothing to how he was going to feel back at Auntie Jennison's.

'Before you say anything, Travis,' she said, 'there's bad news, I'm afraid. I can't believe it… there's you, me and your dad, and it took Bill, who isn't a visitor, to see the problem.'

'What problem, Auntie Jennison?' Travis asked.

'When we push the scarper button, where does it take you?' Auntie Jennison replied.

'Well, back to where you came from, of course,' Travis answered.

'Exactly, Travis. But, you see, your granddad hasn't had his scarper button on him for twenty-five years, and if you gave it to him now and he pushed it, because he's moved on but the button has been inanimate, it would mean he'd end up back in 1978; and we know that didn't happen, because he's not here now,' Auntie Jennison said.

'So that means that I didn't find him.'

'It looks like it's the end of the road, Travis.' Auntie Jennison sounded totally dejected.

'Hang on, Auntie Jennison,' Travis said, 'it doesn't necessarily mean I didn't find him, it just means I couldn't bring him back. I can still try to go and see him at least.'

'Not the same, though, Travis, is it?'

'No, Auntie Jennison, but I can't just stop now. I'm going to see Chrissie and see if I can get a Visitor's Order for the prison.'

Travis sat on Chrissie's back doorstep waiting for him to put in an appearance; he'd waited about twenty minutes when he saw Chrissie come out of his shed.

'Back again, Travis? It must be a year since I saw you last,' Chrissie said. 'I bet you need some help. I can always tell, you know, when someone needs some help; I like helping people.'

It came back to Travis what a nightmare Chrissie was. 'Yes, Chrissie, I do need some help…'

'I knew it! I'm never wrong, you know. Here, Travis, what d'you think? I did twenty-three minutes' visiting today – that's my new record—'

'That's very good, Chrissie,' Travis said, cutting Chrissie off. 'Listen, I need a Visitor's Order to get into Samson Prison.'

'You'd better come into the house, then, Travis. You'll have to excuse the mess, I don't seem to be very well organised now that Mum's gone.'

'Oh, I'm sorry, Chrissie… I didn't realise.'

'No, it's all right, Travis. I go and visit her now and again, so it's not like she's really dead.'

'Is that where you've been today, Chrissie?' Travis asked.

'Yes; you see, it gives me comfort, Travis. I haven't got anybody else.'

'Chrissie, you really shouldn't. It's not a natural thing to do and it will only end up in problems.'

Putting it mildly, the house was a tip. Travis had seen tidier skips. Chrissie moved a pile of clothes so there was somewhere to sit, and sitting facing Travis, he said, 'Now, when d'you want to visit Samson?'

'As soon as possible, please, Chrissie,' Travis answered.

Chrissie rummaged around in the rubbish and produced what appeared to be a remote control, except it was about twice as big as the ones in Travis's house.

'Not too big, then, Chrissie?'

'The newer ones are a lot bigger than this, Travis.'

Chrissie pointed the remote control at the wall and pressed a button; from somewhere down near the skirting board Travis heard a whirling sound and a large oblong screen rose up into view.

'Must get some oil on that, Travis. Did you hear that racket?'

Chrissie pointed the remote again and the single word 'searching' came on the screen. The face of a youngish lady appeared and seemed to be looking directly at Chrissie. 'How can I help?' she asked.

'I need Samson Prison, please,' Chrissie said.

'Vid link?' she asked.

'Yes please,' Chrissie answered.

The screen immediately went blank and the word 'connecting', flashed on and off on the screen. This time a youngish man appeared. 'Samson; how can I help?'

'I need a Visitor's Order please,' Chrissie said.

'Who are you coming to see?' the young man asked. 'Surname first, if you please.'

Chrissie looked at Travis.

'It's Travis,' Travis said loudly, looking at the screen.

'First name?'

'Thomas.'

A pause and then, 'Sorry caller, there's no Thomas Travis coming up on my screen. There's no one of that name here.'

'Could he have been moved?' Travis asked.

'I'm sorry, I haven't got that information.'

'Well, isn't there someone there who would know?' Travis asked.

'I'm sorry, caller, I haven't got that information on my screen and even if I did I couldn't divulge it.'

Chrissie butted in. 'Thank you,' he said. He pushed a button and the screen went blank.

'So he is something to do with you then, Travis, that child killer?'

'He's not a child killer, Chrissie, and he's my granddad,' Travis said.

'I believe you, Travis. If you say he's all right, then that's fine by me. But there's something about his name – just something – and I've heard it recently; well, not exactly recently, but I'm sure I heard it. Hang on a minute.' Chrissie pointed the remote at the screen again.

As before, 'searching' came up on the screen, and then the face of a woman. 'How can I help?' she asked.

'Yes, info please,' Chrissie said, 'on one Thomas Travis.'

'Full search?'

'Please,' Chrissie said.

'Nationality?'

'English,' Travis answered.

'Date of birth?'

Chrissie looked at Travis, who shrugged his shoulders.

'Not known,' Chrissie said.

'Any known address?'

'Try Samson Island.'

'Is that with a "p"?'

'No, without,' Travis responded.

'Yes, here we are. Display results in tile form?'

'Yes please.'

The screen went blank and then almost straight away it was filled with small oblong boxes, each showing Travis's granddad's face. A series of dates were underneath each photo and a cursor appeared on the screen. Travis and Chrissie watched, fascinated, as the history of Thomas Travis at Samson unfolded on the screen: clips from television, old newspaper cuttings and an interview conducted with Thomas when the pods were completed.

'Here we are, Travis, this is the bit we've been looking for,' said Chrissie, and they watched as the information came on the screen. 'He's still there, but now he's a free man. You know what that means, Travis; you can just go to Samson – no Visitor's Order, no nothing – and pay him a visit.'

'Yes, that's right, straight over on the helicopter and Bob's your uncle. Thanks, Chrissie, I couldn't have got this far without you! You're a star.'

'Look, Travis, you know I like to help… It makes me feel, it makes me feel… well, important. So is there anything else I can do?'

'I need to go back home now, Chrissie, but thank you. Everybody will be waiting for some news. I'll come back to see you again, Chrissie, honest.'

'You couldn't stay for a while, could you, Travis?'

Travis felt mean, especially as Chrissie had been such a help to him. 'Tell you what, Chrissie, I'll stay for for a chat for a bit, if you like?'

Travis overstayed at Chrissie's, and by the time he put an appearance in at Auntie Jennison's, she and Mr Pomphrey were both on tenterhooks.

'Here he is! Put the kettle on, Bill. Do you want anything to eat, Travis? You must be famished.'

'I'd like a drink, Auntie Jennison, but I had some cake at Chrissie's, thank you,' Travis said. 'I know he's hard work, but I couldn't just rush off; he was so helpful.'

'You're such a good boy, Travis, so thoughtful. Come over here to your old auntie.'

They all decided Travis had done quite enough for one day, and Travis for once agreed. He felt quite exhausted after the day's excitement and was tucked up in bed by nine o'clock.

The previous day had taken its toll on him more than he realised, and he slept right through until midday the next day.

'Oh, Auntie Jennison, why didn't you call me? I wanted to go to Samson today.'

'Travis,' said Auntie Jennison, 'I want you to go to Samson as much as you do, but it would be no good you going if you weren't wide awake. No, Bill and I decided to leave you to sleep.'

'But that means it's too late to go today now! Oh, Auntie Jennison…'

'Just listen to me, Travis; it seems quite certain that you can't bring Granddad back now, so there's no urgency any more. When you go next, at least you'll be wide awake.'

'I know you're right, Auntie Jennison, it's just it's the—'

'It's the impetuosity of youth, Travis,' Auntie Jennison butted in.

'Here you are, you two,' Mr Pomphrey came into the room. 'A nice cup of Earl Grey for Auntie, and a Coke for you, Travis. Tell you what, how about all up the pub for lunch?'

Auntie Jennison's eyes lit up at the prospect.

Time dragged all the next week at school. Travis was disappointed, as he could go to Auntie Jennison's the following weekend, but he had to do two days back at school after that before breaking up for the Christmas holidays.

Travis and Mr Pomphrey arrived at Auntie Jennison's on

Saturday at about the same time as they had the previous week. Alex went round and round on the spot as soon as he saw Travis. Auntie Jennison, as usual, went OTT when she saw him and then immediately insisted that Mr Pomphrey went off to the kitchen to make the tea.

'Mr Pomphrey seems to be a long time, Auntie Jennison,' Travis said.

'Yes, doesn't he just! He's probably doing the washing-up. There was a fair bit; it didn't seem really worth me bothering with any this week, as I knew Bill was coming down.'

'I see you've acquired a new ashtray, Auntie Jennison.' Travis's eyes alighted on a silvery-coloured ashtray on the mantle.

'Yes, and d'you know what, I've really no idea whatsoever where it came from!' said Auntie Jennison, not batting an eyelid.

'It looks remarkably like the ones in the pub that we were in last weekend, Auntie Jennison,' Travis said.

'D'you think so, Travis? Well, that would be quite a coincidence, wouldn't it?' Auntie Jennison looked somewhat surprised.

Travis thought he'd push his luck; he walked over to the mantle and picked up the ashtray. 'I'd swear this is one of the pub ashtrays, Auntie Jennison.'

'Oh dear, Travis, I don't suppose Bill brought it home with him… mind you, Travis, I shouldn't say it, but he's getting a bit forgetful. Yes, that's what must have happened, he must have brought it home. You know, we'll just have to keep an eye on him in future.'

Next morning, Travis had to go through his checklist with Mr Pomphrey. Then, both feeling happy that at last he was to see his granddad, and sad knowing that Granddad would have to stay where he was, he went out to Auntie Jennison's shed.

Now that he'd managed to get to the helipad once, he had no problem with the walk to the link station or buying a ticket. Brimming with confidence he settled back in his seat on the train. Casting his eyes around the carriage, he could see there were a lot more people on the train this time. He caught his own reflection in the glass. Yes, he thought, my hair looks almost long enough now. Travis felt his confidence grow even more.

Most of the passengers alighted at Penzance Central, and Travis was left in the carriage with just a handful of people. That's good, he thought, no queues at the helipad.

As soon as Travis got off the train, he could see there was some sort of a problem. People were milling around everywhere, and there didn't appear to be any queues for tickets. Travis wandered over towards the overhead information signs, but looking out at the helicopters he could immediately see what the problem was. Although he'd chosen a summer's day, it was blowing a gale. Huge chains were anchoring the helicopters to the ground and it was obvious that nobody was going anywhere.

Travis toyed with the idea of buying a ticket, but decided not to, as the wind could blow all day. He looked up at the information board. Not much help, he thought. All it announced was delays owing to high winds. You've only got to look outside to see that, he thought. Travis found himself a spot where he could keep his eye on the weather and waited. Two hours went by and Travis came up with a brainwave. Finding a spare cubicle in the gents he pushed the scarper button. Sitting back in Auntie Jennison's carriage, he reset the coordinates and came out in Chrissie's garden in 2044.

Chrissie was home this time. 'Travis, what a lovely surprise! It must be almost six months since I saw you last. Are you staying for a chat today?'

'I'm in a bit of a rush today, Chrissie,' Travis said. Chrissie looked crestfallen. 'I'll stay for a little while, though, OK?'

Chrissie's face lit up. 'Come in, then, come in.'

Chrissie's house was even more of a tip than Travis remembered it from his last visit. He was appalled at the way Chrissie was living.

'Find somewhere to sit, Travis – move that stuff out of the way.'

Travis picked up an armful of bits and pieces and deposited them on the floor. 'Are you still visiting your mum?'

'Yes, it's the only visiting I do now, Travis,' Chrissie answered. 'Now, how can I help you? What do you want me to do?'

'Well, to begin with, Chrissie, it's more how you can help yourself! For a start, just look at you! You're living like a tramp.

D'you still wash?' Which was quite good coming from Travis, with his track record of soap and water...

'Course I do! It's just that since...'

Travis interrupted and said sharply, 'Don't give me any of that old rubbish. Just get and sort yourself out, Chrissie, if you want me to be your friend.'

'Yes, Travis.' Chrissie hung his head.

'The reason I'm here, Chrissie, is because I need weather records for the helipad from last year. Here, I've written down some suitable dates for you.'

'Anything you say, Travis, anything.'

Chrissie rummaged around for his remote control, eventually found it and dutifully pointed it at the wall.

Armed with the information he needed, and spending just enough time with Chrissie to be sociable, he gave Chrissie a promise that he'd go back to see him again.

'If I come back and you're still living like a tramp, I won't ever come back again – understand?'

'Yes, Travis.'

Travis, feeling like a schoolteacher dealing with a naughty boy, pushed his scarper button.

As soon as Travis was back in the carriage he decided to pay Chrissie another visit to see if he had got his act together, and he arrived at Chrissie's platform two weeks after his previous visit. As Travis went to leave the shed he noticed a white envelope pinned to the inside of the door. *To Travis* was written on it. Travis tore open the envelope and started to read the paper inside. It said:

Dear Travis,

Thank you for being my friend. I know I've let you down. I do live like a tramp; I've tried to improve, but I just can't go on any longer. By the time you read this I will be with Mum for ever.

It's what I want, Travis. I'm going to see her now, and when I get there I'll stay until I'm asleep.

Goodbye, Travis, and thank you again for being my only friend, the only one I've ever had.

Chrissie

Travis read the note over and over, and, with tears in his eyes, ran to the house. He peered in through the windows: nothing and nobody. Distraught, he pushed the scarper button.

Chapter Thirty-four

Mike Harding opened the post and called out to his wife, who was in the kitchen. 'Pam, the tickets have come for the governor's leaving do; it's next Saturday.'

'Look, dear,' she said, walking into the living room, 'I really would rather that you went on your own. I saw enough of that place for years; you'll all be talking shop, and I'll hardly know anyone there anyway.'

'Somehow I knew you were going to say that, so if you're sure, I'll sort out the travel arrangements.'

'Promise me one thing though, Mike: promise you'll go over by boat – you know what I think about helicopters,' Pam said.

Mike laughed. 'Anything to keep the peace! The boat it is.'

Mike's vid phone started ringing; the caller ID told him it was Thomas, and a rather sombre-looking Thomas Travis appeared on Mike's screen.

'Good morning, Thomas. How are you?' Mike asked.

'Not so good, Mike. I suppose you've heard the news.'

'Yes, the governor and I had a chat. I'm really sorry, Thomas, especially after all you've done at Samson. I have tried to phone you, but I couldn't get through.'

'I know it's a bit childish of me, Mike, but I've had my phone turned off; I suppose you could say I've been burying my head in the sand. Anyway, putting all that to one side, the reason I phoned you is to find out what arrangements you are making for the weekend.'

'Well, to start with, I'm under petticoat rule and Pam told me that I must come over on the boat.'

'I'm not surprised; she never did like the helicopter. Isn't she coming then, Mike?'

'No. I can't say I blame her; once you get away from Samson you realise that there's a big wide world out here. Wait and see, Thomas, there'll be a day when you look back and say that you were glad to leave the island.'

'Can't see it, but I hope you're right, Mike. Anyway, it's just as well I phoned you, because they're sending a liberty boat to Penzance for people who don't trust the helicopter. The weather forecast is good and the boat is due to leave Penzance for Samson at...' Thomas paused for a moment. 'Ah, here we are, at two o'clock, or as the governor would say, fourteen hundred hours.'

Always well organised, Mike Harding had all his travel arrangements sorted out the same day. He would arrive in Penzance at noon on Saturday, and that would give him an hour for lunch and then plenty of time to get down to the quay for the liberty boat.

'Right then I'm off now, Pam,' Mike said, slipping the invitation tickets into his pocket.

'Have a nice time then, dear, and don't get too drunk,' said Pam with a smile.

Mike kissed her goodbye and set off for the link station. Before long he was at Bristol Temple Meads finding his seat on the train. Although he'd travelled on the EMS more times than he could remember, he still marvelled at the speed and comfort, and a mere thirty-five minutes later he was in Plymouth. The link to Penzance was as full as it could get; Saturday trippers, Mike thought. There was a slight delay at Liskeard, and an announcement came over to say that extra carriages were being hooked up. But by the time the link pulled into Camborne Station, the lost time had been made up and Mike Harding watched out of the carriage window as the last travellers for Penzance boarded the train.

A mass exodus ensued at Penzance Central and Mike, although a big man, felt himself being carried along with the crowd. He strolled into the town, and fifteen minutes later a very relaxed Mike Harding was sitting in the window seat of a little restaurant ordering his lunch.

'Lunch time, Travis,' Travis's mum said, 'go and wash your hands, there's a good boy.'

'I'm not hungry, Mum, honestly.'

'Look, Travis, it's no good blaming yourself for what happened to Chrissie. Tell him, Tom.'

'Listen, Travis, he would have done it anyway. Think about it, son; you know I'm right.'

'But Dad, I said he was like a tramp!' Travis was close to tears.

'Travis, he'd been living like that for a long time. What you said to him didn't make any difference; he was going to do it at some time anyway. Now come on, son, try to eat something, please.'

Travis didn't go to school on the Monday, but as Tuesday was the last day of term before Christmas, his mum cajoled him into going in order to try to get Chrissie out of his head. By the time he came home on Tuesday evening he seemed more like his old self, and his mother thought her therapy seemed to have worked.

'I'm going round Mr Pomphrey's now, Mum,' Travis said.

'All right dear.' She felt quite relieved; almost back to normal, she thought.

'How are you feeling today, Travis?' Mr Pomphrey asked.

'Very much better, thank you, Mr Pomphrey,' Travis answered.

'I take it you haven't thought about going to see your grand-dad, though?'

'I've thought about it, Mr Pomphrey, but that's as far as I've got. When are you going to fetch Auntie Jennison?'

'More, when are *we*, Travis! I've spoken to your dad and he said the three of us could drive down to fetch her tomorrow; he thinks it will keep your mind occupied.'

'So that I won't think about Chrissie, I suppose.'

'Well yes, that's it, Travis.'

'I think that's a super idea, Mr Pomphrey… on one condition.'

'What's that, Travis?'

Travis smiled. 'No stopping on the way back for pub lunches.'

Auntie Jennison's arrival was the usual poppy show. Alex, Charlie, Auntie Jennison's huge suitcase and various accoutrements, accompanied by a haze of cigarette smoke and the usual blowing off noises, made Barbara smile as she watched Auntie Jennison alight from Tom's car.

'Come along, silly dog!' Auntie Jennison tut-tutted through clouds of cigarette smoke. 'The pup's peed in the car. Barbara, fetch some disinfectant, there's a good girl. Tom, take my portmanteau in. Travis, don't just stand there boy; poor Charlie thinks he's being left behind. And Bill, don't forget the parcels, and do be careful with them. I hope the central heating's on full – I'm freezing.'

'Nice to see you again, Auntie Jennison,' Barbara said.

Auntie Jennison hadn't finished yet. 'No one would stop for a pub lunch, Barbara, and I'm absolutely famished. Is Becky here yet? Travis, go careful with Charlie, will you? Stupid boy! No lunch – can you believe that, Barbara? What is it you say these days? I'm all stressed out! I was really looking forward to a pub lunch. I need a fag; I shall feel better after a fag or two.'

'But Auntie Jennison, you've got one there, look, in your hand,' Travis said, pointing.

'This one's nearly gone, brainless boy. I shall go straight for a lie-down, Barbara. It must be that journey without so much as a stop – not a stop! And Barbara, I shall need a hot-water bottle and the electric fire.'

Auntie Jennison flounced off into the house, leaving everyone to carry out their allotted tasks.

'I didn't know you could go cold turkey over ashtrays,' Travis remarked.

His dad was still chuckling when he and Mr Pomphrey were sitting in the living room taking a well-earned drink.

'Looks like young Travis has got the measure of Auntie Jennison's little weakness, then, Tom?' Mr Pomphrey said.

'Yes, Mr Pomphrey, I'll have to have a chat with him about it. I don't think he understands that Auntie Jennison can't help it; he probably just thinks she's just a thief.'

'When you say it like that, Tom, it sounds terrible – a thief! Well, yes, I suppose she is really. Do you suppose there's any cure for her?'

'No, I don't think so. If you remember, she carried on getting ashtrays for herself even when she didn't smoke. The trouble is, she can't see it's wrong, and most of the time I don't even think she knows she's doing it,' Tom said.

'Oh, she knows what she's up to, all right! Look at the tantrum she threw just now,' Mr Pomphrey said.

'Still, it could be worse,' Tom said. 'At least she isn't like she was years ago.'

'What was she like then, Tom?' Mr Pomphrey asked.

'She was an absolute nightmare. It used to be bicycles – anybody's bicycle – except children's bikes; she'd never take a child's bike. She used to take them, and I used to take them back to their owners if I could find out where they came from. Nobody's bike was sacred; she even had the vicar's. It wasn't too bad when she took the postman's bike. I managed to get it back to the post office, and I told them that I'd found the bike in a ditch.'

'Yes, interfering with the mail is a very serious offence, isn't it?' Mr Pomphrey said.

'Yes, it certainly is, Mr Pomphrey. The police knew it was her who was responsible for all the thefts, and they came to the cottage one day with a search warrant. Auntie Jennison was most indignant. They went all around the cottage; they were there for hours, but they found nothing.'

'Did she have any there then, Tom?'

'Oh yes, she had them all right – fifty-seven of them!'

'Fifty-seven!' Mr Pomphrey exclaimed.

'Yes, fifty-seven,' Tom answered.

'So where were they, then?'

'She had them neatly lined up on the platform. Of course, the police had no way of getting into Auntie Jennison's shed, although they tried and tried. Auntie Jennison asked them how many bicycles they were looking for, and when they told her she told them there was no way that that many would go in such a small shed, so eventually they gave up trying and went away empty-handed.'

'So what happened to the fifty-seven cycles then, Tom?'

'I managed to smuggle them back outside the police station and let the police find them. It took a long time because Auntie Jennison kept adding to the collection. Then she committed the cardinal sin – she stole the police sergeant's bike.'

'She never did!' Mr Pomphrey exclaimed.

'Oh yes, Mr Pomphrey, and then she had the cheek to go shopping on it. They spotted her and chased her in a police car. The trouble was, she thought it was all a game. They had three police cars after her and a motorbike, not to mention the ones on foot.'

'What happened when they caught her?' Mr Pomphrey asked.

'Well, that was it, they never actually caught her! She got fed up in the end and parked the bike outside the police station. She walked in and said, "I know I've been a naughty girl, and I promise – no more bikes".'

'What did they say?'

'They knew it was her, and that she was the one-woman crime wave, but deciding as she was old, and they'd be made a laughing stock if it went to court, they just gave her a roasting and let her go.'

'So was she as good as her word?' Mr Pomphrey asked.

'Yes, Mr Pomphrey,' Tom replied, 'although she said she couldn't understand what all the fuss was about. As far as she was concerned, she had merely borrowed them. Auntie Jennison never took another bike from that day on; she started on ashtrays instead.'

'Hello, Dad! Hello, Mr Pomphrey! I heard you mention Auntie Jennison. Am I missing something?' Travis asked.

'Nothing really,' his dad said, 'but I do need to talk to you about Auntie Jennison… later on, all right?'

'Yes, Dad. I can't find Mum and I wanted to know if Becky was coming today?'

'No, she's coming with the twins tomorrow, and Mark will be here the day after on Christmas Eve. Do you want to come down with me to pick her up?'

'No thanks, Dad, I'll stay here with Mr Pomphrey and Auntie Jennison, if that's all right, Mr Pomphrey?'

'Can't be done, I'm afraid, Travis. You see, Auntie and I are going shopping, and because of what we're going to get you can't come. Sorry.'

'I bet it's presents for me,' Travis said. 'That's all right, Mr Pomphrey, I'll go with Dad.'

'It's not only presents we're going out to buy, Travis. Don't say anything to Auntie Jennison, but I'm going to sneak off and buy her an engagement ring.'

'Tell you what, Mr Pomphrey,' Tom said, 'let's have a little engagement party on Christmas Eve and you can give her the ring then.'

'Oh, what a lovely idea! Thanks, Tom.' Mr Pomphrey sounded delighted.

The next evening, after Travis and his dad had collected Becky and the twins, an elated Mr Pomphrey gave the family a sneak preview of the ring while Auntie Jennison was out of the way. She almost caught sight of the ring when she came in the room, but a quick-thinking Barbara surreptitiously slipped it on her own finger.

'Come along, you lot, stop standing around – there's work to be done,' Auntie Jennison said. 'Christmas Eve tomorrow, and not a decoration to be seen. Tom, go out to the garage and fetch the trimmings; Bill, you'd better help him; Becky, we need the steps – and Barbara, drawing pins, lots of drawing pins, and sticky tape.'

'What shall I do, Auntie Jennison?' Travis asked.

'You, my precious, you can come and give me a cuddle and a nice big kiss!'

The whole family pitched in and put the Christmas decorations up, and for the first time ever Travis was allowed to put the fairy lights on the Christmas tree.

It really looked like Christmas and felt like Christmas in the Travis household, but Travis knew he still had a job to finish, and tomorrow would be the day.

Chapter Thirty-five

Sleep didn't come easy to Travis that night. Thoughts of Alex, Chrissie and his granddad coursed through his mind. What would tomorrow bring? Would he see his grandfather?

He looked at his bedside clock: ten to two. I'll never get to sleep, he thought; but sleep he did. Despite his plan to be out of the house as early as possible, it was just after ten when, after checking and double-checking everything he would want for the journey in true Mr Pomphrey style, he was ready to set off. There was no one around to say goodbye to, and Travis suddenly remembered that the family were going off for some last-minute shopping. He decided to scribble a note telling everybody where he was going, but he changed his mind because he didn't want to worry his mother, and abandoned the idea. Instead, he went around to Mr Pomphrey and called out, 'Mr Pomphrey, are you at home?'

'Come in, Travis, I'm in the living room,' he replied.

'Mr Pomphrey, I'm going to Samson Island today, and I need you to help me out. Mum will worry if I'm gone a long time and if she knows what I'm up to.'

'What d'you want me to do, Travis?'

'Somehow, Mr Pomphrey, I want you to let Mum think I'm with you.'

'Auntie said they'd be gone until at least one o'clock, so I could say you were having lunch with me and staying for the afternoon, if you like. I don't really like telling lies, but as it's in a good cause...'

'Oh, thank you, Mr Pomphrey, I knew I could rely on you.'

'Now, Travis, have you checked that you've got everything?'

'I've been over and over it, Mr Pomphrey.'

'How about food? You're bound to get hungry.'

'Trust you, Mr Pomphrey! That's the one thing I never thought of.'

'Sit there, Travis, and I'll go and cut you some sandwiches. Corned beef all right?'

Travis nodded his head in approval. 'Yes please, Mr Pomphrey,' he replied. Finally, armed with Mr Pomphrey's sandwiches and all his other paraphernalia, Travis eventually set off for Samson.

He sat in the Pullman and studied the weather reports that Chrissie had got for him. Settling on Saturday as being the best day of the lot, he pushed the 'go' button.

The platform at Camborne was quite familiar to Travis now, and he set off from it towards the station with a jaunty step. It was the same man in the ticket office at the link station whom Travis had spoken to before, and he greeted Travis with a smile; Travis was beginning to feel like a seasoned traveller. There were more people on the station than the last time and the train, when it came in, looked full to overflowing, but Travis was lucky and found a spare seat almost straight away. At Penzance Central the train emptied almost right out, and Travis could feel the anticipation of seeing his granddad rising inside him. The train pulled out of Penzance Central, and Travis looked through the window at the large station clock: three minutes past midday. Won't be long now, he thought.

There were only two queues inside the helipad building and Travis noticed that the desk for Samson was closed. He started to panic. The other two queues were for St Martin's and Tresco. Travis, unsure, joined the queue for St Martin's. It seemed to him that he would never get to the front of the queue but eventually he found himself looking up at a tall, slim man sitting on a high stool behind the ticket desk.

'A single ticket to St Martin's, please, sir,' Travis said.

The man looked down at Travis and peered through his thick glasses. 'A single?' he said, looking enquiringly at Travis.

'Yes please, sir,' Travis said.

'We don't do singles, sonny,' the man said.

Travis hated being called sonny but he bit his lip and replied, 'A return then, sir, if you please.'

'How old are you, sonny?'

It jarred on Travis to say it but he answered, 'I'm ten, sir.'

'Thought as much,' said the man, 'thought nine or ten. Where's your responsible adult?'

Travis realised what he meant. 'She's a bit late, sir, she told me to go on and get my ticket.'

'Did she indeed! Do you know what I think? Well, I think there is no responsible adult, and you know you've got to be fourteen to travel alone. So what are you – a runaway?'

'No sir, honestly, my Auntie Jennison will be here in a minute.' Travis could see the man was about to come from behind the desk and grab him.

'Come on, mate, I haven't got all day,' said the man standing behind Travis. He was getting agitated. 'Just let the kid to go over there and wait for his auntie.' The man pointed to the entrance.

'Yes, go on then, sonny, but I'm watching you – so no scarpering off,' the ticket seller said.

Scarpering off? Travis thought that would be quite funny under normal circumstances. Travis leant on the wall by the entrance and every time the ticket seller looked in his direction Travis pretended that he was looking for his aunt. The queues for tickets were getting shorter, and Travis knew the man would be after him before long. Travis listened to the announcement coming over the loudspeakers: 'Link announces the departure of link train to Plymouth.'

Travis made his mind up in an instant; the ticket seller was talking to a customer and pointing at something on a paper in front of him. Travis ran and just made it as the link train warning, 'Mind the doors!' came over the speakers. Ticket or no ticket, Travis was on his way to Penzance Central.

'You nearly missed the train back there,' a middle-aged lady smiled sympathetically at him. 'Are you on your own?' she asked.

'Well, yes and no,' Travis replied. Thinking quickly, he added, 'Actually, I've mislaid my aunt.'

'Mislaid her!' the lady started laughing. 'That's a good one… so tell me, where did you mislay her?'

'I don't think I mean mislay,' Travis said. 'I got off at the wrong stop, so it's more she's mislaid me.'

'So which stop were you supposed to get off at?' the lady asked.

'Penzance Central,' Travis answered.

'So she's waiting for you there?'

'Yes,' Travis lied sweetly.

'I'm getting off there as well. I've only come over from St Martin's to do some shopping, so we can go and find your aunt together, if you like,' the lady offered.

Travis sat in silence; he now had another problem besides having no ticket for the link. Suddenly he blurted out, 'I haven't got a ticket for the train.'

'Don't worry about that,' the lady said, 'just hold my hand and walk through the barrier with me, no one will take any notice.'

The train pulled into Penzance Central and Travis grabbed the woman's hand and held onto it like his very life depended on it. Sure enough, they passed straight through the barrier and out into the street.

'Right then,' the lady said, 'so where's this auntie of yours?'

Travis looked up at her sweetly and said, 'Well, the last time it happened, she said in future to meet her at the tourist information centre.'

'What d'you mean, the last time it happened?'

'I'm always doing it.'

'And I thought you seemed like a nice boy! You just like riding on the link for nothing – go on, get out of my sight!'

Travis ran off while the going was good. Travis looked at his watch. I'll never get to Samson at this rate, he thought; the tourist information office might be a good bet. Perhaps I can get on a ferry without an adult.

The tourist office turned out to be right down beside the harbour; Travis wasted no time and went in the already opened doors. It was a brand new building with an ornate tiled floor and a long wooden counter. Behind the counter stood three girls, all in their late teens or early twenties. Putting on his best smile, Travis walked over to the one who looked the friendliest.

'I wonder, miss,' he said, 'can you help me?'

The girl smiled broadly at Travis. 'If I can… what d'you want to know?'

'I need to get to Samson Island. You see, my auntie and I have got separated and the helicopter ticket seller won't let me on, on my own.'

'Yes, that's right; children must be accompanied by a responsible adult,' she said.

'Can I get on a ferry on my own then?' Travis asked.

'Yes, you can go on your own, that isn't a problem; on the ferry you don't need an adult with you. But there's no ferry to Samson from here; you have to go to St Martin's and then get a connection from there,' she answered.

'Yes, that's all right, I'll do that,' Travis said.

'Are you going to the gardens or visiting someone? Because if you're visiting, you'll need a VO,' the girl told him.

'My aunt and I are going to the gardens,' Travis answered.

'So when did you want to travel?'

'Well, now, of course – right this minute.'

The girl smiled at him. 'There's no connection to Samson today... Well, what I mean is, by the time the ferry gets to St Martin's, the gardens will be closing for the day, and there won't be another boat to Samson until tomorrow.'

'There's still a ferry to St Martin's today, isn't there?' Travis asked.

'The last one today leaves at two thirty, and you can pay when you get on, if that's what you want to do.'

Travis thanked the girl and went out into the bright sunshine. It's the end of a dream, he thought. Tomorrow's Christmas Day at home; they'd kill me if I wasn't there, and anyway it would worry everybody to death. He decided he'd at least go down and have a look at the harbour, as he intended to try again after Christmas. As he came near to the sea he thought of Polperro. The noise of the seagulls was deafening, but there the similarity ended, and although Polperro was busy, it was as quiet as a cemetery compared to Penzance.

Pangs of hunger swept through Travis. With all the excitement he hadn't thought of food all day. He looked around and spotted a bench by the jetty wall. Three people were already sitting on it, but as Travis approached two of them got up and moved away. This is a good spot to watch the boats, thought Travis. He sat on the bench and looked around. At the other end of the bench was the solitary figure of quite a large, elderly man. Preoccupied with looking in his carrier bag for the food that Mr

Pomphrey had prepared for him, Travis didn't hear the man slide along the bench towards him.

'Hello,' the man said, Travis nearly jumped out of his skin. 'Sorry to frighten you like that… You were on the link this morning, weren't you?'

Travis started to feel suspicious of the stranger; he decided to just look blank at the man.

'It's all right, I'm not going to bite you. It's just that you don't see many of those these days.' He tapped Travis's carrier bag. Travis held up the carrier. It's just a Lidl carrier, he thought.

'They got bought out by Billy's supermarkets about ten years ago,' the man said.

Travis started to relax. 'Yes, I was on the link, sir, you're quite right.'

'Thought so,' the man went on, 'and if I'm not very much mistaken you got off at the wrong stop.'

'How do you know that, sir?' Travis was impressed.

'Simple,' replied the man. 'I got off here and you went on to the helipad, but you're back here now two hours later, so you didn't go on the helicopter; and the way you've been looking at the boats, you were supposed to get on a ferry, am I right?'

'Are you a detective, sir?' Travis asked.

'Goodness no, never was,' the man chuckled, 'and anyway I've retired now.'

'Would you like a corned beef sandwich, sir? I can recommend them; Mr Pomphrey made them.'

'That's very nice of you, but I've just eaten lunch. So tell me, are you meeting someone or are you on your own?'

As Travis didn't really know the man he decided not to say he was alone. Instead he said, 'I'm supposed to be with my Auntie Jennison, sir, but she isn't here yet.'

'Auntie Jennison, you say? Now, where have I heard that name before?'

Travis sat in silence eating his sandwiches. He could see the man was deep in thought. Suddenly the man said, 'Of course – I remember now! Look, we haven't been introduced.' The man held his hand out. 'My name's Harding.'

Travis shook his hand. 'Pleased to meet you, Mr Harding.'

'When two Englishmen meet, one's supposed to say, "How d'you do?" Did you know that? And in reply, the other person says, "How d'you do?" as well. So shall we do it again?' Mr Harding asked.

Travis shook his hand again, and they both said, 'How d'you do?'

'That's more like it,' Mr Harding declared. 'So how long is it before your aunt is due to put in an appearance?'

'Oh, I couldn't say,' said Travis. 'You see, she's a little eccentric. It could be any time really.'

'The one I know about sounds eccentric, from what I've been told about her,' Mr Harding said, smiling.

'I'll bet my Auntie Jennison is more so! Actually, I think she's as mad as a hatter,' Travis said.

'Tell me some of the things she does, and we'll see if she's more eccentric than the one I know of,' said Mr Harding.

'Well, let me see,' Travis said. 'She smokes all the time, she steals ashtrays from the pub and she eats sticky peppermints one after the other.'

'Don't tell me – does she suffer from wind as well, by any chance?'

Travis's mouth dropped open. 'Well, yes, she does, but how did you know that?'

'There's something here I don't understand,' said Mr Harding, looking bewildered. 'How old is this Auntie Jennison of yours exactly?'

'I don't know, but she is ever so old,' Travis replied.

'What precisely are you doing here?' Mr Harding asked.

Travis decided to throw caution out of the window, 'I'm trying to get to see my granddad; he's on Samson Island, Mr Harding.'

'And what might his name be, may I ask?'

'It's Thomas Travis.'

'Oh, my God!' Mike Harding looked like all the stuffing had been knocked out of him. 'So what's *your* name?'

'I'm Travis Travis.'

'Travis Travis... but Thomas hasn't got a family and Auntie Jennison...' His voice faded away. 'Here, let me have a good look at you... yes, yes, I can see Thomas in you.'

Travis was growing excited. 'You know my granddad?'

'Yes, we're old friends! I'm on my way to see him now.'

'*Wicked*!' Travis said, catching hold of Mike Harding's arm. 'Take me with you, please, Mr Harding. Please, please take me with you.'

Mike Harding dug in his pocket. 'Here you are then, you'll need one of these.' He handed Travis one of the two tickets he was holding.

'Wow! Oh, thank you, Mr Harding, thank you so much!' Travis was ecstatic.

The liberty boat came in at a little after two o'clock and Travis could see the one word 'Samson' painted on the side. He went aboard with Mike Harding and proudly handed his ticket in. The boat cast off from the jetty and Travis felt that at last he was really on his way. Mike Harding smiled reassuringly at Travis and they settled back for the boat journey.

'How many more times are you going to look at your watch, Travis?'

'I just can't wait to get there, Mr Harding,' Travis said, 'I'm just so excited.'

'Look, Travis, when you see him, don't expect too much. Remember, your granddad doesn't even know he's got a grandson; it might come as quite a shock to him. I don't want you to be disappointed.'

'It's going to be all right – you'll see, Mr Harding.'

'Listen, Travis, it's another hour at least before we get to Samson, and there are a few things that have been puzzling me. Can I ask you about them?'

'Yes, of course you can,' Travis replied.

'Well, to start with, are there two different Auntie Jennisons?'

'In our family there's only one Auntie Jennison, and that's enough, believe me,' Travis said, smiling.

'So she must be at least one hundred and five years old, according to my calculations.'

'Yeah,' Travis agreed, 'quite probably.'

'And the other thing I can't understand is this: I've known your grandfather for twenty-five years and he never mentioned his family, least of all having any children.'

'He only had the one, Mr Harding, and that's my dad, Tom.'

'Yes, but he made no mention… almost like they were lost for ever.'

'There are things you just don't know, Mr Harding, things that are better left alone.'

'Yes, I understand, Travis… Families, eh?'

The boat journey was nearly over. Mike Harding strained his eyes and could just make out the figures of the governor and Thomas standing shoulder to shoulder on the jetty.

'Look, there they are, Travis.' He pointed. 'The two men standing to one side, that's your grandfather and the old governor.' He stood up and started waving.

'You're almost as excited as I am, aren't you, Mr Harding?'

'More than you! Look, you're not even waving,' he said. 'Listen Travis, when we get off the boat, there's something I want you to do for me.'

'Anything you like, Mr Harding. After all, if it wasn't for you, I wouldn't be here, would I?'

'I know you want to see your grandfather badly, but let me have ten minutes or so with him and the governor first, and then I'll introduce you.'

'You're worried about the shock he's going to have seeing me, aren't you?'

'Yes I am, Travis.'

'Look, Mr Harding, I'll go to the pods and you bring him along when you're ready; how's that?'

'I know it's a big disappointment for you, Travis, but I think it's for the best.'

The boat pulled in alongside the jetty and was made fast. The gangplank was put in place and the passengers started to alight. Travis hung back and waited until his grandfather, Mike Harding and the governor, arms linked, walked off towards the Prison Officers' Club.

Travis, never much interested in gardens or gardening despite his mother's best efforts, marvelled at what he knew to be his grandfather's work. He walked around the walled garden and then on towards the pods.

'Closing at six thirty, mind, son,' one of the guards called over.

'Yes, thank you,' replied Travis.

Chapter Thirty-six

Mike Harding bounded down the gangplank of the liberty boat, ran over to Thomas and the governor and warmly shook hands.

'Come on, you two,' said Thomas, 'I never thought I'd see the day when I was in a position to buy you both a drink in the Prison Guards' Club, but that's what I'm going to do.'

'*Establishment*,' corrected the governor. 'Gin and tonics all round, then, Thomas. What d'you say?'

'Yes, but not too much for me... remember, I don't drink,' Thomas said.

'I think when you hear what I've got to tell you, you'll need a large brandy,' said Mike.

'Come on then, Mike, spill the beans,' Thomas said.

'When we've had that drink,' Mike replied.

Travis kept looking at his watch. It was almost six thirty, and the guard was approaching. 'Come on, son, closing time,' he said.

'I'm waiting for the prison governor, actually, sir,' Travis replied.

'Oh yes, and I'm Father Christmas! Come on now, out you go,' the guard said.

Travis turned to leave, but just at that moment, in through the entrance of the pod walked the governor, followed by Mike Harding; trailing on behind came Travis's granddad. The guard backed away. Travis couldn't help himself. 'Told you so,' he remarked cheekily.

The trio came nearer to Travis. 'Here we are, Thomas,' said Mike Harding. 'Here's the reason for the large brandy I bought you.'

Travis stepped forward, at last face to face with his granddad.

'Thomas Travis, I'd like to introduce you to Travis Travis.'

Travis stepped forward and held out his hand. Thomas took Travis's hand and stared intently into his face. 'How d'you do?' he said.

Travis pumped his granddad's hand up and down, and through tears mumbled, 'How d'you do?'

Thomas, visibly shaken, stepped back and slumped onto a nearby bench; Travis was now in floods of tears.

'Are you all right, Thomas?' the governor asked. 'Who's the boy, Harding? Stop playing games, man.'

'It's not a game, Governor. This young chap is Thomas's grandson,' Mike replied.

'My grandson...' Thomas echoed.

'My God!' said the governor, and sat down beside Thomas. 'I think I need a brandy as well!'

'Come over here, son, and let me have a good look at you,' Thomas said.

Travis approached and his granddad placed both his hands on his grandson's shoulders and stood him squarely in front of him.

Travis looked at his grandfather and said. 'I'm Tom's boy, Granddad.'

'Tom had a son... Well, I never... and my Sarah?' Thomas looked quizzically at Travis.

'I'm sorry, Granddad,' Travis said, shaking his head.

His granddad paused and a sad look came over his face. He sat in silence for a while and then he said, 'How old are you now, Travis?'

'I was eleven on 9th December, Granddad – two weeks ago,' Travis blurted out.

Mike Harding and the governor turned and looked at each other. 'The boy doesn't even know what month it is!' the governor said, 'what the devil's going on here?'

'You're eleven.' Travis's granddad caught hold of Travis's hand. 'Tell me, are you wearing anything around your neck?'

'Strange question, Thomas,' remarked the governor.

In answer, Travis undid the top buttons on his shirt and lifted the scarper button out for his granddad to see.

'My God!' Travis's grandfather shook his head in disbelief. 'And you're so young.'

All this was completely lost on the governor and Mike Harding. 'I think an explanation's in order, Thomas,' the governor said.

'Can I have a few moments with my grandson, chaps? There are things we need to discuss.'

'Yes, all right, Thomas, take all the time you like. Come on, Mike. We'll be in the club when you've finished.' Mike and the governor turned and walked away.

'Have you come to take me back, Travis?'

'That was the plan, Granddad, but Auntie Jennison—'

'Is Auntie Jennison still with us?' Thomas broke in.

'Still with us, and she's getting married,' Travis said.

'Getting married! I can't believe it.' Thomas shook his head.

'She's marrying Mr Pomphrey.'

'Well, well! Yes, I remember Bill Pomphrey, our next-door neighbour.'

'Granddad, I can't take you back. You see, Auntie Jennison doesn't think your scarper button will work.'

'I haven't got it anyway, Travis, it's long gone.'

'It was, but I've got it here.' Travis delved into his pocket and took out the scarper button.

'Why doesn't Auntie Jennison think it will work, then, Travis?'

'Because she says that you didn't get back to 1978, and that's where you started from.'

'That's true.' Thomas hung his head. 'So it looks like I'm stuck here for ever.'

'Granddad, I just had a thought. Although you started in 1978 the scarper button came with me and I started in 2004; it might just be worth a try.'

'If my button won't get me home, Travis, I don't know what I'll do! There's nothing here for me now.'

'We could always try mine, Granddad.'

'I couldn't let you do that, Travis; anything could happen. Listen, let's go and find the governor and Mike and take it from there.'

'OK, Granddad.'

Travis took his grandfather's hand and led him out of the pod. At the entrance, Thomas paused and looked around. 'Will this be the last I see of this place, Travis?' he asked.

'I hope so, Granddad, I really hope so.'

'Me too, Travis.'

Travis and his granddad walked into the club, and the old man called Mike and the governor to one side. 'Travis and I have to leave shortly – well, that's to say Travis will be going anyway.'

'What the devil are you drivelling on about now, Thomas? Don't give him any more to drink, Mike,' the governor said, 'he's obviously had enough!'

'The liberty boat doesn't leave until nine thirty, Thomas. I don't understand you either,' said Mike.

'Let's walk over to my office, gentlemen,' Thomas said. 'I think you're both owed an explanation.'

Thomas and Travis set out for Thomas's office; the governor and Mike Harding quickly finished their drinks and followed on behind.

Thomas put his hand around Travis's shoulder and looked at Mike Harding and the governor across his office desk. 'This young man, my grandson,' he said, 'is a time traveller; he's come to see me from the year 2004.'

'Granddad, no!' Travis shouted.

Thomas patted Travis's shoulder. 'It's all right, Travis, I've known these men for twenty-five years, they're my friends and they deserve to know the truth. Travis has come to try to take me home, back where I belong,' he said.

The governor and Mike Harding looked at each other. Mike Harding was the first to speak. 'Well, that explains a lot of things – the carrier bag and the white bread sandwiches for a start! No one eats white bread any more, and nobody says "cool" or "wicked"... and your hair's a little short, isn't it, Travis?'

'You believe Granddad then, Mr Harding?' Travis asked.

Mike replied, 'If your grandfather said black was white, I'd believe him, Travis.'

The governor just stood there speechless, as Thomas gave them a full account of 'visiting'. Eventually, he spoke. 'It's all like a dream, you know, this, Thomas... So this is goodbye, then?'

'If I'm right about my scarper button, Jeremy, once I leave here it will be for ever. You see, the power has been passed on now to Travis,' Thomas said.

'I can come back and see both of you, though, if you'd like me to,' Travis added.

'Yes of course, Travis,' Mike Harding said. 'You can bring us news of your granddad.'

'I'll bring you a Christmas card, Mr Harding.' Travis suddenly remembered that it was Christmas Eve at home and he glanced at his watch: ten past seven.

'Do you want me to try now, Travis?' Thomas asked. 'Only, you look agitated.'

'Yes please, Granddad, they'll be starting to worry about me at home.'

Thomas and Travis shook hands with Mike Harding and the governor, and Travis handed his grandfather the scarper button.

'On the count of three, then, Granddad,' Travis said.

Thomas lifted his scarper button up in full view and counted, one, two, three... Travis watched as his granddad's index finger time and time again pushed the scarper button, to no effect.

'It's no good, Travis, I'm here to stay!' Thomas sank into his seat. His head went down and his shoulders slumped.

'Come on, Granddad, let's try mine,' Travis suggested.

'No, it's no good, Travis. I can't let you take that risk – anything could happen,' Thomas replied.

'It's our only hope. Come on, Granddad, we'll push it together!'

'Yes, go on, Thomas,' Mike Harding said. 'It's your only chance. Say goodbye, Thomas, and go for it.'

Travis caught hold of his grandfather's hand and took his index finger. 'Ready, Granddad?' he asked.

Thomas looked at the governor and Mike Harding. 'Goodbye, Mike, goodbye, Jeremy.'

Travis counted, 'One, two, three,' and simultaneously he and Thomas pushed the scarper button.

Travis came running up the stairs of his platform along the corridor as fast as he could. He banged open the shed door and stood alone in the cold night air. A flurry of snowflakes started to fall. He waited. No good, he thought. He took a couple of steps towards the house. It didn't work; Granddad's still there... Shoulders slumped, hands thrust deep in his pockets, he walked off slowly towards the house.

'Aren't you going to wait for me?' a voice behind him asked.

'No, I'm not, Granddad,' Travis replied, and shot off towards the house. In he went through the kitchen and into the living room, leaving all the doors wide open.

The whole family had gathered: Travis's mum and dad, Becky, Mark and the twins. Mr Pomphrey and Auntie Jennison were dancing to the strains of Slade playing, 'Well here it is, Happy Christmas'. Alex came running over to Travis, who scooped him up with one arm. He ran to the CD player and yanked the plug from the wall. Mr Pomphrey and Auntie Jennison stopped dancing; everybody stopped talking and stared at Travis. With his free arm, Travis pointed at the kitchen doorway.

'Look, everybody,' he said, 'we've got a visitor!'

The End

Printed in the United Kingdom
by Lightning Source UK Ltd.
112866UKS00001B/7